The
High Price
of a
Good Man

The
High Price
of a
Good Man

Debra Phillips

ST. MARTIN'S GRIFFIN ❧ NEW YORK

www.stmartins.com

Design by Kathryn Parise

LIBRARY OF CONGRESS CATALOGING-IN-PUBLICATION DATA

Phillips, Debra.
The high price of a good man / Debra Phillips.
    p. cm.
  ISBN 0-312-30525-7
  1. African Americans—Fiction.   I. Title
PS3566.H4772H54 2003
813'.54—dc21

2003041273

First Edition: July 2003

10 9 8 7 6 5 4 3 2 1

Like the stars at night without a sky
Like a question without the why
A restless bird without its wings
A song without words to sing
Early morning without its dew
Such is the sweet missing of you

Dedicated to my mother, Daisy Mae Davis

One

First of all, just for the record, I love me some me.

You heard right. And I'm not ashamed to say it either. I truly love Miss Queenisha Renae Sutton. The tall, well-endowed, fine honey-coated sistah that I be. Every inch of me is special, even if those inches are blown out to the fullest. Call it conceit if you want. Call it an overblown ego if you like. Call it what you want, but that's just how it is.

See, that's what's wrong with a lot of folks nowadays. Specially my ebony sistahs on the prowl. The ones that be looking for the elusive "good black man." Sistahs be tripping. Keep trying to love everybody else more than they love themselves. But not this amazon sistah. "If you can't find somebody else to love you," my mama always told me, "then you have to love your damn self." Mama should know because she and God have a close and personal relationship, and because of this, God has blessed her with infinite wisdom.

"First, you have to love yourself, and others will follow." She was always saying stuff like that, my mama, and some of it went straight over my head like a scent and mixed with the air. But some of it, the good parts, stuck to me like new skin. That's why we women lacking in the ways of love have to listen to the wisdom of our mothers. True, there may be a few mothers who never found out the truth and wisdom about life and love themselves, but on the other hand, there are plenty of mothers who did. Those, I say, are the ones to listen to.

Good old "mother wisdom." I listened as much as I could, but everything is everything with me, and my philosophy is what you see is what you just might get, but only if you play your cards right. Like me, for instance. *Hmph.* I can't be worrying about why my nappy, reddish-brown hair don't grow long and wavy down my ample back when a six-dollar box of relaxer and a nice laser-done weave will do just fine. And no way. You won't find me sitting around feeling sorry for my tall, sweet, honey-brown self, all of six feet tall and a size sixteen, thank you very much, just because diets don't like me and I don't like diets.

Amazon diva that I am, when I dress to kill, I strut all my stuff with my head held high like a twenty-eight-year-old proud bird. Some eyes do see and appreciate, while others—well, heck, they don't even matter. Some say I have a very pretty face, something about my almond-shaped eyes being filled to the brim with a light of hope, and all warm with mischievous brown. But that ain't nothing, 'cause they're only saying something that I already know. I don't lay claim to being no professional prizefighter, but having big heavy limbs and heavy fists do have its advantage. The big and the bold, like myself, we don't mind handling our business if the need arise. If I have to throw down, so be it, and may the best woman win.

I'm the oldest of two daughters born to Odessa and Clayton Sutton. My mama left my daddy in Money, Mississippi, and headed for California when I was three and my sister, Kellie, was age one and still pulling at her tit. My daddy, Clayton, knew that he couldn't let a good black woman like my mama get away, so he tried putting his alcoholism on hold and followed suit within three months. My daddy. God rest his soul. Daddy probably would have been a professional California hoe-chaser by now if he hadn't slipped back into old ways and drank himself to an early grave. And that old saying about it takes a village to raise a child? True, and not so true. Compton was the small village that helped my mama raise me and my sister, Kellie. Helicopters hovering—the sound of bullets flying and ambulances racing through the murky night was as normal as the air we breathe. People never forgot to lock their doors at night, and not many of the tiny, rotten-frame houses that lined our shabby street went without security bars. The mean streets of Compton—a place long steeped in bad reputation, true enough, but it's not so bad as most folks imagine. And then again, some days it's worse.

Compton was okay, but I wanted to get out, and I did. Keeping it real with a good college education, I now earn a living from nine to five as an executive buyer for a major department store. I don't care to give the name right now. But I can say this much, though, they don't hire a lot of African-American women in the kind of position I have—but for me, they pay a sistah well, so I can't complain. Not when I'm buying my second condo in the upscale part of Cerritos, California. Not when my bank account would make the average working man wanna cry. And if I can't get a baby Benz in the color I want, no sense in having one at all. That's why I'm sporting a cold silver one equipped to the full.

I may not be the one who coined the saying that a little hard work never hurt nobody, but I know it's true. Sometimes it breaks my heart to say it, but unlike some of my fellow sistahs of today, I have no plans to take care of a man. Nope. Sorry. Not this large and lovely sistah. Not to say that I wouldn't buy my number-one squeeze a nice gift every now and then, but if he's the kind of man that's looking for a woman to pay for every date, wash his dirty drawers, buy his clothes, pay his car note, and dish out some spending cash on top—*hmph!*—then his eyes be bugging, and he's looking at the wrong honey-brown woman.

Which brings me to why I'm having a big problem with this fool, Marcus, sitting up here now in my face telling me that he don't have the money to pay for the cozy lunch we just ate. Ain't this a trip. I feel like pulling a Tyson on him, reaching over and biting off his ear and spitting it out on the floor. But cool, I tell myself. I can be calm. For the last ten minutes he's been sitting across and smirking at me, waiting for me to take my wallet out. And I'm waiting, too. Waiting for him to be joking with me about inviting me to lunch and having no money to pay.

"Marcus, you really got some nerve. You know that?"

"Aah, c'mon Miss Lady. Give a brother some slack. I'll set you straight when my funds roll in. I promise."

I'm making one of my faces, and I know it. Poetta swears that I always make faces when things don't go my way. She's probably right. If looks could kill, Marcus would be on the floor right now clutching his own throat.

"No, you hold on, now, Mr. Think-You-All-That Marcus. Let me hear it again so I can get this straight. I was all the way in Cerritos, relaxing at my own crib and minding my own business when you called me up. I didn't call you. You called me, and asked me out for lunch. Right?" I could feel my pulse throbbing at the side of my temples. Sometimes when I get a little excited, I have a tendency to get a little loud, but I was making a point of keeping my voice down and leaning in over the small and quaint pink cloth-covered table where the bill for our meal lay waiting like a copy of the state deficit.

"I said I'ma take care of you next time, girl. Why you sweating me and making a big deal out of it?"

"A big deal? Marcus, perhaps you don't understand the basic rules of dating. You ask the woman out, you pay. The woman ask you out, she pays." I clucked my teeth and shook my head. I couldn't believe that this was going to be the stumbling block of what could have been a nice relationship. Looks like I've been foolish enough to even think it was the beginning of something special when I should have known better. I hadn't known the man but a good three weeks, but after a few phone sessions I thought there was hope for us—a budding seed of a relationship. Guess I was wrong. Dang. I hate when that happens. And I had it all planned out in my head, too, how I was gonna rock his world between the sheets after our date. Now the only thing I feel like rocking is a big rock upside his head. "Well, how much money do you have with you?" It's the look on his face rubbing me the wrong way. That combination smirk-sneer.

"About two dollars and forty-five cents." He pushed the bill holder over in my direction. "Stop making a big deal of it, and handle our business so we can go to the pad and get our freak on, woman. You know you wanna."

"In your dreams. The only freaky thing that you and I could do right now is me struggling to remove my boot from your behind."

"Ooh, aggressive. I like that in my woman. Aggressive and kinky."

"Well, you don't have a woman at this table, so pull out some cash so we can get on with our lives." I couldn't stop glaring at him. Such a waste, too. Marcus T. Turner had been one of those chance meetings three weeks previous. Surrounded by my natural habitat, stores at the mall, and doing what I do best, I had been shopping that Saturday three weeks ago, hauling around a slew of packages and trying to have an intelligent cell phone conversation with my homegirl, Poetta, when I bumped into the tall, slender, and somewhat handsome Marcus T.

Granted, he wasn't what you could call a superfine brother. In other words, a possible diamond, but still raw and without the shine. But he was a smooth talker. Had a good look working for him with those slightly hungry-looking light brown eyes that looked like he could sop you up with some gravy and two biscuits. Clean-shaven, delicious cocoa skin, except for that floss-thin black mustache hanging over the most kissable thin lips I'd ever seen on a man. If I didn't know any better, lips like his usually came from a skilled doctor's scalpel. Marcus had the lips I dreamed of: flawless.

Okay, okay, so I have this thing about lips. Some folks have a foot fetish, but I have this thing going on in my head about lips. If a man has thin, nicely shaped lips, it's like the icing on the cake. But if a man's lips look big enough to curl up and cover his own face, I don't want no part of him. Marcus had these thin and perfect-shaped lips. When he smiled at me, I could see that he didn't have perfect teeth, but a girl can't always have everything in one perfect package. Sometimes it takes a pinch of the good parts and a dash of the bad parts to make it all worthwhile and keep it real. All I'm saying is, the man was all right.

Even as large and luscious as I am, I don't usually go around bumping into men, at least not on purpose, so I figured it had be destiny. Everybody knows that the good Lord works in mysterious ways by sending a man your way when you're not looking for one. I know 'cause my mama told me this ever since I was knee-high to a poodle and terrorizing from my crib. But honest to God, a tall and voluptuous woman like myself hauling a bunch of packages around and trying to talk on a cell phone while strolling through a semi-crowded mall needs to pay more attention.

Marcus and I, we bumped, and packages went all over the place. I probably would have gotten mad at him if it hadn't been for the fact that it was mainly my fault and Marcus was so apologetic, and did give me a good view of his well-defined rear in those well-fitted black dress slacks he had on as he bent over to retrieve my things. A wide smile had pulled at my lips while thinking how nice his gray silk banded collar shirt looked on him. Moving swift like the wind, he had my packages spotted, swept up, checked, and back in place, the whole time he kept saying how sorry he was. Sorry this. Sorry that. And then I was saying something, too, like, "Excuse me Poetta, gotta go." Click.

Poetta hates it when I cut her off too abrupt by hanging up on her, but I felt like I had an emergency to deal with—some 911 of a possible hunk. Just looking at that man making such a fuss over my fallen things was enough to take my breath away. I didn't see no ring on those fingers, and such nice hands, too—large and well kept. A recent manicure. Another plus in my book. No nasty-looking black, bacteria and goo all up under his fingernails to possibly contaminate my intimate and special places. Things were looking up.

"Mercy me." I had to fan myself. "There's nothing to be sorry about. I'm sure you didn't mean to." After I composed myself, he helped me over to a stationary wooden bench where I perched to take inventory of my things while he stood over me smiling and looking ever so patient. Even though he didn't have perfect teeth, I liked his smile right off. Sometimes, if you angle your head the right way, even a few crooked teeth can be quite sexy. The man had to be a good six feet two, and that was another plus in my book. Six feet and two inches of testosterone towering over my six-foot frame was right up my alley. I had to look away several times to blush, which isn't the easiest thing for a woman of my complexion.

"So, what's your name?" he wanted to know.

I had looked up at him again and thought that our chance meeting might be something to check out. "Queenisha Renae Sutton. But my close friends call me Queenie."

"Well, it's nice to meet you, Miss Queenie. I'm Marcus." He held out his hand, and I took it for a brief shake. "Marcus T."

I have to admit now, that day I was impressed. In my mind, that middle *T* had to be for something good, like tall, teasing, tantalizing, or terrific, and the way he said his name, his confident tone, sounded like it held some kind of importance to him. He sat down beside me along the bench. After we talked awhile, it seemed the right thing to do to give him my beeper number.

"No home number?" He mocked disappointment.

"Beeper first, home next."

"Oh, it's like that, huh?"

"Yeah, it's like that." Sometimes a sistah have to learn the hard way, like I did, about giving out my home phone number. Now my number two policy when dealing with a man is, never, ever tell a man your address or home phone number until you're absolutely positive you wanna be hearing from him on a regular basis. This alone cuts down on hang-ups and phone stalking.

Marcus beeped me the very next day. Five days into beeping, and me ringing him back, and him saying the right things, he'd earned my phone number. Matter of fact, he's been calling me every day since then. Like clockwork. No sooner after I arrive home from work and have my banana-mango scented bubble bath and a spot of tea—well, more like a spot of sherry—my phone would burr with its own urgency, and to my delight, it would be Marcus. After a short while, I got to liking all the things he was saying, that tint of possibility in his words, and I guess my words were checking out, too. After two weeks and a half, he asked me out to lunch. And before I answered, I had to recheck my mental stats on the man:

NAME: Marcus T. Turner
LIPS: Thin, perfect . . . kissable
MARITAL STATUS: Single, but looking for the right woman
JOB: Construction worker (pays well)
CAR: Ford Mustang 5.0 (in the shop for repairs)
LIVING ARRANGEMENTS: Sharing apartment with brother Gerald in Culver City
GOALS: To someday own his own construction company

Marcus checked out good, so I agreed to have lunch with him that following Sunday. And though I don't like the idea of chauffeuring a man around on the first date, he had explained to me how his car needed major engine work, so I agreed to drive from Cerritos to Culver City to meet him at a nice, cozy little restaurant a few blocks away from the Fox Hills Mall. After weeks of holding back our lustful thoughts like a dam holding back water, we would be on our very first romantic date. But that was then.

And here we are. A balmy-looking Sunday afternoon, late June, and I'm beginning to feel like I would have had a better time at the dentist's office having a root canal. I could have been somewhere doing what I do best, like shopping or kicking it with my best friend, Poetta, and her sister, Marva. Doing what girls do when they hang.

Instead, here I am sitting across from this lightbulb-shaped head Marcus T., who just polished off a filet mignon, a large salad, baked potato, two glasses of wine, and a nice hunk of Mississippi mud pie, and now he sitting here talking about he don't have no money to pay. He was looking good, too. Had on a nice burgundy and tan knit shirt and some nice-fitting burgundy slacks, and I'm secretly hoping he gets severe heartburn and a bad case of intestinal gas once he gets home.

"Let me hear it again, Marcus. Just in case my ears are playing tricks on me. You saying that you don't have any money with you at all? None?"

"None. Haven't received my check from my last construction job yet, but they say it's in the mail. But, Queenie, girl, don't sweat it. I'll even pay you back if it'll make you feel better."

My chicken Alfredo was turning on me. The room's drone of customer voices, the clink of silverware against bowls and plates, all faded away. I could feel the slow burn of acid reflux inching its way back up through my esophagus. No money to pay. *Umph.*

What kind of fool did he take me for? "Marcus, don't 'Queenie girl' me. Only my closest friends call me Queenie, and right now"—I waved a stiff finger across his face—"you are not my friend."

He looked surprised. "What? 'Cause you paying for the first date? Big deal. This is the new millennium, and women pay for dates just like men. And besides, I'm worth every penny of it. Come home with me, and let me show you. I promise, you won't regret it."

"Maybe so, maybe not, but we'll never know, will we? I just think you have some nerve pulling a stunt like this."

"Queenie, why you wanna be that way? Thought we were going to have a nice day together? Woman, I have plans for us. Devilish plans." He winked an eye and added, "I know you like to freak, and I'm just what you need."

I didn't have to see him gyrating his pelvis beneath the table; I could feel it. The man had gall, I had to give it to him. "You mean big plans as long as I'm paying?" Gritting my teeth at the same time, I opened my purse and fished around for my wallet. I didn't know which was upsetting me most, the ease of him conning me into a lunch at my expense or his devil-may-care attitude about it. Such a nice little restaurant, too. Nice decor. Not exactly what you could call cheap. What was that name again? Chateau-à-la-'bout-to-get-an-attitude. Instead, I gave him my most sweetest look. "Okay, okay. You win this time, Marcus."

"Woman, you tripping. It's just lunch, not a car payment."

"You got that right," I added, huffy. "I am not the one who pays to have a man." And to think that I had dressed up for him with my navy blue ankle-length velour skirt and top. I'd worn my black lace shawl and light black boots thinking that the June sky, a sneaky lace of sun and a few clouds, could be unpredictable.

"I think you're overreacting a bit." His eyes danced in a head that couldn't possibly hold common sense.

"And I think," I said with much attitude and a harsh whisper as I placed a fifty-dollar bill on the bill tray, "that if I had known that lunch would be on me when you were the one that asked me out, I wouldn't have come."

He looked almost hurt by my remark, but only for a few seconds. "Why you making a big deal of it? I said I'll pay you back the next time. I promise."

"The next time? Negro man, paahleezz. What makes you think there'll be a next time?"

"A little sassy now, aren't we?" He grinned like he was enjoying every minute of it. "But that's slick. I can deal. I like that in a woman like you."

The waitress, a blue-eyed, too thin, and pale girl with long, stringy brown hair, came up quietly and took our bill and my money away. I felt sick to my stomach but smiled in spite of it.

"A woman like me?" I asked, suddenly intrigued by his choice of words. "What's that supposed to mean, a woman like me?"

Picking up his glass of white wine, Marcus smiled and sipped at what remained in the glass, then gulped it as if he were suddenly dying of thirst. Looked like he wanted to fix his crooked-teeth-mouth-self to ask for another round, but my eyes dared him. "You trying to pick a fight, aren't you?" he said.

"Tell me, Marcus," I prompted with a true eagerness that had to be showing on my face. "What's a woman like me?"

He sat there, easing back in his seat to contemplate my expression. I swear, sometimes I feel like I can read minds. Ever since I was a young girl, growing up in Compton, I've had the feeling that some folks' thoughts scroll around in their eyes like neon signs that blink and reveal their message. You have to watch carefully. It's all in the eyes. I can almost see Marcus's thoughts scattering around in his pompous head.

I'm cool, though. I'd known men like Marcus before. Men who sought out larger females, thinking that their size made them more vulnerable and so needy of a man and easy prey who'd do anything just to have and keep a man. Even if that same man treated her like the crud on the bottom of his shoes. But I don't say anything. I wait to hear him say it.

"You know." He grinned in a teasing kind of way—funning with me, using his hands to gesture width. "The-more-to-love woman. A big girl like you. You nice and all, smart, witty, and for real you have a very pretty face, but—"

There it was. That all-familiar *but*. Wonder what had taken it so long to come out? That one little word, *but*. Seemed like all my life, I have heard that same little three-letter word come from so many mouths that even when I didn't hear the word itself, I saw it passing like some circling bird of prey in people's eyes. "You all right, Queenie, but . . ." Or, "I think you're a terrific woman, Queenie, but . . ."

It has taken me years to rise above it, to slap its meaning to the far corner of my life like some pesky fly that had buzzed around me for too long, and to keep stepping. Marcus T. was just another fool trying to work my nerves—another buzzing fly that needed to be put down.

"Oh, I see." I sat back in my own seat and looked out the window of the booth. The humid June sky was dotted with moving clouds, and the thick air seemed like it would never cool off. Traffic along Slauson Avenue never ceased moving. Made me think of ocean tides that never cease. One car after another, fleeing faces in colorful ships. So many people rushing here and rushing there. I wondered briefly what destination they all could be on their way to, then wondered what threads of good and bad weaved together to make the fabric of their lives. Did they, too, have to constantly fight the battle of the folks who tried to make a fool of 'em? The room was hotter. I shouldn't have worn velour.

"Hey, I—I mean, don't get me wrong," Marcus threw in after a brief quiet spell, stumbling over his words. "I mean, I ain't mad at'cha. Hell, me myself, I like a woman with some extra meat on her frame. Always have. Stuff to grab and hold on to."

A small chuckle from me. "Whew. Lord, I'm so relieved to hear that, Marcus." I do my proper Southern belle act, fanning myself. "I mean, what ever would us big-boned women do without men like you?"

"See," he snorted, and sat up straighter, looking more serious. "Why you wanna play a brother? I'm talking serious biz, and you joking."

"Guess because a brother needs to learn that all big women don't always make an easy target for a man who thinks he's doing her a favor just by going out with her. Yeah, I'll admit I like sharing intimate time with a nice, ebony brother, but make no mistake about it, Marcus, I like to be the one asking him out. It ain't that serious."

The waitress brought my change, and I left the three dollars for a tip. I got my purse and keys and stood up to leave. "I don't have a problem paying for a man's dinner, Marcus, but I should be the one asking him out when I do so. You didn't even know if I had enough money on me to cover this meal or not. You just *assumed* that I did. It was nice, but I'm outta here."

He looked shocked. "But what about us spending some real time together at my place?"

"What about it?" I couldn't get myself together to leave quick enough.

Marcus didn't bother to stand up. He sat there, looking stupid, looking up at me like he couldn't believe that I was actually leaving without him.

"I got some hot videos and bubbly at the crib. A little chronic if you flow that way. Don't you wanna spend some quality time with me?" He puckered and blew a kiss at me. "Let ol' Marcus make you feel good and make it up to you."

"Maybe that's your problem right there: too much chronic and all that smoke clouding your better judgment. Thanks, but no thanks, but I don't flow that way. As for us spending some quality time together, this was it." I stepped away from the booth, turned, and walked toward the exit.

"Hey, Queenie, wait up," he called after me. "Can a brother at least get a ride back home?"

I stopped and half turned around. "You the one like to assume so much—just assume you already have one. The bus stop is right outside."

"That's cold-blooded."

"Have a nice life, Marcus. And don't bother calling me."

Was he stunned or stupid? Don't know; don't care. I didn't bother to look back at his expression as I braced my back, squared my shoulders, and walked briskly to the door.

Two

Sometimes the company of a sistah friend can be more comforting than a man. Meaning your very best friend. Your homegirl. Your confidante. A best friend knows the comfort zone, and usually, how to put you in it. I blame her mama for that name. Poetta Chenell James. I was Poe's savior that first day we met, back in second grade at Mona Park Elementary. It had been Poetta's first day at school, when three bully girls tried to take her lunch money. "Which one of you girls want the first beat down?" I still remember my words when I boldly stepped in front of the ringleader, Edna Marie. Edna had ran off crying, even though I didn't get the opportunity of putting a finger on her.

I had saved the day, even though that brave act landed me a trip to the principal's office and Poetta a trip to the nurse's office, where she got a lollipop and cuddles. That's my buddy, though. No matter what.

After that lunch with Marcus, the comfort zone didn't sound so bad. That's how I was feeling by the time I got back to my car and headed down to the 110 Freeway and sped on. After talking with Poetta earlier that day, my best friend had mentioned that she was feeling a little under the weather, something about having the sniffles and a cold trying to come on. And me, being the loyal friend that I am, I'd promised her that I would stop in and check on her after my date with Marcus. And just because I knew that she would have done the same for me, I even stopped off at Vons and got her a few get-well items, you know, a few pieces of citrus fruit, some Vapor Rub, a carton of orange juice, and some zinc throat lozenges.

In no time, I was parked in front of the split-level, fake Spanish-style facade in Paramount that was Poetta's house. We're like night and day, but all the same, Poetta and I. Been friends back in the days when real men chased women and paid for all the dates and Afro hair-styling was in, and women thought it was cool to walk around on sky-high heels that secretly conspired to damage their backs and uteruses. We have a few dog days thrown in every now and then, but mainly it's a friendship long-shaped by loyalty and respect.

Unlike some folks that might have been jealous of her, I considered Poetta kind of lucky in the sense that after her mother passed away four years previous, she left Poetta with a nice chunk of life insurance money, payable in monthly installments, and a three-bedroom house that was completely mortgage free. Nothing fancy, though, but just enough house to get by on. Leaving the house just to Poetta and not jointly to her and her sister, Marva, tore a rip in their sisterhood for a while until they finally were able to resolve it. But Poetta's mother, God rest her soul, she knew what she was doing. Marva was okay, but it wasn't no secret that Marva was money hungry, too quick to flip her coin, and couldn't hold on to water for too long. Besides, Marva, according to her own words, had "professional coochie skills," and with those skills, she knew how to get anything she wanted from a man. Marva already had the things most women still seek—a big, fancy house; two big, fancy cars; a monthly spending allowance to die for; and a man that loves the dirt she walks on but is too old to remember it.

Quiet as kept, if Poe's house were my mine, I'd throw some new paint over the god-awful pink that look so out of place with the rest of the neighboring houses, and maybe do something with the old-fashioned windows that give the house a sad, unloved look; have the lawn professionally done; plant a few flowers. Instead of Poetta, it's always me the one talking about painting this and French windows that and fixing the place up a bit while Poetta is always too preoccupied with her burning candles, fixing other folks' problems, frying hair, chasing after one charity drive after another and pretending she so busy living larger than she really is. She sweet, though. Kindhearted, too.

I gotta say this, that for a sistah who don't keep a nine to five, Poetta got a lot going on. Unlike me, so she claims, she can't see herself stuck on somebody's dull and stupid job, so she falls back on one of her natural talents—one given to her by the master above—the beautifying of hair.

Whatever you could possibly need, my girl Poetta can hook it up: long, thin individual braids; braid wrap; goddess braids; a fancy weave; or a jamming perm. You name it. All done right out of the comfort and privacy of her own home.

Once I turn onto the quiet, magnolia-tree-lined street where Poetta lives, I can always tell that I'm getting closer to her house by the wispy balls of tangled human and synthetic hair migrating discreetly across the asphalt and lawns along her street. Tiny, man-made tumbleweeds, I call 'em. I'm surprised her neighbors haven't called out the city ordinance on her. But my best friend got it good that way. Her neighbors don't mess with her, and in return, she don't have to put a voodoo hex on her neighbors. It's not perfect, but it's an arrangement that works.

I parked my car in the driveway behind her four-year-old Toyota that still needs an engine, and got out with my small bag of offerings. Heat tried to burn a hole in my head as I made my way over the rotund stepping stones leading to her door. I love coming to her house, sharing her food, her time, her friendship, but I have wished for a better neighborhood. Too many teens roam the block, and not a weekend goes by without a loud and rowdy party going on. Sometimes the sound of gunshots ring out loud at night. Helicopters are almost permanent fixtures suspended in the sky near her house, which is too much excitement for me.

I wasn't paying enough attention, as usual, and a tangle of attacker hair caught my footing and threw me off balance right at the first step of her porch, where I stumbled and fell, sending the few items from my grocery bag scattering. Shooting pain zipped through my hip, and I must have hollered or yelped loud enough to bring Poetta—dressed in some long orange-and-brown African-print dashiki and black stretch pants—out to see what was up.

"Queenie? What happened?"

"Girl, you need to do something about all this hair mess in your yard 'fore somebody gets hurt!" I hollered up at her, feeling foolish for not watching my step. A hot pain in my back punctuated my frown.

"Umph. You'll live."

"Some help up would be nice."

"I know. It's my fault you fell. Sorry."

Poetta took her time coming over to help me up. Had the nerve to take a few seconds to stand and look up the street one way, and then the other. I don't know what the heck she was looking for, but it didn't seem like the right thing for her to be doing while I'm lying hurt on her grass. I swear. She my homie and all, but sometimes the girl just weird and spacey and don't even know it.

"Excuse me, some help here."

"Queenie, you gotta be more careful with yourself before you tear yourself up."

"And you need to be more concerned about my large and luscious behind hurting down here on your lawn before I have to sue you."

"If you watch where you walk sometimes, you wouldn't always have this problem. Here," she offered, outstretching her hand and making a face. "Let me help you up."

Now, that's just like Poetta, always finding fault but it's never blowing in her direction.

"Thought you supposed to be so sick." I slung the straps of my purse over my shoulder, dusted myself off, and rotated my neck to make sure it was still working right. Somehow she didn't look all that sick to me as she picked up my few items from her half-dead lawn and helped me up the short stairs and into the house.

"I am," she said lamely before leading me through her door. "But thanks to Mother Nature, they have herbal teas for everything that ails you."

"For everything?" I should know better than to inquire. Poetta brewed and sipped tea for everything from going to bed at night to helping with pooping and pissing in the morning. What tea couldn't fix, chanting and burning candles could, according to Poetta. She claims her mama taught her well.

"Like I said, for everything."

"What about a dried-up coochie?" I snickered, trying to be funny.

"Have tea for that, too. My own special blend I make up myself. I call it Moistplus. Now stop trying to be cute, and c'mon in the house."

"Yeah, right. I got your Moistplus, all right." Inside the house was too warm, as usual. Probably from the wall heater burning at full blast combined with all those darn candles burning in the background. That's another weird thing about my girl Poe. She got this thing about fire and candles. Something else her mama taught her. Poetta's mama, Mama James, had migrated from somewhere down in the Louisana bayou. Rumor I heard was that Poetta's mama had been run out of Louisiana when too many folks accused her of being a modern-day witch and there were threats on her life. Mama James left Poetta's father and drove herself and her two daughters out here to California, where hexing folks wouldn't be so noticeable. Don't know how much of the story is true, but Poetta definitely inherited candle-burning and chants from her. No matter what time of day or night, Poetta's house is always filled with the flicker and glow of burning candles. Scented candles, solid-hued candles, unscented candles, plain-shaped candles, and odd-shaped ones. Something spooky or something to be proud of, it's the only place I know of where you can use the rest room any time of day or night by candlelight.

"Girl, it's too hot up in here. No wonder you trying to come down with something. There's no circulating fresh air coming in." I fight the urge to start opening up windows.

If she heard, she igged me. Some time ago, Poe once told me that the burning of candles helped to control the flow of everyday living— helped things to get right after being wronged. Said that evil keeps away from the flames of justice. Whatever the heck that's supposed to mean. Her words had bothered me then, and sometimes, they still do. But I keep it to myself.

What bothers me even more is the fact that the girl even have a few weak or misguided followers that slip her a few dollars to "fix" things gone wrong in their mundane lives. Usually some cheating husband acting a fool or forgetting how to come home at night, or some mysterious ailment that a modern doctor can't seem to pinpoint. Funny the things that people choose to believe in.

Sometimes, I'll be sitting around at her house all quiet and observant when her so-called "clients" come through, but my ears be checking it all out, and I be laughing up a storm on the inside and wanting so bad to tell those foolish women that the only thing that Poetta can "fix" in their lives is their jacked-up hair. But it's not my business, so I leave it alone.

Somehow it's still a mystery to me, but about fifteen years back, Poetta became convinced that the burning of specific candles could cure or fix any problem from bad breath to bunions on the feet. She even went so far as to share some of her knowledge with me, but I can't remember all that hocus-pocus mess. Let me see now. . . . Oh, yeah. You want money to come your way, you say a special chant, burn two green candles with money underneath. Somebody put a hex on you, you burn a white and a black candle at midnight and recite your enemy's name three times. You want a no-good man to leave, you write his name on the egg from a black hen and throw that egg over the roof of your house. You think your man has a woman on the side, you burn his dirty drawers and bury the ashes with a pair of your own dirty drawers. Oh, and let's not forget the one where you have to burn three gray candles while burying his drawers at the stroke of midnight.

She'd carry on like this for weeks and months, me making fun of her silly beliefs in rituals, but as time passed that same laughter turned to deep and silent worry. Once, a few years back, when Poetta's sister, Marva, complained about her loss of a sex drive, Poetta convinced the girl that writing her name under a burning red candle under a full moon would take care of her problem. Now, don't get me wrong, and I'm not trying to say that some kind of hex was done and it worked on her sister, Marva. Oh, no—heck no. Queenie don't even believe in that mess. But I do have to admit one thing now, that girl Marva haven't been right with herself since. According to Marva, not only did her sex drive return, but thoughts of sex stays on her mind con-

stantly, like automatic breathing. And you didn't hear this from me
. . . but, if some kind of spell did work, it worked too good because
that girl, Marva, will lie down with any male that ask, even with a
blind dog on a wet day.

Like I said, me myself, I don't belief in all that hocus-pocus-place-a-
spell-on-somebody's-behind-mess. As it was, in the beginning of
Poetta's madness with chants and candles, it was hard for me to get
used to her always burning a candle for this and burning a candle for
that, but after a while I just summed it up to a harmless craziness that
was part of her. Kind of like body odor, not pleasant and not too
unpleasant, but just there. I just strive to be a good friend to her like
she is to me. "So, what's the haps with you?"

"As you can see, I've been keeping busy." She seemed pleased with
herself as she gestured to her clutter along the floor. "Charity starts
in the heart."

"So I see." Along the carpet was a few stacks of pink and blue flyers.
How quaint, I thought, looking around and thinking that it's times like
this that make me wish that I was more into donating my time to help
out some worthy cause besides myself. With her faithful hair customers and heavy dose of candle-burning on the side, Poetta practically
lived on this kind of stuff. "What's all this?" I asked, knowing good
and well that it had to be part of some gimmick to help raise money
for somebody's charity. Just last year alone I counted five different
charity drives that Poetta was part of: Save the Dolphins, Save the
Ozone, Save the Children, Save the Crackheads, and Save the But-
terflies. Hell, like it ain't crowed enough on the planet Earth. I can
see the Save the Children efforts, but if you ask me, maybe everything
wasn't meant to be saved. Just nature's way of keeping balance on a
self-destructing planet called Earth. And maybe, just maybe mankind,
especially Poetta, just need to stay out of it.

"So what's the subject this time?" I asked teasingly. "Save the fleas?"

"Queenie, make fun if you like, but at least I care about life."

"Yeah, right." For a while, some time back, the Save the Baby
Whales Organization was getting more play than the March of Dimes.
I remember thinking that it's a sad-state of the world when people
consider saving whales more important than saving starving children

living homeless on the streets, not to mention all the starving children in third-world countries. But who am I to be judging? All the same, it never stopped Poetta from going full force in her efforts. It's amazing the sort of causes that some folks will actually give money to. Still, though, I have to give my sistah girl her perks. I poke fun from time to time, but on the serious side, I have to admire Poetta for her tireless efforts. If people like her didn't stand up for some silly causes in the world, who would?

"Thought you were so sick," I reminded her again, raising a suspicious brow.

"I am, a little," she said pertly, closing the door behind us and coping her place back along the carpeted floor. She faked a few coughs, then a sneezed before going back to folding flyers to be stuffed into preaddressed envelopes. "Herbal tea did make me feel better, but I still have to mail out these notices for the AIDS Date-a-thon Gala in two weeks. We're hoping for a good turnout this year. Better than last year at Lakewood Mall."

"Where's it held this year?" I went into the kitchen to put my purchases away and came back out with two cans of light beer. "Here. Join me."

The girl musta looked up and rolled her eyes at me like I'd asked her to piss in a cup for a random drug test. "Queenie, you know Jimboy don't like me drinking in the middle of the day."

"Excuse me," I said with a raised brow and glaring back down at the top of her wrapped head. "But Jimboy left this morning, and you said he won't be back in town for another week. Remember?"

"True that, but I still honor his wishes. It's called loyalty."

"Well I won't tell 'im if you don't," I proposed, still holding the cold beer out to her. "It's not like you're married to 'im. The man don't have to know every time you fight, flirt, or burp, does he?"

"Queenie, hush up."

"If I can have a beer, you can have a beer."

"Well, that's you, Queenie, and I'm me. I don't drink behind my man's back if it's not his wishes."

Well, hell, just get a gun and shoot me for living. Maybe you should burn a candle on his behind and bring 'im home early so you can have a beer when you feel like it. I sat the extra beer on the coffee table and kept my thoughts to myself. "Okay. I'll leave that one alone."

"Please do, and I appreciate it. I have a lot to do today."

"Good for you." I found myself a spot in my favorite chair. Poetta's house might not look like much from the outside, but it's pretty clean and cozy on the inside, and furnished nicely, too. Large and plush pillows on an oversize brown sofa. A large matching chair. Nice oaken end tables perched on a cream-soda-hued carpet. It's my home away from home. At least when Jimboy's not around.

Ever since Poetta hooked up with Jimboy and let the man actually move in with her, I made it a point to keep my distance when he's in town. But thanks to his job of hauling fresh and frozen chicken carcasses across country, his presence wasn't too regular.

"She can't have a beer behind his back. Don't that take the cake." I shouldn't be that way. I don't have a real problem with Jimboy—I mean, not really. He's all right in a undress-every-woman-with-his-probing-eyes kind of way. Personally, I couldn't have a truck driver for a man. Too many lonely nights just to say that I have a man. But Poetta loves the ground he walks on and claims that his sporadic absence gives her more time to meditate—more time to get in touch with her spiritual self. Guess that's all that really matters. I watch her folding and stuffing.

"Looks like a whole lotta work to be doing for free."

"That's why they call it charity work, Queenie. But you wouldn't know much about that."

"Guess not. Queenie don't like working for free." I pull the tab on my can.

"Queenie don't much like working for money either, so what's your point?" she says, looking up, grinning.

"Got that right," I throw over at her. I sat, sipping my beer, and watched her work for a while. Sometimes I envy her simple contentment with life. Even with her spacey weirdness, Poetta has a spiritual peace that I often try to draw on. Sometimes I think it's her spiritual peace that keeps us tethered as friends. Her creamy, peanut-hued face is always so open, so at peace with the world that it sometimes takes me to a different level, one I have a hard time getting back from.

Some years back, she won a Janet Jackson look-alike contest. Maybe not Janet now, but Janet in her younger years before she discovered nipple rings and sex—rounded and high cheek bones, smiley eyes and that glazed-over look of sweet innocence. Poe could pass for Janet's sister if she wanted.

We might be best friends, but at the same time, we are so different—so completely opposite of one another. We share twenty-eight years each of living on the planet, and our birthdays fall on the same day, the tenth, but a month apart. Where I am tall and slightly thick, Poetta is thin, short, petite, and mostly quiet with sparkling dark eyes that take in all life around her and analyze it. Her aura is usually calm and mellow until you get her dandruff up. Then, all hell could break loose. Her eyes are so dark brown that they appear black, and I can't recall a time when long and thin braids didn't live atop her perfectly rounded head.

I heard once, as rumors sometimes go, that Poetta's father relocated to California to join her mother and then turned gay in his later years. Poetta claims that after twelve years of marriage, her mama came home one night and found her father in their bed with a man. It had freaked me out hearing about it, not that my homie told the whole neighborhood or took out an ad in the *Press Telegram*, but we don't keep secrets like that. I was freaked hearing about her dad turning gay because I didn't know such a thing was possible—folks just up and turning gay. Don't know how much truth was in it, 'cause Poetta and I both were seven when we met and I never got a chance to meet her father. But being armed with that knowledge alone seem to have its own effect on Poetta. I saw it in the way that she held fast and tight to her man, when I knew that she could do better.

Even when we were young girls running wild in the 'hood of Compton, Poetta always had a male in her life: a boy dog, a male cat named Tookie, a male turtle named Scamp, a boyfriend, a man to call her own, or somebody else's man. Simply put, like a lot of black women, Poe had to have a male on the back burner of her life for her life to worth anything. Used to trip me out, but after a while, you get used to things.

As the years slipped by, Poetta has avoided her father like the plague. As if being gay were something that could be caught from close contact, like the flu or TB or something that can be passed down in the bloodline like eye coloring or thick lips.

"So tell me," I ask between sips of my beer, enjoying every bit of the coolness rushing down my throat. I wanted to talk about anything to keep her from bringing up the subject of Marcus T. "What's this Date-a-thon Gala about?"

"Girl, pleeease." Poetta looked up, feigning surprise at my query. Candlelight catches a glint from her eyes, giving her a childlike look for a moment, mischievous but smart. "Like you don't already know. The same as last year 'cept it'll be at Fox Hills Mall. Two separate bid wars for dates with attractive and successful people, and all monies going to AIDS research. You'll have a ball."

"Excuse me." Now it's my turn to feign surprise. "And what makes you think I wanna be at some dumb fund-raiser where people have to bid on dates?"

"Because it's for a worthy cause, that's why."

"So."

"Because you're my very best friend, and behind that tough-girl exterior you put up, you're really a kindhearted person who is sensitive and generous."

"Heck, I'm your only friend, but I'm not trying to hear about paying for a date. Queenie pays for no one." I didn't dare mention how lunch earlier with Marcus T. had been on me.

"Because Billy Dee Williams will be there."

"So what if—? Wait . . . Did you say Billy Dee Williams?"

"That's right." She looked up to see if I was taking the bait.

"Girl, I know you're not talking 'bout the one and only, superfine and suave Billy Dee Williams, the actor that I've had a crush on for practically my whole life. Poe, don't play with me!" She knew that she was wrong to be trying to play me that way, slip-sliding on the thin ice of my emotions. Since I was knee-high to a dwarf I've had a serious crush on Billy Dee Williams, and she knew it.

"And I told Billy how much you loved all his movies, too."

I shot up from my seat, spilling a tiny spot of beer on old carpet. "Poetta! Girl, don't play with me. You talked to Billy Dee Williams 'bout me?"

"Uh-huh. I sure did." She smiled up at me, happy that I was interested.

"You'd better not be lying to me. Poetta, I'm not playing!"

"Look, are you gonna help me with the Date-a-thon, or not?"

"And Billy Dee Williams will be there?" I wanted to make sure that I was hearing her right. I knew that she used to work a short spell for a major film production company some years back, which meant that my girl did have a few connections, but Billy Dee Williams? Dang. Heck, for all I know, she could have been burning candles on his behind, too . . . and . . . Who cares! Heck, to see Billy, not only would I help, I'd sponsor the whole function if I had to.

"That's right." She smiled sweetly, displaying perfect white teeth. "And you know if sister Marva knows that Billy Dee is coming, she'll try her best to claim the man for herself, so you can't be half stepping. You gotta be there, and be there early."

"Wow," I said, almost drooling in my beer. "Billy Dee."

"Girl," Poetta threw in like some afterthought. "We are going to have some fun. You'll see. All kinds of folks will be there from the actor's guild. You won't believe the celebrities. You'll see."

"Poetta," I said proudly, resisting the urge to rush over and give her a big hug. "Girl, you something else with the hook ups." I felt better already. All thoughts of my dreadful date with Marcus T. faded away like smoke from a room. Who needed chopped meat like Marcus when they could have a chance at filet mignon of Billy Dee?

"Then you'll come to the AIDS Gala?"

"For Billy Dee? Hell, yeah," I said. *That's a no-brainer*. "You can count me in."

"All right then. Now bring yourself on over here, and help a sistah out with these flyers."

That's my homie, I thought, smiling ear to ear. My girl, my ace boon. Always looking out for a sistah.

I placed my beer on the coffee table and eased down along the floor with her and started folding and stuffing. For the moment, just like in the old days when we had sat out back of my mama's house making mud pies in the summer heat, we were bonded in goodwill and happiness. Two friends, thighs spread-eagle in front of a short stack of dream-filled flyers.

Poetta made a sly expression. "So, how was your date with Marcus?"

"Girl, Marcus farcus. Forget that fool. All I want to think about right now is Billy Dee."

To that, all she said was, "And you shall."

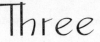

Three

Hate. Such a strong word, but unfortunately, a reality. A person could spend a lot of time in life hating things that you can't change, like the size of your feet, the sound of your voice, or the sway in your walk. And then again, you can keep telling yourself that you simply will not hate it, and that you will do your best to deal with it. For instance, the way I have to deal with going in to work the next day. No matter how much I like my job, I hate dreaded Monday.

Two, three, sometimes five days a week, it's the same thing—like some part I must perform in a badly written script I did not write. I park my car in the designated spot in the Macy's concrete parking structure and take the elevator up to the third floor of the corporate office, where my office, along with a cohesive collection of other departments it takes to run a successful department store, resides. The executive floor, they call it.

Once the elevator opens up to the third floor, I draw a deep breath, my back stiffens, my heart races as my breath catch and release somewhere inside my chest. My hands start to feel sweaty as I cautiously poke my head out from the elevator. I look to the left. I look to the right. I hold my breath. Everything looks clear. The itchiness along my backside calms down. I feel it's safe to exhale. I look to my left one more time, just to be sure, confident in the fact that I don't see him. I step out from the elevator and stroll casually to the spacious corner office that is mine—my own private space for as long as I work for Macy's.

Fifty feet away and counting backwards. I pass the green-eyed devil that goes by the name of Claudia Freeman, whose sole purpose in life is to keep mess and scandal alive in the workplace. She, of course, has been blessed to come to the right place to find employment. If red hair were a strong indication of intelligence, Claudia would be listed as the smartest white woman in the world. With each passing week, her hair takes on a new shade of red: ruby red like the inside of an overripe grapefruit one week, fire engine red like an emergency the next, and now, to my subtle horror, blood clot red, like a tragedy. *Hmph.* I may have forgiven her for generating that vicious rumor about me sleeping with my boss a few months back, but I certainly haven't forgotten. You never forget. The idea is, I have to keep reminding myself on a regular basis to maintain a professional relationship at work at all times. I tuck my indifference away as I near her desk. Claudia spots me first from her tackboard cubicle. Mischievous green eyes light up.

"Morning, Miss Slut." Playfully, she gives a cute wave and smile.

"Hey, Miss Hoe." I smile back. We were rival enemies once, but a good slap to her head in the privacy of a locked rest-room stall cured all our problems and put mutual respect back in its place. She probably would have reported the abuse, but after reciting her address and assuring her that I'd drive straight to her house to set up my new residence should I lose my job behind that slap, she let it go. We good to go now—play-friends for life. We got it that way.

No time to stop and shoot the breeze. I keep my focus in tow. Forty feet and counting. I spot a few more early starters and wave. A few more good mornings through tight, morning lips. A few more feet to go, and I still don't see no sign of him.

"Morning, Mack. Hey, Jesse. How's the wife and kids? Good to hear it."

I wave to my left. "Morning, Jamal. Hope that rash cleared up."

I can't wait to get to my office and close my door and lock out the rest of the world. Once I get to the end of a paneled wall—freestanding tackboard screens, actually—I say a quick prayer and peek around look for any sign of him. Ten feet away, I see the closed door to my office. I can almost feel the joy surging like a new river through my veins at the thought of being home free. I look to my left, then look to my right, clutch the handle of my briefcase tighter, and get to stepping fast toward my office, where I stand and wrestle briefly with the doorknob. In one big whoosh of relief, I swing myself up into the place, which is supposed to be my designated area of working privacy—my sanctum, my temporary safe harbor away from my working peers. I made it! Finally, alone at last. Sighing with relief, eyes squeezed shut, I stand with my back pressed against the thin wooden brown door as I say a little prayer of thanks. "Thank you, Lord. . . . Thank you Jesus. . . ."

But no sooner I open my eyes, the signs that he has beaten me to this place, again, are right before me. I see the soft candlelight flickering along the top of my desk. Alongside it, a single long-stemmed rose stands in brazen red in a crystal vase. I see the beautiful layout of thinly sliced cantaloupe melon and bowl of cherries. Chunks of cheese and a steaming cup of coffee sit next to the short floral glass of orange juice. No doubt freshly squeezed. The bran muffin, large and oozing its cinnamon warmth waits for me next to a bed of thick sliced bananas. I see it all and think out loud, "What the hell—?"

And then I see him—Mr. Raymo strolling out casually from my adjacent private rest room, drying his hands and smiling his silly little smile that makes my behind feel funny as my sphincter muscle tightens with a spasm that always triggers a mysterious pain in the center of my back.

"Goodness, no. Not now."

His name is Raymundo Carlos Morales Castillo. Better known as Raymo the pest around our quaint and friendly little department. God must be punishing me for something I've done in a previous life, because six months after I landed the job as senior buyer for women's fine wear and accessories, Raymo came on as senior buyer in the men's department. I was happy to meet him in the beginning. He was nice and smiley, a little short, quite a talker, and clearly no concern or threat to me. Not a bad-looking Latino man, wonderful personality, so I thought at the time. He seemed like a man in a stable frame of mind, smiled a lot, and knew how to dress to a T. As much as it pains me, I am forced to look at his position within the company as being equal to mine, which means I have no solid grounds or higher rank to pull to have him dismissed from his duties as one of the department's top buyers for men's clothing. Aside from the fact that Raymo is doing a wonderful job of harassing me with his unfocused delusions of love, I think he's a great guy. Yes. It's true. Raymundo Carlos Morales Castillo is madly in love with me, Queenie, and he doesn't care who knows it.

I'm still not used to it myself, but it's a revelation I've been telling to Poetta for months now. Just like last month, I ran it by her again. "Girl," I said to her over my second wine cooler while sitting in her kitchen. "You know the office nerd, Raymo, is in love with me, and he just won't leave me alone and I don't know what to do about 'im."

"Who? That short Latino guy you keep talking about?"

"Yep, that's him."

We were sitting in Poetta's candlelit kitchen waiting for some of her gut-burning chili to get done. Everybody that knows Poetta knows that she makes a mean chili that if you eat it by lunchtime, it can clean out your entire system by the end of the day. I keep teasing the girl that she ought to bottle the stuff, stick a label on it, and sell it as gut cleaner, but she never takes me serious.

"I might have to shoot 'im just to get 'im to leave me alone."

"Queenie, the man has a crush on you. How bad can that be?"

She obviously didn't understand. "A crush is one thing," I had rebutted, looking every bit of serious. "But this man is driving me crazy. I'm seriously thinking 'bout filing sexual harassment on him, which I know my boss, Jay, won't appreciate." I recall her helpful tidbit of advice as if it were yesterday.

"Queenie," she'd said, waving her frivolous hand because nothing was really important to discuss about a man unless it was something about her Jimboy. "I can help you out. Have him where he won't be able to stand the sight of you."

"Figures." If I was telling her that Jimboy had a mean crush on me, she would be ready to work some kind of hex on the both of us, blow graveyard dust in our faces, burn two candles at midnight, and consider us fixed. Not that Queenie believe in hexes, but I just know Poetta.

"Bring me a lock of his hair, and I can fix it."

"Yeah, right." She must be insane. "Thanks, but no thanks." What did she think I could do, walk up to the man and ask for a patch of his hair? "He don't have that much hair to be giving some away."

"So what if the man has a little crush on you. You should be flattered if anything. It's cute and probably harmless. Sleep with 'im. You'll see. Once and he'll get over it and calm down. Good loving always calms a man down. Once he's had you, he won't be sniffing so hard behind you trying to get some. It's like a cure."

I stared at her like she had two heads and both heads could talk and chew bubble gum at the same time. "Are you crazy? That might be a possibility if I was taking a combination of Valium and Prozac. Obviously you don't understand what I'm saying here. The man is not my type. Reminds me too much of . . . you know who."

"No, who?" She feigns ignorance.

I had igged her on. "B'sides, I don't know how many times I have to tell him that I'm just not interested, and I wouldn't sleep with 'im if one day all the male special equipment in the world mysteriously dried up and fell off from their owners, and his was the only one left in tact. No way, José."

"Queenie, is he that bad? Never say never."

"Oh, I can. Bad? Yes. I mean no. I mean yes, he is . . . sorta. I mean, he's not ugly or nothing like that, but—"

"But what? What's wrong with 'im?" She had looked like she needed more convincing.

"Well," I had reflected, not knowing what to list first. "He's too short for me. Don't care for short men. Short men usually have short you-know-what, and you know how I feel about that."

"Queenie, please, that's a myth. And?" She put a spoon to her mouth to taste her chili concoction, then prompted with, "Go on," like she was taking a survey. "What else is wrong with the man that you can't date 'im?"

"And . . . and he's half-bald with small dark-brown eyes. Small light-brown eyes I can deal with, but not dark brown. And too nervous and jittery acting, like he can't control where he puts his hands, all touchy-touchy, and feely-feely. I hate that in a man. Heck, I might have more hair on my chest than that man have on his head." I stopped to reflect on his eyes. The same dark eyes like Monroe had. Eyes that couldn't be trusted. "Too much like Monroe for me."

Goodness. What made me bring up that name? Monroe had been my first Latin lover. The first one to break my heart, and as far as I was concerned, Monroe had been the last.

She laughed. "More hair on your chest? I hope not. Monroe hurt you bad, but Monroe is not Ray. Give Ray a chance. Think of some good points about 'im."

"Nice lips, though. I gotta give 'im that much. Always smells good. But still, reminds me of Monroe. Nah. No more Latino lovers for me. I can't feel the trust."

"Stop comparing and give 'im a chance. He could be the one, Queenie. From what I've heard, Latino lovers are the bomb! You never know."

"Poe, you crazy. Sex is not the answer to everything."

"No, and you're just too picky about men."

"It's not that easy," I had countered.

"Only with you, Queenie. You make love so difficult. It's not a cut-and-paste kind of thing. It takes time to nurture."

"Yeah, right, like you the expert. But I'ma break this guy if it's the last thing I do. Might have to go postal and take my pistol to work and pistol-whip 'im to get my point across that I'm not interested."

"Girl, you tripping. He can't be that bad. Like I said, sleep with 'im. He'll calm down. You'll see."

It had been pointless. I couldn't make Poetta understand. Heck. I couldn't make Raymo understand. No matter how strongly I tried to convince him that I could never be the woman for him, he just wouldn't give up.

Now, here he is again, in my office. A too-friendly trespasser. We looked at one another for a few seconds, speechless.

"You are late, my precious ruby," he says with his heavy accent.

His voice, whenever he speaks to me, comes out in a deep, slow, and seductive drawl, and I can tell that he is all too serious.

"Raymo." My first instinct is to laugh, but annoyance holds me back. I must keep a straight face. I must. How else will this man understand that I mean serious business?

"You are feeling well rested?"

My shoulders slump. "Raymo, no . . . not today. I am not in the mood for your antics today. Please leave my office immediately before I have to call security."

"And they shall come, and they shall see that I have come only for the goodness of pleasing you. They, too, shall see the love I have for you."

My words don't register. Not when he has the nerve to stroll right to my chair, pull it out, and beckon with his outstretched hand.

"Come, now. You must sit. You are hungry, yes?"

"Yes . . . I mean no." I don't budge from my spot. "I'm not hungry, Ray. Don't want no trouble this morning. I just want you to leave my office right now."

"Look." He gestured toward his breakfast layout, like I hadn't said a thing, obviously pleased with himself. "I have prepared for you your favorite to ease your morning. Come, now, my sweet, you must eat now."

"Look, Raymo, it's a nice thing you've done here. Really. But . . . I really wish you would stop with this bringing me food, gifts, and flowers and tokens of your unfocused attention. It's not natural, Raymo. Not when I don't feel the same way about you."

"You don't like the homemade tamales I left on your desk last Friday?" He held up his two hands like a surgeon after scrub down. "These hands . . . I made them with these hands. Me, all by myself. I am known to be a good cook, yes?"

Heck. I couldn't lie about that. They were the best damn tamales I'd had in my entire life, but . . . "That's not the point. And, yes, they were delicious. But this has got to stop. It's not natural for you to carry on this way when I can't show you the same feelings in return."

Three swift lifts of his too-thick black brows. "There is never anything unnatural about love. Love is natural." He paused to smile warm and gooey-eyed. "Come. You must eat now."

It's useless. Already I feel exhausted, like I've worked two weeks in a row on somebody's railroad without a break. "I'm not hungry," I lie, knowing good and well that the piece of wheat toast and glass of juice I'd grabbed on my way out this morning hadn't been enough to sustain me. "Leave now, please." His cologne is strong but nice. I feel like asking the name of it, but I fight the urge.

Walking back over to me, he stands right in my face. Well, almost in my face because his face is about an inch below my chin. Actually, I can see the top of his head, where a small runway of hair has been cleared for his baldness to take off. I have nothing personally against shorter, balding Latino men with small lips that tear up the English language on a regular basis. Really, I don't. The man wasn't bad-looking at all. And if he didn't try so hard, I could probably . . . No. No way. He sure smelled good. Almost intoxicating. I wanted to pinch myself for even thinking about that. Ray is a good-hearted person, just not the man for me.

Okay. Better scenario. Picture this: me, a good size sixteen sliding slowly, 'rumpalicously to a size eighteen. Tall and beautiful, standing at least one inch over this man even with my low pumps off. He is dressed impeccable, I can't deny. Always smells good, too. He is all of five feet eleven inches compared with six feet of womanhood. Not short by average, but short for me. One of my breasts, not to toot my own horn, would make up the size of his head alone. He is a small man trying to play hardball in a big woman's world. Perhaps it's my imagination, but it looks to me like my twelve-year-old brother, if I had one, could overpower him in a good wrestling match. But again, I could be wrong. Books can't always be judged by their covers. Did I mention dark brown eyes? I'm sure I did. Add to that, a thick black mustache that half hide even white teeth. Handsome in his own way, but not what I'm looking for right now. And there you have Raymundo Carlos Morales Castillo. Mr. Raymo.

Not so close, Raymo, my mind screams. *Not so close!*

"You cannot fight it, Queenie. The destiny of love. You will never know the true meaning of pleasure until you have known Raymundo."

"Excuse me, but I'll take my chances. And you won't know the true meaning of being pain free if you don't leave."

"You play hardball, this is true, but you cannot fight it forever, love. Something that is meant to be. No matter how hard you try, Queenie. I am all the man that you will ever need in your life. You cannot see this, yes?"

Little man, pul-leeze. Don't even try laying your little peanut head against my bosom . . . Raymo. "I wouldn't do that if I were you. I'm not playing."

"I will love and cherish you like the queen you are meant to be. The queen in my life, yes."

"Not today, Raymo. Now, enough is enough, please leave."

He reached and picked up my free hand, held it too tight for me to pull it out from his grasp. "A hundred years can pass, and I will always love and cherish you. You are the sunshine of beauty that melts my heart. I cannot help how I feel, Queenie. Do not punish me because of how I feel for you."

"Okay. That's enough, I said." I drop my briefcase, pull my hand out from his sweaty grip, stoop a bit to heft his too-light body up. I open my office door and walk out carrying Raymo, all 150 pounds of him slung over my shoulders, back to the door of his own office.

All eyes are on us. I know it looks crazy, me dressed in my satin eggshell white blouse and baby-blue business suit and stepping hard with my eggshell white pumps with Raymo slung over my shoulder like a limp bag of mulch. Me looking every bit of serious, and him still professing his undying love. I mean, give me a break.

"A strong woman I love. Strong hips for babies, and one day you shall see, Queenie, all the love that I have for you. Then you will be sorry you did not appreciate me, for I have dreamed the dream of lovers, and your face was the face I saw."

I keep my lips tight. "Uh-uh, hmm." *Maybe when hell freezes over.*

". . . Love is the gift that all wish to receive. You cannot run from true love. There is no place to hide . . ."

I heft him down, stand him on his feet, allowing him a few seconds to compose himself, straighten his own suit, gather up some dignity, if there was any left to gather. "You are some kind of woman. Strong and powerful, like an ebony goddess. You are, yes?"

His slurpy look up at me makes me want to scream. Still, I say nothing as I brush off his nice suit. The one he looked pretty nice in. One thing for sure, nobody can say that Raymo can't dress. Must spend his whole paycheck on nice suits and shoes. Dang. "Thanks for breakfast, but if I catch you in my office again, I'll tear your little head off and use it like a bowling ball."

"And I love you, too." He blows a kiss my way.

Sick, sick man. He actually perked up at hearing my threat.

"But then," he said, his eyes flashing with mischievousness, "If my head is off, you will not be able to feel my warm lips along your lovely body should I kiss you all over."

I stare down at him, eye to eye. "Then I'll just strangle you."

"Yes, but you shall have to put your lovely hands around my neck to do."

Enough is enough. "Raymo!" I scream, ignoring all prying eyes, inquiring minds, and nosy looky-lous. "Get some professional help! Okay!" I turn and hurry, marching like some one-track-minded soldier on a mission back to the sanctum of my own office, where the phone is almost ringing off the hook. "Who the heck—"

Quick, I closed my office door and locked it. Never mind the blinds for now. I snatched up the receiver, hoping it wasn't my boss. After Raymo, I certainly wasn't in the mood for his shenanigans either this morning. "Miss Sutton here. How may I help you?"

And there was that voice. His voice. Raymo's. "Yes. You may help me by stop playing this childish game. You know that I am the man to treat you like a queen."

"I do?"

"Yes, you do. But you are fighting it."

"What the—? Ray, give it a rest!" I slam the receiver back down and hurry over to my chair and flop down. I ramble through the middle drawer for aspirin, Tylenol, anything that could help with the headache that was starting like a small storm in some vicinity of my head. I almost feel sorry for him. "Little, crazy, mixed-up-in-the-head man."

I had been dreading it for months, thinking about it, but dreading it, too. As much as I hated it, I knew what I had to do. Too much time had slipped by with Raymo constantly sexually harassing me, and it wasn't getting any better. In the beginning it wasn't so bad. Perhaps even—I can't believe I'm even thinking such a thing—kind of cute, but in a twisted kind of way. All I know is after the third week of his employment with the department, I was a little flattered by his interest, his little sexual innuendos. Certainly, he didn't have a lack of females in the department being interested in him. What woman don't like a man that can cook from scratch?

He was like a bee that took to me, honey. And in a way it was sort of amusing—him, at least in my eyes, being such a small statue of a man having the gall to think that he could take on a woman of my substance, of my caliber. Did he really think he could court the Queen? Didn't he have sense enough to realize that he could only be the appetizer on my plate of life, but never the main course? Why couldn't he see this himself?

A beautiful and voluptuous woman, such as myself, could sip all the juice out a man like Raymo in one sitting and toss him aside like an empty carton. Oh, my. I had to slap my own face. Just the thought of sipping anything on Raymo made me shudder. If he didn't look so much like a shorter version of Monroe. Monroe had broken my heart. I couldn't let that happen again.

After downing three aspirin, I flopped down in my leather executive chair and let my mind run wild with the details of what I needed to do. Ray. What a persistent man. His lips always trying to kiss me, hands always trying to touch me. Could our lips truly feel right together? I doubt it. Ray and Monroe—one and the same. What did I need with another Latin lover breaking my heart? Wasn't one enough? Sexual harassment. That's all it was, and as much as I hated the thought of filing an harassment claim on Ray, I didn't see any other way to make him stop. "One more chance," I mumble under my breath. "One more."

Four

Yesterday, Monday, I let it slide. Now it's Tuesday morning, more red roses on my desk. Enough is enough. I should have done it months ago. If I couldn't get Raymo to cease with his foolishness of being in love with me, I'd have to find somebody who could. I was sick and tired of him, and sick and tired of being sick and tired. No more Miss Nice Lady. I was going for the hard artillery. I thought about calling the office of Johnnie Cochran, but he might already have his plate too full for my case. Then again, I believe I read somewhere that Johnny handles only criminal law.

"The hell with this!" I shoot up from my desk and march to my door and throw it open, then march down the hallway, around the corner, and down another hallway to Jayron O'Conner's office.

Jayron is the man, the top honcho over all buyers. In fact, Jayron had been the person responsible for me getting hired at Macy's some years back. Unfair workload, need time off for personal matters, or a strong urge to blow off some steam—Jay was the man to see when problems arise within the department. Though it's true that we've shared a few lunch excursions, honest to God, each time it had been to discuss issues and matters dealing with our department or my job performance or the possibility of a big promotion in my favor. Despite those rumors, I'd never entertained the thought of actually sleeping with the man. Not really. Fantasizing about us being buck naked in a stainless steel room, him tied with silk rope and me standing over him with a leather whip—well, that one don't count. Besides, I had consumed two glasses of sherry before I went to bed that night. Alcohol sometimes does that to me, even small amounts.

Jay is okay, at least most of the times. I wouldn't exactly consider the man a good friend, but usually, Jay did a good impression of being a fair, honest, and a decent boss that a troubled employee could talk to. That was most of the time.

Swallowing the lump in my throat, I knock hard twice on his closed door, and after a second or two I hear his deep, throaty voice telling me to come in.

"Queenie. Morning."

"Jay, top of the morning to you, too."

If anybody had it going on at Macy's, especially in the department where I worked, it had to be Mr. Jayron O'Conner. Inside his office is more like the inside of an elegant model home of two rooms. The expensive kind. Beautiful cherrywood desk, Italian leather executive chair. Cherrywood file cabinets and matching chairs. Large potted palms everywhere you look. All sitting pretty on an expansive handmade oriental rug, an impressive, not to mention very expensive rug. The sound of traffic beneath it, the view from his office window looks out on a magnificent balcony-enclosed rose garden that was probably planted expressly for him. Every time I enter his office, I feel myself drawn to that great sweep of window, if only to stand and gaze out at red and white Double Delights and Snow Beauties before Jayron brings me back to myself by asking, "What the hell can I do for you, Miss Queenie?"

His tone and choice of wording never changes. What the hell can I do for you? What the hell is on your mind? What the hell took you so long to get back from lunch? Maybe that's what I like about Jay— he's like a rock that never changes. He's so straight to the point. Such a put-his-foot-in-your-shit-right-away kind of guy. You can't help liking that in a man.

"Jay," I say, pausing to make sure I'm about to say it right. I fold my arms over my ample bosom, the way I always do when I'm having a problem and look out the window in front of me. Sometimes a woman's large breasts can be distracting, even for her. "I've decided to file a sexual harassment claim."

Behind my back, I can hear his shocked gasp. I imagine his thick pink lips turning down in a contemplative smirk, his emerald green eyes almost popping out from his pale face with freckles that had to be turning as red as his thick hair. All that Irish blood starting to boil up.

"Now . . . now Queenie, let's not be too hasty. Things can be worked out."

I can feel him sweating. A few circulating rumors had it that a few of the office females found the man handsome, somewhat of a hunk, and that whispered rumor about the man being hung like a horse always teases somewhere at the back of my head, but it's just something I heard. I wouldn't have the nerve to find out if it were true. Not with my boss. But in my book, he's all right. He's got this constant sniffing thing, like a permanent cold lives in his head and his sinus needs clearing—always looking at his watch like each second you spend in his presence is time wasted and can never be recaptured. Ticktock, ticktock. If I didn't work for Macy's and was into bigheaded men, I could almost see myself with someone like Jay. That nice brown Boss suit he's wearing has to be feeling a tad too tight by now.

Jay has been with the company for twice as many years as me, and if anyone considered themself one loyal employee, it's Jay. Behind my back, he has to be running nervous fingers through all that thick red hair, making me wonder if it's all real and his, or perhaps surgically implanted.

"What the hell for, Queenie? You do know that harassment suits don't make good job choices, right?"

"Neither does being harassed day in and day out at work by a man you have no romantic interest in, Jay."

"My God, Queenie, a few pats to your rear end, a sly pinch to a breast every now and then, I really didn't mean anything by it."

I turned around. "What the hell—? I'm not talking about you, Jay. I'm talking about Raymo. I can't take it anymore! The man is driving me to drink!"

He looked a tad embarrassed. "Raymo? . . . Oh, yes . . . Raymo."

"Yes, Raymo."

"Just what the hell did he do?"

"Jay, haven't you been paying attention to what's been going on?"

"Drink? Sounds good to me. What's your choice?"

Perhaps he had a hearing problem. The man even had the gall to reach into the side drawer of his desk and pull out several miniature bottles of liquor, much like those small bottles they give you on airplane flights, lining them up along his desk like toy soldiers. Unsmiling, I walk around to the front of his desk and take a seat.

"You're not listening to me."

"Hell, yes, I am. Let's see," he says, all into it like he's the new bartender in town and I'm some new paying customer he needs to impress. "I have whiskey, rum, and vodka. I rather fancy the vodka myself."

"Jay, I'm serious." I don't blink.

"Might be out of orange juice, though. Can you handle straight?"

"Yeah, straight to the point." I see where this is going: nowhere quick. Jay is in denial as much as Raymo. But what did I really expect from an Irish blood who dated black hookers who only wear blond wigs? Rumors get around. *Think I don't know, huh?*

"Look," I almost yell, hoping to get his full attention. "If you're not up to hearing this, I'll just leave now and go call my attorney to see what I need to do."

"Okay. Okay. I'm listening." He halts his playing with the tiny bottles of liquor and sits up straighter in his chair. "Who the hell is it again? Casey down in the mail room? I see the way he looks at you sometimes. Like . . . like you're a giant slab of country-style ribs, and he's the sauce. Or is it Martin in electronics? Let me tell you, I never believed those rumors about you and him from the beginning."

"Rumors? Martin who? What rumors? See, that's what I don't like about working at this place, too many people keep mess going and running their pie traps. What rumor about Martin and me? Never mind. Look, I don't even wanna know. Didn't you hear me the first time? I'm talking about Ray."

"Ray Castillo?" He'd said it as if were the first time he'd heard the man's name. "You want to file a sexual harassment claim on Raymo?"

"You darn right on Raymo. The man is nuts, and he won't leave me alone."

He grins, looking straight at me. "Little, nice-to-everyone and can-cook-like-a-pro Raymo? The sharpest dresser—besides myself, of course? Raymo?"

I could see more laughter in his eyes. "Then you know who I'm talking about. He keeps sending me flowers and candy and mushy-sounding cards, not to mention the daily offerings of food."

"Food? What kind of food?" He licks his lips slyly, before going into a chuckle. "Wouldn't be any of those wonderful sopes he makes?"

"Heck, I don't know. You name it, but mostly Mexican food, you know, burritos, chiles rellenos, or homemade beef tamales."

He was fair-out laughing. "Really? Daily offerings of homemade tamales?" he asked when he could catch his breath. "And you can't see how lucky you are?" He laughed some more. "Raymo?"

"I don't see what's so funny, Jay, 'cause I keep telling the man that I'm not interested in him as a boyfriend, and to leave me alone. I'm not playing around; I've had it with him."

It seemed the more I talked, the harder he laughed.

"Oh . . . oh my God," he laughs, throwing his head back and clutching at his chest. "Food, flowers, perfume, candy. Hell, some women would love to have a man that thinks about them like that. And you, Queenie, you have a problem with it?"

If only I could twitch my nose and have lightning streak down from the sky, through the roof, and strike him. "I'm glad you find this amusing."

Finally he stops laughing and tries to put on a straight face, but the corners of his mouth, as I'm looking dead at him, won't act right, refuse to cooperate. "Okay, okay. I'm sorry, Queenie," he managed, laughter still trying to percolate up from some place inside of him. "It's just that . . . well, the thought of you and him together in my head . . . I couldn't help it."

"Jay, I'm not kidding. You really don't know what I'm going through."

"What kind of tamales did you say?"

"What?" It was my turn to look at him like he was crazy.

"You said he brings you homemade tamales. What kind?"

"Uh . . . beef, sometimes pork. I don't know, and what difference does it make?"

"Homemade, you say?"

"Uh . . . I guess. Yes. Homemade. Look, never mind about the tamales. Okay . . . I see where this is going. Obviously, I made a mistake in coming to you. Silly me. I shouldn't be bothering you with this at all. I just wanted you to know before I filed, you know, so it wouldn't be such a shock to you."

"No . . . no, it's no bother. Hell, the next time you get tamales, just send them over to me. I've tasted the man's homemade tamales before, and you don't know what you're missing."

Then maybe you should date 'im, I think. "Look!" I all but scream. "The man is harassing me, which is interfering with me doing my job well!"

There it was again. This time, snickering. "Geez . . . I can't help it. It's just that . . . he's got so many other prospects if he's looking. I mean, he's got Lola in accounts payable. Now she's close to a knock-out, and what you could call an eight on the scale of ten. And there's Pat in women's lingerie. Ohh, yes. Make a man wanna drink her dirty bathwater, that one. Tina in customer service is short and sweet, but Maria in cosmetics is a true knockout. She's an eleven plus. Oh, yeah. Know what I mean? The kind of woman that wet dreams are made of, and they're all single females for the picking." He shook his head just thinking about it. "Hell, Queenie, you're a good person and all, but . . . well, hell, you have too many hang-ups, and your personality is too . . . too overbrewed."

"Well, too bad this isn't about my personality, Jay. It's about a misguided man stalking me at my workplace."

He looks dreamy eyed. "Yep, that Maria in cosmetics would be just perfect for Raymo."

I want him to see the annoyance in my face. "And your point is?"

"I mean," he says testily, trying a funny twist to his face and feeling his way around the right wording. "It's them, and then there's you. You're a very pretty woman, but—" He gestures with his hand in my direction, and starts laughing as I rise up from my seat, turn and march to the door, then stop and look back at him. The big red fool was having a good time with something I see as a problem.

"That's not funny, Jay." So much for fairness. *Crazy fool!* I couldn't wait to get out of his face. "Guess I'll see you in court, then."

"I'm so sorry," he chuckled. "Queenie, don't be mad at me. I'm sorry. You know I'm just teasing with you. Hell, stop being so sensitive. I thought we could tease one another every now and then?"

"Never mind, I'll handle it myself!"

He holds his hand up like there's more to be said, but he can't for laughing so hard. "Well, whatever you do, be gentle. Ray may be misguided, but he's harmless. Oh, yeah, Queenie, before you go, I'm afraid I have good news and bad news."

Great. Just what I need at the moment. "And what might that be?" I wanted to hear, but in a way, I didn't.

"It appears that we have major clearances coming up, which means that I will need top buyers pulling a double tomorrow to get the fall-winter orders in. Could be an all-nighter. We're talking teamwork here."

"And who might I ask will be working with me to get this task done?"

"It's, ah . . . it's Raymundo. He is the man for the job, just like you're the best for women's apparel."

"Oh, heck no! Jay, no! When is this?"

He mocked a frown. "Wednesday. Sorry to do this to you on such short notice, Queenie, but I was just made aware of the department's needs a few hours ago myself. My boss came down hard on me about us acquiring three new designers, and you know how much work is involved in that. I have no choice."

I make a face, knowing it can't save me. "I'm beginning to dislike this job."

"I knew I could count on you and Ray. You two are the best, and I need teamwork."

"Unbelievable. And the good news would be?"

"Overtime pay with an end-of-season bonus. Oh, and about that other matter, that harassment thing. Don't worry. I'll have a little talk with Ray. I promise. He'll leave you alone after I get through with 'im.'"

Tight-lipped, I turn and stomp back to my space, where I slam the door of my own office behind me. *The nerve of that fool, Jay!* Could it get any worse? Pulling a night shift with the man I can't stand being around is asking for too much. I was sick of Jay and Ray. The Ray-Jay blues. I don't know who the heck Jay thinks he is, but I have a good mind to pull out the yellow pages and get busy looking for an attorney. Obviously, the man must think I'm bluffing. If so, he has no idea who he's messing with. Queenie don't play. If I have to, I can let my fingers do the walking.

Five

I don't want to be at work the following Wednesday night. But I have to. My boss, Jay, said so. Like his word is the gospel. Called me at my crib to remind me, again, of what needs to be done. Said that if I didn't show up for fall-winter acquisitions, I could kiss my own sweet behind good-bye as I haul my personal belongings out the door. Said that true, I was one of the best in the company, but nowhere near irreplaceable. Love my boss.

Two senior buyers from each department working. Two on each floor. Men's wear and women's wear, the top two. Working in teams. Teams as in Ray and I, together, working.

"Let's just do this and get it over with." It's 9 P.M. Too bad if I sound in a bad mood. Having to leave my place and come back to work, who wouldn't be?

Opting for the casual look, after I'd gone home and napped, ate, and showered, I'd slipped on my best rumpled look; thin white T-shirt, black sweats, white sneakers. Seeing how I would be around Ray for most of the night, I used no perfume and very little makeup to make myself as unappealing as possible. The last thing I wanted to do was give the man the wrong impression, that I was making myself look good for him. Would have worn rollers in my hair, face cream, my cotton flannel pajamas and thick bunny slippers, but feared a problem with security.

Ray kept his gaze down, going over some papers. "I'm almost finished, thank you very much."

"Looks like you've been at it for hours already."

Lips that barely moved. "You could say that, yes." He kept his gaze down like it might be too painful to look up at me.

From his tone I sensed a problem. Something felt different, but I wasn't quite sure what it was. We are in his office, and for the first time I take notice of its size. Would have been in my office except for the fact that I had warned Ray that the next time he set foot in mine, I'd tear his head off and use it like a bowling ball. His office is larger—much larger than mine. *How ironic*, I muse. Him being a small man, me the large and lovely. Seemed to me that I should be the one with the largest . . . Never mind. Nicely done, as well. Earth tones everywhere you look. Stylish decor about the walls, pictures, mask, abstract art—all reflective of both African and Latino heritage. A huge oak desk facing the door, to the side of that, a matching conference table. Not bad at all.

"Have a seat," he says without commitment. "But only if you want to. I would not want you to think that I am sexually harassing you."

"Oh," I lightly snort. "It's like that now. Sounds like someone is a tad upset after their little talk with the boss. Good!" I pull out a chair at his conference table where our fall-winter acquisition presentations lay scattered. Catalogs, style videos, swatches of material, all shades of color and texture to be examined. Hours of work lay ahead, and I'm not up to it. Something is different, missing, like fresh air. Food. No food is laid out. No candles. No beautiful roses. Just him and me. "Better a little talk with Jay than an attorney." I pick up a catalog and flip through a few pages. I could be at home sleeping, watching cable, or painting my toenails.

I don't have to ask Ray if he's been home and came back—I know his answer. Dedicated workers never leave work until it's all done. Ray is no exception. I'm missing the trimmings, his offering that I have come to dread and expect. Dreading all that attention, but expecting him not to change—at least not so soon. Not after one warning talk from the boss.

"I can't believe all of this. I don't know where to start." I take up another catalog from one of the new lines of dressy wear and evening gowns. I flip and look, but my mind is not in it. "Who am I fooling? I'm already tired."

Ray is too quiet. Sitting at the same conference table, opposite end, jotting down notes, quantity, style specs. I can't decide which is worse, him talking too much, or him not talking at all. I'm not used to this. "Think I should go for full order with the new people? They have quite a selection, and I hear Robinsons-May is throwing major orders their way. What do you think?"

Silence.

"This is nice." I turn a photo up to show him one fancy gown, a pearl-white, sheer chiffon number with a sequined bustline. "Probably too fancy for our customers, you think?"

Silence.

I heave in a deep breath. "Look, Ray. You can be mad all you want. You had that talk from Jay coming, and you know it."

He doesn't stop writing, like I haven't said a thing.

"I mean, I don't want to see you lose your job or anything like that." I stand up from my seat as if doing so can help me make my point. "You seem to be a nice person, Ray. A little pesky at time, but everyone in the office thinks you're nice. It's just that you, well, you're just too much like him."

A spark of interest sends his eyes up to spotlight me. "Him?"

"My first love, Monroe. I don't know. Maybe I shouldn't be saying all of this. I had to go to Jay because you wouldn't stop. I wanted you to stop trying so hard to make me like you that way. But you wouldn't." It is the first time that we have been so alone in the office—his office. The first time I have opened myself up. The first time he has listened.

"And you say that because I remind you of him—this Monroe guy—you would have me fired from my job?" The first time his eyes have looked so serious.

"Fired? Oh, no, Ray! I don't want to see you fired, no. Maybe transferred to another location to work." *Like the moon*, I think. "But not fired. I just want you to stop trying so hard to make something be between us. That's all I ask."

"Did he bring you flowers, this Monroe?"

"No. He didn't."

"Did he think that you might be hungry at times?"

"No. He didn't."

"Did he write you poetry that he cannot show you?"

I had to stop and think about that one. Poetry? "No. Not that I know of."

"Did his dreams consist of you each night?"

I couldn't think of what to say to that one.

"Then you are mistaken. He is not like me, this man." Raised brow, he is looking up at me, over some papers in one hand, an expensive-looking pen in his other. "I am so sorry to hear of this man that has hurt you, but you cannot compare him to me."

"This is too weird for me. I can't be here. I can't do this. Not tonight." I feel tired, suddenly. Feel like all my strength and energy have seeped out. Someone opened a valve inside me. "And it's so cold in here. Dang. They must leave the air on all night." I sit back down rubbing the goose bumps along my bare arms. We need a new subject to talk about.

Without a word said, Ray gets up to grab his coat along the rack, moves to where I sit at the large square conference table. "Here." He drapes it over my shoulders gently. "You should not be cold."

Any other time I would have snatched the thing off me like a burning cape and flung it back in his face. But this is different. This is not a time of a man's relentless pursuit, but a friend doing a kind thing for another friend. This is something I like, something that makes more sense. "Thank you."

"Tell you what," Ray says, perking up. Inspiration has somehow struck him. His second wind. "You look tired. I can do your accounts for you. I am almost finished with what I have to do. I can do yours, as well."

"No." I shook my head. I couldn't possibly be hearing him right. Hours and hours of perusing through video catwalks, catalogs, freeze frames, material. Was he insane? "Ray, it's way too much work after doing your own orders. I couldn't."

"You can, and so can I. You need rest. I know your flair, your taste. I have paid very close attention to your ordering style."

"Ray, I couldn't let you do that. Wouldn't be right, and what about boss man? He'd have a red cow if he found out."

"And who will tell him?"

He raised a brow. He was serious.

"You go head. Go home. Get some rest, and I will have your accounts all in order and ready for the processing department by morning. You will not be disappointed."

"Are you sure?" I wanted to leave, needed to go. I stood up and let his coat slide from my shoulders, catching it before it found the floor. I couldn't think of one other soul that would take on such a horrendous task. I looked at my watch. 9:35. I see him working into the wee hours. Could his offer be a trick, some cruel attempt to sabotage my accounts and show me in bad light to my boss? Would he?

"Yes, I am sure." He sniffed, watching for my reaction.

Ray went back to his seat, adjusted the maroon silk tie loose over his maroon silk shirt, sat back down. "You must go now and get some rest." He sniffs. "Don't worry about a thing. Ray will take care of everything."

"You sure you can do it?" I move to hang his coat back along the rack, guilt riding over me. Some guilt, but not enough to make me refuse his offer.

"Queenie, yes. You go and rest now."

"This is an awful big favor to do for someone, Ray. What's the scoop? What's in it for you?"

Pen in hand, he looks back up at me with a hint of a smile. "Appreciation. This is all I wish from you."

He didn't have to keep telling me. I stepped away from the coatrack, got my purse from the floor. One long look at all that work, and it was so unbelievable. "If you say so."

I look over at him, a hardworking man back at it. Deep into it. It touches something in me, but I can't say what. "Thanks, Ray." I took one step.

"What? No appreciation kiss to the cheek?"

I should have known there would be a catch. There's always a catch for a deed too good to be true. But the warmth and comfort of my bed were calling. What harm would a friendly peck to the cheek do? There is no one to see and start rumors. I walked over to him. A small price to pay, really.

Tilting his head, his cheek out, his hand pointing to a spot. "Don't worry, I won't tell Jay."

"Oh, that's funny, Ray." Bending to reach my lips to his cheeks, the smell of his cologne is intoxicating. I purse my lips to press there, at that spot he points to—on target until he turns his head in midpurse. Our eyes lock for one brief moment, our breath mingles. Then he turns his face back to offer his cheek. I kiss it fast and straighten myself up. "Thanks again, Ray."

"You are welcome, Queenie. Friends?"

"Friends."

Confused by the feelings running through me—feelings I have no explanation for, no reasonable rationale, I walk from his office. Walk away—away from his open door. I stop and look back to see his hard-working silhouette cast by the room's dim lighting. I see something that I can't quite put my hands on, but it's there. *What a nice guy. Too bad he's not my type.* I expect his mischievous eyes to follow me, but this time, they don't.

Six

I swear. Sometimes I don't know why or how I let Poetta talk me into some of her crazy schemes. But here we are, a week and a half later at Fox Hills Mall. More people had turned out for the AIDS Date-a-thon Fund-raiser than I imagined. The place is literally packed with nicely dressed men and women of various races—the women, no doubt, present for the same reason, as I was, which was to get an up-close-and-personal glimpse of the one and only Billy Dee Williams. But thanks to my girl, Poetta, I would finally get a chance to actually meet the man in person. Of course, I had to promise Poetta that I would contribute some money to the cause. I couldn't bring myself to actually tell Poe to her face, but I wasn't spending more than a hundred dollars at the most, Billy or no Billy. Queenie pays for no man.

"How much longer we have to wait?" I felt antsy and restless, couldn't keep the impatience out of my voice no matter how hard I tried, so what was the point. "I can't be up here all day now. Not on a Saturday. I have places to go, people to see."

Poetta gave me one of her girl-just-be-cool looks. "Be patient, my dear friend. Be patient."

"I am being patient, but Billy need to hurry up and come on. And these are not the most comfortable of seats, I might add," I said shifting uneasily in my folding chair.

The perfect day for a fund-raiser. The clear and brisk Saturday held a promise of soothing warmth throughout the day. Inside the mall was a bevy of activity, probably more curious lookie-lous than fund-raiser participants. A platform stage and folding chairs were strategically placed in the center of the mall's lower level so as not to block or hinder any possible shopper's passage. The low drone of voices swirled and mixed in the air with mellow piped-in music. Excitement, anticipation—you could feel it.

We were seated, the three of us—Poetta and her scandalous sister, Marva, and myself—along the second row of chairs. Looking around me, I could see that there wasn't a vacant chair to be had. To be honest, I would never have imagined that such an event as bidding money to date someone you don't even know would be so popular, but it goes to show you that you can't know everything.

"May I have your attention," a tiny black woman with large eyes was saying from her stand along the stage. "First of all, I want to thank each and every one of you for coming out to be part of this very worthy cause. We're just waiting for a few more of our scheduled guests to arrive before we can get started. We should be starting in about fifteen minutes. Thank you all for your patience."

"Dang," I sighed impatiently. "Some more waiting."

Marva, seated on the opposite side of Poetta, leaned in and asked, "Poe, who's that tramp?"

"Marva, you know that's Gwen Rhineheart. Remember? The program coordinator."

"Oh, yeah. She's that snotty heifer you kept talking 'bout."

I cringed in my seat, hoping that no one else heard Marva. Why was it that this woman couldn't have a decent conversation for once in her life without calling somebody out of their name? "I just want Billy to hurry up and get here." I sniffed and patted at my hair.

"Heifer, please," Marva sneered in my direction. "Billy wouldn't want yo' big butt."

I leaned over and hissed back. "Put a sock in it, Marva, cause I don't wanna hear it!" I rolled my eyes at her, hoping she got my message. "Get on my nerves," I mumbled under my breath. I can't stand her behind. I've been knowing Poetta's sistah, Marva, for as long as I've known Poetta. Keeping it to myself, Marva was what I like to refer to as a *frienemy*, which is that perilous combination of a friend and enemy. A friend only because she is so close to her sister, Poetta. Frankly, the girl is not my cup of tea or my type for the friendship group, and I could write a book on all the reasons why. But just to list a few—Marva is on her fourth marriage, and this time to an older man. According to Marva, money and old age are her strict prerequisition to a happy marriage. Her current husband had to be at least forty-five years older than she, and I was clocking her at the uphill of thirty, a mere two years older than Poetta and myself. The world according to Marva, she's God's gift to the older man with young and vibrant money.

Secondly, she's too cute, and she knows it. One of those kind of sistahs who thinks her cinnamon-brown beauty is the only beauty to behold, and that beauty should be noticed the minute, the second she walks into a room. Her attitude screams, "Hey everyone, I'm here!"

Okay, okay, so I'm bit jealous. Well, maybe not jealous, but aware and cautious of her species. No man is safe around her, and it's no secret that the woman is so hot that if you touch her skin—ouch—you get a burn. But still, I have to give the girl her perks. I mean, I know that most men like 'em thin and petite like Marva. And she's got this crooked little wicked smile, and these big, brown doelike eyes that look so innocent until she opens her mouth and you hear her speak. A lot of women think her down-her-back brown hair is a fancy weave, but trust me, I know better. It's all hers, though. Thick and healthy hair probably generated from all the man-made protein she's ingested over the years, and I'm not talking protein shakes, here. Anyway you look at it, Marva can be the most friendliest thing to your face, but the minute your back is turned, you gotta be a tramp, heifer, or a hoe. And I've heard her call folks worse but she means no harm when she calls you outta your name this way. It's just the way she is. All these things, mind you, are just part of the total package that makes her Miss Marva. The perfectly flawed woman.

Let's just say that I'm used to Marva the way some folks are used to mucus forming in their nose. It's nasty at times, but it's a fact of life. Even these little things about her aren't so bad. I can deal with the bad mouth and the bad attitude, but what keeps me on guard is the fact that the girl has a sickness when it comes to her lust. A deep-down sickness like a cancer hiding out inside her essence or hiding inside her draws, one or the other. Guess it's safe to say that Miss Marva is like a lot of females who refuse to admit it, but suffers from a common malady known as COC, which is the layman's term for Coochie Outta Control. I don't hate the player, just the game, so I call it like I see it. The girl had already slept with two of my boyfriends by the time we got out of high school, not to mention four of Poetta's, and three of her mother's boyfriends.

Make no mistake about it, husband or no husband, Marva will sleep with anybody wearing pants: your baby brother, your too-young cousin, your half-dead husband, or your could-be-gay uncle, or your male dog, Spot. It's bad. But don't get me wrong. She's still sweet and special in her own precious way—like most slutty women. And she don't mean no harm about it. It's just Marva being Marva. It was a hard teaching, but I learned my lesson from her the hard way. To this day I take no man of mine around her overheated behind for fear that the special place between her thighs might have magnetic powers. Poetta, her own sister, don't let her in her house when Jimboy's at home.

There's a problem, for certain. Sad part is, even Marva don't really know what her problem is, or what she needs to do about it to get it under control. It's sad, but that's how she is. That COC alone is enough to keep you suspicious of her, but coupled with the fact that she can't say five words straight without throwing in some form of profanity, it can be a bit much for a newcomer. In other words, to know her is to love her.

Once, when we were in elementary school, Poetta told me that her sister came out of her mama's stomach cursing when she sneezed the word *shit*, and she's been cursing ever since. Right then a vision had popped into my head of the doctor holding baby Marva up and whacking her on her newborn tail, and she crying out the word *damn*!

Time to change the subject in my head. "I really like that navy blue suit Miss Gwen have on. That's sharp."

Poetta had told me how Gwen Rhineheart, the program coordinator extraordinaire, had did her best to get some big-time corporations to cosponsor the fund-raiser this year by donating some of their products for refreshments. As a result, a well-guarded and impressive-size buffet was set up on the opposite side of the stage complete with little fancy finger sandwiches, coffee, tea, Pepsi, and assorted slices of cakes and cookies.

I was proud of the fact that I'd taken the time to eat a good breakfast at home, which helped me to steer away from the refreshment area of sweets and more sweets and concentrate on Billy Dee. And nothing was going to get in the way of that. Not even that scandalous-looking spandex dress Marva was wearing. It was some kind of greenish-black metallic affair complete with a little matching jacket and matching pumps. "A darn shame," I mumble to myself, shaking my head. "Should be at home somewhere adjusting the flow on her husband's oxygen tank instead of here looking for a man." *She makes me sick. One thing for sure, the girl knows how to dress for her own agenda.* "Darn her."

"Did you say something, Queenie?" Frowning, Poe looks over at me like I'm crazy.

"No. Not really. Just going over some things in my head. Job stuff. That's all." But I knew I looked good, too, in my black crepe pantsuit with the coordinating knee-length jacket. The slight trim of gray satin along the lapel of the jacket set off the pale gray satin blouse I wore beneath it. Usually I don't wear pumps on the weekend. Not with my fallen arches. But my gray chintz pumps went so well with the rest of the outfit that I didn't have a choice. I looked good, but I was hot as Tabasco sauce. "All this surrounding body heat is making it extremely hot in this mall." I fanned my face.

Making a face, Marva gave the coordinator a good looking-over. "Umph. That heifer need more behind to be trying to wear a suit like that."

"Sis, cut it out. Try saying something nice about somebody for a change."

"What? It's not my fault she don't have no behind."

"Poe, what's taking so long?" I asked, hoping to hush Marva up. "And where all these celebrity folks suppose to be at, anyway?" I took a quick peek over to my left at Poetta. Once again she was doing an Erykah Badu look with her head wrapped up in a fancy-looking, colorful rag that matched her caftan. Not that I got nothing against Miss Badu. I mean, it's no secret that the sistah got the pipes that can blow. But I think a sistah should keep her hair fly at all times, just in case that Tyrone guy do decide to drive up with a big truck to help your man leave your behind. At least a sistah be looking good when the time comes.

"Most of the celebs are here," Poetta announced quietly, pointing over to one of the mall's vacant store spaces. "See that door over there? That's where they're being housed. Right in that empty space where they have it all papered up so you can't see into the window. Billy's probably back there right now, mingling with a few folks. You know, before it's time."

My heart felt like it skipped two beats at the mention of his name. "God. I still can't believe that a man of Billy Dee's caliber would participate in something like this. Not the fund-raiser per se, but the fact of allowing himself to be auctioned off to the highest bidder. How refreshing."

"Queenie, it's a fund-raiser and a worthy cause. They're all doing it just to help raise money. I'm sure that none of 'em are hard up for a date."

"Well don't hate me because I said it. You are just too sensitive, Poe."

Marva had to lean in and add her two cents. "Isn't that Billy Dee punk already married to some tramp?"

"Marva, you need to watch your dirty mouth." I balled my fist at my sides. God. I wanted to reach over and slap her silly. "You need to check yourself. Don't be bad-talking 'bout Billy that way. Billy's no punk!"

"Heifer, pleeeze," Marva hissed, looking insulted like I just called her a virgin. "I'm talking bout Billy's tramp. Not him."

"Good grief, you two. Marva, please . . . and you, too, Queenie. You both need to chill out." Poetta gave us both a stern look in each direction like she was somebody's mama.

I just shook my head. I could tell that Poetta was a little embarrassed the way she kept darting her eyes around and her hand feeling up and around that fancy rag on her head. "I wish the both of you would be quiet."

"No problem." I mock the zipping of my mouth. I despised that rag on her head. I saw it as part of the mystery that Poetta was changing more and more with this new man of hers. I don't know what it was exactly, but girlfriend was going through a serious metamorphosis. Just two months before Jimboy came into her life, she was a woman who practically lived in designer warm-up suits and expensive running shoes. Not saying that anything was wrong with it, but lately it's more of an "Afrotiqueky" look with flowing caftans with matching turbans or one festive-looking African dashiki after another. Things sure had changed. My only guess was that all that candle-burning had simmered out her need for expensive designer clothes.

Poetta looked over and caught my eyes and smiled. I took the number card, which had the number three printed on it, and looked more to me like a paper fan, and fanned myself with it. All this waiting to see Billy Dee was making me hot.

"The event will be starting shortly," Poetta announced casually. "Just relax and be patient. Be ladylike."

Everybody participating in the bidding was given numbers and registered with the help of a twenty-dollar donation. Umph. *Twenty dollars out already*, I mused. That left me all of eighty dollars to bid on a date. Okay, okay. So I could see myself paying eighty dollars for a date with Billy Dee. After all, Billy wasn't your everyday Joe with nothing to do. There was a worthy cause at work, and of course, I wanted to help to do my part. Eighty dollars, but not a penny more. Besides, secretly I was hoping that Poetta would introduce me to the man behind the scene and I could take it from there.

My backside was starting to hurt from all the sitting, and I could feel too much moisture forming along my back. "Dang," I muttered.

I knew I should have powdered that area with talcum after my shower. When I'm nervous, my sweat glands have a tendency to work over-time. "I wish they would c'mon with it."

"Queenie, chill out," Poetta cooed, waving her hand like it was supposed to help soothe me. "When we get back to my place, I am going to hook you up with a tea that will help you to relax."

"I can hardly wait."

Finally, Gwen Rhineheart, fund-raiser extraordinaire, was back on the stage at the mic. "Welcome, ladies and gentlemen."

"It's about time," I heard Marva yell out. "Just bring out the choc-olate beef tips, and let's get busy!"

"Lordhavemercy." I shook my head and wondered what Marva's rich old man at home was doing while she was out looking for some new sex and about to spend his hard-earned money for it. But never mind. I focused on Gwen on stage.

"Once again, I want to thank you all for finding the time in your busy schedules to come out and be a positive part of this event. We're about to get started, but first a few announcements. It's been reported that the owner of a late-model black, Sedan DeVille, license number 555JJ59, your lights are on, and you might wanna go out and take care of that."

I glanced over at Poetta, who was looking over at me. What did we care about somebody's Caddy? Just get on with it.

Gwen went on with, "And as you know, the main participants for our event today, which happens to be our sixth year, are celebrity look-alikes who are very much active in the filming industries. Most, if not all, have actually played along the sidelines as stand-ins for the real McCoy, and . . ."

"What? Look-alikes?" I did a slow burning look over at Poetta, who kept her gaze straight ahead. "Excuse me, Poe, is she saying we won't be seeing the real deal, but look-alike celebs?"

The girl had the nerve to *ssshh* me with a bony finger to her pink-glossed lip. I tried to sneak a peek over at Marva to see how she was taking the news of fake actors, but she didn't seem to be having a problem with it. I guess the joke was on me. I sighed and focused back on Gwen on stage.

"Unfortunately, our main guest speaker today, the authentic and talented Mr. Billy Dee Williams called and canceled out due to a touch of flu. He sends his regrets and hopes that everyone understands."

"Dang!" I could feel steam trying to rise up from me. "And no Billy Dee. This is messed up!" I stood up from my chair. "Later for this. I'm outta here!"

"Queenie, please!" Poetta snapped, pulling at my coattail. "Will you please chill for a minute."

If though it was any of her business, Marva leaned over and hissed at me, "Heifer, sit yo' big behind down."

I glared over in her direction, contemplating if I should front her the way she was fronting me. Somehow I wasn't in the mood to be called too many names. I was sick of her, too. But Poetta pulled me back down to my seat.

"Friends don't embarrass friends, Queenie."

"And true friends don't lie to friends either, Poe. Heck, I could be at home taking care of whatever I need to be doing instead of sitting up here with a bunch of fake wanna-be actors." I was ready to give girlfriend a good tongue-lashing for having me waste my Saturday. Stewing on the inside, I sat there with my lips poked out, staring and glaring and not paying attention to the slew of gorgeous men arriving on stage, and then the females. After a while I settled back down and paid attention.

Face after face looked too familiar. It was incredible. Where they found all these people was beyond my imagination, but it was like looking at the real deal. Some of the look-alike faces I was sure I'd seen before, maybe in some movie from a distance or something, but the resemblance was uncanny. There was a Diana Ross, a Whoopi Goldberg, a Mario Van Peebles, a Keenen Ivory Waynan, a Vanessa Williams, an Erykah Badu, Michael Jackson, Toni Braxton, and a slew of others. And—oh, my god, L.L. Cool J. Lord have mercy. "Incredible." The list was almost endless. And they all looked so much like the real deal. But my heart didn't skip a beat—didn't start thumping wildly inside my chest until my eyes fell on him.

"Oh, my . . . oh, my goodness." My mouth sagged open.

There must have been over two dozen faces up on that stage, but it was like I couldn't see anyone else up there but him. They had saved the best for last. He was the last one to come on, dressed in a tight knit T-shirt-type black shirt that looked as if it had been painted onto his buffed chest. He had on some nice dressy black slacks, but I didn't give a hoot about that. My eyes were filled with the sharp and defined features of his well-developed upper torso. His skin was like moist pecans glistening in the mall's lighting. The man was a dead ringer for Denzel Washington. Even had the same last name, Washington, except that his first name was Ezekiel. Zeke for short. I ran that name around on my tongue to see how it would feel. It felt great. It was pretty tasty, too.

I don't know why, but suddenly my armpits were sweaty, and my palms felt itchy, like maybe I was about to come into some money, or about to lose some. By the time the bidding wars started, I felt reckless with my little money. And it didn't help much that the bidding didn't start cheap either at one hundred dollars. Every time I held up my bid card for Zeke, some other female held up hers. Even that shameless hussy, Marva, wanted Zeke, but obviously just to annoy me. No big deal. My mind was made up that the man was mine and mine alone. All thoughts of Billy Dee drifted away like thin smoke from my head as I kept outbidding every woman that had the nerve to challenge me.

There was a connection between us. I felt it the second his gaze looked my way, our eyes locking for those brief seconds. Already, I felt like I knew him—had been missing him. He was the man from my childhood dreams: powerful looking, tall, dark, sinfully handsome, and intelligent. The eyes tell it all. The perfect man to make me feel that sense of safe and the one I wanted to father my children. What woman in her right frame of mind wouldn't want that?

Before it was all over, I'd shown them all that I, Queenie, would not be outdone. Not when it came to something that I really wanted. And I really wanted Mr. Zeke Rasheem Washington.

Before it was all over, Marva had dished out $1,500 of her husband's money for a Michael Jordan. Yeah, right. Like there's not a dark-skinned black man that looks like him everywhere you turn. But who cares. I got what I wanted. Even if that one date with destiny did end up costing me $1,250. He'd be mine for one night, and believe you me, I had all intentions of getting my money's worth.

Seven

The following Saturday would be the day, and I wanted everything to be perfect for my date with Zeke. I was glad that we had exchanged phone numbers after the fund-raiser was over. Several times during the workweek we'd spoken, nothing too serious, but a sort of "get acquainted" before our date ritual. So far, the things I had learnt about Mr. Zeke Rasheem Washington were pretty impressive.

Number one, he was single and somewhat new to Los Angeles. That was a plus in my dating book of rules. Single men too native to Los Angeles have a tendency to have too many women to chase or too many women chasing behind them. Who needs another problem? Either way, I might like a little challenge every now and then, but I'm not one that's down for a long, drawn-out competition in the game of love.

Number two, not only was Zeke a struggling actor, but he was a successful screenplay writer, as well. During our conversation over the phone, he ran off a few titles to his credit, but each one went clean over my head in recognition. I took it that he wasn't rich, but did earn a good living from it. Doing the AIDS Date-a-thon, according to Zeke, was his way of giving back to the community. Sharing a part of his success.

Number three, he lived in a nice part of Ladera Heights, complete with a roommate named Sweet Willie Special. A roommate, he claimed, that was there, but not all the time.

I couldn't wait for him to eventually get around to number four, what I really wanted to know, if he had a serious relationship going with anyone. But before he could answer, I interjected with, "And Zeke, please be honest. That's all I ask."

There was a long pause over the phone. I couldn't have held my breath too much longer waiting for his reply, but somehow I did. *Oh, please, God . . . please let 'im be available . . .* "Well," I prompted, eager to know. "Are you involved?"

And then he said in his deep bedroom voice that could melt frozen caramel on the spot. "I do have a couple of female friends, but they're not what you could call my lady or my steady woman. Know what I mean?"

Unbelievable. "So, are you saying that you have no steady girlfriend at this time?" I was intrigued. Seemed to me that no matter what a man looked like, fine or super-duper ugly, there was always some other woman lurking around in the shadows of his life. Face it, my sistahs, no man worth having comes without someone else attached somewhere. But I chose to believe him. Which only served to prove that a man as fine as Zeke couldn't possibly be without a female or two in his life and tell the truth about it.

"I have no one that I'm serious with. I'm not in love with anyone right now. Maybe because I'm having a love affair with my work. Might not seem like it, but trying to write for the big screen and television can be very time consuming, and add to that the pursuit of acting, well . . . it just don't leave a lot of extra time."

"So." I sought to pry deeper, my own subtle way. I wasn't completely convinced that such a handsome and well-put-together brick house of a man could possibly be without a true and steady girlfriend. Will wonders ever cease? "Who cooks you a good home-cooked meal or gives you a back massage when you need it?"

A mild chuckle over the line. "My mom moved to Cali a year before me. She wants me at her dinner table every Sunday, but I try to make it at least every other Sunday. Mostly outta love and respect for my moms. As for my back—" He paused. "—I have an excellent handheld back massager that does the trick. In other words, the only special woman in my life right now is my moms."

I loved his closing remark. Another plus in my book. The man loves and respects his mother. How can a woman go wrong with a good sign like that? But I'm relentless. I can't stop. "Yes, but who gives you that . . . you know, that special attention when you're feeling tensed and achy in special places?"

"Well," he laughed lightly, amused by my inquiry. "There is one young lady . . . nothing too serious, though."

My heart stopped for a few beats. "Your steady girlfriend?"

Why was I pushing the issue about him having a steady woman in his life? Big deal, I mean, why wouldn't he have someone? *Besides,* I kept telling myself. *We've just met. We're just going on one measly date, not to the marriage altar.* I exhaled to help myself lighten up, relax. "Honesty is always the best policy."

"Her name is Reeba, and for some strange reason . . . I don't know, she thinks that she's in love with me. She comes around once or twice a week. Sometimes she cleans for me or cooks. A body massage every now and then. But mostly just to kick it with me for a while. She's okay. It's a relationship, and then again, it's not. I think of her as a good friend, but she thinks of me as more. You know how some women can be."

"Yeah, I do."

"She's hard to explain, Reeba."

"Reeba, huh?" I sniff at this unpleasant news. News I asked for.

"That's right."

"Well, now I know."

I knew, all right. I didn't have a clue what kind of person this . . . this so-call Reeba chick was, but one thing I did know, I had to come up with a plan to deal with her. It had been a long time since I'd met a "keeper," and I was willing to go the distance. My mind was already made up that I was going to be Zeke's steady woman, and the last thing I needed was some Reeba chick hanging around, trying to persuade him in another direction.

Zeke and I talked a few more times after that, and by Thursday I was looking forward to our date on Saturday with the same anticipation as a child looking forward to a promised trip to her favorite toy store. I had no business trying to fantasize sex into the plan, but somehow I was so attracted to Zeke and the things he was saying, the way his deep-space voice vibed over the phone that a slow-burning flame was about to get started between my thighs even before a match was struck.

At Poetta's house, that following Saturday, while I sat in her big and cluttered kitchen and allowed her to put the finishing touch to my hair, I could barely control my excitement. It was well after six in the afternoon, and outside her thick-curtained window, I could see the last of the ebbing sunset sinking into a blaze of red and orange. The still warm breeze sneaking in through her window held a whisper of gardenias. Poetta's front yard was a disaster, but she did try harder with her huge backyard of flowers.

I'd been shopping most of the day to prepare for my date with Zeke, and only because Poetta agreed to do my hair up for me, it seemed only feasible that I would shower, dress, and leave for my date from her house. I had two outfits that I had bought expressly for the occasion, a lovely silk pantsuit in lavender, and an ankle-length dress of dark purple velour with a matching jacket with rose-shaped buttons of shimmering crystal.

"Which one?" I asked Poetta for the umpteenth time. "Should I wear the pants or the dress?"

Poetta had some bumpers heating up in her curling-iron oven, which seemed like a waste of gas with all those candles burning all around us. I swear, here it was almost the middle of summer with stubborn heat still lingering outside, and Poetta had about thirty candles strategically placed about her kitchen with flickering flames. White candles, black candles, red candles. With all that heat in the room with us, her curling iron could have heated up without direct flames. It made me uncomfortable. What better timing to inquire about all the candle-burning she was doing lately?

"Girl," I said testily, keeping a rein on my tone. The last thing I wanted to do was get the girl all worked up and upset while she's handling my hair. "I'm 'bout to burn up in here with all these candles all over the place. You not try'n' to work no hex on nobody up in here. Are you? What's up with the candles?"

"You know me, Queenie: I need my flames. It's part of me."

I faked a cute laugh and angled around to get a good look at her face. Maybe she had devil horns growing under all those braids. I know the truth stalling when I saw it. "Need the flames how?"

"To help balance sin and harmony and keep evil away, that's all. Nothing to be worried about."

"You saying you have too much sin in your life or what?" Not trying to be nosy, just trying to understand.

"No. I'm saying that there's so much going on in the world all around you, Queenie. These are serious times we live in, and you need to be prepared. Nothing to worry yourself over."

"Yeah, Poetta, but every time I'm over, you got all these candles burning and burning. Shoots. Ain't that much sin in all the world for all the candles you be burning."

"Queenie, what I say? I said don't worry 'bout it. It's nothing to hurt anybody. Maybe I just like candles."

"In the summertime?"

"Summer or winter, it's my house, ain't it?"

"Oh," I said, properly put in my place. "It's like that."

"Yeah. It's like that. So, if you don't mind, let's change the subject."

Just like Poetta. Always her foot up in somebody else's business, but the minute you try to stroll through her secret garden, you get stopped dead at the entrance. I like to think that we can talk about anything, but just last month when I tried to ask her about her love life with Jimboy, she had looked at me like I asked her what flavor edible panties the man liked best. Jeepers. True, I wanted to know more about the candles, but it was painfully clear she wasn't ready to tell me.

"Okay, back to me, then. The pants or the dress? Which outfit you think I should wear?"

Too busy arranging ringlets of curls atop my had, Poetta didn't answer right away. She kept angling her head one way and then the other way, staring, fixated, at the top of my head like it might change shapes at any given second and she didn't want to miss it. "Well . . . I don't know. The one that makes you feel the most special. You the one going out on a date with the man."

"Maybe the dark purple and my boots," I tossed in, fishing for her input. The one that makes me feel special? Heck, no. She wasn't getting off that easy. "Dark colors are more slimming, I'm told. Umm . . . Don't you think?" I looked over to where each outfit, still encased in clear plastic, hung from a cabinet knob, complete with Robinsons-May price tags still on.

"Um—well. I think they both look nice, Queenie."

"Well, Poe, which one? If I wasn't asking, you'd be telling me anyway."

"Either one, Queenie." Tight-lipped, she kept her focus on my hair. "They're both nice, but I just think. . . . well . . ."

"Oh, no," I sighed. Not one of her sentence breaks. I hate when she does that, starts a sentence but don't finish it. Like that time we went to this nice house party where some affluent people would be, and I'd come out from the restroom with my dress half tucked into my pantyhose, my behind all out for everybody to see. I don't know what made me ask her that night if I looked okay. She'd said the same half-fetched sentence that night, too.

"Well, I just think . . ."

Took five minutes of hard badgering for her to tell me what was on her mind. "What? You just think what, Poe?"

Finally she'd let me have it. "I just think you'd look even nicer, Queenie, if your butt was completely covered up."

I was so embarrassed that night, I felt like crawling to a corner of the room and staying there for the rest of the evening. But that's my homegirl, Poetta. Just like me, you have to really know her to love her.

"You just think what, Poe?"

"Nah. Nothing."

"You think what? Just tell me."

"Queenie, it's nothing. Really."

"Woman, you'd better tell me what you think, and tell me now!" I reached up and stopped her hand in midcurl. A few inches over, and I would have touched hot steel. I don't know why it mattered so much, but anytime Poetta had an issue, I had the time to hear it. I needed to hear it. "Tell me."

"Girl, don't be grabbing up to these bumpers, unless you looking for some pain! What's wrong with you?"

I released her hand. "You think what?"

She heaved a sigh. Another way of stalling for time. "I just think you're getting way too carried away behind this date. I mean, it's just one date, not a commitment. I just don't wanna see you hurt, Queenie, that's all."

"Carried away?" No, she didn't say that. "Carried away? Poe, you illing, you know that? What makes you think I'm carried away? I'm just looking forward to a nice and friendly date with a very attractive man. No harm in that. How's that being carried away?" I didn't care if she did hear the indignation in my voice.

"Yeah, but you know how you get, Queenie. Especially when you really like somebody."

"You don't know what you're talking 'bout."

"I think you do."

"Poe, how am I carried away, huh, how?"

"By going out and buying not one, but two new outfits. And you need your hair done again when you just got it done last week. And three new pairs of shoes, too. Obviously, girlfriend, you've forgotten that I've known you since second grade. Two outfits and three pairs of shoes sounds like carried away to me."

"Poe, you tripping."

"Am I?"

Was it jealousy or what? Poetta might have been a minor part of helping to put the charity fund-raiser together, but in no way did she try to secure a date, a luncheon, or even coffee or tea with any of the handsome men that had participated in the event. Even though I hadn't bothered to ask her why, I just assumed that her going out on a date with some superfine actor look-alike while Jimboy was out of town—well, maybe her man Jimboy wouldn't have appreciated it. Never mind the fact that Jimboy himself was hardly ever around. Maybe she was jealous that I had something exciting to do and she was facing another Saturday night of sitting around those flickering candles all by herself.

Refusing to sound upset with her and end our day on a sour note, "I'm not carried away," I said calmly, forcing sympathy into my voice. "Zeke is different, the ultimate challenge. And, yes, I must admit that I'm a little excited about going out with him. That's all. I mean, I'm not blind. I know that a handsome man like him must have a whole heap of females try'n' to get a taste of him. I know this. But tonight is my time, bought and paid for, and I want to look nice. No big deal."

"If you say so."

"Well, I do say so."

"Queenie, call it what you want, but I know what I know."

Feeling a little uneasily with the conversation, which by the way was none of her business, I pretended to study my newly manicured nails. The fire-engine red was kicking, but somehow didn't seem shiny enough. "You got some nail gloss I can use?"

"Queenie, just don't allow yourself get sucked in by another pretty face and hard body. You know how you are sometimes when you think you're in love."

"And what's that supposed to mean?"

"You know exactly what I'm talking about."

"No, I don't, but maybe you should just tell me, seeing how you're such an expert on my love life."

"When you think you're in love, you're like moist clay, easily molded. Sometimes molded in the wrong direction."

Now, that hurt. Who was this little built-too-low-to-the-ground, wax-burning, hex-calling heifer with not enough meat on her bony frame to be giving advice about how to steer clear from the perils of dating?

"You know what, Poe, I'ma act like you didn't even say that." I wanted to remind her of how much she'd changed since she'd met Jimboy, who by the way, was forever off somewhere hauling something to some destination that was a mystery most of the time. "Hmph."

But I bit my tongue. After all, the girl *was* handling my hair. Words of advice—regardless of how bold you might consider yourself, one thing I've learned over the years, never insult or upset the folks handling your food, your money, or your hair. "You have nail gloss or what?" A feeble attempt to change the subject, but she wasn't done yet.

"You do remember how madly in love with Monroe you were?"

"Monroe? Who, me? Queenie? Girl, please, he wasn't man enough to file my toenails down," I lie.

"Yes, you. Ms. Queenie. Don't act like you don't remember." Poetta slapped the side of my head lightly in a playful manner.

"Girl, ooouch!"

"Well, don't be sitting up here acting like you suddenly have memory loss."

"Maybe because you're talking out the back of your head."

She would have to bring up Monroe, again, despite the fact that she knew that it was still a touchy subject. Seven years passing, and it was still a subject filled with painful memories that can't seem to stay buried. I didn't need her to keep reminding me of a man that had lied about not being married for two whole years. Two whole years of wining me, dining me, and seducing me in the plush surroundings of a Beverly Hills apartment that I was led to believe was his alone.

My first handsome Latin lover. I had loved Monroe more than life itself. Perhaps a phase I was going through in my early twenties, but Latin lovers were touted to be so hot, so sizzling, I couldn't resist. Loved him. At least, now, I think it was love. More like being in love with the idea of being in love. Of that, yes, I was guilty. I closed my eyes and thought about him. Monroe Chavez. Delicious. Monroe had been my first slip away from my norm of chocolate-dipped men. Forbidden fruit. Dark hair, dark eyes, mysterious. Tall and suave, that kind of chiseled face that make you wanna slap yo' mama for saying you can't see him anymore. I was twenty, and his ten-year age jump over me had driven my mother to having a nervous twitch in her left eye, but even that didn't matter. We were unstoppable.

We'd met during my second year at college, Monroe and I. Spent every moment together in the teaching mode. I taught him how to eat and appreciate soul food. He taught me the mamba, on the floor and between the sheets. Two months later, I was in love and ready to

settle down, be his wife, keep his house, have his children—little Latino and black treasures.

Monroe. God, when would that name stop intruding on my life? I
would have climbed the highest snowcapped mountain during an av-
alanche for Monroe. I would have swum bleeding and butt naked
through shark-infested water to rescue that man. I would have shot
Monroe dead off in his big feet if I'd had a gun that day I'd gone to
that same apartment to surprise him with a home-cooked meal. Picture this, the shock on my face when his young, thin, and very pretty
Latino wife opened the door to me and my two bags of groceries
expressly bought to fix a good home-cooked meal for her husband. It
had been his best friend's apartment all along.

I had been too gullible, and perhaps a little too trusting back then.
A man told me something, and I took his words for the truth. But the
Monroe experience had been a lesson well learnt. Never take a man's
word for granted. If he tells you that there is no one else in his life
at the time you first meet, chances are he's lying. No matter how poor
that man is. No matter how ugly that man is, there's always somebody
in the shadow of every man's life—each and every one of 'em. Another
woman waiting, barely passing through or newly left, or hiding out
somewhere in the darkness of truth.

"I don't want to talk about past mistakes."

"I bet you don't."

"Poe, talk about something else or be quiet."

"Like I said, I just don't want to see you hurt, that's all."

"That was the old me, Poe. You live; you learn. Zeke is the new
challenge, and he's not married. It's different this time. I'm in better
control of the situation now." I didn't want to dwell on bad stuff, but
Poetta wouldn't leave it alone.

"I hope so. Like I said, you know how you get when you think
you're in love."

"Nothing's wrong with love, Poe." I wanted her to shut up
about it.

"True. But real love takes its time. Not something that can be
bought and sprayed in the air and there it is."

"Sure, you're right." *Like you would know.* I know what I know. I know that if you really want something in life, you have to reach out and get it. Long gone are the days when shy or timid women sat back and waited for the man to make the first move.

"And Queenie, don't go hopping your hot behind in the bed with 'im just because you paid some money. The man is not a male prostitute."

I make a shocked expression. "Now, you know that is not me, Poe. Don't be insulting."

"And I don't care how superfine he is, don't be letting 'im feel you up and slobber all over you. It's not like you'll be seeing 'im again."

"Yes, Mommy." I decide to humor her. "No panty-draws for him."

"Oh ... and ... if you see the man in tight pants, try not to stare at his bulge like you usually do."

"Poe, stop lying!" I can't resist laughing at her words.

"Queenie, yes, you do! I don't care where we go, you always spot men in tight garments with large bulges, and you know it. It's so obvious, not to mention embarrassing."

That heifer. "You must be looking to know this." I almost turn beet red. "I do not ... well ... What's wrong with it? I mean ... if a man didn't want folks looking at his bulge, he wouldn't be wearing tight garments. That's how I feel about it."

Holding her curlers in midair above my head, Poe retaliated with, "It's embarrassing. That's what's wrong with it."

"Then don't watch to see me look. Jeepers." We share a brief laugh.

"Girl, you hopeless."

Poetta placed the curling iron down and took up a can of sheen and sprayed my head for a long time like she was creating a new ozone layer. She stood back and admired the way her creation of curls were arranged with stylish sophistication. "There," she said, pleased as she passed me a handheld mirror. "You like it?"

I ooohed and awed my reflection for a few seconds. "I love it. How much I owe you?"

She paused as if she had to think about it. "For being such a good sport about the fund-raiser, this one is on the house."

"Yeah, right," I said, getting up slowly from my chair. My back felt stiff from sitting too long, and my left leg still felt asleep. "On the house, huh?" Like the other times haven't been. I couldn't recall the last time I had to pay Poetta for hooking my hair up. "Thanks, Poe."

She lowered her head with a sly look. "Queenie, you know you welcome. Just watch out for that man like I said."

"Yes, Mother." I grinned at her, but I could tell that she was serious. Right then it came to me that perhaps she knew more about Zeke than she was telling me. But, no. I knew Poetta too good for that. When it came to the dirty 411 on men, she wasn't one to hold back.

"Make fun if you want, Queenie. Just remember, a too-handsome man is like a wolf in sheep clothing."

That would explain why she's with Jimboy. "Yes, my goddess of wisdom."

"Oh, you bugging now. Make fun if you want."

I gave Poetta a scrutinizing look. She was serious. But nothing she could have said or done could deter my date with Zeke that night. Nothing. I was consumed by that feeling. That same feeling a woman gets when her mind tricks her into believing that she has finally met the right one—that special man that God himself has made and placed down on this earth just for her.

I had a date with destiny. I wanted to tell her that, but before I could open my mouth to get the words out, she said, "Oh, and if you're having dinner out by the water, I would opt for leg coverage. Wear the lavender pantsuit."

Eight

Santa Monica Pier's Seahawk Inn was the perfect place for a romantic date. Who wouldn't want to dine in plush, tropical surroundings over-looking the ocean? The place was almost overcrowded with palms, ferns, and trailing vines hanging from a vaulted ceiling. Looking more like a tiny airplane runway, small running lights lit the pathway of mauve, beige, and moss-green carpet. The massive room was high-lighted with a center aquarium almost as tall as the ceiling itself. Amid the effervescent bubbles of blue, yellow, and orange coral, silvery eels slid through the water like liquid mercury while delicate angel and clown fish hovered curiously to watch diners. Laced cloth tables with glowing candlelit centers gave the place a cozy comfort to ease any possible tension I was feeling. Piped in music, soft and soothing, played like skipping whispers through the lightly scented air. Rose petals.

What was that tune? A jazzy version of "Strangers in the Night."

"This place is the bomb," I said, probably a bit too eager. Instantly, I felt a flicker of embarrassment that I was sounding like a giddy child in a candy store for the very first time. Like I've never been to a posh restaurant before. "Very classy," I corrected as I looked around and took it all in.

"Glad you like it," replied Zeke, watching my expression.

"I do. I love the water."

"I do, too."

The ocean view outside the sweeping glass window where we sat was full of dark and mysterious crashing waves. The light of the full moon glistened off what looked to be endless dark glass. To the right and left of us, sailboats of various sizes were anchored where they swayed and bobbed in the water like restless children. "Look at all those expensive toys for the rich. Must be nice."

Zeke nodded. "You wouldn't necessarily have to be rich to own one of those smaller boats, but having a good bank account probably helps."

"This is really nice." I was speaking more of the idea of being in such a nice place with Zeke than I was of the opulent atmosphere itself.

"It's okay, but I've seen better," he said, adjusting the band on his wristwatch.

A chubby, dark-haired waitress came over and asked if we wanted drinks.

"A glass of white wine, please."

"I'll have the same," Zeke chimed.

One minute flat, the waitress was back with our drinks and two menus. Nervous as I was, I felt like gulping my drink down and asking for another. *But I'm a lady tonight*, I remind myself. *A perfect lady.*

"You come here often?" I asked, looking for a reasonable topic. Something easy on the brain to help smooth out my edges. One thing for sure, Zeke didn't need me to tell him how handsome he looked in his seven-hundred-dollar smoke-gray suit. I could tell that he definitely had the know-how on how to hook up a good look. I knew the suit's cost because the same designer name suit was carried in Macy's, and it wasn't cheap. Even his perfectly matched blue-and-gray tie and gold tie pin seemed in order. A sharp dresser, another point up.

"Actually no," he responded with a tint of wistfulness in his voice. "This place is okay, but I would have chosen a much nicer spot. Perhaps the King's Castle a little farther down the pier or the Reef out in San Pedro."

"The King's Castle? Hmmm. I'm impressed. I've been there once."

"Is that right? Nice, don't you think?"

"You got that right." *The King's Castle*, I mused. Not only did he have good taste, but he was obviously a man who didn't mind being reckless with money. The one and only time I'd graced the place he spoke of was with a group of friends from work gathering for our annual Christmas party. After one glimpse of my share of the ridiculously high bill, I vowed that I would never set foot in the place again, and I haven't.

My interest piqued, I asked, "If this place is not your choice, then who chose it?"

Zeke shifted slightly in his chair and lowered his menu before looking around. I loved his eyes, the way they captured and held so much expression without his lips having to cooperate. Beautiful bedroom eyes.

"The way I heard it," he said, lowering his voice as though he was about to divulge top military secrets. "The owners of various restaurants contribute their share to the AIDS fund-raiser by donating expense-paid meals to the participants. This is one of such restaurants." He patted his left breast pocket. "Got our meal vouchers right here."

"Well, good for you," was all I could think to say. *Meal voucher? Hmmmm. Hope that's not a sign of future cheapness.* I may not care much for spending money on a man, but I'm quite the advocate for the opposite.

We both viewed our dinner menus in silence. Little did he know that I was doing my best not to jump into prying deeper into his business. I couldn't help it. There was so much I wanted to know about the man. Even if our date was only for one night and we would probably end up going our separate ways and never seeing one another again in life, I still wanted to know. Heck. I felt like I had a right to know. Did he come from a big family? Did he believe in God? What was his favorite color? Did he like silk boxers next to his baby soft skin or cotton? So many things, yet so little time.

"So, Queenie," he said, breaking my reverie. "Tell me about yourself."

"Where should I begin?" It was already a little after eight, and Zeke had made it clear, more than once during our previous phone conversations, that right after our dinner date, he would have to depart for a so-called late-night appointment with a fellow cowriter. It seemed that the two were hard at work on a script together for a major production company. According to Zeke, time was of the essence when big money was on the line.

"Start wherever you like."

A tiny, blond-haired girl with large blue eyes came over and took our order. I swear, I don't know what it was about the man, but I could barely concentrate on what to order for sneaking a peek at him over my menu. One fine specimen. So dashing and virile looking. Babies by a man like him would have to be stars someday—actors and singers. *Silk or cotton? Wonder what he likes to wear next to his . . .*

I cleared my throat. "Uh, I'll have the baked salmon, steamed vegetables, a small garden salad, and a glass of unsweetened lemonade." After fasting all that day, I was ready to eat two cows and a side order of grilled pig. But, no. I'm in control. *I'm a lady tonight*, I remind myself.

"The chicken and lobster dinner for me."

We handed our menus to the waitress and settled back into a cozy silence for a few seconds. *You'll never know if you don't ask the man. Just ask!* I fiddled with my hands for a while, sitting there, waiting for our food to come and feeling like a gate inside me was trying to open up.

"So," he said, turning his full attention back to me, eyes piercing mine. "Tell me now, what's Queenie about?"

"I don't want to bore you."

"I'm not easily bored." He smiled more with his eyes than with his lips.

It was so unlike me not to jump right in and talk about myself, being my own favorite person and all. I should tell him about my plans to become a successful entrepreneur one day, and how I have struggled through working a full-time job and college at the same time to earn a BA in retail management. How my job as a top senior buyer for Macy's afforded me the ability to put away a good sum of savings so that one day I can live my own dream, to possess my own chain of clothing boutiques specializing in the more-to-love woman. A place for the larger woman needing to dress for success. One store in the beginning. A seed planted. A slew of stores later. My own cultivated garden. Sipping my wine, I fought the urge to tell so much too soon. Instead I asked, "You first, Zeke. What does a creative person such as yourself do for fun and relaxation?"

It's like my mama always said, "It's best to allow a man to do what he likes second best, which is the art of talking about himself."

"A lot of things and maybe not enough. Sometimes I stay so busy that I forget that all work and no play makes Zeke a dull boy, or better I should say, a dull man."

You got that right, I thought, smiling shyly. *Not one thing is boyish about you.*

He angled his head sideways in a cocky way that gave him an impish look. Up close, even in the candlelight, I could see that his Denzel look was more surface camouflage than anything. Anybody with good eyesight could see that Zeke was more down to earth and more sincere than the real man could ever be. Cool and collective, like a calm river flowed beneath his surface. Not only was he sinfully handsome, charming, and debonair, but also a good conversationalist. Elbow on the table, I rested my chin along the bridge of my hands as my mind floated away on his words.

All my life it seemed—well, maybe not all my life, but since I first became aware of the opposite sex, somewhere around age six—I've always had this mental list tucked away in the back of my mind of what would be the man of my dreams. The list, like some sacred scroll etched in my brain, has grown and evolved over the years, but the basics always stays the same.

I'm a witness to it all the time. Females pooling their judgments, their expectations, and warning signs about men. I had my own lifetime of tidbits on what to look for in a man, what to put up with, and what to put your foot down at. It all came to me the way it did to most females: spoon-fed to me by my mother, blown like ancient moon dust into my face by my aunts, and whacked upside my head by so-called well-meaning girlfriends. And let's not forget the pure get-my-feelings-stomped-on experience that all women must go through. Oh, yeah—Queenie has had her share.

As far as I was concerned, men fell into three possible categories: the good, the bad, and the just-a-waste-of-space-on-the-planet type. The good type for me consisted of good-looking, average to good body, good-hearted with a reasonable good attitude toward life. A man that truly loves women. Definitely a good job, hopefully with clear and focused life goals already established. Why waste a perfectly good life? Oh, and good sex. Some females like to put sex at the top of the list, but I know better. All the good loving in the world can't make up for a man who leeches on you or treats you like dirt. The good-sex part should be the icing on the cake.

If you respect life, life will respect you. I never forget that time is flowing like a restless river, and too many times in the past I'd occupied myself dating a few men from the bad category. But ultimately, they never panned out to be more than what they were in the beginning. Not bad guys in the eyes of all women, per se. But just a bad choice for me. As far as the third category, Queenie don't waste her time.

Like every other hot-blooded, heterosexual female on the planet, I, too, am questing for the perfect man. That one special man that I can love and devote my life to—allow my back to be thrown permanently out of line from too many days of wild and careless lovemaking. Then allow my body to become stretched and misshapen with his babies growing inside me like wild, sprouting seeds. This man I seek is not perfect in all the aspects of perfection, but perfect for me. A pinch of compassion, a dash of dreams, and two scoops of some good lovemaking qualities would help.

That man, when I finally find him, my raw gem in a pool of fake stones, I'll place high on a throne of goodness and cherish him for the rest of his earthly days . . . forever and ever . . . and. It feels like my search could be over. Zeke could very well be that man. How does one explain a feeling that is so intensed, so new to themself? If I was a book, he was turning my pages. Lost in my own reverie, while Zeke talked I did my specs on him:

MARTIAL STATUS: Single, never married, but hopeful.

LIPS: Perfect and begging to be kissed by me.

JOB: Actor, screenplay writer.

CAR: Beemer, sporty two-seater, convertible. Sea mist blue.

LIVING ARRANGEMENT: Owns his home. Shares with a roommate named Willie.

GOALS: To become a famous actor and producer.

What I wanted in a man was what I wanted, and I wasn't planning on settling for less. So far, no complaints. According to my own quality control, Zeke had it going on. The man had everything that defined itself as a good catch in my book. So far, so good, but still, there were a few things that had to be checked on—like his everyday personality and outlook on life. And of course, that icing on the cake, his performance between the sheets. The last thought made me feel a little warm and tingly. Immediately, I had to fan myself. "Is it hot in here to you, or is it just me?"

". . . and that was how it all came to be," he was saying. He stopped and regarded me, puzzled. "You're hot?"

Too lost in my own reveries, I didn't have the faintest idea what he was referring to. "I'm sorry. Just go on." Embarrassed, I sipped my drink. Thank goodness for an alternate distraction.

Our food came, and I felt a tad shameful that I really hadn't heard much of what Zeke had said. A few bits and pieces. Something about being a tennis buff. And traveling a lot, and something about most women not liking his roommate. I did hear the part about him considering himself adventurous.

"So what's the farthest that you've been so far?" I looked over at his plate of baked chicken, baked potato, and half a lobster tail and felt envious. I was thankful that the rumbling in my stomach wasn't loud enough to be heard. To add to that, my small piece of salmon, garden salad, and steamed veggies seemed pitiful. I bowed my head for my silent grace: *Lord, thank you for this meal before me, and dear Lord, if you make this man fall in love with me, I promise to live right and go to church every Sunday for the rest of my life. I promise not to pray and ask you for another thing as long as I live. Amen.*

"I think you were right. It is getting a little too warm in here," Zeke said. "Mind if I take off my coat?"

"Course not." *How polite of him to ask*, I mused. *Wish you could take it all off right here at this table, and throw in a lap dance while you're at it.*

"Let me see," he said, picking up his fork and pondering my question. "Been to the Caribbean Islands twice. Hawaii once, and saving up for Paris."

"Would that be Paris in Vegas, or Paris, France?" I chanced a grin.

"Real cute, Queenie. I'm referring to France."

"Just kidding. It sounds great. I'm saving my money, too. But instead of traveling right now, I plan to start a business someday."

"Is that right?" Looking mildly amused, he picked up his fork.

"That's right. One day this lady here will be a rich entrepreneur. A business woman extraordinaire."

"Well, good for you," was all he said.

At least he did smile when he said it, but still it bruised my spirit a little that he didn't even bother to ask what kind of business.

"I'm starved," he chirped, picking up his knife to cut into his meat.

"Me, too."

What followed was mostly small talk, and during the whole time I must have caught Zeke stealing quick glances at his watch a half a dozen times. I had no business thinking that we could see each other again, not because of some fund-raiser that had brought us together in the first place, but by our own free choice. The thing was, I didn't want to seem too forward by posing the question and putting the man on the spot. Zeke cut and ate heartily as if he couldn't feel my uneasiness trying to take over the night.

Lord, please let him be the one. Please Lord, please, I prayed silently. I should know better, but can't help myself. Sometimes we want what we want and don't have a clear reason why we want it. Because. But it all seemed so settled. We had both driven our own cars to the restaurant, only because Zeke had insisted that it would save time by him not having to drive to one side of town to pick me up, and then drive to the opposite side of town to get to the restaurant. The cold, hard truth stared me boldly in the face, that after our dinner, we would climb into separate cars and drive off into separate directions. It was a painful realization that I didn't want to think about.

Somewhere after coffee and dessert of strawberry-topped cheesecake, Zeke stood up and excused himself to go in search of the rest room.

"Be right back," he said, almost with too much glee. "Give these to the waitress when she brings our check." He lifted his coat and reached into the breast pocket and withdrew our meal vouchers before draping his coat back along the chair. The faint sound of keys clinking against each other perked up my ears.

"Sure." I nodded amiably, half hating that our date was drawing to a close. *I'll never see him again*, I thought as I watched his confident stroll away from me. Never experience his smile again, never know if he reached his goal in life of becoming a successful actor. And if somewhere down the line the good Lord blessed him for participating in such a worthy cause, I would never know. I felt an ache in my heart. Already, I was missing him. "What a hunk of a man."

He was a keeper, for sure. So laid-back and down to earth. So kind and sweet. So incredibly stupid to leave his car keys unattended in his coat pocket with a woman he hardly knew. Didn't his mama teach him anything about females? Forget about getting to know him first. I was ready to have his baby! Tonight if he asked me.

"Mrs. Zeke Washington." Yeah. I liked the way it sounded rolling off my tongue.

I got up and slowly went to his chair and picked up his coat, turned it upside down, and lightly shook it. His ring of two keys fell to the floor with a light thump. Two brass keys on a small, silver ring. Car ignition, trunk, and house key, perhaps? Sweet and simple. I liked that in a man. I didn't care if it didn't make sense that I hardly knew him. I didn't care who saw me pick those two keys up and tuck them away in the vault of my ample bosom. Well, not too ample, but big enough to hide a small treasure—just what those keys meant to me.

Lovingly, I placed his coat back along the chair, stopping only briefly to see who might be watching. Most faces were too busy talking or being wooed with food and wine to pay me any attention. Only one pair of bold eyes watched—a gray-haired white woman with too thick glasses and too much makeup on was noticing. She sat across the way from our table staring over at me like she was getting paid to do it. But after I gave her a mind-your-own-damn-business look, she rolled her eyes back to her own dinner partner.

"What? You doing a documentary or somethin'? You need to be minding your own man."

I scrunched my face up at her. *People like you make me sick!* Who was she to be worried about how I was handling mine? How could she possibly understand that when it came to the man of my dreams, destiny needed a helping hand? I couldn't just let Zeke walk in and out of my life no more than she could see without those too-thick bifocal glasses perched on her nose.

Hmph. The nosy woman even had the nerve to look over in my direction again as I took my seat. Good thing I was being a lady that night, or I would have marched right over to her table and told her a few choice words and put her cooked rare steak on her head like a bad hat. But I was handling it. I looked her dead in her pink face, daring her with my eyes. "Honey, get real. Sometimes, a woman gotta do what a woman gotta do."

Nine

"Queenie, I really can't thank you enough for giving me a lift back to my place."

"It was my pleasure, Zeke."

Confusion clouded his face. "The darnest thing about my keys, though."

He shook his head before opening the passenger's door, pausing in his seat. The cool night air rushed into the car like a restless spirit, only to settle down to soothing. "I'm sure they'll turn up at the restaurant sooner or later."

"I hope so. But still, I just don't understand how they could have gotten away from me like that. I'm usually pretty good about keeping up with my keys. I don't know. Anyway, I'm really grateful for you going out your way to bring me home."

"It was no problem."

We sat outside his two-story, English Tudor–style house. Me, shameless as I wanna be, and Zeke ever so grateful that he didn't have to cough up the small fortune it would have cost for a cab from Santa Monica to Ladera Heights. The songs of crickets calling for mates filled the night air. I looked up at the full moon and smiled. So beautiful. The clear, California sky gave me the feeling that each star that twinkled so bright did so just for me.

"So this is where you live."

"Yep. This is my casa."

I looked over at the address posted along the tall palm tree next to his driveway. "Not bad. Not bad at all." He owned his own home, an ambitious black man doing what needed to be done to obtain his pie in the sky—reaching his goals. This was good. This was real good. It's my opinion that if a woman have to be involved with a man, it may as well be a man climbing the rungs of success. I studied his address silently. 3326 Kemp Street. A beige house with dark brown trim. Seeing as how it was a place I wanted to see again, I memorized it.

"I mean . . . I backtracked everywhere near that place for those keys and—"

"I know, I know. But don't worry about it. I'm sure they'll turn up at the restaurant and they'll call you. You did leave your phone number with the manager, right?"

"Yeah, but still . . . this is so embarrassing to have you drive me all the way-back. It really ticks me off."

"Zeke," I said as soothing as I could. "It was no problem. It's not like I have a curfew and have to be home and in bed by a certain time."

"God, what a night." He pulled a roll of breath mints from his pocket and offered me one, then popped one into his mouth. "I've never lost my keys like this. Never. I can't thank you enough."

"And you're welcome again, and stop worrying. They'll turn up."

"Yeah. I guess you're right," he said somberly.

"Mind if I use your rest room before I head back to my side of town?"

I thought I detected a slight hesitation.

"Sure. C'mon in."

I got out and followed him up the pebbled stone driveway to the house's facade and pretended to look away when he fetched a fake rock from a pile to the right side of us, obviously a spare key holder, and let us in.

"Just ruined my plans, that's all. My appointment is shot. I just can't believe it."

"Zeke, stop ailing over it."

"Easy for you to say. I'm missing money, and that bothers me."

Talking about his keys was the last thing on my mind. Getting into his house was the first. Judging by the looks of his place, the man was into mirrors and glass. Where there should have been drywall were panels of glass. Block glass walls. Brass and glass coffee and end tables. A black marble pedestal table with a glass top perched on plush misty gray carpet. Gray and misty blue walls. The place looked spotless for two men sharing. I was impressed.

"The rest room's that way," he pointed, and then turned his attention to a small stack of mail.

"Thanks." I followed his pointing finger and headed down a short hallway of closed doors, all except for one, which was the room I was looking for. I couldn't believe how clean and neat everything was. A few pieces of African art along the walls. Black and gray designer embossed towels neatly displayed. Cute soap dish filled with pastel soap shaped like sea shells and a matching rug and toilet cover in smoke gray. A place for everything and everything in its place. Smells of a woman's touch everywhere. I hurried up and did my business, flushed, washed my hands, and headed out.

Surrounded by large burgundy and dark gray pillows, Zeke was sitting at the edge of a magnificent light gray leather sofa flipping through channels with a remote control and looking a bit restless, as if he was about to get up and leave back out any second.

"I really love your place." I said, panning my view, hoping for a offer of a seat. A glass of wine and kick your shoes off and stay awhile invite. *Too soon*, I told myself. *Too soon*. "Aren't you going to show me around at least?"

When he looked up from the giant television screen, irritation flicker in his eyes, but only for a second.

"It's kinda late, but I guess a quick tour can't hurt."

"I don't mind if you don't."

"Hey, what the heck." He cut off the television and stood. "The living room. The kitchen's over there. Two bedrooms downstairs. Two bedrooms up. The two lower-level bedrooms, one is my video library office, and the other is used as a den when company comes over."

"Nice." I commented, noticing his taste in ultramodern decor. I followed him up the stairs, holding on to its oaken handrail. Another rest room done in gray, maroon, and black. Okay. So far so good. "You decorated yourself?" What was I fishing for? The man had already told me that he had a woman in the shadows. A woman I couldn't wait to meet.

"A room or two myself." He beamed proudly. "The rest was done by my friend Reeba, the young lady I told you about. Reeba dabbles in freelance decorating in her spare time. In fact, that's how we met. I needed someone to hook up my pad, and a friend gave me Reeba's card."

"She sounds interesting." Like I cared.

"Reeba's cool. You'd like her."

Reeba. There was that name again. A woman I knew that one day I'd have to deal with. Reeba the good friend that thinks she's in love with Zeke. Reeba the tasteless interior decorator who shouldn't be allowed to decorate the inside of a dog kennel, let alone a brother's dwelling. Reeba, Reeba, Reeba. I didn't know the woman, but already I hated her. "This Reeba sounds like quite a gal."

Grinning. "She's all right most of the time. But it's like I said, I'm not ready for nothing too serious right now."

"I don't blame you," I said, thinking that any man would feel that way if he hadn't met the right woman yet. "Love can be so complicated."

"Got that right." He grinned.

After we all but skipped by the closed door of one bedroom, his roommate's I surmised, I just had to ask, "So, just where is this wonderful roommate tonight?"

"Never said he was wonderful. Did I say he was wonderful?"

Okay, okay. "Excuse me for asking." If I didn't know any better, I could say that the man looked insulted by my remark. Penis envy, perhaps?

"Willie. His name is Sweet Willie."

"Sweet Willie?"

"Yep. Sweet Willie Special. I call 'im Willie though. And you can believe, he's quite the character. But let's talk about something else."

I read people. Even consider myself good at it. Just a few words, a certain facial expression, but mostly body language. Most people never think about how much is said through body language. The quick batting of an eye or the pursing of the lips after a question has been asked. The way Zeke stuffed his hands in both pockets of his trousers, looked down at the floor, and averted his eyes before looking back up at me with the oddest expression, his roommate, Sweet Willie, wasn't exactly his favorite topic I took it. He seemed uneasy—like my asking had grazed along a sore spot. Just like a too-handsome man. With good looks usually comes a big ego. Could it be jealousy of his roommate dancing in those eyes?

"If you must know about 'im, he's gone a lot. You could say that he's on tour right now. Big job up in Vegas. He's deep into show biz. Give or take a few days, and he'll be back in town."

On tour, huh. How interesting, I thought. Two guys living together and both in the entertainment business. "How fascinating."

"Sometimes, but not always."

After a quick peek in Zeke's cherry-paneled bedroom, my breath snagged somewhere in my throat. Moonlight rained down through a ceiling portal unto the pie-shaped bed, which sat perfectly centered in a room of glass and cherrywood paneling. A glass-enclosed fireplace—gas, of course—was trimmed in brass. Three short steps lead up to the maroon, satin playground of ecstasy just waiting to happen on that same large, round bed perched on a step-up pedestal. To me right then and there, that rotund-shaped bed was the place of specialness. That quick peek was a peek into paradise. Already, I could see my large and luscious self sprawled along that bed, Zeke and I, together. Could see my love-clouded eyes gazing up through the moon-shaped portal and see beyond the stars as if I could see forever.

"This is beautiful," I hear myself say, stepping into the plush light gray carpet that almost swallowed my feet. But enough was enough. I'd seen enough for one night. "Imagination. I like that in a man."

"Looks like that's all there is to see of my casa. It's no mansion, but I call it home."

"And it's a lovely one, too. I love it."

"Thanks."

I followed him back along the stretch of landing leading to the stairs with my head caught up in the clouds with thoughts of delicious possibilities. I could see so many things that night, all in my head waiting to be born into reality. I could see myself living in a house like this with a man like Zeke, see myself elegantly descending the majestic stairs one at a time, down to the place where my admiring friends would be waiting. Their smiling faces all aglow with envy.

My mind was making plans. If I worked my cards right, I would be the leading lady in Zeke's life. Me, Queenie—love goddess on pause. The number-one lady cooking all his meals, tending to his needs the way a new mother tends to a needy baby. My mama always said that the fastest way to a man's heart was through his stomach. And when Mr. Zeke got a taste of my greens and hot-water corn bread and hazelnut-topped sweet potato pie, I just knew that he would be thinking that he died and went to heaven before his time.

All these thoughts were kicking around in my head. I should have been paying better attention to my feet. Halfway down the stairwell, my right foot zinged when it should have zagged, and I stepped down wrong, and it felt like somebody hauled off and kicked the balance right from under. I felt the panic jump inside me as I lurched forward with my shoulders trying to go in one direction while my body went in the opposite. I couldn't right myself fast enough to keep from bumping hard against Zeke, and—oh, my God—sending the man tumbling down fast like some out-of-control snowball from an incline of snow. One of us yelped out loudly, probably me. But by the time I regained some semblance of balance, Zeke—my Zeke—lay at the bottom of the stairs, withering in pain, his face twisted as he clutched his right foot.

"Oh, my God, no."

"My ankle. I think I hurt my ankle." He closed his eyes with pain.

I hurried down the rest of the steps as fast as my legs would take me, my heart feeling like it was about to leap out of my chest. "Ohmygawd. Are you okay?" I knelt down close to his face, the minty smell of his breath was in my nostrils. "Zeke, I'm so sorry. Are you hurt badly? Tell me where it hurts again. Say something."

I helped him sit up so that his back could rest against the wall. I could see his lips dry and cracked looking and moving slowly in a face contorted with pain. "Is it your back?"

He grimaced. "No."

I pressed lightly along his rib cage, something I'd seen done plenty of times on ER. "Is it your ribs?" I licked my lips. Just saying the last words only reminded me of how hungry I still was. That dinner I'd eaten earlier had only teased at my stomach. Some ribs didn't sound bad at all. I looked up with a wistful thought.

"Speaking of ribs, you ever had Tony Roma's ribs?" Licking my lips some more just thinking about it. "They make some of the best open-pit smoked ribs in town—"

"Queenie." His voice was was so low, barely a whisper.

I put my ear closer to his face, right at his lips. "Yes, Zeke, I'm here. Tell me what you want me to do. Tell Queenie."

"Queenie . . ."

"I'm listening. Just say it, Zeke."

"Queenie, just go home."

"Oh, I see. It's like that, now?"

"Yeah," he said, rubbing his right ankle. "It's like that."

Hmph. Big baby. Obviously the man wasn't at death's door if he wanted me to leave 'im and go home. And I did. But not until I was convinced that nothing was broken, no serious injuries. One glance at his rapidly swelling ankle, and I was almost convinced that I should scoop him up and drive him to Kaiser—willingly or kicking and screaming—just to be on the safe side. But through his moaning and groaning with pain, Zeke convinced me that he'd be okay once he drew some warm bathwater and soaked for a while. Besides, no bones protruded from skin. No major artery was spurting blood.

"Okay, if you think you'll be all right, I'll go on home."

"I'll be fine." He frowned, painfully. "Really. I just need to be alone."

After I helped him up, resisting the urge to scoop him into my arms like precious cargo and carry him back up the stairs to his bedroom and lay him out along the big round bed, I got him all settled and cozy on the sofa. I could have doctored on him all night, really, but it was time to call it a night. After I propped his right foot up on a pillow along the glass coffee table, fetched him something cold to drink and some ice in a plastic sandwich bag I found in the kitchen and placed it on his ankle, I said my good-byes.

"And Queenie," he said as I stood at his front door, a happy but a wounded look along his face. "Despite all that's happened tonight, I still had a nice time. And thanks again for the ride back to the crib."

"Me, too, Zeke," I said, my hands turning the living room doorknob. "I had a nice time, too. I just feel so bad to leave you this way."

"I'll be all right. Really." He waved me along and then shifted his elevated leg on the coffee table.

"You sure?"

"I'll be fine. It was a freak accident, but I'll live."

"Okay, then."

"Thanks, Queenie."

"You're welcome, Zeke," I said as I opened his front door and headed out.

Ten

Three more hours to go at work the following Monday. I'd made it through the biggest part of the day. Things were going smooth. Ray has only passed my office and waved twice, smiling and waving. I waved back, but keep my expression serious. His wavings are small intrusions to my life, no bringing of homemade food, no chocolate or roses. No sneaking into my office to set up his special buffet as an offering of his undying love. Not on this day. This is a good day, and I'm doing good because he's doing good to keep it like friends should. No unexpected surprises, and for once in a long time, I'm having a blessed day at work. Maybe things are changing, after all. I should have threatened to file an harassment claim on him earlier.

This new Ray is not so bad. I thought about ordering a gift for the man for helping me out last Wednesday by doing my mass ordering. I had my doubts at first. Kept thinking about all the ways Ray could make me lose my job if he'd wanted. But that Thursday morning following, true to his words, everything was done and taken to the processing department. All signed and delivered. What other friend I knew would do something like that?

I go to the oaken credenza where I last recall seeing the thick book of yellow pages. A thank-you gift to Ray and a get-well gift to Zeke is in order. Just because I don't like the man don't mean that I can't thank him for a job well done. And with Zeke, just because our one and only date ended bad didn't mean I should write him off. Not when he was in my every thought, like punctuation at the end of every sentence. Zeke. My Zeke. A gift for a friend and for a special friend, soon to be lover.

First Ray, I mused. *Umm. What does a woman gives a man who she believes to be a pest most times? Cologne? Flowers? A gift certificate to a health spa?* I couldn't think. I spotted the book at the bottom of my cabinet, but before I could pull the heavy book out, the phone rang, instantly making me think of Ray, probably thinking he could collect more for his good deed of finishing my major orders. I shouldn't be so quick to accuse, but who else would have the nerve to be calling my office before I had my morning infusion of caffeine? Irritated, I went over and snatched it up, ready to give Raymo a good tongue-lashing, but the voice I hear on the opposite end wasn't Raymo's; it's Poetta, and from the tone of her voice, her words screaming in my ear loud enough to wake the dead, she has a problem—a real problem.

"It's over! Queenie, my life is over!"

"Poetta? Girl, what's wrong? Talk to me!"

And then she says the most stupid thing—she says, "In my will I'm leaving everything to you, Queenie. Everything. I just want you to know."

Click. The line goes dead.

"Poetta!" My stomach knots up, and for a second or two it feels like I can't catch my next breath. I don't know what she meant by leaving everything to me, but I wasn't taking no chances. My thank-you business with Ray had to wait. I had to get to my best friend before she did something dumb.

After ringing up Jay and telling him I was sick to my stomach and going home for the day, but would come in early, early to make some of my time up, I hightailed it to my car and drove like the police speeding into Compton to rescue some white women being held hostage by two gun-wielding black thugs.

The minute I pulled up in front of Poetta's house, I got an eerie feeling at the sight of the place—a feeling like I was about to enter the *Twilight Zone* with my eyes wide open. It was just last Saturday I'd been at her house, and funny thing, I didn't recall seeing no fire-flickering candles from the edge of her roof. Real candles burning real flames and sitting over in tiny candle holders that appeared to be suspended by fishing twine.

"What the heck—" Not only were there candles burning from the top of her house, but white block-shaped candles lined up at the bottom of the front entrance like small wax soldiers waiting to do battle. A walkway of flames.

"Ohmygawd, the girl has finally flipped her lid." I couldn't believe what I was seeing, I mean, burning a few candles inside your house is one thing, but this . . .

I got out and hurried to the door and tried the knob, surprised that it wasn't even locked. Poetta was getting too laxed in the last few years by thinking that she could go to sleep at night with her windows up or not bother with locking her doors. Where did she think she was, in the back woods of Mississippi somewhere? Just too laxed, but I couldn't think about that long when I spotted her slumped in the corner of the room, her body all crunched up along the floor. I quick-scanned around the room. Insane as it was, a fire roared in the fire-place in the summertime. Heat outside and heat on the inside. Reddish-orange flames licked and crackled hungrily in the room, from the candles burning, from the fire in the fireplace. I couldn't even imagine what crazy thing had happen to slide her down loony lane so early in the day. More so, I couldn't recall the last time I'd seen Poetta look so torn up. I mean, the girl was tore up from the floor up, and here it was almost eighty degrees outside, and girlfriend had a cozy fire roaring inside her house. *What next? A giant bonfire on the front yard?*

"Poe, what's wrong, girl?" Her thick reddish-brown braids looked angry, stood like multiantennae on her head, and she was wearing some kind of beige camisole with the matching taupe pants. A refreshing change from her Badu look. I went and stood over her, looking down at the pathetic heap of woman, whose puffy face and swollen red eyes looked as if she'd been crying pretty hard. My strength in the light of weakness was now before me like some defeated rag doll, spent and beaten down by life. "Poe? Talk to me. What happened?"

She didn't answer. Didn't look up to acknowledge me. I stooped down trying for eye level, which is something that's not even easy for a full-figured and voluptuous woman of my weight whose sole exercise routine for the last few years had been lifting a box of doughnuts to take in to work twice a month. I could hear bones and joints knocking and creaking, crying out with protest. "Poe . . . Poe what's wrong?"

I noticed that she was clutching some kind of stuffed rag, or some kind of pincushion tight to her chest. I wasn't sure what the heck it was, but I reached over and tried to pry it away from her. Wrong move. That girl looked up at me like I was Satan himself come to take her home. She grunted, clutched the thing even tighter to her chest as if her life depended on that rag.

"Poe, what's going on, girl?"

The more I looked at the thing, the more I realized that it wasn't just a rag, but some kind of doll fashioned from dark cloth—a doll with real-looking human hair at the top of its dark gray cloth head. Its center had an opening that folded in like a cloth-made stomach. It was eyeless and mouthless and some kind of silvery stick pins protruded from what I perceived to be—what? Its arm? A tiny patch of real-looking hair protruded from the center of the thing, from what seemed to be its belly.

"Poe, what is that thing? May I see it?" I asked, reaching for the doll again, but clearly Poetta wasn't going for it. I could tell by the cowering look in her eyes as she twisted the rag doll closer to her like some frightened child, she meant business. Frankly, the whole scene was beginning to give me the creeps.

"No!" she screamed, trying to hide the thing behind her back.

"Poe, let me see it!"

"Queenie, I said no!"

"You little twit! I said let me see it!" I lunged and grabbed it and wrestled it away from her clutch, stood up and moved away from her, holding it up for a good viewing. I didn't know what the big deal was, but the more she had refused to let me take a look at it, the stronger my nerve to see it. I had it in my hand, held up to the light of the flames. It was made of a smoky gray material with dark brown seeds for eyes, a piece of something that looked like toenail for a nose and a piece for its mouth. Nappy stuff, dull and dark looking, perched atop its head looking like snipped hair from somebody's head. I was making a face and couldn't help it. Whatever it was, it was ugly and nasty looking. "Now, what the heck do we have here?"

Talking 'bout a sister looking pained. "Queenie, give it back!" she screamed, running up to me, all in my face.

"Girlfriend, you just hold on now." I didn't know what the heck her problem was, but as her closest and best friend, I felt called upon to find out. "Not until you tell me what it is."

"I said give it back, or . . . or you'll be sorry," she cried out. "I'm not playing."

"And I said not until you tell me what the heck it is. And for your information, I'm already sorry . . . sorry for knowing a weirdo like you." Maybe not the best thing to say at that time, but the way I felt. I loved that girl like a blood sister, but she had her days.

"Never mind what it is. Just give it back to me and stay outta my business."

I don't know if it was just me, or all that fire all around us, but I was heating up pretty quick. Aside from the fire roaring in the fireplace, it must have been over a hundred candles burning just in the living room alone. I didn't even want to think about the rest of the house. Standing at the gates of hell would have been cooler.

"Queenie, give it back and leave me alone."

"First tell me what this is, Poe, and you can have the damn thing back."

Poetta settled back down, lowering her defense. "What for? You wouldn't understand," she said, watching that little stuffed, gray-cloth doll like any minute, any second it could suddenly sprout wings and fly away. Dang, she was really tripping.

"Maybe that's your problem, Poe, you spend way too much time locked up in this dark and dreary house burning candles and chanting spook spells to make your life better, but I don't see it happening. You need to join the real world and get a real job!"

"And that's your opinion. You worry about Queenie, and I'll worry about me." She walked up on me closer, like she wanted to throw down a few rounds. This was not the calm and peaceful Poe I was used to. "Give me the damn doll!"

And smug about it, too. I pushed her back, and she landed on the floor, but not too hard.

"Queenie, you give it back or I'll take it," she all but hissed.

"You'll take it? Oh, that's funny. See, I left work to come see about you, and now you won't tell me what the problem is. You think you can take it, take it." I was just about to tell her to try me again, but before I could open my mouth that girl, Poetta, she was like a flash of lightning the way she streaked up from the floor and snatched that nasty-looking doll from my hand and threw it on the carpeted floor. Before my mouth could close up, she jumped down on it like she was about to perform some kind of sumo wrestling with the thing. I watched in shock as she took out that stick pin and stuck that doll in the leg with it over and over again like she was in somebody horror movie, grunting and screaming to the top of her voice.

"Two-timing! Wife-cheating! You lying snake in the grass! Couldn't keep it in your pants! Could you?"

"Poetta! Poe, stop it!" I couldn't stand seeing her this way. Of all the years I'd known my girl, she was the calm one, the sensible one. The one who always kept her emotions in check.

"You're a dog!" she screamed, banging that rag thing along the floor. "Just another big, phony, poke-anything, cheating liar!"

My heart was racing along with her words, my head starting to spin from being so caught up in her frenzy. "Who, Poe, who? Jimboy?"

"I should cut your penis off!"

"His penis? Poe, who are you talking about? Jimboy?" Who else could it be, but with all her so-called clients, I couldn't be sure. If she heard me, she didn't acknowledge it.

"—anything! You'll screw anything!"

"Who, Jesse? No. Couldn't be him. Who? Clinton?" But duh. Couldn't be him either. Why would Poetta care so much about who Jesse or Clinton screwed? "Jimboy, right? Girl, I don't know what's got into you, but you have finally lost your mind." When I really opened my eyes and saw what she was doing, sticking that damn pin in and out of that damn doll with the patch of real hair, curly black and thick and looking too close to curly and tight pubic hair, I knew I had to do something, but quick. But what? I went over, stooped, and snatched the thing from her hands again. She make a lunge at it, but not in time before my toss flung it to the fireplace. "Look, just stop this. You scaring the heck outta me!"

Now don't go getting me wrong, 'cause it's like I said before, Queenie don't even believe in no hoodoo-voodoo mess, but I swear on my granny's grave, God rest her spicy soul, that little cloth-made doll made a small scream when it hit the fire. Not a loud booming scream like something you'd hear on some low-budget horror flick, but a tiny, tiny scream that was short-lived. My hears caught it, and I know what I heard. And then it was over.

"Whoa . . ." I felt the hairs on my back side stand up when I realized what my ears had picked up. A scream, a yell, whatever the heck it was, my heart raced inside my chest when I had heard it. The sound reminded me of the movie, the older version of *The Fly* when homeboy with the tiny human head was caught in the spider's web and he cries out for help. Damn spooky was what it was. "Did you just hear something?"

But even spookier was Poetta screaming and hollering and running around like a nut trying to find something to help her fetch that spooky doll from the fire. "Queenie, no. Oh, no! You'll kill 'im!" she screamed, looking around for the fire poker that was never kept where it should be. "No! Queenie, help me, he'll die, you'll kill 'im!"

"I'll what? Poe, what the heck are you talking about?" *You crazy!* my mind shouted. "Kill who?"

"Jimboy! You just killed 'im! Oh, no . . . no."

"Poe, you're crazy—it's just a doll!" And not a very good likeness of the man, if anybody asked me. "A stupid doll!"

"Get it out! Help me get it out!"

"Girl, you tripping hard. I'm not sticking my hand in that fire."

She stopped searching for the poker and got up in my face yelling and screaming and going off about dolls, spirits, and killing folks. It was the first time I'd ever seen her eyes so large and wild looking. Crazy. I mean, I thought I was the costar in a scene from *One Flew over the Cuckoo's Nest*. Veins bulged like overstressed dams at her temples. I'd never seen Poe like this before, and what I was seeing was giving me a bad feeling, sending a shiver up my spine.

"I should have stayed my behind at work!" My hands were trembling, my head spinning from the madness of it all, one big whirlwind of madness, and I didn't know what to do, so I slapped her.

That's right! I slapped her!

It wasn't the kind of slap that was hard enough to loosen any teeth or cause permanent brain damage, and it wasn't like I was trying to hurt my homie, 'cause like I said before, Poe and me, we go way back. When we close, we closer than twins. An attempt to bring good sense back to her, my slapping was done out of love. She stopped for a second, looked totally shocked, but still looked wild about the eyes. Trying to bring her back to reality, back to herself, I slapped her again. She stopped and looked confused.

"Queenie? . . . What the hell?"

Stunned, she stopped in midbabble and did something I wasn't expecting. She slapped me back, hard and sassy with it. *Oh, hell no! No, she didn't just hit me!* I slapped her again. She returned my slap and advanced me two more, one to each side of my face.

It was on then.

I threw her little bony Badu butt on the floor and straddled her like a wild horse that only I had the power to tame and ride. "Crazy woman! You crazy heifer! You don't be slapping me!" I screamed to the top of my voice, wrestling her arms, trying to restrain her. I had no idea what kind of madness had happened in her life that would make her crazy enough to try'n go up against me, but she had to be outta her rag-wrapped mind. Friend or not, if she was looking for a butt-whooping, all she had to do was take a number. "You dizzy cow! What's wrong with you?"

"You murderer!" She screamed back at me, her eyes red and bulging. "You killed 'im! You beastly woman, you killed my Jimboy!"

"I don't know what the heck you're talking 'bout! I didn't murder no dang body, at least not yet!" I tensed up my body for more strength, trying to take her thin arms and tie them into a knot, but little as she was, she was stronger than I thought.

We could have went on wrestling along the floor and stirring up dust for a good while if it hadn't been for the thick and growing smell of smoke that hooked our attention. It did more than hook our attention, it made us stop at the same time, arms tangled, a thatch of hair clutched in both hands, made us sniff the air at the same time.

"What's that smell?"

I froze above her. "You smell something, too?" I climbed off and Poetta sat up along the floor with her thin braids sticking up on her head like dark popsicles as we both sniffed the air again. "Smells like somethin' burning."

"Sure does."

"You didn't leave something on the stove cooking, did you?"

Poe shook her head. "Of course not."

She sniffed; I sniffed. I can't say who looked up first, Poetta or me. Maybe we both looked up at the ceiling at the same time, and what we saw wasn't a pretty sight. "Oh, my God! Fire!" We saw the fury of hell above our heads. We saw the breath of Satan breathing down on us.

"Ohmygawd, Poetta!" I screamed. "Your ceiling's on fire!"

Eleven

God looks after fools and drunkards. How true, how true. And then there's always the afterwards. After the rain, the sun. After the madness, the calm. After the war, the peace. After we scattered about the house ranting and raving, going for pots and pots of water and finally scrambling outside the house in search of Poetta's trusty water hose, which, by the way, she couldn't remember the last time she'd laid eyes on the thing, we knew it was hopeless. After Poetta courageously removed a few small items from the angry, hot house spitting orange and red hatred, flames licking the summery air, all we could do was stand outside along the dying grass and watch the flames do their job.

Who called the fire department? We still don't know. But before we knew it, a red engine roared up to the front of Poe's place, and a bevy of oversuited men jumped out dragging hoses and shouting and barking orders back and forth. The fire department—who had called them?

After the firemen happily chopped away half of Poetta's house like a team of vandalizing hoodlums who didn't know any better, I helped Poetta—who I had noticed by then was way too quiet and staring off into space—to load up the few things she did manage to save into my car.

The flames all out and nothing more to see, I thanked the good fireman who suggested that Poetta get in touch with the local Red Cross to see about obtaining some kind of assistance. If Poetta did hear the man talking to her, she didn't let on. I went around to the driver's side and climbed in and paused before starting the engine.

Poor Poe. She stared expressionless and straight ahead without blinking. Her hands were clasped in the center of her lap, and the way her small shoulders were hunched made her look even smaller. It broke my heart just seeing her that way. Mrs. Reed, one of her neighbors, had been kind enough to give her a blanket, some big, bulky, and itchy-looking green thing that Poetta had wrapped around her shoulders and half pulled up around her neck. Black spots of soot and ash along her face, her thick and dry-looking braids that stood every which way along her head, that itchy, army-green blanket wrapped around her, and the way she was staring so motionless ahead of her, she looked a pure-dee mess.

I took a deep breath and let it out slow. What the hell had just happened? What had it all been about? "Well," I said slowly, not to sound mean or nothing. "I hope you're satisfied. *I* knew all that candle-burning all over the place would eventually amount to something."

No sooner had I said the words, I regretted it. It was the wrong thing to say at the wrong time. What kind of friend was I to be blaming her at a time when she needed me the most? Hadn't Poetta always been there for me in my time of need? Of course I never had the need to burn down my own house, but that was besides the point. Hadn't she helped me through plenty of ups and downs and kept me from getting my behind whipped? Sure she had, I reasoned in my head. Like that time when we were just kids and my mama caught me and Billy Ray Martin out in the storage shed behind our house with my panties down and Billy Ray Martin squatting down with his eyes almost as big as binoculars with him trying to see how girls pee. It made a little smile come to my face just thinking about it. Me the teacher, Billy Ray my student. Even though that was over twenty-something years ago, I bet that mentally challenged Billy Ray still don't know how girls pee. And my mama wasn't no help either. My mama, yellow as she was, had almost turned beet red when she showed up out of nowhere and snatched me up from the floor of that storage shed and shook me so hard I'm sure I heard my teeth rattle. Mama's left eye was still twitching, and she was shaking and fussing at me when Billy Ray Martin took off running like a black cat being chased by a big stray dog. After she grew tired of shaking me, my mama must have snatched my panties back up so hard, my crack had a bad rash for weeks; then she yanked at my clothes the whole time trying to drag me to the house where I knew for sure a good peach-tree switch would be waiting to dance me around the room. Funny, the things we remember from childhood.

I still remember breaking away from mama, who was hollering and screaming for me to bring my "hot behind" back. But fear of a beating had steered me straight from our backyard and down the dusty street behind Billy Ray. I broke away and ran like the young fool I was. It was like I was a gangbanger with the wrong colors on in the wrong neighborhood. I ran. I ran straight to Poetta's house, where she hid me for two whole days in her bedroom closet, sneaking food and water to me by day and staying up to talk and giggle with me late into the night.

A runaway child was what I was back then, and worried folks had looked for me. Looked long and hard, I was later told. I was a fugitive from the justice of my own mama. With Poe's help, together we were partners in crime—she, lying to our parents about my whereabouts by day and feeling darn good about it by night. But it didn't last long before Poetta's mama discovered me sleeping in the closet one morning and took me home to my frantic mother. The whole time Poetta's mother was at our house, I could tell that my mama was so happy and relieved to see me by the way she kept hugging and kissing me and ranting. "My baby, my sweet, precious baby." The perfect picture of a understanding and loving mother for her child.

"My baby—Lord, thank you, Jesus—my baby is safe." Those had been her very words. But the minute we were alone, my mama kissed my cheek and went and got her mothering tool, a stiff leather belt, and opened up a brand-new can of "whup ass" on me.

"Poe, what exactly happened?" I asked, coming back to the present.

At first she seemed like she didn't even hear me—like I hadn't said one word. The more she refused to talk, the more pissed off I was feeling about leaving work early, ruining my expensive pantyhose and my favorite two-piece suit. I wasn't looking no better than her with my hair sticking up every which way on my head, black spots of soot on my face, but I forced myself to be patient, like a good friend trying to understanding what she'd been through. "Poe, say something. Talk to me."

Maybe she was in some kind of trance. All I wanted was to understand her position. I wanted to understand how I would feel if half my house had just burned down because of my carelessness, because of some sick and twisted fascination with fire. And I got to thinking . . . maybe . . . maybe somebody had put some kind of reverse-it-back-to-you-hex on Poetta. Not only that, but what if we both had burned up in those hellish flames and our spirits had to part ways? Mine, of course, going to the golden gates of heaven because I don't believe in devil-worshiping, while Poetta's soul, on the other hand, would go from one hell to another one. Devil worshipers can't go to heaven, can they?

"I need some quiet time, Queenie," she said softly, like a small child.

"I understand, Poe." Which was the honest-to-God truth. I flipped down my sun visor, thinking to ease the glare from the noonday sun. But there was no sun on a gloomy day that can't find hope. I headed for my own house. I was speeding along on the freeway with all kinds of crazy thoughts crowding my head and trying to take control of my mind. Putting Poetta up in my place for a few months until her house was repaired wouldn't be a problem, but if girlfriend thought she was going to be chanting voodoo spells and burning hex candles up in my crib, hmph. She had another thought coming. Queenie don't even play that.

"But I still wanna know what happened."

She sat silent, looking tight-lipped.

"Look, Poe," I said, hoping the agitation in my voice was more than evident. "You called me at work today, shouting in the phone like some crazy person about your life being over, or something like

that. I didn't call you; you called me. And here I am, missing half a
day from work just to see 'bout you, and you won't even tell me what
the problem is. Don't you think I deserve to know?"

I gave her a sideways glance and kept my attention on the road.
She didn't speak, but the way her head went down and her shoulders
heaved as if all the vibrant life pushed out of her with that last breath,
I felt the tears before they came.

"Poe, I can't help you if you don't tell me what the problem is." I
kept looking back over at her as much as I could without jeopardizing
our safety along the highway. I knew I was going a little under the
speed limit of sixty-five, but I didn't care. Cars sped up behind me
only to switch to another lane to keep from rear-ending us. A horn
sounded from somewhere behind us, but I ignored them all to concentrate on what was ailing my best friend. It pulled at my heartstrings
to see her so sad—so broken up. Her chest was heaving and racking
with tears.

"What, Poe? Is it your sister, Marva? Don't tell me. Lord, no. Is
she sick or something?" My eyes grew wide in horror. "Ohmygawd,
no. It's worse, isn't it? Marva finally has AIDS from sleeping with every
man within a fifty-mile radius, isn't it? Darn! I knew it. Poe, I tried
to tell that sister of yours to get herself some professional help for her
sex addiction, but—" No, couldn't be Marva. Poe had mentioned
something about cutting off a male's member, had to be Jimboy unless
she had another boyfriend, a secret lover I wasn't privy to.

"Did something happened to Jimboy?"

Tears soaking her face, Poetta shook her head for no. I tried to
study her face between keeping my eyes on the road and reaching for
a tissue to give her from my glove box, but all I could see was the
side of her head. Maybe it was something to do with Jimboy and
Marva both.

"It's not AIDS? Then what? Cancer? Ohmygawd, cancer. The big
C. I knew it! Marva has cancer? All that old sperm from that antique
husband of hers probably corroded her insides, and I knew it. I tried
to tell her that stuff that old men have is like battery acid; it's not
good for a young woman . . ."

She cried harder. I know I should know what her problem is, but

Poetta, being a person of complexity, it could be anything. Having a house burn halfway down would be enough to make me cry.

"It's not your sister Marva's husband? Who, then?" My eyes watered. Soon, I was crying copiously along with her without shame. I wasn't for sure what great tragedy had invaded her life before the fire, but whatever it was, I, too, felt her pain and suffering. After all, Poetta and I, most of the time, were like two peas sharing the same pod. I wanted to be there to absorb some of her pain the way a sponge absorbs water. I could barely see the road in front of me for the tears in my eyes.

My nose was becoming congested, and my chest was starting to ache the way it always does when I'm feeling troubled or grieved. *Sniff.* "Tell me, Poe. You can tell me." Feeling bad, I snorted and wiped my nose with the back of my hand.

Finally when she spoke, her voice sounded thin and weak, like somebody's child after being scolded too hard. "He—he had a wife."

"He?" Felt like a light went on inside me. *He* didn't sound like a sister Marva problem. My eyes dried up on the spot. "He who?" I knew darn well who *he* was, but my mind was on pause.

"Who else, Queenie? Jimboy. He had a wife and two kids!"

I didn't mean to stare at the side of her head. Honest. And a good thing my eyes weren't piercing lasers. Oh, heck no. "You mean to tell me that we're sitting up here crying and slinging snot over some man? Over Jimboy?"

"I loved him."

"You what? You love—Poe, your house almost burned completely down to the ground. You could have been killed, not to mention me, as well, and you sitting up here, looking like you ran out of Prozac two weeks ago, not to mention that you're homeless, and all because of some man?"

She shot me a dagger look. "Just because you can't love somebody don't mean I'm the same way, Queenie!"

Oh, no—she didn't go there! "Girl, you tripping. You have been inhaling too much smoke, obviously." I hurried up and pulled my car to the shoulder of the highway, put it in park, and cut the engine. If we get hit from behind, so be it. And she was crying again, only harder, as if tears could actually make it better. "You know, Poe," I said, doing my best to keep an even tone. "You have done some crazy things over the years, but this—this takes the cake. How can you be so vulnerable as to let a man control so much of your emotions that you'd wreck your own life? How?"

"You don't know love like I do, Queenie."

"Bullshit. Sounds like the title for a good book I should be writing about you. You don't know love like I do. Poe, your problem is, you don't know the difference between falling in love and falling into stupid."

"Guess I'm not like you, the tower of strength." She made an ugly face.

"Maybe so, because to me, Miss Queenie, it ain't that much love in the world." I felt so upset with her that I had a good mind to tell her place-a-hex butt to get out of my car! But, no. That wouldn't be right to put her out. Not on the freeway. Not to my best friend.

I was quiet for a few seconds, then took a deep breath. "So . . . how'd you find out?" I mulled it over about Jimboy having a wife all along. Now that explained a lot—like why he rarely called her when he was out on his so-called trucking jobs. When he did return home to Poe, seemed like the longest he could stay would be one or two days before claiming to have another haul. I mean, how many frozen chicken carcasses can there be to haul back and forth in a week? Come to think about it, driving a rig across state is the perfect setup for a cheating man. "Did he tell you himself?"

She took her own sweet time answering. I waited.

"She called me," she said, and sniffed, studying her soot-covered hands.

"His wife called you?"

"Said she found my number hidden in one of his coat pockets." She sniffed. "I don't know why he would have to carry my phone number, seeing how he'd moved in with me."

She started crying again, but this time quietly—a peaceful cry.

His wife? I thought about that, too. A few pair of pants, a few pair of shoes, a couple of shirts here and there hadn't really looked like a total move-in to me. Looked more like the best of two worlds. Some double-life-living mess. "He's just one man, Poe."

"I loved 'im, Queenie. I can't help how I feel."

I'm listening to her but not listening. Love. Sure. I'd been there. Done that. I had sense enough to know that life is a bitter teacher and love really don't love nobody. Too bad Poetta didn't have sense to see that.

"Well," I said, trying to take charge of the situation—put it all back into its place. "Stop crying. You're probably better off without someone like that in your life. I know it hurts right now, Poe, but you'll get through it. We'll get through it together. You'll see."

She gave me a brave smile that looked more like herself. I felt better, too, just knowing that I would do what little I could to help. I started the car back up and pulled back onto the freeway. "I think you should have a doctor look after those burns on your hands."

"Yeah." She huffed at the suggestion.

"And I'm sorry about that little fight before the fire." I leaned over and hugged her. "It's not that bad. Some fresh aloe might help those burns. We'll see if I have some at the house."

"Sure. I'm sorry I slapped you." Already blisters had formed on the burned skin where she had tried to put out flames that tried to claim her hair kit. "Maybe you're right," she agreed, and went back to staring straight ahead like a woman in a trance. "You're always right, Queenie."

"Well, good. You finally noticed."

Twelve

Coming up, you learn a lot of things from your mother. Children are their mother's sponges. Soft. Absorbent. Mine taught me a lot. Things like how not to let a man play you for a fool for the second time around, or before you can really hope to find and love a good man, you have to be a good woman first. And no man can truly love a woman who don't love herself.

Mother wit, I like to call it. Some of that wit comes out like thin smoke and goes in one ear and right out the other, never to be thought of again. But some of it, the parts that talk to your deepest soul, the parts that makes sense, stays with you in the recesses of your existence—kind of like stored computer data, to pulled up later for future use.

My mama always said that good food heals the spirit and mends the body, and a person in need of healing is a person in need of some good food. And my mama knew her stuff. That's why I was feeling as good as it gets taking care of my buddy, Poetta. Driving that girl home to my house where I could patch up her half-melted spirit. I could smooth her out.

Food heals the soul, I kept chanting in my head. In my spacious and overwhelmingly yellow kitchen with all the latest in kitchen technology, I bustled around, preparing a good and nourishing meal for Poetta, who was still in bed the next day, looking like somebody's thrown-away stepchild.

Outside my condo window, a timid sun was smiling down on the city of Cerritos, and it felt good to be doing something to help somebody. Poetta would be all right once I served her some of my fresh baked biscuits—homemade I might add—fresh sliced apples steamed in cinnamon water, fried ham, and some of my lightly scrambled eggs with a side order of pure maple syrup. I only eat the pure maple because I've been told that it's the most healthiest for you. And believe it or not, I do think about my health from time to time. Not only that, but it's good on the palate, and I was determined to heal whatever was ailing Poe, be it man troubles or the temporary loss of her own living space. And just to give Poe a good laugh on top of it all, I'd even searched the recesses of my overbooked closet and found the nurse outfit that I had rented and accidentally forgot to return for the office Halloween party a year back. Faithfully, I keep the outfit enclosed in plastic, and when I retrieved it and put it on, it still looked as white and fresh as ever, complete with the little matching white nurse's cap. And it still fit! Just for fun, I even took the time to use my black eyeliner to pencil in black freckles all over my face. If my memory served me right, me showing up to the office Christmas party dressed like a freckle-faced nurse last year and offering free exams to all the young tenderoni males had been quite a smile-maker. Giddy inside, I was hoping that the outfit, black-dot freckles on my face and all, would do the same to help cheer up good friend.

Poor Poe, I thought as I stood at the yellow-tiled kitchen counter and gazed out through the wispy, open curtains. *You'll be all right.* I hummed a tune as I put the last finishing touches on the tray of food I would take in to my patient, my best bud, complete with a single yellow rose from my own bunch from the supermarket two days earlier. "One yellow rose to help some cheer along," I said to myself on my way to her room.

I kept hoping for some cheer, some kind of appreciation, but the moment Poe seen me walk into the bedroom with the tray of food, the girl made a disgusted face and looked away, looking like some-body's sad and tossed-away puppy.

"Hey, girl. Hope you feeling better." I put on my happiest face, determined not to allow her melancholy fever to affect me one bit as I walked over, sat the tray down along the side of the bed, and then eased over to the window to open up the window blinds and let some light into the room.

"Thank you, but no sunlight for me."

"Sorry," I said cheerfully, letting her words roll past me. "But sun-shine is just what the doctor ordered. You'll be all right once I get some vittles in you."

"Vittles? Queenie, if you talking 'bout food, please say so. Besides, I'm not hungry," she said with a stubborn-looking pout. "And what's with that silly outfit? You going to a costume party or somethin'?"

"Poe," I sighed, keeping my wits about myself. "Never mind where I'm going, but you have to eat something. Stop try'n' to be so difficult when I'm try'n' to be nice."

"Nice when nobody asked you to be." Stubborn arms folded across her chest.

"Maybe so, but at least I'm trying."

For a spell, we shared a brief stare down. "You'll be all right," I said, determined not to let her sour mood invade me. "You'll see."

But to that she just rolled her eyes and looked away, then gazed stubbornly back at me. "Easy for you to say."

"Hope you slept well. I know I do when I sleep in this room." It's one of my favorite rooms at my place, and I keep it simple. Peach-hued walls, peach-hued carpet, blinds at the window the color of rip-ened peaches. Not a whole lot of furniture, except for the bed and nightstands and my oak rocking chair. Simple but functional. In the full-size brass bed of my extra bedroom, the same room I like to think of as my thinking room because I like to sit in the smooth oaken rocker next to the window and look out on the world and do my thinking, she was here in my special place and doing her best to get on my last nerve.

"If you call listening to crickets sing all night, I guess I did."

"Good," I chirp. "Maybe later if you get up, get cleaned up, and put on some clothes and go out for a walk, you'll feel even better."

"Maybe I don't wanna feel better right now."

"Poe, being witchy about it won't help none. Some fresh air will do you some good."

"Queenie, just bite me and be done with it."

"Don't tempt me. With that attitude, I just might."

Poe was propped up on two of my best down pillows, still looking a mess from her ordeal. Her hair was lying much closer to her head, but there was a beat-down look about her that couldn't be missed. At first I thought that there was still some black soot from the fire up under her eyes, but a closer observation confirmed that those dark circles under her eyes were darkened skin, which had to be from exhaustion or lack of sleep. Still tore-up looking. I shook my head. All over some no good man that didn't mean her no good to begin with. I just didn't understand why it was that some women allowed themselves to be treated like doormats for the sake of love. If I looked long and hard enough, I could see straight into her eyes to her soul. Hurting big time is what I saw, and nothing I said was going to ease that kind of pain except time.

This thing with Jimboy and Poetta was obviously more serious than I had imagined. I went over and sat at the edge of the bed, picked up the steamy mug of liquid, and held it out for her.

"Here," I said. "Drink this."

"What is it?" She sniffed, scrunching up her face like she smelled something horrible.

"You heard of chicken soup for the soul?"

"Be serious," she countered. "Who hasn't?" She eyed me suspiciously. "And—?"

"Well, chicken soup for the souls of white folks and good ol' down-home pot liquor for the souls of black folks. Try it."

"Pot liquor for breakfast?"

"Why not? Girl, didn't your mama teach you anything? Nothing can warm your insides and get all up inside you and clean you out and rearrange your whole disposition like a good cup of pot liquor. So hush up and drink up before you hurt my feelings."

She took the cup from my hands and sniffed it. "Ooh. Kinda lively smelling for collard-green juice, ain't it?" She sniffed again. "Good, Lord. Some plain old green tea would do just fine. What's in this stuff?"

"Let's see," I said playfully. "You have collards, turnips, mustards, and a couple of bunches of fresh spinach with pureed tomatoes, onions, and garlic with a few teardrops of pure virgin oil. Not to mention a little sea salt and fresh ground pepper. Only virgin olive oil 'cause oil that's been had too many times might have a bad reputation." I chanced a few chuckles, but she wasn't having it.

"What?"

"Get it? No longer a virgin—the oil—never mind, Poe."

"Girl, pleeze." She grinned, looking a little more like herself. "You are so crazy."

"Oh, and my secret ingredient, one tablespoon of good whiskey. I added that to your cup."

"That explains it." She sniffed again before taking a sip. "Might grow hair on my chest, but not bad, though." Another sip. "Not bad at all."

"Just for my best bud."

"Queenie, I know you haven't been up long enough to cook a pot of greens this morning?"

"Nope. Cooked 'em yesterday. Cooked up a bunch of food to last me awhile. No big deal. I always cook up a storm to last me. Some good ol' greens, pot roast, whipped potatoes with gravy and black-eyed peas and corn bread. No Jiffy in a box stuff either."

"And you wonder why you can't lose the weight."

"Who says I'm really trying to? Honey, Queenie loves Queenie just the way she is. Whoever don't like it can go be with the devil."

"Uh-huh. Yeah."

For a hot moment, she seemed interested, then, like some light clicked off in her head, she put her mug down and went back to looking depressed. Leave it to me not to beat around the bush. "Look, Poe, on the real side, I just want you to know that I'm really sorry about you and Jimboy. I mean it. I liked 'im, a little. I really thought he would be the one for you. You know, the whole deal, marriage, a house, kids, two dogs, and a few grandkids down the line. Guess we all have to learn the hard way about men sometimes."

"I don't wanna talk about it." She put her cup down along the nightstand.

"Yeah, you do, so let it out. You really loved 'im, huh?"

She took a deep breath. "I just feel so foolish for not seeing the signs. Especially when they were right there in my face. Right there." Her fist pounded the bed. "Gone all the time. No way to contact 'im until he contacted me. Nowhere to be found on holidays." She went quiet as if she had to think about what she'd just said, then added, "Guess I didn't wanna see 'em. Didn't want to believe that he could let me become so attached, so involved with 'im, knowing that he was another woman's husband."

"You mean you honestly didn't know he was married?" I looked skeptic.

"Hell no! Do I look like a fool to you? I would never violate the sacred bond of marriage. Marriage is a spiritual bond between a man and woman. Vows are spoken to a higher God to love only that person. When another woman invades that bond, it's the greatest sin she can make herself part of. Adultery is the purest of sin for the man and the woman. Haven't you learned anything about this?"

I thought about saying yes, but swallowed the word, thinking, *Me myself, I like my sin partially diluted. Sin too pure is more than what I need.*

"Another woman's husband. Hmph." I could feel my blood heating up. It wasn't enough that a man could be so reckless with his own marriage vows, but the fact that he could feel nothing about having another woman fall in love with 'im, just to have her heart broken, burns me up. "See? That's what's wrong with women today, Poe. We're too quick to believe what men tell us and accept any and everything too easily just to be able to say that we have somebody—like it's some trophy for a woman to have a man. Oh, yeah—I have a man. Big deal. But that don't make it right. I'm telling you, there's nothing worse than a lying, two-timing, double-crossing, low-down, dirty married man. Don't know the first thing about what it means to honor their wedding vows. Instead of saying 'I do,' they should change the vows to 'I really don't plan to,' 'cause that's the way it seems. Heck, Poe, married men are the main ones that think a marriage license means that they've been granted a license to go cheat. Who cares about who gets hurts in the end. Yeah, it starts off with pleasure and fun, and turns to hate and hurt. One thing for sure, Poe, somebody always gets hurt. Sometimes it's the wife, or the mistress, or even the children involved. In the end, somebody always gets hurt."

She picked her mug back up and sipped carefully at her hot brew. "Yeah, well . . . guess I won't have to worry 'bout 'im no more if he's dead. Thanks to you."

No, she didn't. Did she? "Why you gotta go there, Poe? How many times I have to tell you my beliefs don't sway that way with that hocus-pocus put-a-spell-on-somebody's-behind mess?" I stood up with my hands on my hips, looking down at her like some nurse upset at her patient for not cooperating with getting a shot. "You need to give it a rest."

"Believe it or not, Queenie. You were there. You were the one who threw his spirit into the fireplace. Right into the flames. Now he's dead!"

"Girl, you tripping! You just don't give up, do you? You really expect me to believe that Jimboy's soul or his cheating-butt spirit, or whatever, was in that tiny, ugly little rag doll? You must be on crack."

"You condemned his soul!"

"Poe . . . so you saying the man is dead now?"

"I didn't stutter, did I?"

"Is he dead or what?"

"Dead, Queenie. Read my lips. Real dead."

"Look, Poe, don't be a smart mouth. And how the heck would you know if the man is dead, seeing how you claim you haven't heard from 'im in days and have no way of contacting 'im? How?"

She made a smacking sound with her mouth and frowned. "I just know, that's how. Shoots."

And she was serious, too. The way her eyes were bugging, the way that vein always finds it way to the side of her head when she's upset. Bulging and pulsating. Irritated, I paced the room from one end to the other. "I guess this is what I get. I try to be nice, but no, I have to be accused of crazy stuff. It's just no pleasing you, Poe, is there?"

She shot daring eyes at me. "Queenie, I'm just telling you what I know."

That was it. I threw my hands in the air. "Girl, you too much. I'm through with you for now. I can't take this mess. I'm outta here."

"Where you going?"

Like she cared.

"I don't know, but any place away from here. I got things to do, so you do what you do, and I'll check you later."

"Be that way, then."

"Maybe you'll feel better when I get back. There's plenty of food in the fridge, and you know how to work my cable box." I headed for the door but stopped and spun back around. "Oh, and one more thing, Miss Poe." I gave her a stern and serious look short of wiggling a warning finger in her face. "My place is your place, and feel right at home, but don't—and I repeat, *don't*—be burning no candles up in here. I mean it. No candles. Promise."

"I promise, but you leaving me won't make the truth go away, Queenie."

"I know, I know. I'm being mentally punished for something, but I have to go. Maybe I'll go find a voodoo shop and get a doll like you." I watched for her reaction, but she didn't look up. "Remember, Poe, no candle-burning."

Whether she heard me the last time or not, she stared straight ahead at the wall like a mental patient on too much medication. I needed to find a better place to be. I closed the bedroom door on my way out.

Thirteen

Fire, candles, and now voodoo dolls. Dang. Poe is sicker than I thought. If she thought she had me believing that jive about spirits living in little ugly dolls and folks dying because their ugly doll gets burned up—*hmph*—she had another thought coming. She just didn't know how close to being put out of my house she was for talking so crazy. But I'm cool. She may have ruffled my feathers for a minute, but I still love her like my blood. Besides, I have bigger and better things on my mind.

Poe wasn't the only one needing some nursing back to health. I needed a better place to be, and what better place to go than go check on my other patient, the home of Mr. Too-Fine-for-His-Own-Good, Mr. Zeke. The man was lucky and didn't even know it yet. His very own private nurse, complete with good nutrition and uniform and about to make a house call.

Before I left my place, I prepared Zeke a plate of some down-home cooking, going heavy on the mashed potatoes and gravy, and poured the rest of the pot liquor from the greens into a tall thermos and bagged it all up. "Yes, indeed," I said to myself on my way out. "How lucky can a man get?"

I had held on to his hot property for as long as I wanted. His keys.

It was time to return Zeke's car and house keys, and I had my story down straight on how those keys had come into my possession. Over and over, I rehearsed my story in my head as I got in my car and headed to his house. I figured that with his ankle messed up, he was just another poor soul in need of some good nursing, and the way I saw it, I was just the woman to give it to him.

Perhaps I was being a little too presumptuous, a little too full of myself by planning a pop-by to his house when I hadn't known the man a good week. But I couldn't help myself. Something about that man just wouldn't let me forget the way he smiled, or the promise that had danced in his eyes. He was hurt because of my carelessness, and I couldn't sit back and let him go in need. Not with that messed-up ankle and him hopping around in that big house all by himself. He was definitely in need. Besides, I needed something to take my mind off Poetta and her crazy problems. Zeke would be perfect for a change of pace. Maybe it was his sexy body or his kindhearted mannerism, or maybe it was just the simple fact that I was horny as heck and felt that I hadn't got my money's worth out of him, and in no way would I let myself be shortchanged.

I took the long way from Highway 10 so I could stop off at the Krispy Kreme doughnut shop at Crenshaw and Martin Luther King Jr. Boulevard. Half a dozen still-warm doughnuts and two steaming cups of coffee just in case the man had a sweet tooth trying to act up. Krispy Kremes—only the best. By the time I reached Zeke's place, the morning air was still a little dewy cool, but the persistent sun was doing its best to knock that coolness off. I spotted his car in his driveway but didn't dwell on the mystery of how he had retrieved it with his sore ankle. Wasn't my problem. I was feeling too good to be worrying over minor details. The lively chirp of birds filled the air as I gathered up my breakfast offering and headed for his door and rang the bell.

I rang again, then started a countdown in my head. Eight, seven, six, five, four. Just to make sure, I rang one last time and stood back, wondering what could possibly be taking the man so long to hop his fine self to the door. What if his ankle was worse than he'd thought? What if he couldn't get up because it hurt too much and he needed some help? What if I just stop tripping and use the damn key I was bringing back to him. Duh.

Pulling the key out from my uniform pocket, I stuck it into the lock, heard the click, and eased the door open, calling out his name at the same time, but getting no answer.

"Hey, Zeeekkkeeee! It's me. Queenie."

Still no answer.

"Zeke, are you here?"

Nothing.

"Zeke Washington, are you dressed and decent?" I smiled to myself and mumbled, "I hope not."

I closed the door behind me and stood motionless in the entrance foyer, listening for any signs of life, but heard only the sweet hush of silence. I sat the two cups of coffee in the cardboard tray down along the coffee table. "You might not even be at home." Silly me. Just because his car was returned and parked in the driveway didn't mean the man had to be home. But just the same, I had to make sure.

"Zeke, it's Queenie!" I called out again as I headed up the stairs with my two bags of goodies. I was hoping a brother was hungry, because I know I was. Fooling with that crazy woman, Poe, I hadn't even had the time to get my own grub on. I was hoping for a quaint little continental breakfast with Zeke, just a little something to cheer each other up. "Helllloooo," I called again, listening for any signs of life, but the house was as quiet as a mausoleum after closing hours. I'm thinking that maybe he stepped out to go get some milk or some butter or something. A short hop down to the corner convenience store wouldn't be too hard to navigate. But I wanted to make sure. I kept my pace up the stairs.

I stood at his closed bedroom door and tapped lightly. "Zeke?" Be just my luck to open up the door and find bodies in motion, wild rabbit humping all over the place. It would serve me right, too, for being so presumptuous to come visiting without calling first. I hate when folks do that to me. I hate it.

When I didn't hear his voice answer the first knock, I knocked again before opening the door. Sprawled on the satin sheets of the big round bed was Zeke, and it looked like he was doing some hard-core sleeping. The covers were half off his feet, and I could see that he, or somebody, had done a good job wrapping his swollen ankle in a beige cloth bandage.

"Zeke." No answer. I moved over to the bed and stood over him. "Zeke, you sleep?" No doubt about it, the man was knocked out. I smiled ear to ear; looking down at him gave me such a warm feeling. Even in sleep, he looked so handsome, even with his face twisted and that thin line of drool easing from the side of his mouth. "Ahhh, look at 'im."

Down along the floor I noticed a small pill bottle and sat my bag of goodies down as I picked it up and read the label. "Umph. Vicodin." I'm not pharmacist or nothing, but did recognize the medication as being a highly potent pain reliever. Good old Vicodin. Three years back, when I fell and dislocated my shoulder, my own doctor had prescribed the same medication for me. It was good, all right. Good for pain and comalike sleep.

"Poor baby. That ol' ankle musta got to hurting pretty good." I put the pill bottle back along the floor, grabbed up my bag, and stood and spread the covers over his legs and feet, but not before taking a quick peek up under. And he sleeps in the buff. Good gracious! My quick peek last longer than it should have, but I finally managed to pull myself away and headed from the room with enough delicious visions to last me the rest of the week.

I don't know what got me to thinking about a good hearty dinner for later, but I was headed back down the stairs to the kitchen to see what I could whip up for Zeke's surprise dinner—you know, the good friend trying to do her part to help out—but actually, I was still feeling guilty about his ankle. After all, the man's ankle wouldn't be jacked up if it hadn't been for me. Felt like I owed him some help. A good home-cooked meal would be just the thing to help get Zeke back on his feet. The heck with the leftovers I had brought with me. Zeke deserved better than leftovers. My man deserved the best.

When I was halfway to the kitchen, the doorbell rang. I froze in place, hoping that whoever it was would go away. It sounded again, almost to the point of vibrating through the whole house like some oversize church bell. *Heck*, I thought. *I'm here. Just answer it.* If Zeke was so out of it that he couldn't hear me calling his name with me standing right over him, he certainly couldn't hear the door bell, no way.

Hurrying over to it, I swung the heavy door open. *And what do we have here?* I mused, eyeing the pale-faced white woman standing before me, looking like somebody's Little Red Riding Hood with all that red on. It was a good thing she wasn't somewhere in Compton. She had on some kind of red satin-looking dress that was clinging passionately to her thin frame. Her dark hair was done up in some kind of tossed salad of curls, and a few strands had playfully found their way to her slender face. Red pouty lips perched up under piercing blue eyes that looked as if they could see clean through concrete. *Wow,* I said to myself. *A blue-eyed devil in red satin pumps.* She looked too thin, too pale, too white, and way too out of place for the neighborhood she was in as she stood there eyeing me, and me eyeing her. And that dang suitcase in her left hand. What was that about? I knew that look on a woman's face. It was the look that said, And who the hell are you?

Intimidation has never been my weakness. Chocolate-chip cookies, yes, but intimidation, no. I made my face as stony as it can get—and that's pretty stony, seeing as how I have been known to make babies cry by just looking at them real hard. My face was looking like stone, like the way I feel when I'm standing in line for service and some white chick comes up and the clerk finally comes over and asks her, "May I help you?" Like I haven't been standing there forever. I was looking stony, all right.

"May I help you?" I asked her, hoping to hear that she had somehow lost her way to her grandmother's house and somehow needed some directional assistance.

"Yes . . . I . . . I was looking for Zeke."

"Zeke?"

"Yes, Zeke Washington." She stood back a pace, looking.

Heck. I knew what Zeke she was talking about. "Whom may I say is calling?" If the woman was looking for an easy way in, she wasn't about to find one with me.

She held her right hand out and waited for me to shake it. "I'm Reeba Cottonspin."

She got the message quick when I looked down at her outstretched hand long enough for it to wither and fall off. "Reeba who?"

"Cottonspin. Is Zeke here?" Her eyes batted. Her mouth didn't know if she should smile or frown.

Reeba Cottonspin? Oh. So this—this is the little friend, Reeba. The one that Zeke had spoken fondly of. The one who wanted more than he was ready to give her—wanted a relationship instead of just being his friend. She probably wanted to be Mrs. Zeke Washington and get my Zeke all tied up with too many zebra babies, a huge mortgage, too many bills, and too many broken dreams spun only by the web of delusion of having a white woman. *I don't think so.*

Armed with the few tidbits of information that Zeke had told me, I almost felt as if I really knew this Reeba woman on a personal level. Zeke had told me all about her, all right, but I guess he forgot to mention the part about the woman being white. Not white white, but more like a rosy pink. Delicate looking.

"Well, Miss . . . Cottonspin, I'm so sorry," I said, as pleasant as I could possibly manage, "but Mr. Washington is unavailable right now. Would you like to leave a message?"

Why should I care if all the black men in the world turn to white women, as long as I can have just one, my Zeke. True love shouldn't have to be about color. Not for me. I've dated them black, brown, and white. Men do the same thing. My theory is, can't Mr. Right in black, go to brown, or white. Love is love. But the problem nowadays with black men and white women is things are getting out of control. Black men going around acting like they not black no more just because they have a white woman hanging on their arm in public. Some even going so far as to think that they got something special, something better—like an upgrade on computer software. All because of the difference of skin color. Personally, I don't see what the big deal is. Unwashed coochie—black, white, or brown—it all smells the same.

"That would be nice," Reeba says, a nervous twitching at her left eye. "But I really need to speak with him in person."

"Oh, but that won't be possible," I said in my best professional voice.

"And why not?" she wanted to know. Her eyes prompt for my answer.

"Because I said so." I looked at Miss Reeba, Miss Thang, and tried to figure out why Zeke would want something like her over a strong black woman. I get to figuring in my head. She got pretty blue eyes, true that, but I got pretty brown ones. She got itty-bitty breasts, true that, and I got big let-'em-all-hang-out-with-joy breasts. And just to tell it like it tis, if the girl had some kind of behind, I'd be able to see it from the angle she was standing. But no, nothing. *What a shame*, I thought, shaking my head just thinking about it. Queenie don't have a problem in that department. *When it comes to junk in the trunk* . . . I gave her a good up-and-down once-over and rolled my eyes. Wasn't enough room in her trunk to change her own mind in. Miss Reeba's lily-white butt was flat as flapjacks spilled on a hot griddle.

Don't like to be profiling, but just to be representing a real woman with a real butt, I turned around in my nurse uniform and bend over to check my shoelaces, untied them, then retied them. Butt all melting into the door—just so Miss Reeba could see all that juicy behind that was behind me. *Reeba, eat your heart out*, I wanted to say, but that wouldn't be right. It wasn't her fault.

"Oh, yeah—that's what I'm talking 'bout," I say as I straightened up and turned back around to face her. She looked even paler, but more confused than amused. But she don't fool me. She got my message all right. The only way Miss Thang could match that was to go to a specialty shop and purchase herself an butt-blowup kit. I knew her type. A struggling black brother sniffing behind her probably gave her the notion that she was all that and two bags of chips. It don't matter, though. I wasn't about to let her pale behind up in the place while I was there representing. Heck no.

Reeba cleared her throat. "Is he here, or is he just unavailable?"

Oh, my. Did I detect a budding attitude? "I'm sorry," I said, sounding as professional as possible. "Perhaps it would help if I explain the situation here. I'm Miss Sutton from CDC. That's Community Disease Control. It appears that Mr. Washington has come down with a bout of necroswellhisbidickeritis. It's airborne and highly contagious for those who have not been properly immunized."

She looked stricken. "What?" She craned her long and pale neck around my body in some feeble attempt to look inside the house. "But I just spoke to Zeke yesterday, and he didn't mention—"

"Anything about his condition? Of course not," I said, trying to sound like some authority on the subject. "Dickeritits is not the sort of thing a man would want to reveal, especially to his most intimate of friends, say perhaps to a girlfriend who might be planning to have children someday." I paused and coughed, then watched her with one raised brow. "It's a rare virus still being closely studied by the Center of Disease Control." My right eye twitched in suspicion as I eyed her up and down. "Might you be a girlfriend of Mr. Washington's?"

"What? . . . Who? . . . Me? . . . I—I—well, no, not really."

"A distant relative, perhaps?"

"No."

"The housekeeper, perhaps?"

"Absolutely not," she huffed. "A good friend. We're just good friends."

"Oh, I see." I half smiled.

I swear, I could almost see her prissy thoughts scurrying around in the back of her blue eyes. Eyes that were growing bluer and larger by the second as she patted at her chest and kept trying to peer around me into the house.

"Look," she said, a bit uneasy with this new information. "I would like to hear it from Zeke himself. I'm sure that if he had some kind of—of condition or rare disease of some sort, he would have told me."

"Are you saying that you don't believe me?" I raised a brow to a challenge.

"Not exactly. I'm just saying that if Zeke has some—some kind of weird disease, I would like to hear it from him."

The woman had the gall to punctuate her words with a look of defiance—like I was getting on her nerves or something. *Interesting*, I mused. "Oh, I see, a risk taker."

"Honestly, now, if he's so contagious, how come you're in the house with him?"

Squinting at her, I got all in the door like a wall of solid honey-brown flesh. "Does the word *immunization* mean anything to you? After all"—I patted at my chest—"I am a trained professional."

"I still want to see Zeke. Let me talk to him."

"Very well," I said calmly, just like any professional would do, having to deal with one of disbelief. "Wait right here, and I'll go get the waiver form for you to sign."

Her eyes really bucked, and those red lips of hers were looking kind of funny, too, trying to form themselves into an *o*.

"What waiver forms?" Reeba asked, stunned that I knew more than she about a man she'd known longer.

"It's the standard form that the disease control center uses that states that you have been properly informed of the house's quarantine, and that you are still willing to take the risk regardless." I winked at her before throwing in, "Just for litigation purposes, in the event of your untimely death." Smiling widely, I turned my back to her. "I'll be right back."

"Never mind."

I turned back to face her. It was getting to her. I could tell. Something about the way her eyes looked, that odd angle of her head and the antsy movements of her body. The expression on her face looked like she was smelling something unpleasant.

"Okay, okay. Look," she said, almost too hasty. "Just tell him—tell him that I'll call later when he's better, or cured. Whatever. And here—" She sat the suitcase down on the concrete step to the house as if by coming any closer she might burst into flames on the spot. "Just tell Zeke that Willie will be back tomorrow, and he can't stay at my place anymore. My neighbors are complaining. Just tell him that for me."

"Why, of course." I nodded amiably. "His roommate, Willie, is back in town and he can't stay at your place." *What the hell was that about?* I wondered at the back of my mind. Why would Zeke's roommate, Willie, have to stay at her place, anyway? What kind of freak-the-whole-house relationship was it? *Never mind*, I told myself. It was none of my business, and it was a good thing that I was in the picture now to keep wild and freaky white women like her away from good, decent black men like Zeke. "Certainly, Miss Reeba. I'll make sure that I inform Mr. Washington."

"Thank you."

"No. Thank you."

Yeah, right, I thought as I watched her turn and slither back to her sporty-looking red car. I stepped out and picked up the small black suitcase and stood in the sunlight, watching her start the engine of her car up and drive off. "Black men have enough problems in their lives without the likes of you, Miss Lady," I said to myself under the warm embrace of morning sun. "Good-bye, and good riddance."

Fourteen

We were standing in front of the minister. He was a short, half-bald, another George Jefferson–type man with extremely large hands, and Zeke—more dashing as ever—was looking proud and debonair in his black tuxedo. The stained-glass windows of the church threw splashes of red, blue, green, and yellow against the white Chantilly lace and satin of my bridal gown as Zeke slid the golden band along my trembling finger.

And then the words "You may kiss the bride" flowed into my waiting ears like a sweet melody that would never be forgotten. And we kissed, long and hard, with the smiling and cheering of family and friends embracing us—sucking up our happiness the way sunlight sucks up the gloom from a cloudy day. Mr. and Mrs. Ezekiel Washington.

"Throw the bouquet, Queenie! Throw it!" The sound of cheering was maddening, and—"Excuse me, but could you please throw the bouquet!"

"Excuse me. Queenie? . . . Excuse me—"

A jolt startled me. Eyes popping open and trying to focus. Panic. I sat up and did a quick scan to see where I was. *Oh, yeah. On the sofa of Zeke's place.* My eyes were a little blurry at first, but when they finally did focus, I liked what I was seeing. His face was candy to my eyes. I was staring up into the face of a curious-looking Zeke, who was looking down on me. It was about time he woke up. His expression didn't help much. Glad, mad, or sad, it was hard to tell by the odd look on his face. But judging by the crook in my neck for falling asleep on his sofa, it was a good thing he woke me up.

"Excuse me—Queenie, right?"

"Yeah."

He rubbed his head. "How long you been here, and what are you doing in my house? How'd you get in?" His words sounded slow and grainy, like, Excuse me, but we might have a problem here.

"The front door. It wasn't locked." I know I was lying, but I couldn't help it.

"And you just come in and make yourself at home, is that it? How long have you been here?"

"Didn't you already ask me that?" I massaged the back of my neck, trying to ease the crook out, stalling for the right answer. "A couple of hours, maybe. Waiting for you to wake up. Thought I might have to call paramedics to resuscitate you."

"But—but you're in my house." He looked astonished.

"I was worried about you."

"But you're in my house, though."

"I was worried about you. Came to check on your sore ankle."

Rubbing his hand through his hair, he still looked like he needed more confirmation—more clarification. "About two hours? Who let you in, again?"

Who let me in? I mused. "I turned the doorknob, the door opened, I called out your name over and over, but you didn't answer, so I came in. Who let me in?" What kind of silly question was that to be asking his woman? His new woman. Perhaps even his future wife, and let's not forget the future mother of his children. Our children. It was then that I knew that the truth of it hadn't settled into Zeke yet. The truth being that I was going to be the new woman in his life whether he knew it or not. Signed and sealed. Sometimes men have no idea what they need or what they want. Help in their decisions is what they needed.

Sometimes it takes a woman—a strong, know-how-to-get-what-she-wants kind of woman, like myself—to help a man along. I was going to be Zeke's new woman, and I had known it from the first meeting, the first time I laid eyes on him, and the minute I pulled out my credit card. What I didn't know was what was taking him so long to see where I was coming from.

"I can't believe you're in my house like this." He kept shaking his head as if he could make understanding shake loose.

"And I can't believe you sleep with your door unlocked like that. I could have been a serial killer. Anyway, I came over for a reason. I drove back to the restaurant and inquired about your keys again. Some old dizzy broad tried to give me a hard time about taking a serious look in the lost and found, but a few choice words convinced her to do so, and voilà—your keys." I held up the ring like it was some kind of prize to be proud of.

"You found my keys?"

"Yep. Somebody turned them in. And that's why I'm here, waiting for you to wake up. Guess I must have dozed off while waiting." I paused, then threw some more lies in: "You should be glad I showed up. I saw a couple of thuggish-looking guys hanging around your car, but when they saw me drive up, they stepped. Shame, shame on you, Zeke. This is Los Angeles, you know. Can't go around leaving your front door unlocked."

"You actually retrieved my keys." His half-frown turned to a smile. "Wow. Thanks, Queenie. You drove all the way back up to the restaurant just for me?"

"Sure did." *Somebody stop me*, I think.

"Thanks, Queenie, but you really didn't have to trouble yourself. I had a spare set round the place, and—"

"No trouble. That's what friends are for." I averted my eyes for a second or two. He was wearing a dark blue robe, something looking like terry cloth. When he neglected to close it, I could see his powerful-looking thighs all the way up to those boxer shorts, all white with those cute little red hearts printed all over. I thought back to my earlier peek of seeing him in the buff, but even with boxers on, he looked delicious. His strong muscle-ridden legs were a balm to my tired eyes. "You can always thank me later."

"I can't believe you went back to the restaurant and retrieved them. You all right, Queenie. I really appreciate that."

He went quiet, looking down at me like he couldn't believe his eyes that I was there, in his house, ready and willing to please him. Truth be told, I couldn't believe it myself. Going out of my way trying to please some man has never been one of my strong points, but I wasn't feeling that way about Zeke. Zeke was different, like a new product of manhood placed on the market, and I was the curious consumer, ready to buy and try. I didn't have all the answers worked out in my head as to how I could best get him to see where I was coming from, that if there ever was a woman on this great earth that was meant for him, ready to jump in and give all 100 percent, that woman was me. But that would come later.

"You hungry?" I asked, hopping up as fast as my legs would allow. "I been to the market for a few things to make you a good supper. Nothing too extravagant. A little somethin'-somethin' to help you heal up quicker. Ol' Queenie here will have you back on your feet in no time." I moved past him going to the kitchen to see about his stew.

"Queenie, that's real nice. . . . I mean, really, but you shouldn't have."

He followed me, limping with a dark brown wooden cane to keep from putting all his weight on his ankle. Standing beside me, he sniffed at the delicious aroma coming from my slow-simmering pot along the stove.

"Taste this," I said, taking up a large spoon and spooning some for him to taste. "The best beef stew you ever tasted."

"Nah. That's okay. I'm not much of a meat eater. Especially red meat. Look, Queenie . . . we need to talk."

"Just taste it." I swear, the man was acting like a stubborn child refusing to cooperate, like I was offering up some medicine meant to be good for him. "You'll hurt my feelings if you don't at least taste it."

"Really, I'm not hungry. Maybe you should just leave. I really need my rest. . . ."

"Taste it. Here, let me taste it first." I blew on the savory liquid before putting the large spoon to my mouth. See, it's safe to eat and very good. Taste it."

"Okay, okay, one little taste and then I'm going back to bed to get my rest. I have a lot of work to catch up on, and my friend might be dropping by later, and . . ."

The mention of his friend was my cue to inform him that his little Miss Red Riding Hood had dropped off that black suitcase and I'd flung the thing in his hall closet, and she, his 'friend', wouldn't be by later to visit after all. At least not today, tomorrow, or maybe to-never. But I let those words slip back down my throat. I was being bad, and I knew it—but for something so bad, it sure felt good.

"Be careful—it's hot," I insisted. I slipped the spoon of stew juice into his mouth, and it didn't take long for his whole facial expression to change. Eyes lit up like Christmas lights. Nose crinkling and dimples getting deeper. What was once a frown was suddenly upside down.

"Hmm. That is good."

"See. Try some more."

Another spoonful. "Incredible flavor. And you say it's beef stew?"

"My own special recipe handed down to me by my great-great-grandmother, Abunion."

"Ah-who?"

"Abunion. That was her name. . . . You know southern folks—they—never mind."

In no time at all, I had him seated at the table and shoveling one spoonful of stew after another into his mouth. Add to that, some buttery homemade biscuits and a fresh tossed green salad, and lemon meringue pie waiting on the desert line.

"You look like the type to be a hearty eater once you start eating. I can tell by your build." I sat across from him and tried not to stare. Tried keeping my eyes on my own bowl of stew, but every now and then I had to sneak a little peek up at him to confirm that all was going well. "Look," I said, finishing up my meal, pushing my bowl away. "I'm sorry 'bout coming up in your crib like this without being invited. Guess I got scared when you didn't answer your door. I musta stood outside and rang your doorbell a good two minutes. Thought maybe you'd taken a serious fall because of your ankle and all. I was worried about you, that's all. Guess that's no excuse, though. Not really."

He stopped all eating and looked me square in the face. His eyes were smiling, and soon his lips followed. He shook his head. "No harm done this time."

"We still buddies?" *This time?* This time sounded like he wanted me to come back. I could see the goodness in him, in his eyes, in his smile. My Zeke was a man who loved and cared about people's feelings. A woman can tell this about a man if she's looking hard enough.

"Yeah, we still buds. But what's up with the nursing outfit and spots on your face? You coming from some kind of costume party or some-thin'?"

He wasn't that much off target. "It was a silly joke to cheer you up."

"You're kidding, right?" He sniffed the air as if to clear his sinus. His shoulders slumped slightly, like he was about to unburden a load from them. "Queenie," he sighed, looking me straight in the eyes, then down at his half-full bowl.

"I'm listening."

The brother must have been starving-for-marvin', 'cause I was sure that he was on his third bowl of stew, and his mouth had that look like it still wanted to keep working overtime, even when he had some-thing to say.

"You're a good-hearted person. I can tell. Maybe a little too ag-gressive for your own good."

"Who? Me? Aggressive?" I mocked a frown. *Sure, you right. What other way can I be?*

"Wait, now—hear a brother out. I'm not saying that being aggres-sive is a good thing or a bad thing. I just want you to understand where I'm coming from. He put his third biscuit down in his bowl. "Now, I'm not claiming to know everything about women, 'cause a woman can be pretty complexed and hard to figure out at times. I can tell a little something about you, though. I can tell that you're the type of woman that would make a good friend for me. Smart, understanding, witty, fun to be around, and after grubbing down on your cooking, I know you got it going on in that department, too. It's all good and all, but—"

There it was again. That word. *But.* A good but, a bad but, a little but, or did it boil down to the same old thing—a huge butt? Queenie got a big, big butt. He was looking me squarely in the face, his serious look. The intensity of his gaze made me look away. Was he looking at my fake freckles? I wondered. Was he thinking how foolish I looked?

"But with this career thing of my dreams, I just can't get involved with a woman right now. I really can't. I just don't have the time, the resources, or the energy."

Mr. Know-It-All. *Hmph.* "What makes you think I wanna be involved with you? Just because I was worried about you don't make me trying to get involved. What? Because I dropped by and thought enough to make you a little something to eat?"

"I have my way of knowing." He rubbed his hands through his hair. A nervous habit, I was beginning to think.

"Well, you might think you know everything, mister, but you don't." I fiddled with my spoon—looked into its shine for answers, honest answers, stole a peek up at him, then back to that spoon. Spoons are kind to infatuated females. Spoons never say things that hurt or take budding friendships for granted, no matter how new they may be. "I just think you're a nice guy, Zeke. That's all."

"And I respect that. I think you're nice, too. I just want you to know that we can't get involved right now, that's all. At least I'm being honest about it."

What could I say? I was glass, and Zeke was the man looking right through me.

"The meal was good, and I wanna thank you for that. But I can't eat like this often or I'll swell back up. Have to keep a certain image." He patted the flat of his abdomen.

Now I felt guilt for showing up at his house without calling first. "Muscle men like you don't swell up." I tried to chuckle a little.

Zeke sucked his teeth. "Who you telling? For your information, I used to be over three hundred pounds."

My eyes bucked. "Zeke, stop lying."

"Honest to God. Didn't date much, and couldn't get an acting gig if somebody donated one to me. Image. It's all about image, baby, and good health. It's about health, too."

Even though his lips weren't saying it, I was feeling something else in between his words. Some kind of mutual bonding hovering above us.

"In other words, you saying you don't date fat women."

"Don't have time for dating. Not really."

"You saying you can't be friends with fat women?"

He looked confused by my question, as if I was trying to shake up his thoughts on purpose. "No . . . not really . . . I mean, well, now that you've brought the subject up, I can't think of any of my close friends that are overweight. I didn't plan it that way; it's just the way it is. But even if they were, I wouldn't hold fatness against them. It's not like that. B'sides, who am I to be judging a person by their size when I was there once myself? No. That's not the case with me. I just happen to have all thin friends."

"Oh, I see." It wasn't like it was something I was hearing for the first time. "Maybe it's not meant for everyone to be bone-thin like you, Zeke."

"Maybe so, but that's like saying that everyone should have short-ness of breath and high blood pressure."

I chuckled, even though what he'd said wasn't meant to be funny. "I had shortness of breath one time years back. Went to the doctor, and he told me that it was the cold medication I had been taking. Said I was healthy as an ox. I don't really have a problem with my size; it's other people that do." What I neglected to say was that other people shouldn't matter, but with Zeke I felt different. I was like a child seeking his acceptance—I needed it.

"Look, Queenie." He stood up slowly from the table, securing the sash around his robe. "All I'm saying is it's not about image—it's about good health. You might not be having a problem yet, but with extra weight, it's coming. I see it like this: If you have a problem with folks not liking your size, do something about it. Nobody has to be fat unless they just wanna be. Here, let me show you what worked for me."

I sat there, doing my best not to look disappointed while he half limped away on his cane to go fetch something from a rest-room cabinet. The truth doesn't always have to hurt until it draws anger. *I'm in control.* I tell myself. *I'm still in control.* Thank God life gives us choices. I could have stood up and got my purse and stormed out of his house, but I chose to stay. Some of what he was saying was true, and didn't I hear about strokes and heart attacks all the time? Perhaps it was time to stop fooling myself. In no time he was back at the table with a tall, white plastic bottle of pills.

"Check this out," he said, offering the bottle to me.

"What's this, some kind of miracle in a bottle?"

"Something that works, and it's all natural herbs. Worked for me like a charm to slim my weight down."

I took the stupid bottle and looked it over. I don't know if it was just my imagination, or if he really was acting way too cocky by fetching me a glass of water, a tall glass of water, and placing the glass in front of me. "You think I should take some big green pills? Is that what you're suggesting?" I was shaking my head for no way. "I don't know about this."

"Suit yourself. But if you change your mind, this is the fix. Take yourself a couple of those bad boys, and maybe we can go upstairs to my big round bed and watch some television together. You know, like friends."

Friends. The way he said that last word—the syrupiness of his voice was saying more. "And they're safe to take?"

"They worked for me, and several of my friends. They all took the pills. All natural ingredients."

I screwed off the top of the pill bottle and looked inside, sniffed at the contents a couple of times before shaking two of the green horse-looking pills into the palm of my hand. I stared at those two pills like they were the golden seeds to everlasting life. *Queenie, no. Hell no!* My head felt light. Felt like my heart skipped a beat. Two seeds to Zeke. That's all it took. Two pills, and I could go to the big round bed, and then from there, who knew? Two pills, not three, not four. Only two pills. How hard could that be? "Look like giant seeds."

"Seeds that work." He smiled at me, looking into my eyes.

"Two seeds," I said to myself, waiting for that little voice inside me to say no again. Waiting. But that voice never came. I popped them into my mouth.

I took the glass of water and gulped it down, feeling happy. Two seeds to Zeke, for that time, really didn't seem like such a bad price to pay.

Fifteen

I felt ten pounds lighter the minute I stepped into the elevator at work that following Monday. It was a glorious morning, and there was no mistaking the pep in my step. I couldn't remember the last time I felt so good, so happy, so blessed. That feeling one gets when you're finally getting somewhere in life. A nice home, a jazzin' ride to push around town in, the man of my dreams. I had taken a step with Zeke over the weekend, not a giant step to my ultimate goal, but at least a few baby steps in the right direction. After I'd spent a few hours lounging around with Zeke in his big round bed of satin—no sex, of course, because according to Zeke, "A relationship is like a homemade cake, and sex is like the creamy icing that should be added last, but only at the right time"—we'd shared a bowl of air-popped corn and diet drinks and talked some more about what it was like growing up in Los Angeles.

I'd given Zeke one of my famous massages as he told me more about his roommate, Sweet Willie—how he was picky about who came to the house, and how he could make a visitor very uncomfortable if he didn't like you.

"Sounds like quite a character," I had heard myself saying perhaps more times than I should have. I had heard so much about the guy, and couldn't wait to finally get to meet him. For Zeke to brag on the man so much, talking about everything that Sweet Willie can do, the man definitely had to be a special kind of roommate.

Delicious thoughts of our day together kept swimming around in my head. I felt a surge of empowerment to shed a few pounds, after all I told myself, I wasn't trying to shed pounds just so Zeke would approve of me to be his woman, the only woman in his life, but because of health issues. For the first time I began to really think of what the extra fifty or sixty pounds on my frame was doing to my joints, my blood pressure, and to my heart. For that reason, for lunch I got up a half an hour earlier and prepared myself a nice chicken salad with some light dressing on the side. Besides, what was the point of living life if you didn't set some kind of goals for yourself. Goals keep us grounded, keep us motivated. Zeke was my new goal, and whatever I had to do to get him was fine with me.

Briefcase in hand, I stood at the open elevator door that Monday morning with that crazy kind of energy mixed with fear and dread— that old and familiar dread of what I might find surging through me.

"This just don't make no darn sense," I muttered to myself. I stuck my head out and looked to the right, then looked to my left. Seeing no sign of that pesky Raymo, I looked to the right again. It looked safe enough to step out.

Clutching my leather briefcase to my bosom, I stayed close against the wall as I inched slowly up the carpeted pathway leading to my office. Almost tiptoeing, my heart rate was beginning to pick up along with the distinct sensation that I was doing something sneaky or illegal. Sweat was forming in my armpits the way it always does when I'm nervous or worried. My eyes were alert, looking at every possible angle that he could ambush me from. I was the soldier fighting my way through enemy territory, hiding out in the untamed thicket of the jungle. The sounds of telephones softly burring all around me was the constant calling of enemy bullets. I neared the intersection of standing partition walls and peered around.

No sign of the enemy, but I could still feel hostile eyes watching my every step as I hurried around the corner and reveled in the fact that I was almost there. Almost to my own quiet domain—my own space, the sanctum behind enemy lines. My heart quickened when I heard something like a loud bang. My breath caught. I was frozen in my spot. I couldn't move a muscle as I perked my ears to listen, and that was when I heard him. The whole office could have heard him if it wasn't for the fact that we were both quite early, and not many had made it to their desk stations yet.

"Good mornin', my chocolate delight. I have been waiting for chu, yes. I mean, I have been waiting for *you*. I could not let my lovely start her day without a good breakfast. You are just in time, my sweet."

I don't think so. "No squeezing out the good-feeling juice today, Ray."

Raymo, at least the top of his half-balding head, was peeking over somebody else's cubicle at me, his silly Kool-aid smile all beaming, and he had to be standing on somebody's desk, because the last time I saw the man, he was nowhere near as tall as now. *Oh, Lord. Not him. Not now.* I heaved a disappointed sigh loud enough to wake the dead. And I had thought that the earlier I arrived at work, the easier it would be for me to slip unsighted into my office and lock my door, which is where I had planned to stay all day if necessary.

"Morning, my sweetness."

"Morning, Ray," I huffed. Throwing my nose in the air, I straightened myself up and adjusted my new special tailored two-piece lilac suit and opened my briefcase swing at my side. Walking fast. Walking with my head up. "I'm not in the mood this morning for your foolishness. Remember what we talked about last week? Remember what we said about being friends? So be a good little boy, run along, and play now."

"No, my sweet. There is no little boy here. And true love can never be easily dismissed. This you must believe, yes."

"I'm not playing, Ray. My head is hurting, and I'm feeling a little jittery and not quite myself. Somebody might get hurt, and it won't be me. So, if I were you, I'd keep away from me. I'm not playing."

I tried to make my voice sound as harsh as possible. Did it stop the fool? No. I had made it to my door and was just about to open it when he hopped down from his chicken perch and rushed over and wedged himself between me and my door.

"Wait! Before you go in, I just want to say that I am a driven man who cannot help myself. Do not hate me for this."

I lifted a suspicious brow. "This? And what have you done now?"

"It is not right to punish a man for what he feels, my queen." He patted his chest with one clenched fist.

"It depends on what he's done."

"This feeling for you, my queen, is right here. I will go to my grave loving chu, yes. I mean . . . loving *you*. I will, to my grave."

"True that, and Ray, it might be sooner than you think." I took an agitated breath and let it out. Normally I love it when a man professes his undying love for a woman, even more so for me. Call me a sentimental fool I guess for loving the idea of love. But when it came to Raymo, this was not the place, the time, the woman, or the man. And my head was hurting, not the throb-throb migraines I usually get two or three days before my cycle starts, but a mild underlying current of pain that aspirin or Tylenol didn't know how to help.

"One day, my queen, you will see how much I care for you. One day."

"Look Ray, I don't know why you're back to this foolishness after that talk with Jay, but let me stop you right now," I said, sitting my briefcase down on the floor. I looked around to see who was listening or looking, just in case I decided to break off one of his thin arms and hit him over the head with it. Last thing I needed was a witness. The few employees that had shown up as early as we had tried to seem inconspicuous as they peered around or over their station cubicles. I looked back down at him. He was dressed nice, as usual—in fact, sharp as a tack in his dark gray Hugo Boss double-breasted suit, baby gray shirt, and dark gray satin tie. The sparkle of a diamond buried in the gold ringer along his pinkie finger caught my eye. His cologne was deep yet refreshing. Something new, I supposed. The kind of scent that could drive a woman wild if she had even the faintest interest in him.

"I know, I know, but don't be mad at me."

"Ray, I've been trying to be nice and patient with you, but somehow, for some reason still unbeknownst to me, you just won't give up. You're like that fly that keeps buzzing around a person's special lunch, or that dog that finds a pair of my best pumps and chews 'em up. A pest, Raymo. That's what you are. It's just not getting through to you that you are simply not the kind of man that I could be with."

"That's because you are fighting too hard against something beautiful. Something that was meant to be. But I have been thinking myself, thinking that my love cannot be dismissed. You are fighting in a war against love. Could it be that you are in need of love, but you do not like the idea of me loving you? Yes."

"Do a bear crap in the woods? Yeah, Ray. It could be that." I said, perhaps a bit too hastily. "But it could also be possibly be that I do not like the idea of you being more than two feet near me. Period. What happened to our talk of being friends?"

"Friends sometimes become lovers, yes."

I squeezed my eyes shut for a few seconds—wishing. Wishing I had special powers and that I could just blink him away—twitch my nose like Samantha used to do on *Bewitched*. Maybe I could blink him to the cornfields. My head was beginning to feel like a tiny demolition crew was doing some serious work inside it. I put both my hands on my hips. Little did Mr. Raymo know it, but it was my own position of war. The position I take when I'm feeling fed up with a situation that is driving me to the point of no return. The position of pending battle. I loved my job, true that. And I truly considered myself good at it. But I be damned if I was going to be chased away by the unrelenting pursuit of some unfocused-minded twit who—

"Over dinner tonight we can talk about it." A twinkle in his eyes. "I will cook for you."

"No, Raymo, I don't think so. This—this thing that you are doing to me is not love. It's got a name. Once again, it's called stalking. You are not loving me; you are stalking me! And I'm telling you right now that if you don't stop with this foolishness, I will file a complaint with the police department and drag your good-smelling butt into court. And if that don't work, Ray, I will take your little brown neck and start twisting like this—" I made a creaking sound with my mouth and watched him cringe. "—and twist—" More creaking to emphasis bones breaking and pain coming. "—and twist some more until your eyes pop out from your too-small, Ping-Pong-shaped head."

"Ping-Pong-shaped—that is funny, yes. A funny lady you are. This I like."

He smiled as if he hadn't comprehended a thing I'd said.

"Yes, but to do so—" He wiggled a comical finger at me. "—you will have to put your hands, your sweet and precious hands, on me." He moved in even closer, if it was possible. The man was already standing close enough for me to smell his breath.

"I'm warning you, Raymo."

"And once chu put chor hands on Raymo, he will enjoy and so will chu. But only because Raymo loves chu so much. Chu, I mean *you*, are the woman he has dreamed of for too long. You are in here, my heart. And I cannot get you out because of threats."

"A good beat-down might help."

He tried reaching for my hand and kissing it, but I snatched it back in time.

"When you are angry, you are so beautiful. I have tried to stay away from you, Queenie. I have tried long and hard, but I cannot do so. Your eyes are like darkened amber. Your lips are like—like shaped sunlight waiting to be kissed."

"I'm not playing, Raymo. Stop it."

A silly grin. "Okay. Okay. One little kiss, a peck on the cheek, and Raymo will go away. I will bother you no more today. Another little kiss is not much to ask for a friend."

"You're not my friend, though."

"Come, come, my love. One little kiss and I will go."

He closed his eyes, angled his chin up like some fleshy peace of-fering, his lips pursed.

"One kiss, huh?" I looked around to see how many eyes were watching. None. "Well, here we go," I sighed. "Sometimes a woman has to do what a woman has to do." Dropping my hands to the side, I balled my fist up tight and was just hauling back to give him my best knuckle kiss I could give—a punch I knew would not only knock a few teeth out, but also knock some sense into him once and for all. But before I could get my arm in motion for the delivery, he deterred my attention.

"Look," he piped up, blinking his eyes open and breaking the spell.

"Look what I have done. All for you." His face animated, eyes excited like some kid discovering a bunch of presents under the tree on Christmas morning as he swerved around and opened up my office door.

He was back at it. Red roses were everywhere. Along my desk, along my credenza and the small brown refrigerator that he went to and opened. Sweeping my gaze, I stepped in behind him. "Oh, my God."

"I hope you like Dom Pérignon. Only the best for a queen like you."

"Dom Pérignon? Oh, heck yes—I mean, no, not with you. Not even from you." Beyond the bottle of expensive champagne, the small box was filled with food. Expensive-looking cheese and wrapped deli meats in fancy white packaging. My eyes glimpsed a few small bottles of Evian water and a small bowl of exotic fruit. Prickly pear? Passion fruit? Even some tamales wrapped in clear plastic. "Oh, no. Not tamales again, my weakness," I groaned.

"Just in case chu are hungry later. I mean *you*. In case you are hungry later."

"Raymo," I sighed, feeling the hostility I'd felt for him earlier fading away. "I get no pleasure from being mean to you, I really don't. But—but you have to stop this. I thought we got past this after your little talk with Jay. Remember the talk about sexual harassment?"

"Yes, but this is not about sex. It's about a friend cooking for a dear friend. I know how much you like tamales, and they are fresh from last night. Just for you, made them myself."

My office smelled like a restaurant. I felt . . . I felt weird, too, some strange combination of sad, mad, and glad. Sad for Ray for wasting his time and money on a woman who could never return his love or obsession. Never having that woman even come close to just liking him or wanting to breathe the same air he breathe. Mad that no matter how bad I treated him, he was too thickheaded to see that we could never have anything together. Never. And glad. Glad that I wouldn't be losing my job for knocking him upside his head for being in my office again after being warned. I chose to just put him out with another warning, a final warning.

"Ray, all this is fine and dandy if you like making a fool of yourself. But this is on the real side this time. I'm warning you, and this is absolutely, positively the last time I'm telling you this, so listen good. Stay out of my face! Stay out of my office or you'll be sorry."

That silly smile again. "Yes. You know you really want to thank me. Just one little kiss, and I will be gone."

I shook my head, then went over to him and hoisted his too-light-in-the-butt self up and carried him like some oversize child that needed to be burped out of my office. The fool even had the nerve to lay his head on my shoulder, smiling his crazy smile. And he was so for real about it. Scary. Real scary.

"Ooooh, yes, Queenie. You are so warm, so soft, and so strong. Just like I said, you are strong for good baby-making. So warm, so soft you are. Strong legs, strong arms, and your heart. . . . Your heart is beating too fast."

At the door of his own office I deposited him. "The last warning, Raymo," I reminded him with a stiff finger in his face. Those sappy, puppy-dog eyes gazing up at me gave me the creeps. "Now, you listen, and you listen good, Ray. I'm not interested in a relationship with you now, or no time in the future. Nor in another life. You will never be my type, so get used to it because some things can't be forced. And just so you'll know, I have a man now. His name is Zeke. He's tall and handsome, and going somewhere in life. My Zeke is also a very jealous man, and if you don't stop harassing me, I swear, I will tell Zeke about you, and he will come down here to this place and personally talk to you. Do you understand?"

He only smiled. "Yes, my queen. Your man will come and kill me, just like I would do for you myself, because that is how real love is."

"Screw it!" I yelled, and turned and hurried back to my own office. My head was pounding, and the pressure behind my eyes was increasing. I slammed the door. Finally alone with the world shut out.

I couldn't wait to sit at my desk and collect my thoughts. Not thoughts about working, but thoughts about love, and thoughts about Zeke. We had been talking by phone all week long with me counting the days when I would be back at his place. I had promised him a very special dinner for Friday night, and even though he had seemed hesitant at first due to the fact that his roommate, Sweet Willie would be home, finally I assured him that it would be fine if Willie could join us. I had heard so much about the man, but yet at the same time he was still somewhat of a mystery. Whether his roommate liked or disliked me, nothing was going to deter me from visiting my man. Far as I was concerned, Sweet Willie had better just get with the program. It was already my belief that any good friend of Zeke's was a good friend of mine. I promised to keep the meal light but delicious. I didn't mind cooking, especially if it would get me closer to my goal. Zeke. Just thinking about him reminded me that it was time to take my herbal pills.

"Oh, yeah." I dug in my bottom desk drawer for some bottle water, then found my herbal pills Zeke had given me in my briefcase. I shook two of those dark green suckers out and popped them in my mouth and sailed them down with pure spring water.

Kicking back in my chair, my arms behind my head, I envisioned what it would be like when I was thin. The sexy clothes that I would wear just for Zeke—short miniskirts and knee-high boots, maybe even some Daisy Dukes. Not that I couldn't wear those type of clothes now, but a sleeker me would make a better presentation. Maybe change my hair to a different style—get some new perfume. It would be like second heaven. Thin and beautiful for Zeke.

Sixteen

Making it to Friday is a real mother. Especially after a difficult week at work. It's more like a small miracle within itself. My whole week had been mentally draining and working my nerves, first with an order of DKNY suits that somehow got lost en route to our Brea City store, then a batch of evening gowns—very expensive and elegant ones, I might add—were discovered to have minor flaws in the lining and had to be sent back. Two fashion shows for top-name designers, and I was later for not one, but both. Add to that, the accounting department, a bunch of airhead idiots mostly, was having a hard time producing payment for a shipment of evening wear that had been tagged, trucked out, and racked weeks ago.

One problem after another, and who was the person the vendors were calling every day about their money? Me! Who was catching all the heat from her boss? Me! That's right, yours truly: me, the buyer. Twice, I had to resort to saying a few ugly words to my top vendors and throwing in, "Look, it's not like your damn gowns are at my house hanging in my closet for me to stuff my big and luscious behind into. Stop calling me! The check is in the mail."

When five o'clock on Friday came, I couldn't wait to get myself to stepping outta that place. I had things to do, places to go, and people to see. Not just people, but one person that was special in my book. I couldn't leave my office fast enough, throwing open the door and sticking my head out to look to the right, then to the left. Good. No sign of Raymo. I hauled myself to the elevator and frantically pushed the DOWN button like it was a fire somewhere in the building and I was the first to spot the flames and seek safety. I turned around to see if he was anywhere near me. No sign. *So far, so good*, I sighed as I stood with my back turned to the elevator—watching for him. I heard the elevator clunk to a stop, heard the familiar sound of the heavy doors slide open. One last look to my left, then to my right before I stepped back carefully into the elevator.

"I'd done it! Thank God," I sighed with relief, which didn't last long when I heard that slow, slurpy voice behind me.

"Good evening, my precious. Can I go with you?"

"Ahhhh, heck. Hell no." I didn't even want to turn around to look at him. Didn't want to see that too-damn-happy-to-see-you smile on that man's face. I tensed up. I won't look. I refused to look, keep my back facing him.

"Don't worry, my sweet chocolate, I am not going to bother you. I just wanted to tell chu to have a nice weekend before you left. That is all."

"Look," I said, clearly irritated "The word is *you*, not *chu*, or *chewy*. The word is *you* like the alphabet letter after the *t*: you. I really wish you wouldn't talk to me at all, but seeing how you insist that you do, at least say the word right. The word is *you*."

"Yes, my sweet. You are so right."

"LordhavemercyJesus, give me strength."

The more he talked, the more I tensed. Every muscle in my body firming up like curds turning to cheese. My head was hurting, not a full throttle throbbing yet like the day before, or the day before that even, but a dull ache. And that wonderful smell in the elevator with us, so light and delicate—so sweetly intoxicating—

"These are for you," said Raymo, sounding more serious. "Lovely red roses for such a lovely woman."

I didn't turn to look. I didn't speak. The minute the elevator door opened, I sprinted out of it, running to the door leading out the building. I know it looked crazy, looked foolish, even, but I couldn't help myself. For that awkward moment, Ray's life had been in danger, and he hadn't even known it. The growing pain in my head was birthing murderous thoughts, and by the time I got to my car, I was short of breath, my heart pumping like an out-of-control oil rig. I stood a spell to balance myself and catch my breath. "Calm down, girl, calm down." Raymo. I had left that fool standing there with his offering. Too bad. I wasn't in the mood for him, no way.

First thing on my agenda, home to prepare to go spend time with Zeke. I hurried back to my place and found some Excedrin extra-strength pills for my head and threw back three, showered, fixed my curly weave up in a combination of a French roll and ponytail, complete with a few curly tendrils teasing at the side of my face and at the back. If sexy was the look I was going for, I was definitely there.

I was in my bedroom, packing my overnight bag, just a few items in case a simple dinner date turned into a hot, steamy night: a box of super sensitive condoms (oh, yes), a tube of K-Y gel (give it to me, Gus), a diaphragm (only used once after that freaky incident that landed me at the emergency ward to remove it—goes to show you that decent females with small orifices, such as myself, should never insert anything round, flat, and rubbery inside their honey cave, unless, of course, they wish to experience an excavation team consisting of two doctors and three nurses smiling too hard down at your special place while the doctors shine a big spotlight between the valley of your thighs while taking their precious time removing that darn diaphragm that somehow migrated too far north inside you). On second thought, no way. I tossed the diaphragm in the trash and picked up a canister of contraceptive foam that was hard to find anymore because most drug stores just don't sell the stuff.

"Should I, or shouldn't I?" Even the foam was iffy. I thought of my mama's advice some years back when she told me to beware of contraceptive foams because her last child, sister Kelly, conceived in her late forties, had been a result of using contraceptive foam. The thought of Mama getting busy shivered in my head. Thank you, Mama, for forever traumatizing my mind with that pretty image.

"Not saying it was that foam that made your baby sister turn out crazy," she had volunteered the inside scoop one day, not convincing at all, but speaking her say, "but I'm just saying to watch out for contraceptive foam—that's all."

Maybe I was just jumping the gun with so much preparation, hoping for more than Zeke was ready to give. Hopeful thinking on my part. But I wanted to be ready when it did happen. Not that I wasn't ready to conceive and have Zeke's baby, but some things shouldn't be rushed. I threw the foam into my bag.

"Let me see, now . . . lubrication, my banana-vanilla-scented body lotion, some sandalwood incense, my black and sheer nightie with matching panties that never fit the way they should have, scented candles . . . What else?" I stood back on my thick legs, trying to think, all wrapped up in the possibility of Zeke and I having our first wild night of passion when my roomie, Poetta, had to go and pop up in my face and spoil it. I didn't even hear her enter my bedroom, but there she was.

"Here," she shoved what looked to me like a piece of folded newspaper toward my hand. "I wasn't going to show you this at first, but I think you should know."

"Thank you for being considerate." I kept on packing. "But I'm quite busy right now."

"No. You need to see it, so here."

"Poe, just tell me what it is. Can't you see I'm kinda in a hurry here?" I asked, hesitant to accept the paper she held out. Last thing I needed was some sad news about some young child catching a stray bullet from a drive-by shooting, or somebody's mama kidnapped and found brutally murdered. Poetta knew I hated sad stories, which was one of the main reasons I rarely listened to the daily news on the radio or watched it on television. I kept my radio tuned in to Steve Harvey only. 100.3 FM. The Beat. The station where good music and joking around comes from. No sad news and killers serving long sentences. If it were left up to me, there would be no death row. You kill, you be killed. That would be my motto if I ruled the world. Of course, self-defense would be different. "If it's about our horoscopes, Poe, I really don't have time right now." I brushed her hand holding the folded paper away.

"Queenie, read it!"

"I don't wanna read it. What is it?"

"I said read it!"

"Okay, okay, and don't be hollering at me." This chick has lost her mind. She looked crazy in the eyes, standing there before me in all that white. A white turban-type garment wrapped around her head, her long flowing caftan of white, all trimmed in silver. *What the heck is her problem?* Never mind her. I started reading.

"Read it to me," she ordered, like she was my mama or something.

"Girl, you know phonics—you can read it yourself. Look, Poe, don't be tripping with me because you've been cooped up in this house for days while I'm at work." It had been only a couple of weeks that Poetta's house had burned, not the whole house, but enough of it for her not to be able to live in it until the insurance company handled their business and got her money right for the repairing. Once her house was ready, she would be back into the swing of things, doing her own thing. I couldn't wait. I love my Poe like a sister, but I was ready for her to go back to her own cave.

It don't matter how much you love and admire a person, trying to live under the same roof with that person always puts them in a different light. You notice things. Things that you have never noticed before, like smells from their morning bathroom business when it wafts through the whole house. And how their obsession for the natural feel for dirt and dust to collect around them. How they leave tale tell crumbs from each meal. Little things.

True, my three-bedroom condo was cozy and spacious enough for us to live happily for the rest of our lives if I was the type after the coochie. Make no mistake—I crave the beef tips, grade A and prime choice. The bigger, the better. But seeing how I do love my own privacy, I was ready for Poetta to leave. I wanted her to go back to a place where I could come and visit and leave crazy standing at her door on my way out. You hear things stirring in fullness that you don't want to hear when you share the same dwelling with friends. Their pain tries to seep from them like dark gray mist and settle on you. They have burdens that, ultimately, become your burdens. Their craziness scents the very air that you have to share, fills your nostrils until it finds your inner peace. No rest, no peace of mind. And all I wanted was a night with Zeke. Didn't she know that my boo-baby was waiting on me?

"Okay, what?" I gave in, holding the folded paper to my eyes. It was a small square of words, nothing that would have caught my eyes even if I did read the newspaper. "It says here that—that 'A team of Arizona detectives are working overtime to solve the mysterious death of one Jimpson "Jimboy" McFinney. McFinney died under suspicious circumstances on Interstate 10 when the inside cab of his semitruck suddenly burst into flames. . . . McFinney was the only victim found . . . foul play suspected . . . authorities are seeking to explain . . . what would cause a sudden burst of flames in the cab's interior only that engulfed the victim. McFinney was burned beyond recognition . . . and—' "

I stopped. I didn't want to read any more. I looked at Poe, whose face looked to me like soft stone molded in despair. "And—and you think that I'm somehow responsible for Jimpson's passing. Jimpson? What kind of name is that?"

"Passing is when someone old dies peacefully in their sleep, Queenie. Or a person has been terminally ill for a while, they pass."

"Who would name a child Jimpson?" I tried to imagine talking baby talk and cooing to a baby with, "Hi, Jimpson, hey sweetie, little Jimp . . . baby Jimpee." Dang.

"What was his mama thinking? You think I'm the cause of this?"

"It'll come to you in a minute, Queenie."

"So what are you saying, here, Poe? You think I caused Jimpson's hellish end?" I tried to look serious. "He fell asleep at the wheel with a burning cigarette in his hand. Poe, it happens."

"He hated cigarettes."

"He pulled over to read the paper using a magnifying glass and it caught fire. A freak accident, but it's possible."

"Try again, Queenie."

I put hands on my hips. If I was being accused of being some kind of witchcraft murderer, then I wanted her to just say it straight in my face. "Then what are you trying to say?"

"I'm saying yes. Yes, you had something to do with his horrible end, and yes, you should be feeling something behind it."

"Something like what? He shouldn't have been here in California cheating on his wife, this never would have happened, that's what I feel." I shook my head, fighting back the urge to laugh. A man driving across two states to cheat on his wife and children, filling Poe's head with lies of being a single man and available, his behind perish in flames, and I should feel guilty? I don't think so. "All cheating men go to hell, Poe. Cheating women, too."

"You really don't know what you've done, do you?"

She looked pouty with her lips pushed out, like a child who wasn't getting her way and was about to cry or throw a tantrum. "You're crazy, you know that? Or—or maybe you are spending way too much time locked up in this house reading those so-called spell books you find on the dark shelves of the local library. There is no such thing as putting a hex on somebody, or channeling their spirit into a rag doll with patches of his pubic hair looking like a bad Afro on his head."

She looked up, mildly shocked. "What?"

"Yeah," I went on, feeling cocky with knowledge, "you didn't think I noticed the hair on that little stanky doll before I tossed it to the fire, did you? Pubic hair. That's right! I know nappy pubic hair when I see it, Poe! You my best friend and all, and I love you like a sister, but you nasty sometimes, and you are one sick puppy."

"You should know," she snorted back, crossing her hands at her chest.

"Look," I said, tired of bickering. "Let's not argue; it makes us both crazy. Maybe you need to get out more. Treat yourself to a makeover. . . . You know, get a facial, try a little makeup, do a little something with your hair, for crying out loud. Try pulling a comb through it for a change. Try going to the beauty salon. That's it. The beauty salon. My treat when I return."

"Beauty can't cure this." She all but snatched the paper from my hand and finished the article on Jimboy. "In case you're having trouble reading and understanding this, it says here, 'With no concrete evidence of what could have started the fatal fire that consumed Jimpson McFinney in less than five minutes, authorities are leaning toward the possibility of the phenomenon known as "spontaneous human combustion." McFinney is survived by his wife and their two children, ages nine and seven.' "

"And your point would be?" I still wasn't feeling her.

She looked like she wanted to cry for real. "It's my fault, too. Don't you see? I never should have . . . channeled his spirit into that stupid doll. I shouldn't have done that. It was wrong, Queenie, wrong. And now there are two children fatherless because of us."

"Us?" I wanted to say, *If it wasn't you, it would have been some other love-starved woman.* But I kept quiet. Whether I believed in her powers or not, Poetta was serious as a heart attack. I went into the adjoining bathroom for some toilet tissue. I handed it to her, not knowing what to say. I had no words to console something that made no sense to me. I patted lightly at her back. "It's okay, Poe," I tried. "Everything will be okay." My words sounded light and meaningless, even to me. *Okay? Will it really be okay?*

"Queenie, I gotta go meet his wife, stand in retribution and ask her forgiveness and return his belongings. I have to."

"You what?" My anal sphincter muscle tightened up. "You have to stand in what?"

"Retribution—I have to ask her forgiveness in person. I have to. Don't you see what we've done? We have tampered with the forces to end somebody's life. He had kids, Queenie. Two kids."

"You mean *execution*?" I corrected. "You wanna stand in execution."

"Retribution, Queenie. We have to stand in retribution."

"We? When did you start speaking French? When did *we* do all that?" I stopped patting. "What cheating dog of a married man don't have kids?" I got that funny feeling I always get when time is slipping up on me like a bad joke that's gone terribly wrong, like the time when I had my grimy seventeen-year-old hand in my mama's wallet clutching a twenty-spot, and she walked in the room and spotted my attempt to borrow part of the rent money, and I tried to explain that, "I only wanted to see what dead president's face was on it. That's all." That's the feeling I got.

"We killed 'im. That's all I know." She came over to the bed and sat at the edge and stared at the folded paper.

"We? You mean *we* as in the French version, right? I haven't killed anybody. And just because you've being playing with the man's pubic hair on a rag doll don't make me guilty. Girl, you need to keep it real," I huffed, and pushed past her, going into my adjacent rest room. I came back out with a couple of clean face towels.

"Queenie, his soul will never rest unless we pay retribution to his wife." She folded her hands across her chest and shook her head. "We looking at years of bad luck. For you and for me."

"Poe, stop talking like that!" I wanted to grab and shake her to bring her back to reality. "It's all some spooky coincidence, that's all. No such thing as placing spells or hexes on folks. You understand? No such thing."

She started to cry, softly at first. She would have to be doing all of this when I was on my way out to get my groove on with Zeke. Heck, after dealing with her tired, depressed behind, my groove would be needing its own session of therapy.

"Queenie, you just don't know," she sobbed. Her face was buried in her hands, and all that sniffing, snorting, snot-slinging, and heaving was really getting on my last nerves. Enough was enough.

"Look, don't cry about it. Okay? Everything will be okay with time. I'm on my way out, but when I get back, we will sit down and talk about this and—if you really feel that there's something that we can do to make it all better, even for his wife and kids, then—we'll do what we have to do."

"You really mean it?" She looked up like a child waiting for an answer.

"I really mean it." I folded my face towels and put them in my bag. "I promise. And you know how I am about a promise."

Was she buying what I was saying? It looked like it. She sniffed twice and perked up, bobbed her head for yes.

"Where are you going?"

"To Zeke's place. But just for a few hours," I threw in. "Just a few hours of wining and dining. He's making me dinner this time."

Could have been my imagination, but she really perked up. Eyes cleared up, jaw setting to a different angle. She looked over at my overnight bag waiting along the bed, bulging at the sides.

"Umph. A few hours? Why you packing a winter suitcase?"

"Just a few things, Poe." I moved over to close up my bag from her prying eyes. "Zeke is waiting for me as we speak."

"Queenie, that man don't want you."

The jealous heifer. Just because her cheating man was now somebody's ashes perched over a fireplace didn't give her the right to be telling me the deal. "Why can't he want me, Poe? What's wrong with me?"

"Nothing is wrong with you, but you need to stop trying to make something happen between you and that man."

"Trying to make something happen? You mean like hexing and burning candles on folks? Girl, you a fine one to be talking."

"Queenie, I'm only trying to be honest. One friend to another. Only a true friend would tell you the cold truth. Forcing yourself into a relationship is one thing, and burning candles to persuade one is another. You should know the difference."

"Poe, believe it or not, Zeke and I are friends slipping into lovers. If he didn't want me, why would I be invited to his home?" I glared at her.

"Depends on who did the inviting—you or he?"

"You tripping. Don't be player hating because I gotta man that cares and you don't."

"Queenie, get real. You have Zeke like I have a hole in my head. You might have a man, but it ain't that one. What you have is a man trying not to hurt your feelings, that's all."

"Player hater." I went to my dresser and pull out one item.

"Well, call it what you want, Queenie. I'm being real with you. True, Zeke Washington is fine, but he's not your type. Can't make something be just because you really want it."

"Poe, mind your own business." Normally I listen to her opinions, but this time is different. I don't want to hear it. I unzipped my bag and stuffed an extra pair of red lace panties in and rezipped it. "Heck, if you know so much, how come you didn't know that playing with fire would burn your house down? Leave me alone." Why extra panties? I had no idea.

"That's funny, Queenie. I'm just trying to be honest. You had a couple of good dates with the man, it was a charity thing to raise money and nothing more. Don't go overboard."

"Umph. Sounds like jealousy to me."

"Sounds like a true friend trying to be honest."

I huffed up my chest. "Well, be honest with the back of my head. I'm outta here." I took up my oversize tote bag and walked briskly from the room.

Seventeen

"Ten seconds more to go, Queenie. Nine. Eight. You can do it. Six. Five. You doing good. Four, three, two, and one more time."

I was huffing and puffing. Heck, I was feeling dizzy and about to pass out on that darn treadmill at Zeke's place. I never knew my legs could pump so fast. I was working muscles I didn't know I had, trying to keep up with the pace of the treadmill, walking so fast that once or twice I could have sworn I detected the heavenly scent of—bacon? Or was it the scent of cooked ham from the constant friction of my plump thighs heating up. *Queenie, girl. It's your imagination.* What ever it was, it was making me hungry.

"How much longer?" I panted, sweat rolling down my scalp and into my face.

"Two more minutes," Zeke replied. "You can do it. Be right back."

Finally, the machine was slowing down to a halt. Breathing hard, trying to steady my flow of air, I unplugged the finger monitor and stepped off the fancy-schmancy machine, feeling like I was about to collapse. Zeke had programmed the machine to give me a timed work-out, monitor my blood pressure and heart rate, my distance and fat burned. A good headache must be part of the deal because that was what I was getting. Heck, a machine that could do all that, I kept expecting it to wipe sweat from my buttocks and spray a dusting of baby powder on them.

"I think I'ma die." My heart was pounding so fast in my chest that I felt faint. I eased myself down along the carpeted floor trying to catch my breath, then laid with my back flat along the floor. "Lord, help. I'm 'bout to die."

"No pain, no gain." Zeke was in the kitchen, whipping up some dinner for us, something light but filling, so he claimed. "You'll be all right once your body gets used to it," he called out.

Used to it? What made him think I wanted to get used to bringing myself to the threshold of death and back? All I could do was lie there with my head feeling light-headed. So, this was it. The exciting and romantic evening I was to spend with Zeke? And to think I had brought my best lace panties along for this. Me in light gray sweats. Zeke in dark blue ones. Obviously, we both had agendas for the evening that involved working up a sweat and getting our heart rate up. Only my agenda had simmered and stewed in a blend of delicious results. It was all there in my head. I had visioned candlelight with scents of vanilla or banana or raspberry—while Zeke was thinking more along the line of bright lights to help draw out sweat and body toxins. I had visioned a scented bath with my new banana-scented milk bath tickling at my skin, while Zeke was probably thinking of two more laps on his treadmill. My mind tingled with the notion of a good romp between the sheets later. Just the two of us, the moonlight in the room with us. The caress of satin sheets against hot, flaming skin. Zeke and me, tangled like soft, moist branches from the tree of love.

And then Zeke came back into the room and said, "Time for some crunches."

"Huh?" The only thing I wanted to crunch down on was a stacked BLT with some extra cheese. "Crunches?" I'd heard him the first time, but I was just barely getting my breathing back to normal from the treadmill, and now he wanted crunches? I sat up and watched him stop what he was doing and heft a chair over to where I was. Watched him lie on the floor with his white socked feet and legs in the chair, his back pressed to the floor, hands behind his head.

"Well," he snipped, looking over at me like he was the daddy and

I was the child waiting for parental instructions. "I'm waiting."

"Okay. Okay." So I hate exercise. But before Zeke got through with me, I'd done—begrudgingly, of course—thirty minutes on a treadmill, twenty crunches in sets of four, fifty jumping jacks, and five minutes of running in place. If I didn't know any better, I'd think that Zeke had an obsession with exercise and fitness. Probably had a real problem with plump females entirely. Even though he never actually came straight out and said that he had a problem with the more-to-love female, it was just a feeling I was getting. After treadmilling, crunching, jumping, and running in place, I wanted to confront his fat phobia, draw it out in the open, hit it head-on, and deal with it—but I was still too busy trying to catch my breath and regulate my breathing, not to mention plan my strategy for the seduction later that night. That's right, the seduction. If the mountain won't come to you, go to the mountain, which means, Queenie cannot wait forever.

"You mind if I take a shower to freshen up?"

Zeke looked up from setting the table for our dinner. "Sure, the one upstairs in my bedroom. I'll use the shower down here."

I headed for the stairs, smiling devilishly. "We can save some water if we share."

"That won't be necessary." He smiled amiably. "You just hurry on back down. I'll be waiting."

Zeke don't want me. Hmph. Poetta had some nerve telling me something like that. Didn't matter, though. I didn't care what Poe thought. I just knew that before I left Zeke's house that night, somebody would be seduced. *I'm talking spanked, yanked until it's too good to stank. That's what I'm talking about.* Smiling on the inside, and these were the words circulating in my head as I hurried upstairs to take a quick shower and change clothes.

Mapped out like a well-planned family vacation, my plans were to share a dinner together and watch a couple of videos. Zeke's ankle was somewhat better, but all the swelling hadn't completely gone away, and staying at home and relaxing was just what the doctor ordered. Whether Zeke wanted company for the entire night was a subject that hadn't come up, but that was all in the bag, too, just like my pajamas and bedtime slippers. I was ready.

"Are we ready to grub? I'm starved," I said jovially, coming back down the stairs after my quick shower. "Hope you don't mind me borrowing your terry robe?' I pulled the thick maroon material together, seeing as how I couldn't tie the sash around me.

"I guess not," he replied sheepishly. "C'mon, let's eat."

Later, at the dinner table—if you could call it dinner—I tried asking Zeke several times about his roommate. Every now and then I kept hearing bumping and thumping around coming from upstairs. Not that I wanted Sweet Willie to be all up in our lovefest or nothing, but it kind of bothered me that the guy was home, all lonesome and locked up in his room and didn't have the common courtesy to even come out and meet me. Not even once. Rude. Just plain rude, and I was having a hard time igging it.

"You know," I said, testing the water. "I don't really mind if Willie joins us for dinner. There's plenty of food. Plenty of steamed vegetables, plenty of salad—not to mention plenty of boiled skinless chicken chunks." Yummy. My mouth was watering at the thought of a big baked potato loaded with butter, chives, and sour cream. I reached for another slice of celery next to some steamed slivers of carrots.

"He's fine where he is for right now. And it's Sweet Willie."

"What?" Visions of pot roast danced in my head. I tried to think how long I could keep it all up. I was still faithfully popping those big green horse pills intended to curb my appetite. I was eating mostly tasteless and bland foods. *How much longer?*

"His name is Sweet Willie. He doesn't like to be called just Willie. And no, he cannot join us."

Well, excuse me for living. His words had come rather harsh and snobbish sounding. "I mean, don't you feel funny sitting down here eating and not asking 'im if he wants any dinner?"

"No. Not really."

"I mean . . . the man has to eat, too, Zeke. I just thought that since some food was prepared, he might like to have some. That's all." Dang. I can be persistent when I wanna be. Didn't take a rocket scientist to see that either Zeke was trying to keep me from his roommate or his roommate from me. Can a man's insecurity and jealousy over another man be that deep? If so, why be roommates?

"Yes, he does, but Sweet is very particular about what he eats, when he eats, and whom he eats with. He's very complicated."

"My, my. Sounds like a real character, that Sweet Willie." I forked a steamed carrot into my mouth. *Yuck.*

"Yeah, he is."

"Must be hard living with a person so ticky."

"Yes, you could say that. Never a dull moment with him around, that's for sure."

Zeke managed a smile, but it looked tight and contrite. He seemed a tad nervous, not like his usual laid-back self, like it was something that he was keeping from me, but he still looked dashing in his burgundy-and-black smoking jacket with black lounging slacks.

"Can we change the subject?"

"Don't get a 'tude with me, Zeke. I only thought that now would be a good time for me to meet Sweet Willie, you know, seeing how I've heard so much about 'im."

Could have been my imagination, but it seemed like time stopped for a few seconds. Air stopped circulating. "Look." Zeke slammed his fork down hard enough to rock the glass table we sat at. "I don't wanna talk about Sweet Willie right now, okay!"

For the first time I noticed a bulging vein, tinted green, at his neck, a smaller one at the top of his forehead.

Dang. What is that about? This was new, a man being himself, no putting on airs, no tiptoeing up to the plate. Raw. His outburst rattled me and sent a surge of blood pressure through me that made the fine hair in my kitchen curl back up. *Jealousy, my foot!* Seemed more to me like pure-dee resent. Zeke resented his own roommate?

Now I was really curious. I kept hearing noises coming from upstairs, odd noises like bumps against furniture or walls, a mild thud, a thump, like somebody jumping down from something. Could it be that this roommate of his was so fine, so well put together in comparison to Zeke that resent was the only commonality the two shared? Or was it a money thing? I wondered. Maybe Sweet's career was taking off and leaving Zeke's behind in a cloud of dust, which would make it something that Zeke wasn't proud of. What the heck did I know, it probably just boiled down to bedroom semantics. Perhaps this—this Sweet Willie man was a sensational lover, and females migrated from miles around for his services in the bedroom. That would account for how Sweet got his name. But that didn't make any sense. I'd been at Zeke's place for hours, and the phone hadn't rang once, nor had any other females dropped by for Zeke or Sweet Willie.

My mind was a motherboard of sophisticated circuits trying to compute and solve the mystery. *My man, Zeke, jealous of Sweet Willie? But why?* I changed the subject.

"All these vegetables and no potatoes. Think we'll stay full?"

His calm demeanor was coming back to him. "Sure, we will. You have your vegetables and protein, which is all you need really. It's the sugar and carbs that make people fat."

"It does make sense." Didn't stop me from wanting that big baked potato, though.

"Of course it does. Stay away from the sweets, the rice, pasta, and white bread, and the weight will leave. You'll see."

I smiled. He smiled.

His eyes even lit up when he inquired, "You still taking the pills, right?"

"Yep, like a sixteen-year-old taking birth control pills behind her mama's back."

"Good," said Zeke, finishing the last of his chicken breast chunks. "I'm sorry I snapped at you about Sweet Willie. It's just that, well, he got in late last night and wasn't feeling well. I was up half the night trying to nurse him back to health, and maybe I'm just tired."

I almost missed my mouth with the fork. *Nurse another man back to health? Hmmmm. Okay.* "Too tired for us to spend the night together?" I tried a sexy look on him, running my tongue over the top of my lip slow-like.

The brother stayed on top of his response. "Queenie, have you forgotten already what I said about friends first, lovers maybe later?"

"Not really. But sometimes people make exceptions."

"I don't. I'm pretty much the same all the time. Exceptions? No."

"Never?" I asked, serious.

"Never. Maybe some folks do, but I'm not some folks. Sex is sex, and love is love. You can't rush it. Lust is one thing, but true love is like a flower that must have the patience of sunshine to nurture it along."

Yeah, right. The patience of sunshine. "It's been weeks, now. I wouldn't exactly call that rushing." I kissed at the air in his direction, and Lord if he didn't blush with his fine self. He blushed. That was a good sign. A flag up in war territory.

He pushed mixed vegetable on his plate around with his fork. "I think you're a really nice person—sweet, in your own way. I really like you for who you are as a person, but to be honest with you, you might not be used to a man like me, or used to a man that likes to get to know a woman first. Let me tell you a little something."

"I'm listening." My eyes were glued to his.

"Some men just jump right into a sexual thing with a woman before taking the time to feel the person inside her. But not me. Before I undress the body, I like to undress the mind, caress a woman's spirit. I like to feel the essence of a woman before I feel her flesh against mine. What makes her laugh? What makes her cry? Imprint her smile in my head."

I swallowed a hard lump suddenly in my throat. It was so sweet the way he said it, with feelings, with meaning. My eyes felt misty, like I was struggling to hold back a dam of feelings. His words were pure beauty to my ears. Words aimed at my soul. I had dated plenty of men, smart, young, old, and the likes. But none as deep inside himself as Zeke. I could tell that he was a man that was in touch with himself. I wanted to jump over that table that was like an ocean separating us and pull his head to my bosom—force him to hear the heart that was beating way too fast in my chest, beating just for him.

"Now, Queenie, you have to ask yourself before we go any further with our budding friendship, can you get with that?"

I could get with anything you say. I could get with the things you say, the way you say it. I could get buck naked right now and do a tabletop dance if that would show you how much getting with it I can do. "I can," my lips said, but my mind was saying something else—saying that I would rather get oiled up and get busy on some soft satin sheets. I didn't want to do the long road to getting to know my essence or my spirit.

I wanted to do the short road to nasty, and I wanted to do it now. That night. Right then and there. I should have been honest with the man and said just that. But don't good things come to those who wait?

Then Zeke said, "We can kick it together tonight, but all I can offer you is some friendly conversation and a good movie or two. Just two friends sharing easy times together. No strings attached. So, it's up to you."

"Living room or bedroom?" I raised a brow.

"Bedroom if you like, but only if you promise to behave like a lady." And to that, I smiled. He smiled, too. Need I say more?

Eighteen

Good things come to those who wait. Words of my childhood, handed down to me like precious jewels. Good things come to those who wait. How many times can you remind yourself of those very words before the fog of doubt starts to slip in?

An hour later, after my three-minute shower, after the pat down to dryness, after slathering my skin with my new scented lotion of vanilla-banana scent, and after dinner, I was ready for whatever would step into our path. Almost two weeks of being on the big green pills, some exercising and eating protein and vegetables only, I'd lost all of twenty-one pounds. Not what you could consider a great amount, but enough to warrant Zeke's approval, I imagined. A little pat of my slightly reduced behind was evidence of this.

"I can tell you're losing. I like it," he said, smiling down at me.

Me, too, I was thinking, but kept my mouth shut while Zeke handed me a glass of white wine and put in a video and got it going before leaving the room.

"Gotta go check on something. I'll be right back."

"Take your time," I assured him. "I'll be waiting."

I'd be waiting, all right. Waiting for his speedy return. Waiting for all that had been worth waiting for. Sprawled along the round bed, I

gulped down my white wine from a crystal flute and watched until he
was out of sight, then sprang up with anticipation. I set my empty
glass down on the fancy night table. In the wall mirror behind the
bedroom door I checked myself. Looking good. I smooth down my
slinky golden knee-length chemise, patted my hair into place, and
sniffed at my arms. Banana and vanilla. *Ummmm.* I smelled good
enough to nibble on my own self. I hurried over to the light switch
and turned it off. No. Too suggestive. *You going too fast, Queenie, slow
down. Don't rush it and rock the boat.* I turned it back on, dimmed it.
The subtle look was what I was going for. Seduction was one thing,
but a man didn't have to know that he was being seduced.

From somewhere else in the house I could hear Zeke's voice talking
in low timbre, talking, and then singing. The man didn't sound too
bad either. But then again, why wouldn't he? I turned the light switch
off completely, settling for the illumination of the television. The
movie, *The Best Man*, was on, but even as cute as Taye Diggs is, my
mind wasn't on no movie. Been there, done that. I went over and
climbed back along the bed and waited. Lying on my stomach, I closed
my eyes and let my imagination run wild. A little touching would be
first. A good back rub, perhaps. What man could refuse a good massage? More touching. Just the right touch is all it would take. Hot
fingers on hot places.

I was lost in my own sweet reverie. After that, things are still a
little fuzzy to me. I got that feeling, soft and weird as it was, like time
was moving in slow motion, and somehow I was caught up in it. My
every move snagged on fractions of time. The room was half-dark.
Me, lying along the round bed. The sound of the television volume
turned down. There was music, only it was in my head. A sweet melody rocking me—soothing.

I started humming to it, the tune in my head. Could have been the
wine, the tune in my head was getting louder, more steady, the feel
of the night air slipping through the opened window where a soothing
night breeze found its way in. All I know is that the whole feeling was
surreal, and I was coming into my own. The moment that I had been
longing for, plotting for, and fantasizing about had finally come . . . I
felt his hand, strong and promising along my bare leg as it trailed up

the path to my rear end. One hand, gentle as a feather, moving up to places of sweet dreams.

"You have such nice hands," I complimented, but he was quiet, perhaps focusing on what he was about to do. Slowly I got that feeling—the feeling you get when you want something so bad, knew you deserved it, felt positive that it, no doubt, would be like no other experience you'd ever had. Because it was all about how much you wanted it. The man of my dreams was massaging ever so gently the small of my back and running his strong hands in delicate circles—just the right touch along my anticipating spine. He had my chemise pushed up, exposing bare flesh, but I was not embarrassed, felt no qualms about being so exposed, so there and ready for whatever he wanted to do. My spine felt tingly, as if it were coming to life for the first time as strong, masculine hands trailed down my derriere onto my legs and gently molded and massaged each one, then back up my legs to my back. It felt good, and while it's happening, I'm thinking, *I don't know what school of body massage the man might have attended, but it is obvious that he had paid close attention to the teacher in class. He'd mastered the art.*

"Oooh, Zeke, that's feels so good." He didn't say anything, a small grunt as he went into gentle open-hand chops to my back. A couple of times his strikes seemed a little heavy-handed, with enough striking force to knock away some lung tissue, but it was all good. Strong women don't break so easy. Then, he was back to massaging, taking his time to push heavy, stiff fingers into my muscles, working those fingers like some master baker working his dough. "You are really good at this, you devil you. Shoots, if I didn't know any better, I'd say you were trying to seduce me."

I felt him straddle my legs. His weight startled me for a second or two. "Dang, you don't look so heavy." But never mind. I allowed my mind to slip beyond that. His skin against mine felt . . . felt damn hairy, but smooth. Then I heard Zeke's voice booming in the room from some distance away.

"Get off of her!"

"Huh—?" *Get off?* What the heck did he mean by 'get off'? I didn't get it at first—didn't want to get it—but that nagging voice somewhere at the back of my head, where the music had stopped abruptly, wanted to know what was going on. Either Zeke was a trained ventriloquist, or there were two Zekes in the room, but how in the world could his heavy body be on top of me and his voice coming from the far end of the room? I twisted my head around as far as it would go. If I had twisted any harder, I would have done the head pivot part on *The Exorcist*, trying to see who the heck was massaging my backside up and down if it wasn't Zeke. And it wasn't him! "Oh, my god!"

"Willie, I said get off of her!"

"Willie?" *What the Sam Hill is going on here?*

Standing in the doorway, Zeke flicked on the light. It was Zeke standing in the doorway, all right, and he was standing there with a tray of drinks and two bowls of cut-up fruit. I couldn't move with the weight still pinning me down and pushing relaxation out of me in one long swoosh of air. The weight on my back is not just heavy, but tremendous. I tried to twist to my side to dislodge my suitor from his perch, but I couldn't move. The more I struggled, the more pinned down I was. The silken material of my chemise hiked up, my backside out, all of it, exposed like golden brown rump roast from the oven.

"Sweet Willie, you know better than this," Zeke admonished, and then added, "Shame on you!"

"Ohmygawd, no! Get him off of me, get him off!" Sweet or not, I didn't know who Willie thought he was, making my acquaintance in such an intimate way, but I couldn't wait to look into his foolish face and give him a piece of my mind. Before Willie climbed from my backside, he kissed me sweetly on my back.

"What the hell!" I scrambled up from my position, snatching up the bedcover to hide what everybody in the room had already viewed. My breath stopped for a few seconds when I was finally staring at the Sweet Willie I'd been dying to meet, and what I saw was not a pretty sight. Willie was a beast that stood all of five feet tall and was covered with reddish-brown hair all over. Sparse reddish hair was at the top of his head, standing straight as if to attention. His dark brown eyes, surrounded by bloodshot red, were looking at me in a way that I didn't appreciate, and lordhavemercy, if I didn't see glints of intelligence in those little beady eyes that sat too close together.

"I see you two have finally met."

"My god, I can't believe this. You live with a monkey?"

"Sweet Willie, come over here right now." Zeke patted the side of his leg, and like some obedient child, Sweet Willie went to his side and stood, looking monkeyish.

"Ohmygawd. What the heck kind of monkey is that?"

"Queenie, calm down. He's quite harmless." Zeke sat his tray on the dresser and took one of Sweet Willie's hands and patted the top of it. "He's quite familiar with the English language."

"Ohmygawd. I can't believe this." I'm standing on his bed with the spread clutched up to my chest. Something was in my throat, and for a few scary seconds it felt like I couldn't catch a good breath. I pointed at the thing gazing at me. "Sweet Willie's a . . . He's ah . . . Sweet Willie . . . He's an animal . . . a damn monkey?"

Zeke's expression changed to stern. "Hey, watch your mouth. He knows what you're saying, and he's very sensitive."

My mouth was hanging open from being too speechless as I watched the animal do something with his hands. To my amazement, Zeke responded with some hand signs of his own. "Ohmygawd. You didn't tell me your roommate is a monkey, Zeke. I don't think this is funny."

"And no one is laughing. For your information, he is not a monkey; he's a trained and highly intelligent orangutan. And he says hi, and that he likes you."

"He what?"

"Willie can express himself with sign language, and he says he likes you."

"Okay, I can take a good joke. Where's the camera? Show me where the camera is, Zeke." This had to be some kind of joke—some kind of prank. Maybe I was on *Spy TV* or *Candid Camera* and Allen Funt's son would pop out of a closet any second now and shake my hand and point out that hidden camera. And we'd all share a good laugh over it, and sip on cold drinks later while we discussed my contract of how much money they would be paying me for the episode and inform me when the episode would be airing on national television. Maybe that was what it was. It had to be, right? But, can they really show a naked behind black woman being massaged by a—a—monkey? "Oh, hell no!"

He looked disappointed. "There's no camera, Queenie. This is all the real deal. I was waiting for the right time to tell you about Sweet Willie."

"The right time?" I stopped and regarded him like he was crazy "You saying he's really your roommate?"

"Sweet Willie was supposed to stay in his room tonight. He and I had a long conversation about this, and he was supposed to stay in his room." To Sweet Willie he turns. "Bad, bad boy. You should know better. He didn't scare you too bad, did he?"

What can a woman say to something like that? Nothing.

"Once you know him, he's really nice, and he seems really fond of you, Queenie. He says that big woman cute, and taste juicy, and smell like eat. He really likes you."

"Love at first sight by a monkey. How lucky can I get."

"He's not a monkey. Don't call him that, and don't be so upset because he likes you. Not many females get Sweet Willie's approval. He wants to be your friend."

"Well tell 'im to take a number 'cause Queenie don't swing that way. Hell no." I jumped down from the bed and gather up my clothes. The hell with getting dressed, I stuffed my few things into the overnight bag I brought with me. "You could have told me this in the beginning, Zeke. I mean, how hard can it be to say, I live with a monkey?"

"Stop calling him a monkey. He's not a monkey! He's an intelligent primate with years of training. He's actually smarter than some humans I know. A good sport, too. He's leased out most of the times to be in movies, and a circus every now and then, but the rest of the time he's with me. It takes a special request permit to keep him at my house, but he's so well trained and earns quite a bit each year, it's well worth it."

"Unbelievable . . . just a simple romantic evening, that's all I wanted, just a simple evening. But, no . . . it's just too much."

"Here," said Zeke, watching me zip about the room, gathering up stuff and packing my bag to leave. "Let me put him back in his room. He'll stay there all night. You'll see."

I grab up my bag and head from the room. "But no, instead, I get made love to by a—a damn monkey!"

"Hold that thought, Queenie. I'll be right back."

I didn't hear a word Zeke was saying as I started down the stairs with my bag. Never mind that I was still dressed in lingerie and bare-foot. I heard a door being slammed, and Zeke coming behind me trying to explain.

"Okay, okay, I'm sorry, I should have told you about Sweet Willie earlier. I tried to tell you, but I just didn't know how."

"Maybe you didn't try hard enough."

"He's not just any ol' orangutan, Queenie. He's a show animal, and believe it or not, he brings in the most of the money that pays the bills around this place."

"And that makes him a perfect roommate?"

"There's more to it than that—you see, Sweet once belonged to my uncle Reese when he owned a small traveling circus back East." He stopped and took a deep sigh. "When my uncle Reese passed away three years back, he left me some money in a will but Sweet came with strict and legal stipulations that he would be cared for until his death. You could say that I get a nice tidy sum each month as long as Sweet is happy and healthy. Sweet dies, so does the monthly stipend."

I knew I was looking at him like he was crazy. "But you live with a monkey."

"He's not a monkey; he's a highly trained orangutan with more intelligence than some humans you know. He's been trained to feed and dress himself, and he can use a human toilet, he knows sign lan-guage in both English and French, but can understand three foreign languages. He can ride a bike, drive a car, and I've been told that he gives a mean back massage, as well. And if that's not enough, he like females, human females."

"Zeke, this must be your idea of a sick prank, and I am not amused." I wanted it to be a joke, and all he had to do was just admit it—heck, I like a good laugh, too, sometimes. Maybe it was just me who didn't

want to accept the slap-in-the-face truth that I had been almost seduced by—by an ape—a monkey. Hell, whatever the heck Sweet was.

"I don't see what the big deal is. It's not like I didn't tell you I had
a roommate."

"I have to get outta here," I huffed. "I can't stay another minute."

"Queenie, don't go. I really want us to kick it together tonight. We
can watch movies or slam some bones, or play some cards. Whatever
you wanna do. Sweet Willie won't be out of his room no more tonight.
I promise."

"No. Heck no." I was shaking my head and heading for the door
and mumbling to myself. "Damn monkey kissing all on me . . . feeling
on me. Yuck." I didn't let my lips utter what I was thinking, that it
had all felt so—so good. "Dang. What's wrong with me?" I couldn't
gather my stuff up again fast enough, and Zeke had the nerve to be
looking like he was shocked that I was leaving.

"I said he won't be bothering us again tonight."

"I can't stay, Zeke. I just can't."

"Ah, c'mon now . . . it wasn't that bad. Most women like his back
massages."

"I can't believe you could do something like this to me."

"Sweet Willie likes you. He was just being friendly."

Huffing and puffing at the door. "Yeah, he was being real friendly
all right, especially with my backside." I didn't even want to venture
the thought of what that beast might have done if Zeke hadn't come
into the room and stopped him. "You could have told me this mess
in the beginning—playing games, making me look like a fool. Hell,
Sweet Willie just met me, and he's been more intimate with me than
you have, and I've been knowing you longer. You—you have some
nerve . . . must think . . . I'ma—" Mad enough to slap the taste from
his mouth, I snatched his front door open.

"Look, Queenie. I know I should have told you up front, but don't
you see why I didn't? It's not the sort of thing you just tell a woman
right off. It makes them leery. Trust me."

He almost looked sad, and it almost worked. For a minute, brief
and fleeting, I thought about what he'd said, and it made sense. If he
had told me in the beginning that he lived with a primate, I probably

never would have brought my horny self over to begin with.

"Matter of fact, it's one of the reasons why I don't have a steady girlfriend to this day. Because of Sweet."

"You poor thing you." I kept expecting violins to start playing somewhere in the background. "And to think, all this time I have been puzzled over why a handsome young man, single with his own place, such as yourself, didn't have a slew of females running in and out of your door. Now I know why." I was just about to leave when I caught a glimpse of Sweet Willie waving from the stairway. He pursed his big monkey lips and blew a kiss in my direction. Zeke followed my gaze and turned, trying to waving the beast back up the stairs.

"Get back to your room! Now!"

"Unbelievable."

"See?" lamented Zeke, smiling like some proud parent. "Sweet adores you. I've never seen him behave this way with a female he just met."

"He adores me, huh?"

Then Zeke turned back around and looked straight at me and said the damnedest thing. "Maybe if you gave 'im a little kiss, you'll feel better about 'im."

"A little kiss? You want me to kiss your monkey?"

His face was a wide and sly smile. "Just one little kiss can't hurt."

"You know, Zeke. I may have slapped a few monkeys around in my day, but none as large as Sweet. But the way I feel right now, the only place you and he both can kiss is my big black ass!"

"Ahhh, don't be a sour sport, Queenie. We can all chill out and watch movies. I want you to stay. For real, I want you to. Do it for me, Queenie."

"Better yet," I said, standing at the door with the night air slipping in. "Why don't you and Sweet just get cozy, and you can kiss 'im yourself. Later for this!"

Nineteen

"More bleach!"

"Queenie, half a cup is too much already."

"Poe, stop arguing with me!" I shouted, turning the hot water off in the tub, where I was submerged with bath bubbles up to my neck. "I need more bleach!" It had been a miracle that I hadn't gotten myself pulled over and issued a parking ticket for speeding down the highway back to my house. I couldn't wait to get to the privacy of my own house, couldn't wait to wash the aftermath of my evening at Zeke's house off my body. Dressed in a sheer black slip, a black Badu wrap around her head, Poe stood in the room, looking half-asleep and flum-moxed by my odd behavior. "I'll let you know when I've had enough bleach."

"Girl, what's gotten into you?" The container of bleach hung to her side.

"Never mind for right now. Just more bleach, please."

The water was already hot enough to make hot-water corn bread if I added a dash of salt and enough corn meal, but it still didn't feel hot enough to wash away the feeling of yicky-ickyness from my skin. I turned the hot water on to add to the heat. It's not easy to make some thoughts pop out of your head on command, and the thought of Sweet Willie's hairy, monkey-ass hands rubbing and touching me, and fondling my backside only made my skin crawl more. Damaged goods, that's what I was. "Where's that brush we use to scrub the floor with?"

"Queenie, you can't be serious. That's too harsh for human skin," said Poe, turning to primp her face in the large mirror.

"Will you pass me the dang brush!"

Smacking, she stopped primping, put the plastic container of bleach down, walked over, opened the bottom cabinet, and peered in. "Here you go," she said, tossing the stiff and dirty orange brush over into my bathwater. Even all the dirt on the bristles of that brush felt cleaner than my skin. Soapy, bleach-scented water splashed up into my face and stung at my eyes. I picked it up and thought about throwing it at her head. I wasn't in the mood for her attitude.

"Here, suit yourself."

"Are you going to put more bleach in the water or what?"

She was standing by the door, looking over at me with an expression like I must be losing my mind, then picked the plastic container of bleach up and came to stand over me. "No, Queenie, I'm not. Not until you tell me what's wrong."

"Nothing's wrong, Poe," I lied, using the brush along my already sensitive skin.

"Oh, something is wrong, all right," she snapped. "You the one rushed in here at this time of night acting like a crazy woman. You been in that tub for almost an hour now. Queenie, what's wrong?"

"Look"—I glared at her—"either pour some more bleach in the dang water or give me the jug and get the heck out."

"No!" She stepped back like she was half expecting me to throw a bar of soap at her. "No more bleach until you tell me what happened! Did something happen at Zeke's house? Did he assault you?"

I made a face. "I don't wanna talk about it."

"Oh, no, don't tell me his black ass raped you? Ohmygod, no. Did he rape you, Queenie? Did he? You don't have to protect him if he did; just tell me, and we'll call the police right now. Did he rape you?"

"No, no, no. He did not rape me. Look, Poe, I know you're trying to show me some love by being concerned, but if you ever cared anything 'bout me in all the years we have been friends, I am asking you—no, I'm begging you—to just butt out. I don't wanna talk 'about it." I pushed more bath bubbles up to cover my neck. Embarrassed to even tell the ordeal of my night with Zeke—well, with Sweet Willie, actually—all I wanted was to slide myself down into the tub faceup. Never coming back up again. That would serve Zeke right for pulling his little Sweet Willie stunt.

"Okay, be that way, then. I won't ask you again. You acting like he forced you to do something you didn't wanna do, and that's called date rape." She looked disappointed. "You know, just because a woman knows and likes a man don't make date rape right, Queenie. He shouldn't be allowed to get away with something like that. It's wrong." She left her post at the door, probably to go put the container of bleach away. Empty-handed, she was back at the door, her eyes prompting for an explanation. "Well, I'm waiting."

"Poe, just leave me alone about it. All right."

"Well, did he rape you or not? I'm your best bud, and you know I'm asking because I care."

"Thank you, and no, he didn't rape me. Didn't even try to rape me—I mean, seduce me. Now, can you get the bleach and pour some more into the water, please?"

Poe did one of her famous long-sigh routines. If I had a dime for every time she stood before me and sighed long and deep before imparting wisdom, I'd be rich.

"Queenie, I don't know what's going on, but you cannot bathe in pure bleach. It's toxic. It can make you very sick."

"Well, thank you, Dr. Know-It-All. Then can I be left alone?"

"Sure. It's your world."

Her hands folded, she backed out of the room, looking like an opponent afraid to turn her back on me for fear of being shot during departure. "You obviously got some issues to deal with. I know that much."

"Get on my nerves at times," I mumbled under my breath. Always trying to tell me what to do. Sometimes, more and more lately, I was beginning to resent her intrusions into my privacy. I mean, I cared about her a lot, and I know she cared about me, as well, but the part about her always knowing what's best for me was something I could live without. Back in our younger days, we both were too busy getting our fun on with one party or jamming club after another for her to have time to steer my life like she was my manager and owned a lucrative partnership in my life. And besides, here I was the one with the most education, the good-paying job, the nice condo and nice car, and she's the one always giving me strategies on positive living—like somebody died and made her an expert. It was just a matter of time, but it was going to stop. She need be somewhere trying to manage that woolly hair up under that rag on her head. "You don't know nothing!" I shouted after her, feeling every bit of my accusation.

Poe might think she have all the right answers, but I know from experience that she don't. Like that time in our last year of high school when I got my very first chain letter in the mail. We had to be sixteen going on seventeen and full of ourselves like most teenagers. Back in the early seventies, chain letters were popular, and everybody who was anybody and their mama received them. The letter was typed neatly on crisp pink paper and promised good health and good fortune to the receiver, but only under the condition that they make twelve copies and forward the letter on to friends.

Poetta had been at my house the day the black and mysterious envelope arrived in the afternoon mail. I wasn't impressed. All I wanted to do was to throw the nasty-looking paper away and forget about it. But no. Poetta, Miss Know-Everything-About-The-Universe, suggested, "No! Are you crazy? You should never throw a chain letter away! It breaks good karma." She insisted that I follow the chain letter's instructions to the T and mail all twelve copies. Adrenalized by the process, she even provided me with the stamps. And like a fool, I pulled out my trusty little black book and selected my twelve—umm—should I say, my twelve victims.

"Girl, we might end up winning at bingo on Sunday night," I recall her saying, excited about the possibility.

Together, Poe and I had walked to the Compton library, five blocks away. There, I made twelve copies of the odd-smelling letter, folded each one ever so gently, wrote addresses on each envelope, and licked stamps to paste on each one before dropping my batch into the nearest mailbox.

I still remember how we walked back to my house together, Poe in her bright yellow sundress and me in my pink one. I didn't really want to think about the chain letters anymore, but Poe seemed pleased as pie as we walked along. "Chain letters can be linked to the rising house of the moon," she'd said. Her words made no sense to me then, so I didn't comment. "And the moon," she added, "can be filled with promises. You did the right thing, my friend. You'll see."

Her words still ring loud in my ear as if it had been just yesterday. Twelve letters to twelve friends—well, ten friends and two family members, one in particular, my cousin Tom—who all came down with a mysterious rash on their hands that migrated up to the elbows. Where hands had touched those twelve letters, there was rash. Twelve people and myself. The freakiest thing I'd ever seen, and it took weeks to clear up! Thanks to listening to Poetta, twelve folks, once they found out who had sent the chain letter to them to begin with, became twelve very upset ex-friends, now known as my twelve enemies. Oh, well.

Poetta came back to the bathroom door and tossed another hand towel over in the water, trying to be funny, no doubt. "Okay, if you don't want to talk about what happened at Zeke's earlier, let's talk about our drive to Arizona in the morning. What time will we be pulling outta here?"

I looked up at her like she was changing colors. "Our what?" I'm making a face and I know it, but can't help it. Vaguely, I did recall the two of us having a conversation about driving somewhere, but the sordid details of where I was suppose to be driving her to and for what purpose was lost somewhere in my head. "Arizona?"

"Yes, Arizona. You promised that when you returned from Zeke's, we'd drive up to meet with the wife of Jimboy."

I laid my head back along the pink tile of the wall and sighed as deep as I felt. *Lord have mercy. Is she for real or what?* "You're kidding, right? I mean, you don't really plan to go see some woman you've never met before to discuss how you were screwing around with her husband, do you?"

Poe stood her grounds. I could tell by the set of her jaw, the slant of her eye, she was serious as a heart attack.

"It's not about screwing, Queenie. It's to seek forgiveness and pay retribution for something I've done to another human being. You should try it sometimes; it could make you a better person."

"Oh, no, you didn't say that. You sure you want me to drive you? Me?"

"Well, I didn't mean it like it sounded." She tried to clean it up and put a bow on it, but what was said was said. Can't take spilled milk back. "What I'm trying to say is that when we seek forgiveness from people who we have wronged, it makes us stronger as loving individuals. More happiness is channeled into our lives."

"Amazing."

"Queenie. I'm just saying that the more you seek to do positive things, the more positive things come to you."

"But you were sleeping with the woman's husband, Poe. I hardly think she will be warm and receptive of you bringing it to her face. You don't know what kind of psycho maniac filled with jealousy you could be headed to deal with. Besides," I added, perhaps a bit too hasty, "You talking about paying retribution, if you have extra money and wanna pay something, Poe, pay me for all the food you've been eating round here. I mean, I wasn't going to say anything at first, but . . . I could stand some cash duckies myself. Hmph." I didn't need her money, not really. It was the principle of the matter. "It's not like you my honey-dip and you a kept woman."

"And thank God for that, 'cause you wouldn't be my type, no way." She thought that was funny.

"Be funny if you want to, but ditto here."

I hated to bring up the pettiness of money, but since Poe had been staying with me while they repaired her half-burned-down house, my expenses were going up, not down. More food had to be shopped for. She can't drink regular milk because it makes her constipated and gassy. She can eat only special whole-grain bread, none of that cheap white stuff, and I have to buy special toilet paper because Poetta can't use the cheap two-ply brand because it irritates her sensitive skin around her delicate behind.

"Why you didn't mention this before, Queenie?"

"What, 'bout some money? Because I didn't think I needed to. I mean, you know so much about the world and life. You can see things in your tarot cards. I just assumed you knew."

"You know I haven't used tarot cards in months. You're excuse-shopping. It's because you really don't want to drive me to Arizona, isn't it? Just tell the truth and stop bringing up other stuff."

"Poe, I believe in friends helping friends and all, but I need some financial assistant, too." I was feeling light-headed and indignant as I struggled up from the water and stood, grabbing up a large pink towel to wrap around me. "But I won't lie about it—I'm not thrilled about driving to Arizona to see somebody's done-wrong wife. I mean, you have come up with some crazy ideas over the years, but this one takes the cake. You don't know what this woman might want to do to your behind up in her face talking about you used to be her man's mistress. You must be outta your mind. Didn't the movie *Fatal Attraction* teach you anything about how dead serious a woman can be about a man? You need to—" My words cut off abruptly when I realized the way she was looking at me, like she was seeing a tall pile of money, her eyes large and rounded wide, mouth gapped open.

"What?" I did a quick look to each side of me. "What's wrong."

"Girl, look at you. You are slimming down!"

All that fussy, bad feeling slipped right off of me. "Really?" I smiled like some silly schoolgirl being told she was cute for the very first time. "You can really tell?"—I tried to look at my backside, then the other side. I couldn't tell a thing. "Poe, you really think so?" Pride swelled my head or wherever it was that could make you feel slightly dizzy and light-headed for a few seconds. "You're not just saying that to get on my good side?"

"Queenie, you don't have a good side, so no. Hell yes. Look at you. What are you doing to yourself? I'm so used to seeing you in loose-fitting clothes that I hadn't noticed it before. I can't believe you have slimmed down so much so soon."

All smiles. "Thanks, Poe. I'm really working at it." Securing the oversize towel tighter around my body, I supported my balance holding on to the glass tub enclosure as I carefully stepped out from the water. Queenie is slimming down, she said. Slimming down. Yes! I felt a little giddy inside but snapped out of it. "But don't be trying to change the subject, Poe." She didn't fool me. She knew that since I had met Zeke, I was doing all in my power to trim off some pounds and firm up. Never mind that my head was constantly the place of a residual hum of a headache that could escalate at any given second to a pulsating pounding in the corridors of my head. More and more, my heart was feeling like it was racing ahead of me—like it had someplace else to be and I wasn't invited. It was an odd feeling. Not to mention the dizzy spells.

But I was heading toward my goal and about to get my thizzle on. Once there, I knew the reward would be sweet and well deserved. But back to my homie's problem. "Poe, why you have to go looking for trouble? Jimboy is gone. He's the one that was living the lie by sleeping around on his wife; you didn't know the man was married. He was a dog, and now he's dead. Be happy about it, and let it be." I stopped and closed my eyes a few seconds to allow the dizzy spell time to pass. Goodness. There. All better.

"Queenie, I can't be happy about another human being losing his spiritual life on this level. I mean, I know Jimboy is gone from physical existence, but his spirit is still with us. How can he move on into the light if he's not forgiven? And he wouldn't be gone if it weren't for us—"

"Excuse me, are we God now? Poe, he's dead because it was his time to go and he was living his life in sin with you. He knew he had a wife and two kids." I turned and patted at my face in the mirror, noticing that my face even looked slimmer, giving my eyes a pushed-back look. I used my open hand to wipe steam from the glass. "Dang, I never noticed that before." Dark, puffy circles were around the bottom of my eyes. But not to worry. Makeup would take care of that. "Just let the dead lay."

She put her hands on her hips and looked at me in the wide sweep of mirror. The subtle lightning of the rest room made her complexion look like smooth, brown cream, like it wasn't real. A younger Janet Jackson standing in my rest room.

"You don't understand because you are not in tune to your spiritual side, or anyone else's. Yes, the man has passed, but he wouldn't have if wasn't for you, not us, Queenie, you! This is something I have to do to bring peace to my own karma—"

"Tell Karma to mind her own damn business!" I picked up another towel and dried my legs.

"Very funny," she retaliated with a sharp tongue. "Like I was saying, my karma is out of sync, and nothing but negativity will come my way until I fix it. Maybe that explains my house. Don't you see? I have to go see his wife, and you promised that you would drive me."

"And you just happen to know where the man lived?"

"Yes, I do. I've talked to his wife on the phone."

"You what? You talked to his wife on the phone?" *Has she lost her mind?*

"Queenie, I didn't stutter."

"And who's going to pay for this wild excursion, Poe? I'm not the Bank of America, you know—I have my own—"

"I have some money saved up, and you know I get monthly checks from mama's insurance plan. You won't be out any of your own money for the trip, Queenie."

"Got that right. I'm not the one."

She angled around and leaned against the door frame and picked at her hands. She always had nice hands. Nails that grow long and strong with no help. Slender fingers shaped to dainty. Small but nice. Hands that could hook a jamming style up on a tore-up head in no time. Hands that I have witness turn over tarot cards and tell folks what they want to hear.

"He left a few things at my house, papers and receipts in a box. A few clothes. Never had a reason to look in his private box before. Things that didn't burn up. I've been through his things and found an address. I've known about the house in Arizona for some time, actually, but he had me believing that it was his mom's house in the beginning—but, I know better now."

She was looking too serious, and it made me uneasy. I've known

Poe for most of my own life, and couldn't recall another time she looked as serious about something she wanted to do—something she needed to do. And there was something else in her face, something dark and brooding that I couldn't quite name. How do you say no to a tortured soul? She had a piece of car at her house that she claimed needed some engine work. That same car she wouldn't trust to drive five blocks away from home. I had a new car, hopeful and reliable. She was going to Arizona whether I drove her down there or not. I knew that much.

"Your karma, huh?" I had been ready to put up a good defense of why we shouldn't drive through the desert looking for the wife of a cheating man, and the fact that it was a good eight-or nine-hour drive from Cerritos to where she wanted to go didn't help, but her voice echoed loud and clear in my head. Those same two words, as if she had the power to will their loudness in my head, over and over again. "Because *you promised*, that's why."

I studied her through the mirror, long and hard. "Well," I said, knowing it was pointless to protest any further. "We can't have your karma out of sync, now, can we?" I was trying to be funny to lighten the mood, but she wasn't having it. "You know me, Poe. I've always been a person of my word. If I promised you something, you can consider it done."

Twenty

A promise is a promise. A strong black woman always keeps her promise. I looked at Poetta. She looked over at me. I do a reality check, just to make sure. "You sure you wanna do this?" It's Saturday morning, early.

"Never been more sure of anything in my life." Poetta kept her gaze straight off into the embryonic day.

"You realize that things could get ugly for you once you actually come face-to-face with this scorned wife of his? Right?" I put on my Bill Blass sunglasses.

"And Queenie, things just might turn out okay. Think positive. Besides, I've talked with her on the phone, and she sounds quite pleasant. We won't know until we get there."

"Pleasant, huh? So did Jeffrey Dahmer before he made a meal outta his new friends."

"I felt her karma over the phone line. She's not that deep." She gives me a comforting smile. "Trust me."

"If you say so." My girl got balls. Gotta give it to her. Riding all day just to get in the face of her recently demised lover's wife is nothing to take lightly. I needed to be somewhere handling my own business and seeing about my future husband, Zeke. But being a woman of my word, I never throw a promise away. I make a promise, I keep it.

"Not only that, but a nice long drive might do us both some good," Poetta threw over jovially. "Air our heads out."

Good enough for me. "True that." I started the car's engine and eased it out the carport. We were on our way to Sierra Vista, Arizona. If it were left up to me, I'd rather be heading to see the Grand Canyon or some other popular tourist attraction plopped down smack in the desert, maybe poke around in Phoenix or Tucson for a day or two. Heard a few good things about Sedona. Sedona sounded like a place to check out. I heard somewhere that the stars in sky at night in Sedona, Arizona, looked close enough to reach up and touch. Quiet as kept, I'd rather be going somewhere fun and interesting. Anywhere but Sierra Vista. Even though I'd never been there before, just the name of the place, Sierra, and the Vista part, couldn't dredge up enough excitement for me to blink too fast about. *What kind of people move to a dry and desolate place called Sierra Vista?* I mused. But there we were, top of the morning, Saturday, and on our merry way to see the wife of Poetta's dead lover.

We hit McDonald's first thing and was on Highway 15 by 9 A.M. with everything looking like it would be smooth sailing. We had our Egg McMuffins and cups of steaming coffee cooling in the beverage holders. Windows down. Morning air blowing through my hair, gently slapping at my face. Nothing like a long drive to the desert in the summertime to help clear the mind or help to get a few things off one's chest.

"So, you met Zeke's roommate? The one you were telling me about."

I sniffed. "Yeah. I met 'im."

"Willie, right?"

"Sweet Willie."

Poetta raise a thin, dark brow. "So? What's he like?"

Big and hairy, I'm thinking, but I don't say such a thing. "He's not like anyone I've every met before."

"Handsome?" She was smiling now, more teeth than I've ever seen before. That mischievousness in her eyes was too funny.

"Yeah," I said. "You could say that he was handsome, in his own dark and jungle-fever kind of way. Goes by the name of Sweet Willie Special."

"Goodness. Not just Sweet Willie, but Sweet Willie Special. Oohh. Sounds like my kind of man." She was almost her old self again. Happy and carefree, the way it used to be before the candle-burning, tarot-card reading, chanting in the dark, and fixing the problems of other folks.

"Yeah." I looked over at her, grinning. "I could see you with a big hunk of male like Sweet Willie." And that was all she was getting from me.

"What about Zeke?He must have a gang of women after 'im. He's quite a looker."

"Yeah," I say, listening and not listening. "But I only met one so far. Came to the house, but I got her straight, though."

"Queenie, you didn't?" She looked about to giggle. "I hope you were gentle with the poor woman."

"What?" She could see me rolling my eyes to heaven.

"Oh, no. What did you do now?"

"Nothing. I just helped a girl to be on her way. Zeke don't need no white woman like her all up in his life messing things up more. Black men have enough problems without mixing more crazy stuff in it."

"But Queenie, a man has a right to date a woman of whatever race or creed or religious background he wants, just like a woman does."

"And I know that, but if all the black men are going to the white women, Poe, what will black women do?"

"I know what they should do," Poetta snorted, about to give her full-fledged opinion. "Black women should be happy that a lot of the black men are going to the white women because most of those black men don't treat a woman good no matter what color her behind is. Look at it this way: One more black man stepping to the other side is one less man to do a black woman wrong. Look at it like that, and you'll never have a problem with the so-called black man–white woman relationship problem."

"I'll keep that in mind." Poetta might have the most in inner peace, but sometimes her opinions on how she sees the world, to me, were just plain whacked. *One less man to treat a black woman wrong. Dang. What kind of thinking is that?*

"And when are you going to tell me about what happened at Zeke's?"

"Poe, I'm not."

"Why not, Queenie?"

"Because it's personal, Poe. That's why."

"Okay, be that way, then."

"Thank you for understanding."

We drove and we drove. Poetta did her best to get me to talk about what had happened at Zeke's place, but I just wasn't giving up the 411. Not yet, not on this drive. My staunch refusal to talk about the Sweet Willie ordeal was more from embarrassment than anything else. How do you tell even your very best friend in the whole world that you had almost been in the throes of passion with a gorilla—a chimp—a damn monkey—or whatever the heck Sweet Willie was passing for. How? Oh, no. Not this time. My lips were sealed.

"Sharing is healing. I mean, think about it," said Poetta, tinkering with the rainbow turbanlike wrap around her head. "If you can't talk about anything to your best friend, who else can you talk to?"

"I'll keep that in mind."

I steal sideway glances at her. Her sundress was made of the same material as her head wrap, and I couldn't help wondering where the heck she keeps finding these matching turban outfits—some Badu outlet somewhere? But never mind that. If anybody knew how to push my spill-it-all buttons, usually it was Poetta. After all, she'd had years of experience at it and knew exactly where, when, and how to push. But not this time. She wasn't getting the Sweet Willie ordeal out of me, at least not yet.

"You know I'm yo' girl and I'm always here for you. Right?"

Silence. I kept my eyes on the road.

"We are still girls, right?"

Silence.

"And no man should come between true sistahship. Isn't that what we always say, Queenie?"

"Hey, look," I said finally, tired of her verbal badgering. "We've been riding for five hours now. My back hurts, my butt is tingling, and my pedal foot is numb. How many times I have to tell you? I don't wanna talk about it. You need something to do, you can drive. If not, please be quiet so I can drive."

"All right," Poetta declared. "Be that way. I'll remember this the next time you want me to share something deep and personal with you."

"And I appreciate it." I focused my attention on the fleeing scenery of barren land, dry and loveless looking. No wonder there's so much violence in the big cities. Too many folks crowded up in one place, and not enough room for criminals to change their minds when they start thinking of doing wrong. What a shame. "Look at all this land going to waste while so many are crowed up trying to live in the big city. Amazing."

"Umph. It's a crying shame. And since you think I'm sponging off of you, as soon as my check comes in the mail, I will be paying you some rent and food money."

Whoa. That was out of the clear blue. "Sponging? Who said anything about you sponging?" She picked up her large purse from the seat, rummaged through it for a Chapstick, uncapped it, and applied the soothing balm to her lips.

"You did, yesterday. Remember? Maybe not in those same words, but you certainly implied it."

"Ahhhhh, Poe. I didn't mean it like that. I just meant—"

She stopped me with a hand up. A brown stop sign. "Don't go there, Queenie," she snipped, huffily putting her purse back along the floor. "How soon folks forget all the things a person has done for them over the years. Especially you. You only remember the things you do for me."

"Well, I beg to differ. How can I forget when you bring it up every other weekend?"

"Don't change the subject," she huffed, fiddling with the front of her dress.

"Poe, I said I didn't mean it like it sounded." I was sincere, I already knew she wasn't trying to hear it. She was obviously stuck on stupid, and the last thing I wanted was to hear her go on and on about something that happened years ago—not the way my head was starting to hurt.

That was another thing about Poe's friendship that rubbed me the wrong way from time to time. I loved her like the sistah I was meant to have, but dang, her memory is like an elephant's. She never forgets. She stores bits and pieces of favors and rescue scenes from our past, like blue chip stamps, obsolete, only to be redeemed later at her own discretion. "If what I said the other day hurt your feelings, I want to apologize now."

She shifted her gaze to out the passenger's side window.

"Hmph. Guess I should have made you feel bad when you needed somebody to go get those birth control pills for you at the clinic so yo' mama wouldn't find out her precious baby was contemplating having sex at sixteen."

Here we go.

"You never bring up stuff like that."

"Poe, let's not go there." Unlike my mama, who had felt that the best way for a teenage girl not to wind up pregnant was to keep her dress tail down, her panties up, and her legs closed, Poetta's mother, God rest her soul, had been different. Three days out the week Poetta's mother had worked down on Alameda at the Free Clinic, where they passed out birth control pills like assorted candy to girls over the age of fifteen. Parent consent or no parent consent. Poe always had those wonderful pills even though she claimed she had no use for them herself. What she didn't use were faithfully passed on to me. I really didn't need the pills, but they were nice to have just in case. I didn't take the pills but soon found out that I should have.

"Or when you needed that three hundred dollars for the abortion your mama never found out about three days before your seventeenth birthday. I should have made you feel bad instead of getting the money for you. All my money from baby-sitting, begging my mama for money, begging my daddy, lying, and stealing to come up with all of it. For you, Queenie."

"I said I was sorry, Poe. Can we talk about something else?"

"Now that I think about it, I don't recall anyone paying me that money back. Do you?"

"All right, okay. Just drop it!" I hated when she did that. Brought up some of the weakest parts of my past to remind me of how she had been my rescuer. How she had to sacrifice a little of herself just to keep me on track. Sometimes, she was my mother, my sistah, my friend, and my foe all rolled up into one. For the moment, with her sitting beside me, digging down into old wounds, I only wanted to keep her words from shoveling salt into them.

I resented her digging. I wanted to stop the car—my car, defined by me paying the note on it each month, but being kind enough to drive her candle-burning behind to Arizona in the first place—and order her out along the desolate highway. Make her walk the rest of the way—make her pay. Give myself a reason to come back later to her rescue and save her from me. Blue chips stamps to my side for a change. Instead, I held angry words back.

"Could you kindly pass me some aspirin from the glove compartment. Please."

"Now what's hurting?" She sat up straighter and blew out air before opening the compartment and reaching in to find two bottles. One bottle of plain aspirin, the other, the large green pills from Zeke. The ones that were suppose to melt all fat and ultimately, essentially, take me closer and closer to the man of my dreams. Choosing the aspirin, she retrieved two from the bottle before closing it back up.

"My head."

"Girl, you still taking those pills you got from Zeke? That stuff might be what's causing all these headaches you've been having lately. Are you aware of that?" She picked the culprit bottle up, opened it, and sniffed the bottle.

"Yes, I am." I took the two aspirin from her and popped them into my mouth, chased them down with cold coffee. "For your information, that stuff is what's helping me to lose weight." I disliked when she always questioned my life purpose, my intellectual. "You said yourself that I'm losing, right? Can't you tell?" I feel a lecture coming on, and brace myself.

"Queenie, these pills," she said, holding the bottle up like I needed to know what it looked like, "could be causing more damage than good. Maybe they're not right for you. Did you check with your doctor before you started taking 'em?"

"No, but my psychic advisor said they wouldn't make me spontaneous combust while driving a twelve-wheeler up and down the highway." That should hold her. Feeling devilish, I smiled.

"Oh, that's real funny," she snapped, capped the bottle, and threw it back in the compartment, slamming it shut. "See. That's your problem, Queenie. No one can tell you a thing because you already know everything. I was just looking out for you, but obviously you still don't know that real friends do that for one another."

Are you for real? my glare over at her was saying. "Maybe not, but I do know that real friends don't drive folks down to places they don't wanna go, and if they don't hush up, real friends sometimes turn their cars around and go back home."

"Fine, then." Her hand mocked a zipping sound with her lips.

"Thank God." Finally, peace and quiet. I smirked over at her.

We drove another hour or so before stopping for gas and snacks. Handing me a fifty-spot for some gas, Poe took up her big black tote bag and went off to find the ladies' room while I bought two bags of no-salt pretzels, two Pepsi Ones, and a pack of sugarless gum and paid for the gas. With the help of heat waves at my backside, I hopped back in the car and waited, and waited and waited.

Ten minutes, no Poetta. Twenty minutes, no Poetta. Thirty.

Even extreme constipation didn't take that long. "What the heck—?" I knew she'd said she really had to go to sit on the throne and all, but a good half hour had passed. "Darn it, Poe."

I slipped my brown leather, open-toe sandals back on my feet, opened the car door, and got out, stood for a moment in the sweltering heat of the desert. So this was Tucson, Arizona. Unimpressed, I looked around and about. Most of the buildings I spotted from the highway held a pinkish-orange look that reminded me of Aztec Indian dwellings with a few tall, ultramodern ones placed in the midst. Dang, it was hot. Not a flying bug or bird in sight. Understandable. What could live in such heat?

I scanned around for the direction of the ladies' room and spotted the blue-and-white sign. Sweat was starting along my body, and the air felt too hot to even breathe. I couldn't imagine small insects and birds living for too long in heat so unforgiving, let alone humans. But with the modern technology of air-conditioners, I'm sure they managed.

"What in the world could be taking that girl so long?" I got my straw hat from the back seat, straightened my yellow-and-orange sundress of smooth flowing linen, and sashayed in the direction of the ladies' rest room, hoping I wouldn't find Poe hanging over the toilet, sick. Sometimes she had problems with her stomach when she traveled by boat, car, or plane. Anything that had the power to move from one destination to another, which was one of the reasons why she rarely drove herself any long distance away from home. I was thinking that all that riding across the desert probably had her liver and stomach all shook up by now.

Poor Poe, I thought as I walked over and stood at the rest-room door and tapped lightly on it. I put my ear to the warm blue paint. Nothing but silence. I tapped lightly again, but there was no answer, but now I could hear her voice, low and secretive, like she was mumbling or whispering to somebody in the room with her.

"Poe? Poe, you all right in there?" No answer. "Poe?"

I tried the doorknob, surprised to find it unlocked. The knob creaked as I eased it open as slowly as I could, just enough to poke my head through. And there she was. Poetta, sitting on a nest of toilet paper along the blue tiled floor. Eyes closed, lips moving in low chanting, mumbling under her breath almost. The rest room was tiny, the kind meant for one occupant at a time. One small window. One toilet, one small and badly stained sink. A flattened hubcap hung from a thin chain along the wall like a decorator's worst nightmare. The only light in the room came from the window and the flickering flames of twenty or so burning candles. Candles along the sink. Candles all around her. A flaming circle flickered in the tiny room.

"Oh, no—not this mess again, Poe. I thought you said you were through with—"

She silenced me with a finger to her still-moving lips. I wanted to step inside and silence her with a slap to her foolish head. *Hundreds and hundreds of miles away from home to burn candles? I don't think so.*

"Poe, get your wanna-be-witch-fire-playing behind up. Get up off that floor now!" I made a step toward coming up into the room with her, knowing that to do so, there wouldn't be enough room for us to change our minds if we wanted to. Just too small. Maybe if I grabbed her skinny behind up and dragged her out to the car, we could continue with our trip. Some little voice inside me told me to walk back to my car, get in, and drive back home without her. But when her eyes blinked open on the quick, and the eerie way she stared up at me with those bloodshot eyes redder than red, looking every bit of glowing red at me. Or maybe it was the reflection of candlelight in her eyes. Hairs stood up on my back, and as freaked out as I was, I half expected her wrapped head to pivot on her thin, brown neck and green vomit to gush out from her mouth. Another voice dared me to leave her.

"Damn, Poe, what the hell is wrong with you?"

"Queenie, go back to the car."

"Not until you tell me what's wrong with you."

I didn't wait for an answer. I stepped back with caution. She closed her eyes back and resumed her chanting.

All righty, then. "It's all good, girlfriend. You just take your time and handle your business. Okay? Just take your time," I gestured to her before closing the door back and stood outside in the hellish heat. Dang. My girl had always been a tad on the odd side, but this—this was getting to be some weird mess. Poe was my girl and all, my homie, my homette. She was like my other side, but in an odd kind of way. She was the closest to a friend I could ever get, but now I'm thinking, maybe—maybe there's more to her than I realized. Maybe she wasn't the same Poe I'd known from grade school and shared so many childhood memories with. I mean, darn it. Burning candles at home was one thing, but chanting and burning candles away from the pad was getting to be way too much.

"Lordhavemercy." I felt helpless as I paced back and forth outside the rest-room door, my mind clicking wild possibilities. Maybe Poe was demon possessed by sleeping with Jimboy. Demon semen. Yeah.

It could happen. Or maybe this sudden urge to go to Arizona had nothing to do with the untimely demise of Jimboy at all, but a revenge trip. What if we were on our way to some kind of Arizona gathering of modern-day witches and voodoo priest? Ohmygawd, no. What if Poe was using me as her accomplice and the both of us ended up fugitives running from the law and burning candles on folks in every state. What if she's been a witch all along? What if, hell—what if I just take my big hot ass back to the car and drink some water before I pass out from dehydration.

"Dang, it's hot out here." My throat was suddenly parched, and I could stand a couple of Excedrin Extra Strength for the ache still going on in my head. Plain aspirin just wasn't doing it. I should get out this heat.

"Shoots. Later for this." I walked briskly back to the car and did just that. Five minutes later, Poe came out and hopped in the passenger side, all perky and smiley and happy like nothing had happened. Why I had invaded her rest-room privacy in the first place, she didn't ask. "Let's go," she said in her usual light and airy voice I've come to know as her happy-mood voice. "Sorry I took so long. You know what long drives do my stomach."

"Let's get this show on the road, then." I started the car and kept my gaze straight ahead to keep from looking at her. When we get back to California, I made a mental note, I'll have to give our friendship one good going over to see if we should continue. Reassessment, it's called. I'm not one easily spooked, but at the same time, bizarre and too weird is not my cup of tea either. *One weird chick*, I mused.

We drove back to the highway entrance and sped on. What happened back at the tiny gas station rest room? Two could play at that game. She didn't ask me anything, and I didn't ask her.

Twenty-one

To say that there is nothing much to see in a summer hellish city like Sierra Vista, Arizona, is putting it mildly. A city so small and unassuming that if you sneezed or blinked too many times driving along Route 90, you'd miss it entirely.

What I saw was a lot of what I didn't want to see: a lot of small places of business that appeared to have long grown to tolerate a hellish existence. A lot of barren land baking quietly in the afternoon heat, hot-looking land void of greenery. Too many roads lacking concrete sidewalks, more dirt, dust, and dried-up tumbleweeds. Dusty plains that existed mainly to play the musical waves of hot, dancing heat.

We passed the small military installation known as Fort Huachuca. I'd heard of the place before from when my cousin Maxine joined the army some years back and was stationed there. That didn't last long. Cousin Maxine was too wild and citified for small-town living, and she claimed that living in Arizona was like living on planet Mars— hot and not enough to do. I wondered what kind of person would give up the freedom of civilian life just to enlist and end up at a military post that had about as much interest and charm as a loaf of white bread. I sipped water from my sipper cup, shifted in my seat.

"Are we close or what?" Just for it all to be over with—the drive, the trip—that's all I wanted.

"Let me check." From her tote bag Poetta pulled out a city map and unfolded it, humming something.

"You do know where we're going, right?" I inquired, still trying to push from my head the scene of all those candles burning in that rest room with Poetta sitting in the middle like some brown, collapsible Buddha. *Dang, this girl is getting weirder by the days. When we get back in the 'hood, we are definitely going to talk.* "Well, do you?"

"Yes and no, but I will in a minute." She powered down her window, allowing our cool air to escape and hostile heat to rush in. "Let's see now, this is Fry Street we're at, and looks like it's the main vein that runs through this town."

"You call this a town?" I tried joking, but her peppery look told me to stop. "Sorry."

"Turn right on Fry. The address I have here is 2279 Coolwater Lane, which is right after Riverrun Drive."

"How original," I mused, for lack of a better subject to talk about. "A dry and arid place with an abundance of heat with street names after water. How cute."

Poe ignored me.

"There"—she pointed—"that looks like our street coming up. Queenie, make a right on Coldwater."

I commandeered a right when the oncoming traffic on Fry cleared up. "Now what?" I asked, cruising the Benz slowly along, waiting for more instructions. Brick houses, not big and not small, lined the dusty streets void of sidewalks. A few dedicated trees braved the afternoon heat. I didn't see one soul walking along this dusty road of no sidewalks. I couldn't blame 'em. Not in this heat.

"Keep straight. We're almost there."

"Good. 'Cause I can't wait to get back to Los Angeles and back to my Zeke. I miss 'im already."

"I'm sure he misses you, too, Queenie."

An odd thought popped into my head. "This lady, Jimboy's wife. Is she expecting you or what? I mean, did you at least call the woman and tell her that you wanted to stop by?"

"Don't worry about it." She smiled over at me. "I have it all under control."

"Under control? Poe," I sighed, sick of her evasiveness. "What the heck does that mean? Either she's expecting us or she's not expecting us. 'Cause if she's not, I don't think it's a good idea to just pop up at some woman's door and announce that you're her dead husband's mistress coming for a friendly visit."

"Queenie, yes. Yes, she knows we're coming, and for your information, a *mistress* is a woman who knows that her lover has a wife. I didn't know he had a wife."

She had that smug look about her. The look she gets when she thinks she knows everything. "Ain't that why you have your tarot cards, to be able to know these things?"

"I'ma act like you didn't even say that. I wasn't his mistress."

"Yeah, you right. So instead of a mistress, that made you his *distress*. You certainly got dissed."

"Queenie, hush and save it for later," she sighed, shaking that Badu-wrapped head of hers. "And you worry too much, and too much worrying isn't good for you. It destroys good karma. You gotta learn to relax more, go with the flow, let the rhythm of life blend into you."

"Oh, we gone blend in, all right. Blend in with the Arizona dirt they bury our behinds in for being so bold and stupid enough to drive this far to confront another woman about her husband. Calling the woman to see what kind of frame of mind she would be in to greet us would have helped, Poe." Like a storm, I was gathering strength. "See, that's the difference between you and I."

"That's you and me," she corrected. "The difference between you and me."

"Like I was saying, I pick life up, turn it over, and analyze it. Then plan my strategy. I follow plan A to achieve plan B. For instance, the man of your dreams won't come to you; you go to him. Keeps life in prospective, no blowup surprises along the way."

"Queenie, that still don't make you an expert on life or love. If you were paying attention earlier, I did mention that I had talked to the woman. Yes, she knows we're coming."

"Good. And yes, I heard you the first time. Just checking. As for life, I may not be an expert, but I usually know the whys and the hows of my own goals and destiny, especially when it come to men." But she wasn't really listening to me.

"That's the house." She craned her neck and pointed. "Queenie, pull over here, right here. This is it. Right here."

"Dang, girl. Slow your roll." I did what she told me, pulled over and stopped, put the car in park and cut the engine. The house looked innocent enough. A gathering of clay red bricks and small windows behind a chain fence. Cactus-type plants sprouted from plastic pots at the front of the house, a few sun-hardy flowers, colorful in bravo. Keeping it real but to myself, I thought the whole trip of us driving all the way to Arizona was whacked, but I'm dealing with it, trying to be in Poe's corner. "Now what?"

"Queenie, wait right here. I'll see if she's in."

"Heck, after all this driving, she better be 'cause I am not coming back." I watched Poetta climb from the car and walk gracefully up to the split-level dwelling and ring the doorbell. I could hear the pleasant sing of voices, like old friends coming together again after a long missing. One minute later, Poe was back at the passenger window telling me to come in to meet Brooda.

"Brew who?"

"Brooda. Queenie, just get your tote, and c'mon. She's real nice."

"The woman's name is Brooda?" I couldn't even begin to imagine a baby being called such a thing. "You're kidding, right?" Parents have to start seriously thinking about the names they chose for their children. What is wrong with some of these mothers? Right away, the name Brooda put me to thinking of somebody old and decrepit.

"Yes. Her name is Brooda Mae McFinney. So c'mon, open up the trunk so I can get Jimboy's stuff out."

"Oh, yeah—you did bring some stuff of his to return to his wife. How thoughtful." I got out and opened the trunk, and stood by watching Poetta struggle with a trunk and a few half-full trash bags tied at the top. I don't know why my energy was dragging so, but the last thing I felt like doing was dropping in for teatime with some chick named Brooda Mae, who could be luring us in her den to wait for the right moment to toss hot grits in our face over some man. Heck no. No man is worth all of that. Dead or alive. "I can wait for you in the car. Just don't take too long."

I watched Poetta struggle to get one of the large trash bags out. I wanted her to hurry up and be done with it. Maybe we could drive around and check out the tiny town of Sierra Vista, then look for a hotel room for the night. On the way back to Los Angeles, I was hoping to stop off and check out Phoenix, seeing as how I'd heard a few good things about the place. The sooner she got Jimboy's junk out my trunk and back to his loving wife, Brooda, the sooner we could start on our merry way back to the real world.

"Need some help with that trunk?"

"No, you think so? Yes. I need help."

Heck. That girl, Poe, had packed more than I thought. A small red trunk I'd never seen before was beneath two black trash bags. Poe grabbed the two trash bags and struggled with them, going to the house. I looked up to see if she was going to come back out from the house and help me with the trunk or what. Shoots, he was her man, not mine. What did I care if his personal belongings got back to his sweet wife or not?

"Girl, try to be nice." I grabbed the stupid red trunk and slammed the car trunk down and headed for the house.

Ohmygawd.

I didn't say it, but I thought it the minute—no, the second—I stepped into the redbrick house and swept my gaze around the room. The living room—at least I think it was a living room, it was hard to tell without the traditional trimmings of furniture—was filled with plants. Vibrant, living, and green, plants grew up the walls to waiting shelves for their willowy stems to hang down from. Large trees in huge planters. Brooda's living room was a living rain forest without the rain. Plants hung from the ceiling like green ropes with leaves looking like handles. Everywhere you looked, there were plants. Plants trailing up the wall, climbing down the wall, like . . . like snakes. *Snakes!*

"Ohmygawd."

Large tanks of slithering things. Creepy things. I dropped the heavy trunk where I stood, perilously missing my sandaled foot. I was getting the willies. Obviously, this was a place of madness, and not the place I wanted to be. Even from where I was standing at the open door, where I felt reasonably safe, where I could break out, running for dear life if I had to, there was no comfort, no feeling of welcome. Looking around, speechless, I was rooted.

". . . and this is my very best friend, Queenie," Poe was saying. And then to me, "Queenie, meet Mrs. McFinney, Jimboy's wife."

"Huh? What?" I wasn't paying attention, but managed to pull my eyes away from those glass tanks of snakes. Brooda Mae. Now she was something to rest my eyes on a spell. What kind of mother named her bouncing baby girl a name like Brooda? I tried to imagine what that would sound like being cooed to an infant: "C'mon, Brooda, come to Mommy." Dang. Horrible on the tongue.

Brooda was checking me out, too. "Pleased to meet you, Miss Queenie."

"Queenie was nice enough to drive me down here to meet you," said Poetta, looking from my face to Brooda's. "I brought the rest of Jimboy's stuff for you."

"Is that right?" asked Brooda Mae. "Well, I'm pleased that you did. Come right on in and make yourselves at home. Any friend of my Jimboy is a friend of mine."

In one of those fancy motorized wheelchairs she sat, her red throne, a thin wisp of a woman the color of stained oak wood. Those dark brown peeps of hers looked at me long and hard, like she was trying to remember what child of a family member I might be. Good thing I wasn't one easily intimidated. Her stare would have been enough to unnerve a homicidal killer with a gun, and from what I could see, Brooda Mae had a body that looked in her early forties, but her face, surprisingly for a name like hers, was youthful-looking, attractive. Shoulder-length black hair sporting the hard-pressed look gave in to a flip upward of curling. A small dainty nose on a small, oval face, and if I was attractive to females, yes, I'd find her lips sensuously inviting. Despite her smile that looked sincere, the whole deal of Poe and I being there in her house, more like being there in her rain forest, still didn't feel right to me. There was no feeling of warmth or cozy lurking in my mind, waiting to settle down into my bones.

"Pleased to meet you, Brooda. Poe has spoke highly of you."

"She has? Thank you. And that was mighty nice of you, Miss Queenie, bringing Miss Poetta all the way down here to meet me."

"Please call me Poe. All my friends call me Poe."

"Then Poe it is," she said, wistful, her hands folded in her lap. "Like I was telling Poe over the phone when we spoke last week, any friend of my Jimboy is a friend of mine. We modern-day women must refrain from going to war over men that can't help themselves for being the way they are. Especially us wives."

"Damn," I heard myself say. Brooda was deep. "It takes a strong black woman to think like that."

"Yes it does, Queen."

"Ah, that's Queenie."

"Yes, of course. Miss Queenie."

"Like I said, a strong, black woman. Hope I can think like that about my own cheating husband, when I get one, that is. Takes a strong woman."

Poe didn't say a thing. Just stood there looking silly, smiling down at Brooda like she was the new Gandhi.

"Sure it does," Brooda Mae said, smiling her calm and sweet smile. Looked like I had been wrong all along about her. She wasn't some monster trying to lure us into a trap, but just another done-wrong woman learning how to roll with the flow, learning how to cope. That old saying if life gives you lemons, make lemonade. I could tell that Brooda had a lot of lemonade in her life. A person couldn't help liking a person like that.

"Interesting place you have here." I commented, looking around again. Looking for those two sweet and innocent children she and Jimboy were supposed to have. If kids were in that house, they had to be well-trained or plain terrified out of their minds to be so quiet. The house was quiet enough to hear plants growing up and down the walls. "It's almost like a greenhouse."

"Rain forest," she corrected. "Before settling down to married life, I spent some time in the rain forest of New Guinea doing research. This here is my interpretation of a rain forest in the city, in the desert. It started off as an experiment."

"Unbelievable."

"I love it," Poe said, finally back from her mental break.

"Thank you. I wouldn't be able to keep it up if it weren't for the help of my children. They do most of the watering and feeding and soil testing. It's quite a task."

Impressed, I throw her another compliment. "I can see how. It's really nice. Are the children here now?"

I caught the odd expression that flashed in her eyes even if Poetta didn't. "No. They're with their grandmother in Phoenix right now. Be home Sunday afternoon. I miss my babies, too, but they love going to see their granny. She spoils 'em so."

Brooda Mae powered over to a small table next to one of the glass tanks. Two pictures frames set amidst hanging greenery, one of a boy about ten or eleven and a girl about nine, both looking just like their mother, except younger.

"John Junior and Johnicka." Brooda put their frames back. "They took it hard about their daddy passing away like that—so suddenly."

Ohmygawd. No, she didn't name that poor child that. Johnicka? I kept quiet.

Poe finally opened her mouth. "Ahhhh. Such beautiful children." She picked up each frame one at a time, gazing fondly at each one. "They look like their father, too. Got Jimboy's eyes."

Brooda looked half-pleased. "Thank you. Jimboy was their stepfather."

"Oh."

"It's okay," Brooda assured her. "I get that a lot."

I was in the *Twilight Zone*. The theme music played in my head. Any second the two of them might break out some party favorites, turn on some music, and start getting their jig on. A celebration of Jimboy, his children, his loving, his death. This was some spooky stuff, and I still couldn't believe that I was there in the middle of it.

And there was more. Poetta looked over at the woman like she just remembered something important. Urgency in her eyes. "Oh, yeah. Jimboy. Would it be okay if I see 'im? I mean, if it's okay with you."

See him? See him where? Oh, Lord, I'm thinking. *Now what?*

"Why, of course. He would want you to, just like his other friends.

He wants you all to see him in final resting. Follow me."

"Sure. C'mon, Queenie."

Hesitant at first, I followed behind Poetta. *Oh, no. Hell no. Can it get any weirder? Lord, please, please don't let Jimboy's charred black ass be here in this house with us . . . please. I just couldn't take it.* "What the heck?"

In an adjacent room, more like a small in-home mausoleum, stood five narrow pillars, each about four feet tall. Stone-looking pedestals. Each one had a large silver urn resting on its top. Five of them. Count 'em: five. Beneath each one, a large photo of a man. The only picture I recognized was the last one. Jimboy's smiling, reddish-brown face with a sprinkle of freckles. It had the look of a man truly happy and content with life.

"Are they all your—your husbands?" I would be the one to ask. But I had to, seeing how Poetta didn't.

Brooda looked pleased as apple pie. "Every last one. All good husbands in their own sweet way. Not perfect, but good."

Like it was no big deal to her that the room contained four other urns, ashes of deceased folks, dead, gone, no more life, Poetta went to the last urn, the one containing the remains of Jimboy. She stood in front of it at first, then went down on her knees like she was about to give worship. I scratched my head, watching as she said her words.

"To the spirit of Jimboy, I ask you eternal forgiveness for the wrong I have bestowed onto your marriage. Forgive me on earth, as it all shall be forgiven in spirit. May you rest in peace."

My mama had raised me to be strong, and to know that the world was made up of all kinds of people. The good and the bad. Anything could happen, but this, this was something bad to put in my diary if I kept one. Something that I could put in my memoirs later in life, or tell to my grandchildren as they sit around a roaring fire. *Can we just go now?* my mind is screaming. *Somebody help me. Help us.* But nobody can hear my plead. *My own place, my own house, that's where I needed to be.*

Rising from her knees, Poe said, "Brooda, I didn't realize that Jimboy was your fifth husband."

"Yes, he was, and my last. We shared eight years, all good until the last two, when he took on a restless nature. Men are like that, you know. Settled in the beginning when love is so new, and restless toward the end. He was the best of all five."

"But he was a cheater," I reminded her, a bit too hasty, like somebody had asked my opinion. Too late. I couldn't take it back. "Excuse me, I mean, he couldn't have been all that good if he didn't keep his marital vows. What's the point in taking vows if you don't plan to keep them?"

"Queenie."

"Poe."

"No, no," Brooda's eyes pleaded with us. "Let her speak her opinion. I suppose you're right, Miss Queenie, but then again, it depends on why people cheat," Brooda said, like all was swell with the world. "A cheating man can still be a good man. I didn't think of my Jimboy having other women as cheating, but as him embracing who and what he was. He was being a man, Miss Queenie." She looked straight at me, like I was the one her man had cheated with. Accusing. "You do know a real man when you see one, right?"

That witch. How dare she question me about knowing a real man or not. She doesn't know me. Do I know a real man? Hell, should be asking herself do she know what a real wife is. "Yeah. I know a real man because I have a real man at home."

Looking amused, Poetta threw in, "My friend Queenie here thinks a real man is one you have to chase to get first."

That heifer. Now she was dissing me. How could Poe diss me in front of this woman that she just met herself? What kind of mess is this? "That's real cute, Poe." The two shared a chuckle on me. In fact, they seemed so relaxed and at home with one another in some odd way that I kept getting the feeling that they already knew one another, maybe from another life. But nah. Couldn't be. Poe and I talk about almost everything that happens in our lives. Somebody weird like Brooda Mae coming into the picture, I would have known about her. All I wanted to think about was my waiting car and how I could burn rubber all the way back to Los Angeles to Zeke. Brooda wouldn't know a real man if one walked up and slapped her silly behind in the face.

"Five wonderful husbands, and they all have died within two years of marriage, except for Jimboy. All dead, and from natural causes, of course."

Sounded like she was giving an oral résumé of her accomplishments. "All five?" I asked, seeing how Poe wouldn't. I needed more info. Discomfort snaked up my back. I couldn't get my face to put on the right expression. And what would that expression be even if I could? Shock? Pleasure? Disbelief?

"All five, but I only had two lovely children from the lot. Jimboy loved children. But of course, you two don't want to hear all of this now. We can always talk later over dinner."

"Dinner?" I gave Poetta a quizzical look. *Heck no. Five dead husbands, a living room full of trees and snakes? No way.*

"Queenie, be nice now."

"Of course we'll have dinner. I knew you two would be coming today, so I cooked supper."

"Uh . . . Poe, you didn't mention anything about us staying for dinner and all. I thought this was just a drive up and drop off some belongings of Jimboy."

"Queenie, stop worrying so much. It's all right. Brooda and I have a spiritual bond, and she is our sistah."

Ohmygawd. A witch reunion. I should have known. Now she's our sistah? Why did I let myself be talked into this mess? I didn't want to come, and now I don't want to stay for dinner with a woman who keeps dead husbands and snakes like some people keep dogs and cats. I wanted my own dinner at my own table at my own house. I felt like running out of Brooda's place and jumping in my car, but I couldn't just up and leave Poetta like that. "We can stop and eat on our drive back home."

"Queenie," Poe said, trying to sound soothing, like she's somebody's mama, again. "You have been driving for over nine hours. We can't hop back on the freeway and drive another eight or nine hours to get back to Cerritos."

"Who can't? With some coffee and you talking to me the whole way I could. I love long drives."

"Queenie, don't be silly. You need to rest."

"Here," Brooda said, powering her chair from the room and past me, almost rolling over my foot with that darn motorized chair. "Let me show you two to your room, where you can rest for a while. After dinner you both will feel so much better, and we can all sit down like old friends and talk."

"That will be fine," Poetta agreed. "Your hospitality, my sistah, is greatly appreciated."

"Appreciated by who?" I mumbled.

"We'll talk later," Brooda said, rolling away.

The room, large and simple. Beige walls with pictures of plants and beige tile floors with a brown area rug. Two twin-size beds. Simple but functional. Heaving a sigh, I walked over and sat on one of the beds, drained by fighting fatigue. "Poe, I don't get it. You gave the woman Jimboy's things; you asked his forgiveness on your knees. You talked to Brooda and the two of you have certainly bonded. I'm happy for the both of you. Why can't we just go? I don't feel right about staying here. I don't know what it is. We can get a hotel room and start back in the morning."

"Because we can't, Queenie. I can't just leave, right now, so stop whining about it. You'll feel so much better after you get some rest. And remember what you did to help Jimboy's passing. Just for that, you should want to be here, too."

Twenty-two

"So, tell me," Zeke said, his dark, glistening eyes burrowing into mine. "When it comes to passion, are you cold like the winter slopes of a snowcapped mountain?" He smiled that smile of his. The one that could make a woman's panties wet by just looking at his silky smooth brown face. "Or—" He paused, sucking the tip of his index finger and taking that same wet finger to touch the flesh of my exposed thigh. "—do you sizzle like hot mercy working with the sun? Like ouch."

He was being himself, just like I knew he would be when the time came. Gentleman by day, horny, sexy devil by night. On his big round bed we were, his bedroom aglow in scented candlelight and aided only by the stars that smiled down on us from the room's skylight—Zeke in leopard-skin thong that fit perfect in all the right places, allowing me a perfect view of his manly bulge. And me in red lace teddy that clung to my body like new skin. Our faces radiate across from one another over a plate of plump chocolate-dipped strawberries. I lift one of the delicate morsels and feed it into his open, moist mouth, watching the way his tongue reaches out, curls itself around it like a pink, wet finger, and me, loving every minute of it.

"Only one way to find out," I heave a deep breath, aiding my tender, erect nipples in pressing harder against their lacy confines.

"Seems like it's been forever. The waiting."

"Here," Zeke says, removing the plate of strawberries from the bed and taking charge of the moment, preparing to claim his prize, and that prize just happen to be me. "Let me move this outta our way. Are you ready for me?"

Zeke scoots over closer to me on the bed, stroking my face with the back of his hand as gentle as stroking a baby's bottom. "We did right by waiting, Queenie. Waiting to know one another better. The way it should be with budding love. Waiting to learn mutual respect for one another. Allowing appreciation to take root and grow. I'm not sorry we waited, my love, and I hope you feel the same way."

My thigh, suddenly restless, shifted forward, exposing the fleshy incline of my hip. Heat, like embers smothering beneath ash, began its journey from someplace inside me, making its way to points of pleasure. "Nothing worth having should be rushed. Not when it comes to the loving bond between a man and woman."

Gently, he kisses me again before ambling up from the bed, taking my hand and pulling me up to stand with him. "I love you, Queenie. I knew you would be the one the first time I saw you. My soul mate. A man knows."

Another kiss, long and passionate, as our bodies melt into one another. I feel words rush up from my inside me to my mouth. Things I want to say, but I can't. Only to look into his eyes and see if I can feel what he is feeling.

"I want to see all of you, Queenie. Every crook, every crevice, every nook. I plan to leave no inch unkissed—that's what I want."

He steps back a pace to pull the thin straps of my red lace teddy down from my shoulders, down farther to free my breasts that pop up and out like two golden brown jack-in-the-boxes. Nipples ready and waiting.

"Ohh, Zeke. I want it to be so special—our first time. Something I'll never forget—something we'll always remember years from now."

"And it shall." He brush his lips across my shoulder, peeling down his boxer shorts to allow his penis to break free like a frisky puppy. "I can't wait another minute to love you, to feel you, to taste the depth of your sweetness."

"And we won't," I hear myself swoon as my hand rub along his thick muscled back.

Zeke stops to pick up a small bottle of massage oil along the bedside table. Deftly, swiftly, he has oil in his hand gliding it along my body, his touch like magic fingers along my skin, my body like a standing harp, hums the tune only his trained fingers can play.

He squirts oil into my hands so that I can rub his chest where the baby fine hair curls around his tiny, dark raisin nipples. I rub the washboard ripples of his chest, softly, rubbing down to his navel. A mild electrical current runs through his manhood, and I can feel its vibration as I smooth my hand along the length of it. The hardness of it against my body makes my breath come in sweet and quick gasps.

"—and for our vows," Zeke says.

"Yes, of course, our vows."

"You may go first."

I gaze into his eyes. "Zeke, no man will ever be as perfect as you are for me. I breathe you like the air my lungs must have to live. Your presence with me is like food that my body must have to survive. Forever will be the place my love is kept for you. You are my man, my friend, my soul mate, chosen by love."

Zeke stared back into my eyes. His heartbeat vibrating against mine. "My queen for now, my queen for tomorrow, and for all the tomorrows to come. I will keep you warm and safe on my private pedestal of life. My soul mate you are. My life, my love."

To the bed he guides me, carefully laying me back along the satin. Breath swoons inside me as he draws close to my leg to kiss it—kissed each space along the side of it as if each kiss would generate new life. He kisses one leg, and moves to the next, no space left unblessed by his tender lips. I feel a rising of my legs, like thick gates being open to allow some magnificent carriage inside. His head there is so nice. The warmth, the heat, so soothing. And he rocks, and my body, like dancing to music, rocks with him. Rocking. Rocking.

There's a gathering of heat inside me. Hotness growing. Growing fast. With each breath, I inhale its promise as it moves like a freight train up the tracks of warmth. My hands grab his head pulling him closer, close enough to pull him inside me. Hips rise and gyrate to the music playing inside me, and then the moan is there in the room with us, gathering speed—gathering strength, louder, harder, faster, and louder. My eyes close automatically as I feel his weight on me, heavy and then heavier. Loving sounds he was making earlier have turned to hard grunts. I feel afraid to open my eyes but I have to, I have to see, and when I do, there he is again, Willie—Sweet Willie straddled over me pouring oil, pouring baby oil over my head. Oil rains down into my face, my eyes, my open mouth. I hear my name being called, a sound that rises and mixes with grunts and the scream that has found its way from my mouth. The sound that has become a scream of horror. Louder, I hear myself, and I can still hear my name being called, once, again and again, but I can't stop screaming.

"Queenie! Queenie!"

"Huh! What?" Something popped my eyes open. Sweat on my forehead. My heart racing. "What the—Where am I?" For a couple of fleeting seconds my mind was blank, and I couldn't think of whose twin-size bed I was lying in. Couldn't think. All the good and weird feelings in that special place melting away like ice cream under their hot staring. I panned my eyes around the room, hoping to find some things familiar to me—something to confirm that I was in my own bed, my own bedroom doing the things I was doing, and doing so in my own privacy. But such was not the case. Not with me lying with my sundress hiked up over my hips, a large pillow pressed hard like somebody's smashed head between my hot, sweaty thighs.

"Looks like she's having some kind of erotic nightmare."

"Ohmygawd," somebody else said. Sounded like Poe, but I was too embarrassed to look up at her. Like somebody's stiff tree, Poetta stood at the open bedroom door, her newfound sidekick, Brooda, beside her. Eyes wide, mouths open—the looks on their faces said it all. Then Poetta, her arms folded at her chest, shook her Badu-wrapped head at me like somebody's mama catching her five-year-old daughter in the bushes doing the nasty with the six-year-old boy next door for the first time. "Queenie, are you okay? You fell asleep and had a bad dream, or some kind of seriously kinky dream."

Brooda looked disgusted, but said nothing more.

"Asleep? I fell asleep?" *Dang. Falling asleep in a snake house, I must have been tired.*

Poetta cleared her throat, walked over to the bed, took up a blanket lying at the foot of the bed, and threw it over me. "You've been asleep for three whole hours. Told you that you needed some rest after that long drive."

"I—I—I guess I was tired after all." *But not as tired as embarrassed,* I mused. I couldn't look her in the face, but I could feel that Brooda woman still frowning over at me from her power chair. "Sorry I slept so long."

Then Brooda said, "There's some clean towels in the rest room. I'll set the table for supper while you—uh—freshen up some." She rolled away from the door.

Poetta shot hot eyes at me. "Good grief, Queenie, couldn't you save all that weird and freaky stuff for when you get back home?" She smacked her lips. "You are too nasty to be doing something like this at somebody's else's house. Good grief."

"Sorry 'bout that."

"A nightmare 'bout Zeke? Hmph. You would think that after that bad date, he would be the last person on your mind."

"I know, I know, and I'm still upset with him, but I can't help it. You just don't feel what I feel for that man."

"Really? Why him, Queenie? What's so special about him?"

I looked her in the face. "Because he's so unattainable, and you know me, Poe. I love a good challenge. Zeke provides that challenge." I had to look away, lest she see threatening tears. She didn't understand. How could she understand why I couldn't give up on Zeke so easy? She would have to know what it feels like to really want something so badly that every wakening hour you're reminded of his absence. What normal female didn't get upset with a man from time to time? But they got over it. Can't stay mad forever. Besides, I didn't owe her an explanation. I looked beyond her unsmiling face.

"Hmph. Well, pull yourself together, and act decent."

I avoided her eyes. "Like I said, sorry. Guess that's why I need to be at my own house."

"But you're not at home, and Brooda was nice enough to make dinner, so the least we can do is show our appreciation. So c'mon, go wash up, and let's eat."

"Poe, are you crazy? I'm not eating here."

"And why not, may I ask?"

"Because—because we don't know this woman."

"I know her. Stop worrying so much. You think if she wanted to do us harm, she would have waited so long? Sitting down and fellowshipping over a hot meal is a great vehicle for healing."

"I'm not hungry," I lied. Truth was, I was starving, and the way my head was swimming in light-headedness, it was time to eat or take a big green pill. The last time . . . When was it? I tried to recall the last time I'd taken one of my green pills. Maybe that was why my appetite was out of control. "I don't need to break bread with the woman, nor do I need a healing. I just need to get back home. I miss my boo, Zeke."

"Uh-huh, yeah, and he misses you, too, girlfriend. Now get your mind out the gutter, go wash up, and let's have something to eat. I'll go help Brooda in the kitchen."

She was hopeless. "Yes, mother," I replied back, but Poetta didn't think it was funny one bit.

Twenty-three

We drank strawberry wine. We inhaled vanilla incense. We talked. We broke bread. We drank and got merry like Christmas. The three of us sat around Brooda's big wooden table in her rust-colored kitchen, Poe acting free and easy and eating like she was at a family reunion and chatting away. She and Brooda had somehow formed their own Wives' Club, and me—*hmph*. I was just a visiting guest. Only in America.

Brooda told us her whole life story of how she had been in the army and stationed at Fort Huachuca for four years but couldn't take another enlistment. She seemed to know a lot about Fort Huachuca, the placed she claimed was often referred to as Fort Hoochie-Coochie and notorious for breaking up marriages due to so much infidelity among the enlisted. Fort Huachuca, the same place where she had met three of her five husbands.

"A good place for raising kids, but not a whole lot out this way to do. Soldiers are regular people that get bored, too. The women no better than the men. Nothing to do leaves a lot of room for drinking, wild parties, and extramarital affairs." She put her half-filled glass to her lips, reflecting. "All of my husbands cheated. Every single one."

Dang. "How sad," I said, not that I gave a hoot, but seeing how she was sharing.

"Not really," Brooda replied. "I never expect for a man to be one hundred percent loyal, so I'm never disappointed. B'sides, men are just made that way. They aren't genetically programmed to sleep with one woman, so they really can't help it."

Poetta looked like she wanted to comment on that last statement but didn't. Letting my indifference ride over me like a runaway wind, I finished up my glass of pale pink wine and smiled demurely. Maybe we were doing a talk show, and I just didn't know it yet.

Food was plentiful on the table. A large pitcher of iced tea, a bowl of cheesy spinach salad with all the trimmings, toasted wheat rolls with butter, steamed asparagus, and a platter of fried meat that I wanted to believe was cut-up pieces of fried chicken. Being appreciative of Brooda's hard work preparing a meal for us, I placed a few small pieces of the fried meat on my plate, but kept my fork working exclusively with the vegetables. I trusted the vegetables. They looked like old friends to my taste buds. Every now and then, I tossed a question out into their conversation, but really didn't care if Brooda answered me or not. I tried to get with the program, really, but I couldn't shake that weird feeling that kept asking me in my head how such a union between wife and mistress was possible. "I should have brought my camera."

Piqued by my statement, Brooda placed her fork down and asked, "Oh? And why is that, Miss Queenie?"

She stretched her wrinkled neck in my direction. Amazing. How was it that such a good-looking face, smooth and flawless, could be perched on a wrinkled and dry-looking neck? Too much makeup, perhaps? Somebody had wasted a perfectly good head by taking it off and placing it on Brooda's body because that's exactly what it looked like. Unbelievable. I wanted to ask about it, but I couldn't find the right way. Poe was saying something close to an apology, for the umpteenth time. Heck, she was sorry, she was so sorry, but what about Jimboy? Hadn't he played a part in the lies and deceit that had ultimately led to their affair? And now that it was all over and Jimboy was dead, who really gave a rat's behind?

"A picture of you two, together this way, and getting along is more than anyone would believe. I should have brought my camera. This is definitely a Kodak moment."

"Maybe it's because Brooda is an intelligent black woman like myself, Queenie. We both see no reason to be fighting and tearing one another's hair out over a man."

"You're absolutely right," confirmed Brooda, looking a little smug.

"It's not like I did something to purposely hurt another sistah in spirit," Poe added, looking over at Brooda and smiling for reassurance. "That's why when I finally found out 'bout you, it was then that I knew that my life's karma would never be right until I faced you. I wanted to be face-to-face to ask your forgiveness."

"All is forgiven, my dear." Brooda reached over and patted the top of Poe's hand the way a doting grandmother might do her young grandchild after coming clean about a lie, comforting. "It's not your fault, sweetie, and I don't blame you. Jimboy was a handsome man."

Handsome? My eyes dart from one face to the other. Okay, maybe big lips and freckles can be handsome. I sipped my iced tea.

"A man that possessed a magnetism that drew women to him like hummingbirds to sweet nectar."

Dang. More weird crap. I picked up a toasted roll and crunched down on it, watching one face and then the other. I could hear the violins playing so sweetly in my head.

"Not many could resist his persuasiveness," Brooda threw in after a brief pause. "So don't worry your sweet self over it. And you coming all the way to Arizona to return his personal belongings to me only tells me what a big-hearted person you are. Jimboy is gone now, another lesson learned. You, and me, we both must move forward with our lives."

"Unbelievable." I shook my head and lifted my wineglass. I needed more wine for what I was witnessing. If I told this same story ten or twenty years from now, how mistress and wife had come together in the peaceful glow of friendship behind a man, who would believe me? "Absolutely unbelievable. And so touching, too." I mocked dabbing at a tear.

"Queenie, did you say something?" Poe trained her eyes on me. Brooda followed suit.

"Nothing. I mean . . . I'm just sitting here trying to absorb all of this—this bonding at the threshold of new friendship. It's a bit weird, but refreshing." How could I have thought the worst about Brooda? It was obvious that she was a woman of gentle kindness, a wife who had been wronged so many times by a man that she took it as her faith, her destiny. She held no grudges, no animosity, no secret plots to inflict harm to the woman who had slept with the man that had stood in front of a minister and the eyes of God and said "I do." She held no bad feelings towards my girl, Poe, and Poe held none for her. Right then I hoped that if I ever had an affair with a married man, I, too, would be so lucky as to have a scorned wife willing to make amends—have that same wife throw forgiveness around like free happy dust. Just the way life should be, live, love, and forgive.

Brooda licked her lips and studied her hands. "We women have to stop letting men control our emotions when they turn their attention to others. Me, myself, I've always felt that one woman can never, ever own a man, just like a man can never truly own a woman. Love is a borrowed thing when you really think about it. Borrowed like the good feelings that go along with it when it's going well, and only good for the time we share it."

Poe looked inspired. "That is so beautifully put."

"Sure, you right," I say, my head a little tipsy, but clear enough to handle my inquiry—Brooda talks a good game, but I wanted to know about five husbands. Some women couldn't find one man worthy enough to marry. Who died and made her so lucky? Literally. "How did you say they passed, your other four husbands?"

"Queenie!" Poetta chided, like she's in charge of me. "Must you be so personal?"

"Inquiring minds want to know, Poe, that's all."

"But you have no right—"

"Please, it's okay," Brooda injected, cutting Poe's drama at the tab with a frivolous wave of her hand. "Really, I don't mind." Her eyes sparkle like I've just complimented her. "Three heart attacks, one stroke, and one by fire. Older men, of course. Guess I thought I was the prize at one time before I had my accident that landed me in this chair. Thought they were marrying a younger woman—yes, they did. All five of 'em. Goes to show you that you can't judge a book by its cover."

I tried looking impressed. "I guess not."

Brooda perked up. "How old do I look?"

"Young," Poetta responds, "real young. You have gorgeous skin. I would say . . . in your late twenties."

My turn. I give her turned-up face a good going over, looking for telltale signs, surgical tightness by the hairline, crow's feet at the eyes, but found none. But her hands, her neck, the skin on her bare arms is another matter. Looking at those wrinkled places could have made her part shar-pei, my favorite breed of dog. "Late thirties, maybe your early forties, like forty-one or forty-two."

"You're both wrong." She smirked before smiling proudly. "I'm fifty-six."

Dang. Fifty-six in face years, but that body had to be pushing seventy-six with all those spots and wrinkles. "Get outta Dodge!"

"My secret?"

"Do tell," I prompted, going along with her bantering.

"Snake oil and snake meat."

"What?" Poe stopped chewing, her jaw seizing up. "Snake . . . meat?"

"That's right." Brooda beamed, looking from my face to Poetta's, trying to catch our reactions at the same time. "And I always have an ample supply right here in my home. Home-fed, and homegrown."

"Good thing I stuck with the vegetables," I mumbled lowly. Poe's face was turning red. She looked like she would be sick. "Girl, you okay?" She nodded.

"You'd be surprised at the miracle youth properties of snake oil. And the meat can be cooked to taste just like chicken."

Coughing, Poe grabbed her glass of iced tea, spilling some of it in front of her, then stood up from her seat at the table. "I think I need some air."

I watched her move away from the table and leave the room, patting at her chest on her way out. "Poe, you okay?"

"I'm fine," she called back over her shoulder. "I could stand a cold beer. Wine gives me a headache."

Looking disappointed, Brooda shook her head. "Sorry, sweetie. Don't keep beer in the house. The yeast in it bloats me. But there's a small convenience store up on the corner. About four minutes of walking."

"Sounds like a plan to me."

Next thing I know, Poe's standing at the door, looking at me. "Queenie, I'll be right back. I'ma run up to the corner for a six-pack. Be back in fifteen."

"Hold up. I'll go with you." I spring up like a coil wrapped too tight.

"No. You stay and keep Brooda company. It won't take me long."

"But I need some exercise, too. I'll go."

"No, you will not. You will stay and rest from your long drive. You've done enough."

"Poe, but I—"

"Be right back." She zipped away from the door and was gone. The sound of the door opening found me. My fork poised, I go back to my spinach salad and vegetables, not even looking at the plater of fried meat on the table. No sooner the sound of the door banging shut had settled, the air in the kitchen changed. I could almost feel crazy gathering up strength like a tempest. Eat your food; eat your food. Shut up and eat your food. I kept my eyes on my plate, but I feel that Brooda chick staring over at me from across the table. Staring hard. Staring like she could will her own homicidal thoughts into my head. *That's it. I've had enough. Poe or no Poe, I'm outta here.*

I stood and wiped my mouth with the white paper napkin. After all, I'm a lady, and that's what a lady does. "Brooda," I said, calm and poised as I could. "I wanna thank you for the lovely dinner and your gracious hospitality. I can't remember the last time I ate a home-cooked meal this tasty and all, but I really must be running. Poe and I have a couple of more stops to make while—"

"Sit down."

"Excuse me?"

"You heard me, you overripe heifer. I said sit down!"

Not a request. Not a suggestion, but a strongly shouted order. I'm sure my brow furrowed. My forehead creased. "No, really, I have to go now. I can catch Poe on the way back from the store."

"You think I don't know that you're the one? You think I'm stupid or something?"

"The one? The one what?"

Her face scrunched into an ugly mask. "I know it's you. I know you're the one, the husband stealer. I didn't just get off the banana boat, Miss Queenie, and you can't fool me by pretending that your little short, meatless friend was my Jimboy's choice. Oh, no, sweetie. I know. I know the kind of women my Jimboy likes. He like 'em big and meaty, like mountain climbing, and that would be you—the mountain."

I'm frowning. I can feel it. "Lady, you must be insane in the membrane. I am not the one."

"I said sit down!" Her eyes, the warm and friendly ones, were now wild and animal-like.

"Girl, you are whacked. Get real, 'cause I'm on my way out."

"Over my dead body!" Brooda screamed loud enough to wake the dead. "I went through the trouble of making sure that my children were not here in this house to see their daddy's whore, just so I could have this little chitchat with you and see what makes you so special. So sit the hell down!"

"Brooda—now look," I tried, my voice cracking. "You need to get your facts straight before you go accusing folks of stuff. You know the saying: Check yo'self before you wreck yo'self?"

"Yeah, I've heard that song."

"Well," I huffed, fearless. "I suggest you apply it."

"Too many women like you in the world, Miss Queenie. Just too damn many. No respect for a decent woman's marriage, no respect for his kids, just no respect at all. You need to be taught respect for a married man. Especially one that was married to me."

"Woman, you crazy!" I took a step to move away from the table at the same time Brooda's right hand went up under the table and came back up with something that looked like a small, black gun. "Oh, hell, your ass is crazier than I thought." She would have to wait for Poe to leave to push all that sweet innocence aside.

"Gave that man eight years of my life, the best eight I had, but you wouldn't know a thing about that 'cause you don't have a husband, only somebody else's husband. What's wrong? Can't find your own man, Miss Queenie. Is that it?'

I hold my hands up in halt. "Now Brooda, let's not get too worked up with this. You have it all wrong. I am not the one that was having sex with your husband. I hardly knew the man. I mean, I knew him, but not like that."

"Liar! He told me all about you! He called you by the name you say is yours, Queenie! Heifer! Don't you know that I know everything about you? Where you live, where you work, about that silver gray car you drive. Hell, I even know your freaky ways in bed with my man."

"You do? I mean, no, you don't. You all wrong. It wasn't me."

"Jimboy was a good man, but it was women like you that made it so difficult for him to be faithful in his marriage. Women like you that have no shame in throwing yourself at decent men. But for every bad deed, Miss Queenie, there's a price to be paid."

Bravo don't always come soon enough, but judging from the look on Brooda's face, the madness stirring around in her eyes, it was now or never. I ducked down quick beneath the table, ignoring the ripping sound of my sundress at the seams, and crawled like a scurrying rat along the floor. The weight on my knees along the tiled floor was excruciating, but it had to be done. The *thump-swoosh*ing of my pulse fast and loud in my ear was the sound of fear. If that crazy woman had a gun, why wasn't she using it? The buzz of her chair's motor told me that she was going in the opposite direction of me. My knees ached in protest as I hiked up my ripped dress and fast-crawled around to the right of her, she powered to the left, but not fast enough to keep me from coming up in back of her where I rose up over her like thick smoke and grabbed the hand with the gun in it. We struggled hard with our wild, grunts and shouts bouncing off the wall.

"Give it to me, you crazy fool!"

"I will not!"

"Give me the gun!"

Brooda was screaming back like somebody was trying to murder her ass. "You want it? I'll give it to you, all right! Husband stealer! Trollop!"

"I'm not playing with you, you dizzy freak!" Small in size, Brooda had the brute strength of two full-size sumo wrestlers. For a minute it looked like she was going to pull me headfirst over into her chair. I kept my hand firmly on her hand, holding the gun. I held on for dear life: mine.

In the real world, there's a lot of things that I feel strongly about and would take a bullet for, but knocking the boots with her man, Jimboy, certainly wasn't one of them. No way. I managed to wrestle the gun from her wrinkled hand and almost stumbled back away from her. I aimed the gun at her flawless and pretty face. "Hell, yeah. This what I'm talking 'bout! Talk that smack now, huh! I said talk it!"

I was the one in control. I had the gun; I had the power as I aimed the gun at her face. I didn't wanna kill the crazy broad, 'cause obviously she had some deep and serious issues, but I wanted to put a few bullet holes in her already useless kneecaps. Just to show her that she can't go around trying to pop a cap on a woman behind no man. All that talk of forgiveness had been just that—all talk. My eyes dared her to speak! Just one word, and I would show her.

I was a little winded and sweaty from my our tangle, but more irritated about the side of my new sundress being split up to my thigh. Dang, and I loved that dress. I wanted to smack her good upside her prissy head for making me tear the sides of it. "Who's talking mess now, Miss Brooda? Huh? Who's talking? Oughta shoot you in your useless feet just for GP and for the fact that I don't like you."

She looked mildly amused, but nowhere near fearful. "Girl, you can't shoot me. It's not in you, violence. My Jimboy told me that about you. That you're kindhearted and put on a good front of being so rough. No, you wouldn't shoot me."

"Jimboy couldn't have told you a damn thing 'bout me, because I wasn't the one dating the man! How many times I have to tell you, I wasn't the one dating your husband!"

"What difference does it make now?" She powered back over to her food and resumed eating like nothing had happened. "Finish your meal."

My hands were shaking, aiming that gun at her. "What the—?"

Just like that, she was back to being calm and nice. She wasn't thinking about me—wasn't noticing how stupid I was looking, standing there with my hair all mushed up, my new dress all tore up the side and me with that black gun trained on her. Standing there, wondering why that same black gun felt so . . . so extremely light in my grasp. For the first time since having the gun in my hands, I'm noticing this—that the darn thing didn't feel heavy enough to have any bullets in it. I turned it sideways to look at it good, pulled the trigger, and out squirted a strong stream of water. Plain old tap water! "A water gun?"

Brooda was fighting back laughter, amused. "Uh-huh. Had you going for a minute, didn't I? Tell the truth—you know it. You probably need some clean underwear and some toilet paper by now." She threw her head back, laughing.

"You pulled a water gun on me?" I waited for her reply, but she was taking her time. "That's sick. You are one sick puppy. You know that, don't you?"

"Oh lighten up," she said, grinning and taking up a piece of bread. "I do it to all my newfound friends. A good way to find out where folks are in their heads. Most folks will tell you anything if they think they're about to die."

My mouth sagged open; I couldn't stop glowering at her. What kind of sick in the head woman played head games like that? "I know what you mean. And some folks will do the same if they think they 'bout to get the crap beat outta of 'em, too."

She grunted and continued eating. I tossed the gun to the floor and grunted, but eating was the last thing on my mind. Poetta might have felt some deep-rooted guilt and desire to make amends or retribution with this wacky woman, but I was not the one. She didn't have no beef with me, and I didn't owe Brooda a damn thing.

It was clear that my welcome had been worn out the minute I stepped into her front door and spotted wall-to-wall glass tanks of slithery snakes. Ewwww. I hate snakes. I probably could have warmed up to the idea of trying a tiny piece of snake meat if I had been told about it on the drive up, or before we sat down to dinner, but having a gun pulled on me, real or fake, was the snot on the cake. I chose to step.

"Later for this mess. I'm outta here!"

Twenty-four

I couldn't calm myself down. Not when I had just lived through a scene from *Tales from the Crypt*. My heart was beating so fast, it seemed like any second it would break away from its fleshy tether and push clean through my chest wall. And thanks to that jolt of excitement from Brooda, a storm of a migraine was brewing somewhere off in the horizon of my head.

"Don't leave. Not just yet." Brooda tried one of her winning smiles, but it didn't look right on her flawless face.

"Like hell I will." I hurried into the bedroom to collect my few belongings, stuffing items in my tote bag fast as I could. I could hear the whining drone of that darn motorized chair moving Brooda's wrinkled behind about, but I couldn't stop. I was on a mission and couldn't get out of her house fast enough. And what the heck was taking Poetta so long to get back from the freaking store? And my car keys, where were my keys? For all the time it was taking, Poetta must have went straight to the brewery plant herself for a six-pack of beer. Too bad! I was leaving even if I had to leave without her.

"Where the hell are my keys?" I snatched the covers from the twin-size bed I'd napped in earlier. I looked on the dresser top. Nothing. I checked the floor around the bed. Nothing. In the trash can, I spotted the pillow I'd had earlier. *Hmph.* Crazy woman, that Brooda must think my honey pot is contaminated to be throwing the whole pillow away just because I had one little ole' love session with it. Yeah, right, like she never had a passionate dream and woke up humping a pillow before.

I dug into the bottom of my tote bag and retrieved my car keys. Finally, I looked back down at that honey-pot-scented pillow folded and stuffed in the plastic trash container. Just to be spiteful, I pulled it out and carried it, wedged under my arm.

"Hope I get some armpit juice on it, too."

On my way out, the plan was to slap that Brooda chick upside her confused head with it. My sandals clicking fast on the tiled floor, I hurried from the room, hoping to part with my usual departure speech: "Had a good time. Let's do this again sometime, but I have to go now." Have my say and rush from the house with a pillow slap to Brooda's head on my way out the door, but as luck would have it, Brooda Mae had a few plans of her own.

There she was, blocking the door—blocking the way of my freedom like some outdated slave master in control of my destiny. She was sitting in that motor chair of hers with a large pair of scissors and a roll of duct tape in her lap.

She looked up and smiled at me—rather pleasantly, I might add. "Going somewhere, my dear?"

"Look, Brooda, I don't wanna have to hurt you, so move out of my way."

She looked like she thought I was playing with her behind. I knew she was a cup of crazy, but it was looking more and more like her cup was running over.

"Oh, don't mind me, Miss Queenie. Just putting some duct tape on some of these tanks here. Smaller snakes aren't so bad, but my larger ones, my body squeezers like my boa constrictors, they so big and strong, they can push a top up and come out when they want."

A lump rose in my throat that I kept trying to swallow. The woman was off her rocker.

"These here two larger tanks on the side." She gestured with a tilt of her head. "These are my favorites. Squeeze and Vise. That's their names. Haven't fed 'em for a cup of days, so they should be plenty hungry about now. Probably hungry enough to swallow a cow 'bout your size." She was half smiling, half smirking. I couldn't tell which was worse.

What the hell. Why was she telling me this? Did it look like I cared about her snakes? "Move away from the door, please. I just want to leave." I sucked up air, trying to help my thoughts come clearer—keep me calm.

Brooda mocked a yawn and casually announced, "But I'm not ready for you to leave right now, Miss Queenie. What's the big hurry? You just got here, and I have plans for us. We have things to talk about. Lots of things, and I want to know everything. I want to know what he did to you in bed, how he did it, and what it felt like. Did you like the things he was doing to you? Spare no small details."

I'm blowing hot air now. "Woman, how many times I have to tell your dizzy behind, I did not have an affair with your sorry husband. Okay? Matter-of-fact, I couldn't stand your husband! He wasn't all that good-looking. He talked stupid most of the time, and he smelled funny the rest. Smelled like a hundred pounds of unwashed chickens, if you asked me. So there! Now you know." I'd hit a nerve—I could tell by the way Brooda took up those large scissors and held them poised in the air.

"You lying witch!"

"Look, Mooda or Brooda—whatever the heck your name is—I'm leaving either way, so get the hell outta my way, or else."

"Or else what?" she sneered back, bold as she wanted to be. Her wild eyes, narrowed to slits, dared me. Dared me! Queenie!

"Oh, no—you didn't." Like a brave soldier, I marched straight over to her, intent on taking those darn scissors from her wrinkled hands and maybe even flipping her over and stabbing her in her butt a few times for threatening me. I was sick of her mess! Sick of her lame accusations. Sick of her subtle threats of doing me some bodily harm like she had two good legs to stand on and I didn't. It was obvious she was looking for some hostile excitement, and I felt it was my duty to break her off a little somethin'-somethin' to remember me by. "You want some of me?" I screamed at her.

No sooner I was up on her, she growled, hauled back, and took a serious swipe at me with those darn scissors. She swiped, and I weaved and bopped her upside her cute head and grabbed her hand with the scissors in it. The honey-pot-scented pillow fell away as I manhandled her, ultimately grabbing her arm and pulling her from her power chair and dragging her behind along the tiled floor.

All I wanted was to remove her and that chair away from the door so I could leave, but that fool of a woman grabbed my leg and tripped me down to the floor with her, had me down along the floor struggling and wrestling with her like we were two participants in center ring at the *WWF Smack Down*.

This cannot be happening to me. This cannot. I managed to get the scissors away from her before somebody got hurt, and scrambled up, trying to make my way to the door, panting, out of breath, but Brooda caught my leg again and latched on. Dropping the scissors along the floor, she snatched them up, growling like a pit bull.

"Let go! Let go of me!" I tried prying her hands away from my leg, but she clamped on tight like a pit bull. And strong!

"You are not leaving yet, and if I scream, my two biggest snakes will rise from their tanks and come!"

"Only in your dreams!" I screamed down at her. I pulled my leg away from her clutch, kicked the scissors from her hand, and hurried to the door. The same door that she'd dead-bolted and the key was missing from. "Dang it!"

I sighed, turning back around to face her. "Brooda, stop this madness. I wanna go home, and I wanna go now. So stop playing around, and give me the key." I balled my fist up at my sides. So help me, God, I'd never in my life thought about beating a handicapped person, but the woman was walking on thin ice. Brooda was about to get her first real beat down. "You wretched woman, if you don't give me that key, I'ma beat you like you stole something." Everybody that had a strong woman for a mama knew that was the worst kind of beating one could receive. I was hoping that Brooda knew it, too. I still remember my mama beating my ten-year-old butt for stealing fifty dollars of her rent money from her purse. Have the darkened welts still on my upper thigh to prove it.

"Imagine being swallowed whole by a snake, you Queen woman. Imagine what it would feel like when I scream and they slither out their cage, looking for you."

"You crazy, you know that?"

"And you're a whore. I just can't stand women like you. You husband stealer!"

"If you still think I wanted a man like the one you had, yeah, you crazier than I thought."

"No worry," she said calmly, as if she were talking to a small child, trying to soothe. "A snake can swallow its prey whole."

Obviously Brooda wasn't one easily intimidated. I wasn't trying to hear her crazy claim, but when I looked around at those snake tanks, I could see two large reptiles, slick and slimy-looking, slithering along the glass, rising up along each container. Dang. Brooda had put duct tape on the lids of the other tanks, all except those two. I looked back at Brooda along the floor trying to sit up, right herself. "Give me the door key!" And what did she do? She screamed—screamed to the top of her voice like somebody was killing her. "Stop that noise! Shut up!"

She screamed louder.

More panic jumped into me as I scanned around for something to help shut her up. The thought of snakes coming out their tanks at her distress call was working overtime on my nerves—prompting me to seek action. Problem; now the solution. That's my motto.

Frantically, I looked around the room for something, anything. A silver plated lamp. No, too large for her mouth, but a good whack over the head wouldn't be a bad idea. No. Crazy woman or not, I wasn't about get a murder rap. The scissors on the floor. No. I couldn't stand the sight of blood, and besides, I wasn't trying to kill the foolish woman, just shut her up. Tape. *That might work*, I thought. *The roll of duct tape along the floor!* Pissed, I went over, picked it up, and went back over to Brooda, who still had a lot of energy for a good struggle. *Dang. What the hell is she eating to be so strong?* I got over her and prepared to handle my business, with her screaming and trying to fight me. Her arms never stopped flailing like wild octopus limbs. A scratch to my arm, scratches on my legs. It looked to me like her hands needed to be tied up before I could shut her up. I tore off one piece of tape—

one piece large enough to get the job done. Grabbing up her hands, I secured them with the tape behind her back. I wanted to bind her legs, but what was the point in that if they didn't work nohow? Snatching up the tape ring, I was hoping to pull off a good piece for her mouth, but that was it. The tape was all gone.

"You'll pay for this!" She was hollering and screaming and almost foaming at the mouth. For a minute I almost felt sorry for her and thought about untaping her hands, but I knew that if I did, ultimately, she would only fight me harder. It was more than obvious that she had serious issues that had nothing to do with me.

"Damn! Now what?"

"Heellllpppppppp!"

I quick checked the snake tanks and true to her words, those two snakes had their slithering heads up above the glass containers at the same time, looking around, thin pink tongues darting in and out—making the fine hairs on my back rise up. I thought I would faint.

"Ohmygawd, no. Ohmygawd!"

Brooda was still screaming for help, and I was thinking that I should be screaming the same thing. Snakes in one room, dead folks' ashes in the other. "Oh, Lord, why? Why me?"

She screamed louder.

"Shut up! Just shut up!" My hands at my ears, I tried to drown her out, but I could still hear her, and the snakes were coming out their tanks. They were rising up—coming for me!

Brooda kept screaming, and the more she screamed, the more those two snakes, large and hideous looking, seemed antsy to get out. They were coming out, slowly but surely. I had to stop her, stop her noise, stop her voice some kind of way. No more tape. Panic surging, I looked around, searching, looking and silently praying for something that would help end the madness. Nothing around me but tanks of snakes, and potted trees and plants. *My dress. Of course!* That would work.

I started with the torn side, and tore a strip going farther up, just enough to put around her mouth. One strip didn't seem long enough, so I tore two foot-long strips and tied them together.

"This will not be the last first and last time for us," she screamed.

"I will find you in California, wherever you are, I will find you! I won't rest until I find you! You can bet on it, Queenie. You one dead woman when I come for you!"

"So you want snakes to eat me, huh? You crazy old hag. I'll shut your pie trap!" The torn strips would be good for a tie around her mouth, but I still need something. Something to place in her mouth to keep her dizzy behind from trying to bite me. I looked around and spotted the pillow—that same honey-pot-scented pillow that she had tossed in the trash like it contaminated and unsafe to be slept on anymore because it had once been between my thighs. Perfect.

I went over to her screaming behind with her gnarling and growling like some wild beast and spitting at me. *The heifer spit on me!* I placed the pillow over her face. But I didn't want to kill her psycho butt, just shut her up.

Her mouth was wide open, screaming to the top of her voice, screaming like the end of the world had come, and she wouldn't shut up! The pillow was too big, too cumbersome. Just too much. I had to do something! I had to! I tried to think, and it popped in my head like it had been there all along. I stood back up and hiked my dress and tore off another strip. For a brief moment I entertained the thought of taking my whole dress off and stuffing it into her mouth. But no. I couldn't see myself standing around buck naked in a house of snakes. I had to do something quick.

"Girl, I'm really sorry about this, but you leave me no choice. All you had to do was shut the heck up, but no. You just won't shut the hell up." I could see the panic in her eyes when she realized what I was about to do. Her eyes were the biggest I'd seen them since being in her house. She tried to protest, tried to scream, which was just what I needed her to do, open her mouth wider. I grabbed her face, then stopped. No. I couldn't. I'd paid a nice price for that dress, and I wasn't about to share another thread of it with her. Standing up, I sprinted to the kitchen and found a roll of paper towels. Never mind wetting it first. Her saliva would do the trick. I pried her mouth open and stuffed a few balled-up paper towels into it, risking being bitten, then tied the strip of torn dress around it. *There!* I stood up, looking back down at her. Silence, at last.

"Sorry, but a woman's gotta do what a woman's gotta do. You lucky, though I could have been wearing my old gym socks, and it could have been worse." I studied her for a few seconds. She looked so normal, too. Like she had plenty of sense. "Goes to show you that you can't judge a book by its cover, can you? Did you say something, 'cause I can't hear you?"

Brooda's eyes screamed bloody murder.

The knot tight and secured around her face. "Much better," I said, my head pounding like there was a ground-breaking ceremony going on inside. Still no door key to be found. I sighed my relief, looked around, and got my tote bag and was headed for the window to see which one I could pry open and climb out of when I heard the sound of a key turning in the lock. I went stiff, listening for the tumbler to click, and to my head-pounding surprise, in walked Poetta, calm and happy as a lark.

Twenty-five

"I can't believe she chose to stay! Unbelievable." I ran those same words through my mind a dozen times or more as I drove like a bat out of hell along Interstate 10, heading back to reality—heading back to California. I don't know why it hurt my feelings that Poetta stayed behind in Arizona with that crazy woman claiming that I was the one who was crazy for tying a helpless, innocent person up like that, but it did.

"Innocent, my foot! Screw the both of you!" I banged my fist on the steering wheel of my car. "Burn in hell, for all I care. You and your new friend Brooda."

I had to be doing close to eighty-five on the highway, keeping my eyes in the rearview and looking out for flashing lights. *Hell*, I thought. *I wish a cop would try and stop me.* I didn't have a gun to shoot nobody, but the way I was feeling, if a cop was to pull me over, he had good confrontation coming. Surely, this was how most police pursuits got started—innocent folks, victims of their own circumstances and upset about something, and some trigger-happy cop comes along to mess with them. Wouldn't take much for me to make the six o'clock news with a dozen patrol cars chasing behind me, the way I was feeling.

That was for sure. All I wanted was to be back on my own stomping grounds, where things made better sense, people who didn't like you made it plain to see on their frowning faces. No Dr. Jeckyll and Mr. Hyde stuff. Back to things I understood and people who acted halfway civilized.

My head was still pounding in spite of the fact that I had popped not two, but three extra-strength Excedrin. My head just wouldn't stop hurting, and a heaviness in my chest was beginning to concern me. My eyes felt a little tired and gritty, and I still couldn't believe that Poetta had chose to stay with that—that horrible woman who had accused me of the unthinkable: of being with her man. Me! Even had the nerve to threaten me behind it. Like Jimboy's cheating behind was worth killing somebody over. A real life is what she needs.

It had to be close to eight at night when I hit the highway going home. Seemed like the night sent more darkness in to keep me company on my long drive back to California. I could have found a hotel room, but I didn't want one. I wanted my own place. Thoughts of Poetta kept trying to invade my mind, but I did my best to block them. I didn't know what to make of her strange behavior, but one thing I did know for sure, something had happened to change our friendship, Poe and I. Whether it was changed for the good or the bad, I still wasn't sure. My eyes, already red from not enough sleep, tried to mist up. My best friend had really treated me wrong back at that house in Arizona, but I wasn't about to shed no tears over it. Another harsh lesson in life. Even your best friend can throw you a curve ball. She had caught me off guard. I hadn't expected such treatment from Poe, and it hurt deep.

Poetta had stayed to help Brooda. "Poor Brooda" this, and "poor Brooda" that. The look on Poetta's face the moment she had stepped into that house and raked her eyes over the scene before her, Brooda gagged, duct-taped, and lying along the floor, wiggling her head—eyes red and large as tennis balls, and me standing there with my tore-up-the-side sundress and tote bag in my hand. I had looked a mess, and Brooda had to look even worse. At most, I was hoping for some sign of sympathy from Poetta for all that I had been through while she was gone. Just to hear her voice, my best friend in the whole world saying something like, "Oh, no, Queenie, what happened? You poor thing. Are you okay, Queenie? Are you allright?"

But no. Hell no! Those words never found their way to Poetta's lips. Instead, the minute she stepped back into Brooda's house, using a door key, I might add, I saw the look on her face. Like she had just entered a crime scene and she was the judge and the jury, and I was, undoubtedly, the perpetrator and already found guilty.

"Poe, dang! What the heck took you so long?" I screamed at her. I was so aggravated by then that I didn't think much about her using the door key to let her own self back in. She had had the key all along. *What the heck—?*

"Queenie—oh, no. No, Queenie, what have you done?"

"What have I done?" I'm sure I rolled my eyes to heaven.

Next thing I knew, Poetta was all but throwing her bag of goodies aside and going to Brooda's side to help her. "Oh, my goodness, Queenie. What's wrong with you? How could you do this? Queenie, you should be ashamed of yourself. Look at this!"

I *was* looking.

Oh, I was ashamed all right—ashamed that there was no more duct tape for me to tie her bony behind up beside Brooda. I was speechless. Even if I did have something to say, didn't look like Poetta would have believed me. Suddenly so sensitive, she had tears in her eyes, but they weren't tears for me.

"Queenie, how can you be so cruel? I leave for a few minutes—"

"A few minutes, Poe? A few minutes! You've been gone for hours to me. Just for some stupid beer! I thought you can't drink beer until Jimboy gives you permission because he don't like you drinking during the day? I wouldn't even be here in this mess in the first place if it hadn't been for you messing with somebody's husband and needing to drive down and see his wife! This is all for you, Poetta! You! Since when is beer so important to you?! You don't know what I've been through while you were out looking for beer!"

"I went to the corner store and got to talking with the cashier. Big deal! So I took longer than I said I would, but that's no excuse to torture a crippled woman while I'm gone!"

"She's lucky I didn't twist her head off! She tried to—to hurt me. She called for her snakes—and they—they." I gestured and looked around at the glass tanks and those snakes, both, were lying peacefully at the bottom of their tanks like they were asleep. "Oh, that's just great!" A fine time for that.

"Queenie, I don't wanna hear it," Poetta had said, pulling off the dress strips and the stuffed paper from Brooda's mouth. "And what the heck is this for?" She held the wad of saliva-drenched paper towels up. "Oh, no . . . No, Queenie, you didn't. How could you?"

"Easy." I scratched my head. "And she's lucky. She almost got the panty version!"

Brooda started crying like somebody's spoiled child that hadn't gotten what she wanted for Christmas, and Poetta was eating her act up.

"Don't worry, Brooda. I'm here now. You're in safe hands." She drug the poor, mistreated woman over to her chair and hefted her up into it. "There. I hope that's better."

Brooda sniffled. "Thank you, sweetie. You are so kind."

"Poe, this woman is not who you think she is—she tried to—"

"Queenie, I am not trying to hear what you have to say that could possibly justify you doing something this awful. There's no excuse."

"But if you'd just listen to me—"

"I said I don't wanna hear it, Queenie. Maybe you should just leave."

"What?"

"You heard me; I did not stutter. I think you should leave us alone. This was supposed to be a time of spiritual healing, and you are not helping matters." Poetta threw her head up in the air. "We want you to leave."

"But I can't just leave you here, Poe. This woman is crazy. And besides"—I had tried to reason, more to myself than anyone—"we girls—we homies to the end. We friends, and I can't just drive off and leave you."

"We friends?" Poetta stood up and walked up on me like she was about to either slap or body-slam me, but she wasn't no fool—well, maybe sometimes, but not at that moment. "Right now we aren't friends 'cause I don't have friends that go around doing bad things to helpless and handicapped people like this, Queenie." She threw the balled-up paper towels at me, hitting me in my heavy chest. "I have been knowing you for too many years, and you never change. But one day you will, Queenie. And when you do, you'll realize that you just can't go around in life bullying and beating people up who don't do or act the way you want them to. Just because you're bigger and stronger, you just can't keep doing it. You can't beat up the world."

"I don't need to beat up the world," I had thrown back at her. "Just that crazy-ass woman sitting in her chair crying for trying to hurt me first. A fake stone at your feet, that's all she is, Poe. So stop tripping about her and get your stuff and let's go home." I had rambled in my tote bag for my car keys. "Let's get this show on the road."

And there we stood. The best of friends at odds over the weird. Then she was screaming at me. Talking about, "Queenie, you're hopeless! Just leave!"

"But Poetta—"

"Just leave! Now!"

"But what about you? How will you get back home?"

"Don't worry, I can take care of Poetta. You better believe I can."

Didn't even give me time to fully explain my side of what had happened and why Brooda had to lie along the floor with duct tape on her wrist and paper stuffed in her big mouth. Poe just assumed that the whole thing was all my fault. My eyes misted up at her distrust. Sweet, innocent Brooda couldn't do no harm. Oh, no. I started to beg her to leave with me, to get her stuff and let's go, but she just kept looking at me like I had two heads and she had only one. "You really want me to leave?"

"Yes, I do, Queenie. Brooda and I want you to leave."

Disbelief kept me staring at her.

"Fine with me!" I had screamed back at her, straightened my back, and all but ran out that house and to my car. I wanted her to see that I was mad, and I was, but on the inside, where she couldn't see, I didn't want her to see that I was hurting. Seemed to me that friendship should have came first, regardless.

But I'm driving home now.

"Screw the both of you," I said again, my eyes trained on the long road ahead. "If I never see you again in life, Poetta, it will be too soon for me." And I meant it, too. At least I thought I did.

I pushed thoughts of Poetta from my head again, but thoughts of her kept threatening to come back. The more I thought, the faster I drove. Thank God for small miracles because it was truly a miracle that I didn't get stopped and pulled over for driving like a bat out of hell. The trip to Arizona had taken almost ten hours, allowing for a few stops along the way to rest, but I was back in Cerritos in seven hours and twenty minutes, stopping for gas and refreshments.

At last, I fumbled with the key in the door of my condo, squirming from having to pee so bad. In my own place at last, I sprinted to the downstairs rest room to do my business, washed my hands, and threw some water in my face. Afterwards, I took the time to stand on my scale. Twenty-nine pounds lighter! Excitement tried to jump up in me, but with so much fatigue taking up space in my body, all I could do was smile. I couldn't believe that I had actually shed twenty-nine pounds!

After washing my face and admiring my reflection in the mirror, I headed for the kitchen for a snake. . . . I mean, a snack. *Lord have mercy*. Thinking about snakes was the last thing I wanted to do. Now that I didn't have that pesky Poe around, I didn't have to worry about fixing a full-fledge meal for two people. Just me now. Twenty-nine pounds lighter. Wow. "Girl, you are the bomb!" I got a beat going in my head: "Go, Queenie, go Queenie, it's your slim day, it's your pay day. Go Queenie." Dancing about the kitchen, I was feeling kinda proud of myself. Twenty-nine pounds lighter was enough for a celebration, and what came to mind was a Hawkins Burger. Hawkins House of Burgers, one of the best hamburgers in all of Los Angeles County. A tiny, unassuming little hamburger stand on Slater and Imperial Highway. A building so small that if you sneezed while driving down Imperial Highway, you'd miss the place. It was nowhere near fancy, the Hawkins burger house, but friendly, family-ran, and clean. I could taste one of their double cheeseburgers in my mouth. But that would mean getting back in my car, hitting Highway 105 to get off at Central Avenue to get to Imperial Highway to get to the Hawkins House of Burgers place. *Nah. Too tired for more driving.* Instead, I settled for a small banana and a tall glass of orange juice while I listened to the messages on my answering machine.

Queenie, just relax yourself. You are at home now. No more crazy.

When the answering machine announced that I had fifteen messages, I thought about Poetta. She'd finally come to her senses and realized that she was wrong for dissing me that way for Brooda. Had to be Poe calling that many times, and she was probably ready to apologize and beg my forgiveness, beg me to hop back in my car and drive another nine hours back to Sierra Vista, Arizona, to fetch her from Brooda's house and bring her back home.

Nah. I don't think so. That's what they have Greyhound buses for. No more driving for me. Not tonight as tired as I am. It would take me at least two weeks before I would even remotely consider driving back to Arizona to get that girl. Serves her right, too. But it wasn't Poetta who had called. Not even one of the fifteen messages.

One call from my boss, Jay, calling to see about me. That was interesting. He wanted me to come in earlier on Monday to work on a special project. Great. Another call from Poetta's dizzy sister, Marva, with her foul-mouth self. She was probably calling to talk to Poe about some new man she was dating behind her husband's back, but the moment Marva's voice came on the line, she was saying something like, "Greetings to my two favorite heifers," I erased the rest of her message immediately. I was not in the mood for her.

Two messages from my mother, just calling to see how her oldest and favorite daughter was doing and to remind me that I still haven't been to her new church on Sunday. Every since my sister, Kellie, married and moved away to Detroit, Michigan, my mama started calling me on a weekly basis just to chitchat and throw guilt-dust in my face to make me feel bad for not coming to her church. If it's not church she's ailing about, it's the claim of me not coming to visit her enough, and that I must not love her anymore. Never mind that I call her almost every other day from work and send flowers to her once a month, and drop in to see her at least every other week. I mean dang, Mama, a sistah do have a life of her own to pursue. Cut the strings, Mama, just cut the strings.

I make a mental note to go see my mama after work on Monday. No matter how tired I might be, I'll go sit with her awhile and catch her up on what's going on in my life and what's not. "I love you too, Mama." I say to the answering machine as it proceeds to the next recorded message. Then Zeke's voice comes on—full of deep bass, and I swear, tired as I am, my whole body comes to attention, perks up. With all the craziness that was going on with Poetta and her new witchy friend, Brooda, I had pushed thoughts of Zeke to the back burner. I want to hate him for what happened the last time I was at his place. He could have told me about his exotic roommate—could have told me. But trying to hate Zeke would be like hating my own intentions. He was the challenge, the top of the highest moutain that still had to be climbed. Still, I was upset. He could have at least warned me about Sweet Willie, but still, hearing his silvery, sexy voice asking about me made my blood heat up. His voice said, "What's up, stranger? Thought we were budding buddies? Hope you're not still tripping over that little scene with Willie. I know, I know. I should have explained about him at the start, but I didn't want to scare you away like a few other females. I mean, it's not the kind of thing a brother just spill out too soon. But now, I'm glad you know. Just calling to say sorry. Maybe I can come to your place and check you out. Let's not let Sweet get in the way of a potentially good friendship. Call me."

I smiled from ear to ear. *A potentially good friendship, huh?* Maybe I was being too hard on the man, and then again, maybe I wasn't being hard enough. Whatever the case was, he wasn't about to skip through the Sweet Willie incident with just one apology. I pressed erase. "I don't think so."

I waited for the next message, surprised to hear Zeke's voice again, but this time a hint of trouble could be heard just beneath his sexy flow. The voice said, "Queenie? You didn't call me back. You must still be illing over that little scene at the house with Sweet Willie. I just want to say that I need to see you 'about something. Call me."

Dang. What the heck is his problem? I wondered, but kept listening to my messages. The beep signaled the end of one message and the beginning of another. Zeke's voice again. The tone of his voice, a quiet desperation.

"Queenie. How many times do a brother have to apologize? Look, I'm sorry about the Sweet Willie incident, okay? I'm sorry. All I want is a chance to make it up to you. My ankle is much better. Thanks to you, and just so you know, you make a mean pot of beef stew. But anyway, I know we can be a team, and I do care about you. So what do you say? Can you give our friendship another try? If you can't come to the house, at least call and give me your address. Check you later."

"Goodness, that man is so hot for me and trying to play it off. I just know it."

I listened to the rest of my messages: my sister, Kellie, calling from Detroit; my mama calling back to see why I hadn't called her or been over to her house; Poe's sister, Marva, asking where we two "heifers" were. Even that fool that invited me to lunch and expected me to pay for it called, Marcus T.—he had the nerve to call my house again talking about another date. "This time, I have plenty of money, so give me a jingle."

"And you hold your breath until I do." Not my fault Queenie so popular. I couldn't recall the last time so many folks had thought about me in such a short space of time. But still, none of those messages had moved me like Zeke's. Sweet Willie or no Sweet Willie, Zeke was unfinished business that had to be dealt with. Easing down on my leather sofa, I kicked off my sandals to massage my feet. Tired as I was, I wanted to see him, too, but on my turf, for a change. Not at the place where Sweet Willie would be. I called his house, and he picked up on the third ring. "Zeke, hey. It's me, Queenie."

He sounded genuinely happy to hear my voice. "Hey, stranger. For a while I thought you left town for good."

"Nah. Had some business to take care of outta town. Just got back in, but I'm glad you called to check on me."

"Look, Queenie, I know it's late, but I really need to talk to you. Would you like to meet someplace for coffee?"

"Coffee? This late? I doubt it. Not after driving for over sixteen hours."

"Would it be okay if I come to your place, then? I could bring some Chinese food. I know a great place over on Slauson and Overhill. I really feel bad about you having to meet Sweet the way you did. At least let me make it up to you. You feel like some Chinese food?"

There's a long pause between us. I want to be mad at him. I really do. But the feeling is slippery. "Not too much Chinese food. I'll make us some tea and fruit salad." I yawned.

"I really need to talk to you, but if you're too tired, it can wait until tomorrow morning."

"Zeke, I'm not that tired. You have a pen and paper?"

After I rattled off my address, complete with instructions on how to get to my place, I hung up, feeling suddenly energized. Pleased, I pulled myself up from the sofa to make preparations. Time for the queen to be with her king.

Twenty-six

Returned from the walking dead. That's what I was. At least that's what I felt like. I should have been thinking about taking off all my clothes and collapsing onto my queen-size bed and sleeping for two weeks straight the minute my key unlocked the door to my place. Home at last, but the man of your dreams don't come along every day, and all I could think about was Zeke coming over to check me out, and how he had been missing me as much as I'd been missing him. There was light-headedness every time I stood up too soon, and the echo of my heart beating, beating like an out-of-control drumbeat. But even that didn't stop me.

Hurrying into my rest room, I took three more extra-strength Excedrin, hopped in the shower, and lathered up with my banana-mango body wash from Body Works. The twenty-nine pounds I'd lost didn't look too bad on me as I dried myself off in front of my bathroom mirror, grinning and playing peekaboo in the mirror with my towel. Pride surged in my head. For once I was doing something positive to help myself to get to a place where I truly wanted to be. I could hardly wait to do show-and-tell with Zeke. After that horror movie scene with Poetta's newfound friend, Brooda, some TLC from a man was the cure for all my ailments.

After lighting a few scented candles, I found a pastel pink sundress with wide-banded straps and slipped my slightly swollen feet into some pink slides. I handled my hair until it looked good, half French rolled in the back, ringlet curls in the front. Residue of fatigue kept trying to surface, but it wasn't enough to stop me from having Zeke over. I wanted to look and smell good even if I didn't feel it.

In the kitchen, I sliced up honeydew melon and chunks of sweet cantaloupe. Even though Zeke said he would stop for some Chinese food, I couldn't resist the urge to set out some of my "homemade" dishes. Nothing says you care like cooked meals from scratch. I took out some frozen soul food, well-seasoned collard greens, barbecue chicken, black-eyed peas, and thought about making some corn bread. *Good thing I always cook in mass quantities in case of emergencies*, I mused. Zeke probably wouldn't eat nothing but the chicken, the melon, and some greens, but I wanted to have a full-course meal on hand, just in case. After heating the food, I spread a fancy tablecloth on one of my patio tables and set the covered food out in my rarely used china serving dishes. Napkins. "Let me see, what else?" Iced apple juice. My nice glasses and my best silverware. I stopped and took it all in. Perfect.

Back on the inside, I ran around like a crazy person, making sure my condo was spotless and neat. It'd been over an hour since I had spoken to Zeke, but from his house to mine wouldn't take no more than half an hour. I thought I heard his car when it drove up, sending me to the window to peek out to see him coming up the walkway. When the man came to the door and I swung it open, it was like being sucked up into the whoosh of surrealness—like being a character in an animated play. For the moment, Zeke was on center stage, standing at my door dressed casually in dark blue slacks fitting good on a trim body. A dark blue turtleneck made out of some kind of stretchy material showed off his pecs and well-defined arms. Large and strong arms that I couldn't wait to be in.

"Hey, stranger." He was actually beaming at me, like someone had installed a new higher-wattage light in his eyes, turned the light of his smile up a few notches. "About time you got back to me. It's been odd not hearing from you. What took you so long to return my calls?"

"Been outta town with my roommate." I didn't dare mention the crazy business that had sent me to Arizona to begin with. I was still standing with him outside my door when he handed me a chilled bottle of wine and held up a bag containing two cartons.

"This is for you."

"Thanks." I held the door wider and beckoned him in. "Please come in. How's that ankle?"

"Much better. Thank you," he said, stepping inside, waiting for me to close and lock the door. "A whole day of soaking in some Epsom salts and staying off it helped. I'm glad you called me back. It's been crazy at my place since the last time I saw you."

"Oh?" I asked, my interest piqued by his remark. "How about something to eat?"

"Well, it's kinda late for me to be eating, but—sure."

Knowing Zeke, food was probably the last thing on his mind. I knew what was on mine: a good body rub and some deep-sea loving followed by sleep. He followed me across the living room to the closed sliding glass door; I opened it, stepped out with Zeke right behind me. The night summer air felt wonderful, and that hint of jasmine in the air reminded me that my potted plants probably needed some watering.

"I wanted to talk to you about something—" His voice stopped abruptly. "Whoa, what's with all this food laid out? You expecting party guests?"

"Not really." I turned and smiled. "I just like to be prepared. So you wanted to talk to me, you said." *Maybe I should sit down in case he wants to get on his knees and beg my forgiveness about his roommate.*

"Right. We need to talk."

"Oh, really. About what?" *What else could it be? I pondered. About missing me? Or that during my short absence, he'd realized how much I mean to him, or how much he wants me? Needs me.* I pulled out his cartons of Chinese food and sat them along the patio table. Busy hands keeps me focused, keeps me calm.

"It's about Sweet Willie," Zeke said plainly, not rushing to spill whatever it was I was anxious to hear. "Like I said, something odd has happened since I last saw you."

The faint aroma of frankincense and myrrh seeped out from the house as I waited to hear the rest of his account. "Like what?" I swept my gaze around my spacious yard. The fenced enclosure was large enough to accommodate a Jacuzzi, a small lap pool, and a large fish pond if I wanted, but I chose to keep it simple with a few potted palm trees and trailing-vine potted flowers. Perhaps he could tell that only a sensitive woman with good taste would have a yard surrounded in a cape of heavenly Carolina jasmine, pink and white pansies beneath. The night sky was clear and slightly warm with a hint of jasmine in the air. My interest growing anxious. "Go on, Zeke. I'm listening."

"It's a little complicated to explain—" He reached and touched the tip of my nose, his finger as wispy soft as a graze from a butterfly's wing. "—but just the same, you play a big part, at least I have a strong feeling that you do."

Zeke pulled a white patio chair out for me. "Have a seat, Queenie."

"Thanks."

"And you are so welcome." All thoughts of food slip away from us.

Such a gentleman. I should be feeling special, but something don't feel right, but I don't know what it is. I try not to dwell on crazy stirring in his eyes, but think of it as a peaceful stirring. He took a seat across from me, looking uncomfortable.

"This is nice," I hear myself saying, only it don't feel like my lips saying it. I can't get over the change in Zeke, his attentiveness, sweet kindness, not that he'd ever been truly mean to me, but a different kind of niceness. "Us here together, on a beautiful night."

He looked around, admiring my plants. "And a nice place you have here, too. Very nice."

"Thank you. Have something to eat," I offered, lifting a paper towel from the sliced honeydew.

Zeke was back looking happy and serious at the same time. I watched him take a fork and pierce a slice of melon and place it on my plate, then one slice for himself.

Smiling, I ask, "So, tell me, what's going on?"

"I been doing a lot of thinking about you the last couple of days. About us."

"Us?" The man said *us*. I blinked too fast as I quickly picked up my sliced melon and nibbled at the dew. A little sweetness to go along with that *us* part.

He was looking at me hard, like any moment I might break and run. He said, "Queenie, I know I said that we needed to take it nice and slow, you know, before slipping into intimacy, but I'm sure I don't have to tell you that intimacy comes in different forms. It's not just about two people giving in to lust and tearing one another's clothes off. It's more than that. You do know this, right?"

I nod, feeling that feeling you get when someone is about to make you privy to something big, something that they think you might not grasp right away. Picking up my glass of apple juice, I sipped and swallowed hard, trying to lubricate my suddenly too-dry throat. "Of course."

"And you've been doing so good, trying to make yourself more—more healthy, and I like that. I'm very proud of what you've accomplished so far. I know it's not easy for you."

"Twenty-nine pounds." I sounded like a child seeking the smiling approval of a parent. "I've actually lost twenty-nine pounds so far."

"Really? Twenty-nine?" He picked up his melon and took a few juicy bites before tossing it back to his plate.

"That's right, twenty-nine." I felt like standing, pulling up my dress for show and tell of my waistline, but I resisted.

"Let me congratulate you." Zeke kissed the top of my left hand, then the top of my right hand, the warmth of his lips against my skin sending currents of excitement jolting through my system.

He leaned over and kissed my left cheek, going to the right, his lips brushed lightly against mine, making my breath slip away too soon.

"Wow," I moaned as he pulled away. Fluttering in my chest made me pat at the spot above my heart.

"I have something for you."

"You do?" I queried. This was all so new for me, so unexpected. I had known all alone, even from that first day I'd laid eyes on him, that he would be the one. "Is it a surprise? You know how I feel about surprises."

"Something like that."

Zeke reached around his neck, digging down in his neckline, and pulled out his chain. The gold one—the one with the ring around it. His promise ring. My eyes misted up like the sentimental fool I am as I watched him remove the chain from his neck and put it around mine, careful of my hair. Just like in high school, he gave me his promise ring.

"I want you to wear this. For as long as you like. It's a symbol of us. A symbol of our—our relationship in its infancy. Of course, we still have some growing to do, but I feel strongly that we've come to this bridge."

The way he kept gazing off into my apple-red eyes—red from lack of sleep and too much driving—I kept expecting his lips to lock with mine. But it didn't happen. I was cool with that. Good things come to those that wait. Isn't that the old saying?

"C'mon," he said, rising and taking his plate up. "Too many night bugs. Let's go inside."

Ohmygawd. I put my glass of apple juice down and followed him back into the house, where he stopped in the kitchen to dispose of our plates in the sink, then dug into his pants pocket for something.

"And here. This for you, as well, Queenie."

I double-blinked. "Zeke, what is it?"

"A key. Not just any key, but a key to my house. I want you to feel welcome to come and go as you please."

He placed it in my hand like it was something special—like the key to the White House, or to the president's Air Force One. I couldn't think of a thing to say as he took my hand and led me to my sofa. Now I was really beginning to feel strange, a combination of Hallelujah, Praise the Lord, and What the heck is going on? Had he finally woke up and realized that I was the best thing to happen to him since two-ply toilet paper? What had taken him so long to realize how lucky he was to have a woman like me on his side? A strong, proud Nubian princess.

I was sure that we would, eventually, go to *the room*, the big *room*—my bedroom with the huge, king-size bed, but instead, Zeke led me to the sofa, where we sat down side by side. Before I could ask what was up, he angled around to face me, all serious like, and jumped into a long-winded explanation about his monkey being sick or too lonely since I've been gone.

"Now, I know this is hard to believe, Queenie, but please hear me out."

"What?"

"Give me a chance to explain."

"I heard you the first time. You said that something is wrong with Sweet Willie and you don't know what to do." I'm thinking, *Does the word* veterinarian *mean anything to you?*

"It's true. Queenie, I know it sounds crazy . . . but ever since the other day, when you stormed away from my house, he's been in some kind of emotional slump. He won't eat, he don't sleep, he don't play, and he won't talk to me."

"Talk to you?" I heard the *Twilight Zone* music again.

"You know what I mean, he won't do his sign language. I don't know what to do. I've been calling you and calling you, and where the heck have you been?"

"Excuse me?" A jolt of indignation shot me up from my seat. Was he crazy or what? "So, this isn't really about me at all; it's about your monkey?"

"Orangutan. He's not a monkey. A trained orangutan. He's almost human."

"To me, he's a monkey, Zeke!" I looked at that key in my hand. There was more behind him giving me that key than he was saying. "You're telling me that something is wrong with your monkey, and you need me for help?"

He was all in my face, his eyes reading mine. "I've called you for two days! A friend helps a friend, Queenie."

"And like I said before, I was out of town! Not that I owe you an explanation of my whereabouts."

"Queenie, don't be upset with me."

"Upset? What the hell makes you think I'm upset because you want me to help you with yo' damn monkey! I'm flattered, okay?"

"Queenie, look, all I know is Willie was fine the last time you were at my place. He was playful, he signed with me the rest of the night after you left, he talked about you. How pretty you were. How he liked you good. That's how he said it. He liked you good. He took to you like no one else that's been to the house. He's never done that before. And once you stormed away, all mad, he went to his room and sat in it, and that was that. He hasn't been out of his room since— well, maybe to go poop and all—but something is wrong with him. He's depressed, and I think it has something to do with you not coming around again. In fact, I'm almost sure of it."

I hate it when my ears heat up, especially when I'm about to boil over inside. No, he wasn't sitting up at my house bringing gifts of chicken chow mein and spicy egg rolls and talking about his monkey! "Are you for real?"

I couldn't believe what I was hearing. His words were going in my ears and rambling around inside my head, but they weren't making any sense. "Something is wrong with your monkey, and you're seeking advice from me?"

He couldn't have looked more serious. "Isn't it obvious that I need your help? Understand that if something happens to Sweet, that's the end of the money I get for him, and we're talking about a lot of money here. I mean . . . maybe you could come by the house for a while and sit with him. Just for an hour or so. I could pay you some money."

I looked at him like he was crazy. The more I think about his request, I can't stay upset for thinking how absurd it is. "Zeke," I said kindly, shaking my head to keep from laughing, "if you had called me saying you 'bout to choke yo' monkey around, I would have been happy to hop in my car and zoom over and help you. If you catch my drift—you know, slap yo' monkey. But a real monkey? Oh, no. I'm sorry, but you on yo' own with this one. Queenie don't do monkeys." As far as I was concerned, end of discussion. "Maybe you should leave."

"Okay. I hear what you're saying, but at least go over to the house and say hi to 'im. What can it hurt?"

"I will not. Sweet Willie is not the one I want to date."

"Queenie, please. This is serious business, and believe me—" He paused and kissed the top of my hand, gently, lips hot and lingering. "—this is very important to me. And when you help me with the things that are important to me, then I can see my way to the things that are important to you. If you know what I mean."

Meltdown. I feel it strong. I'm that small plane flying too low to clear the mountaintops. I try to pull up, steer myself above it, but can't.

He kissed my hand again. "Will you do this one little thing for me?"

"Ohhhh, hot mercy. I think I like the sound of that." I was tingly. I couldn't deny it, even though I didn't want to feel what he was saying, but to humor him, and only to humor him, I sighed and tried see his side of it. I held his door key up. "And yo' key? What's up with that?"

He cleared his throat and grinned. "I have an all-day job project tomorrow, and if you could just go to my place and check on him, I would be so grateful."

"Zeke, I don't know." I shake my head. It's not what I want to hear. "Tomorrow is Monday, and I don't know. I promised myself that I would spend some time with my mother after work. She misses me, too." Which one to visit first? Mama or Zeke's monkey? Decisions, decisions.

"You could check on him during your lunch time." He kissed the top of my hand. "You could check on Sweet Willie again after you go see about your mother." He kissed higher along my hand. "I'll be home late, but when I come in, maybe we can party some. A private party, you could call it. You do like private parties, don't you?" Another kiss to my hand with his eyes looking up to see my reaction because I could pass out from his hot lips touching skin. "And let me warn you, I do an awesome striptease act."

"You are such a tease." No, I didn't want to go check on Sweet Willie while Zeke had to work on a movie project, but when I really thought about it, he was a package deal—like women who came with children. To deal with Zeke, obviously, I would have to deal with Sweet Willie.

"Say yes, Queenie." He gazed into my eyes as I gazed into his. He needed me to do this one favor. I could see it. "If I go, I won't be staying long.

"Just for a little while to check on him is all I ask."

I thought about it hard. What was I getting myself into? "He better not try no monkey business with me, or I'll step. No kissy-kissy or touching. I'm not the one."

"You'll be amazed at how gentle and well trained he is. Normally I would have my friend Reeba check on him, but she's not speaking to me anymore." He winked at me, then kissed my hand again. "But who needs her?"

"Got that part right." The mention of Reeba, that name sent a hot stabbing through me. "Don't worry about it. I'll check on Sweet for you."

"Thanks, Queenie. You're a real friend." He stood up and straightened his slacks. "Look, I really have to get to bed early to be able to get up early to shoot at five sharp. You know how it is." He started to the front door.

"But what about eating?" Who was I fooling? I needed sleep more than food.

"It's all for you. I can't. Not this late in the night. Maybe tomorrow night at my place. I'm sorry. Hope I didn't inconvenience you."

Don't be silly, the little voice in my head says. *I always set up dinner for two on the patio at night. No problem.* I clutched his door key in my hand. "It's okay. I'm probably too tired to eat right now myself."

We said our good nights at the front door. A quick kiss to my cheek, and he was gone, leaving me to finger that promise ring hanging around my neck.

Twenty-seven

Monday morning, and all is right with the world again. God bless America, and life is good, but despite all the good feelings I was having about the progress with my relationship with Zeke, my heart was still slightly troubled—like someone had covered my entire body with wonderful blessings, but somehow had missed a spot.

I still couldn't get Poetta out of my mind and how she had tricked me into driving her so far away from home just so she could dis me by choosing Brooda over me after all we'd gone through. I loved that girl like a favorite sistah, and she knew she could come to me for anything, even if one day she found out that her own uterus was no good and needed mine to carry a baby or two. I would have her baby—that's how much I loved that girl. Thinking about her had tampered with my flow of well-being the rest of the night after Zeke had left my place. Still no word from her—no call, no card. Nothing.

"Dang. I can't believe my girl didn't even call to see if I made it back home safe or what. That's messed up." For a brief spell, her behavior troubled me. But forget that for now. She can find another surrogate to have her babies, for all I care.

It had felt funny, too, being at the crib all by myself and all, no Poetta telling me what I should be doing, or trying to get in my business or secretly working some hex out of my rest room. But I'm cool with it. I'm dealing and chilling.

In my car, on my way to work I put my Jill Scott CD in and groove to "A Long Walk." Jill had the cords to soothe. I felt well rested, but my head was still hurting. Not a blinding blue kind of headache, but a dull pressure like somebody forgot to let some of the water pressure out. I don't feel like going in to work, but I know that if I dared to call in sick again, there would be hell to pay. Bossman, Jay, was usually a pretty fair and understanding person when it came to needing some time off, as long as you kept afloat with your work, but I knew I couldn't take the chance of not showing up for important meetings. I had two reps coming in to show me some of their fall-winter line, phone calls to make, appointments to keep, not to mention a few folks to call for a good chewing out for late arrivals and back orders still not received. Maybe a good cup of coffee would set me straight. "God, I don't feel like this mess today."

I tried to fill my head up with good thoughts. What it would be like the first time for Zeke and I—buck naked or half naked, which way did I prefer? Zeke's visit to my house last night had only planted more seeds in my garden of longing. But I was glad we're taking our time. My body had been a raging fever sitting next to his, but I'm waiting it out. Being given that key to his house, even if it did mean dealing with Sweet, would make it all worth it when it did happen.

Waiting for love wasn't so bad. At least I had a man that stood up for what he strongly believed in, and not a man that would take up my invitation to jump my bones just because my legs were the open door that suggested, "Come right on in." I was lucky and proud that Zeke was a real man with real morals and life values, like a rare gem in today's society. But now it was time to focus on the thing that fed me, paid my bills, and kept a roof over my head. My job on Monday morning.

"Dang. I don't feel like seeing these idiots today."

I couldn't have held my head up any prouder as I stepped from the elevator onto my floor and headed for my office. Plans of spending a quiet later night dinner with Zeke danced in my head, even though I knew his menu would be a small portion of meat protein, no starches, salad, and steamed vegetables. And afterwards, Zeke had said, the private party would begin. *Oh, yeah. That's what I'm talkin' 'bout—the private party.* Goodness, I could hardly wait.

A look of festive celebration was everywhere I looked. Colorful balloons hugged the ceiling as part of somebody's birthday celebration. Probably Mary Jenkins, three cubicles down from the elevator. I recalled hearing some mention of it coming last week but was too busy with my own life to remember to get the woman a gift. Darn it. Already I knew that there would be cake and ice cream later, delectable sweet stalkers to tease at my diet, but I felt strong and victorious over food. The heck with Mary Jenkins. More good spirits kicked up a notch inside me as I made my way to my office, swinging my briefcase, pep in my stride.

"Hey, Queenie, looking good there," one of the office secretaries called out as I passed her desk.

"Thanks." I radiate. Guess my weight loss of twenty-nine pounds was noticeable. "Just doing what I do, Miss Thang." I put on the biggest grin I could manage, and if any more pride could fit into my head, it would explode, for sure.

"There goes sexy mama," another fellow employee said.

"Looks like somebody's been working out hard," I heard another voice call out.

Even that heifer, red-rooster-headed Claudia Freeman, had a nice comment as I strolled pass her work cubicle. "Queenie, I don't know what you are doing, but you need to keep doing it. You are looking good this morning."

"Thanks for noticing, Claudia," I shot back, and it would have been nice if I had thrown her a bone of a compliment, but I wasn't feeling it. "That red bird nest on your head is looking pretty sporty, too." She laughed, and I did, too, and kept stepping. I kept straight to my office, opened my office door, and stepped in, and *bam!*

My whole damn office smelled like . . . food. Probably from the large and greasy bag sitting atop my desk, sitting on a large white plate with a single rose on it. Sitting right where I would be sure to find them, right beside the bag of food were two separate items: a tall, clear, and golden box of my favorite Italian candy, called Tabui. "Oh, no . . ."

This had to be the work of Raymo. Didn't he know that Tabui was taboo for me ever since last Christmas when he'd given me a box of the heavenly chocolate truffles filled with chopped pieces of hazelnuts and I had eaten the whole box by myself in three hours! After that I was hooked, buying up two boxes a week. It was one of my weakness, and Raymo knew it. Why was he doing this to me?

I walked over and felt the bag. Hmmm. Still warm. I opened it and looked inside. Tamales. Eyes rolling back in my head, I swallowed hard. The scent was almost intoxicating, calling up to me—daring me to eat just one. A warm bag of more fattening temptation. And that was when I lost it.

"Raymo!" I screamed, my voice as loud as the fifty-foot woman destroying the town, looking for her man. "Raymo!" I had warned him!

I didn't sit my briefcase down; I flung it to the floor, snatched up that box of Tabui truffles, and that bag of warm tamales—no doubt homemade. The delicious aroma of warm, shredded beef and steamed *masa* tried to get the best of me as I went looking for Raymo, but I wouldn't let it.

"Raymo!"

I spotted his narrow behind dressed nice, as usual, in a dark brown Hugo Boss suit, expensive gators on his foot, and him reeking of something that would be nice to smell on a man if it were a man that I desired. He was looking pretty good as he stood at the office water cooler, the office water trough, filling his paper cup and talking with another male buyer from the fourth floor.

Bad enough that he kept giving me gifts of food, but it was more than that. Raymo kept trying to keep me fat, keep a wedge between me and the man I was falling in love with. For the first time, I saw it as more than that. It was a cleverly disguised ploy to keep me from getting to my goal with Zeke, and I wasn't about to let him get away with it.

"Raymo!" I screamed, loud enough for the whole building to hear if they wanted. I didn't care. He turned around to face me, his eyes growing big and wide like somebody's child who has realized that his mama has found out the awful thing he has done and come looking for him. I saw panic streak through his eyes. He looked like he might break and run, but was too rooted with embarrassment to move.

"Queenie, my sweetness. How are you this—this beautiful morning?"

"Ray," I said, marching over to him, narrowing my eyes to slits, balling a fist at my side. "I have begged you to leave me alone and stop this ridiculous puppy-dog crush you have on me, but no. The last time, I specifically warned you to stay the hell out of my office, but no. You just won't listen, Will you?" I threw the box of chocolate truffles at him, knowing I had to be out of my mind because I knew for a fact that the box of candy cost every bit of twenty dollars and they were too damn delicious to be throwing away. The box of Tabui hit the left side of his face. Office workers came out from their cubicles to see what all the noise was about, and if they were looking for some early morning drama, I was just the woman to provide it.

"Queenie," Raymo tried reasoning. "It just a few goodies, no big thing."

"Oh, yeah—it's a big thing, all right, Raymo, because I have warned your silly behind to leave me the hell alone, but you persist! But you know what, Raymo? I have a man, a real man! And he's not some short, no-neck fool like you. Look at you! You're too short, silly looking, half bald, and let's not forget a little dick, 'cause all little, short men like you, Raymo, have tiny little dicks! Like this!" I indicated three inches with my two fingers spaced apart. "So, for the last time, stop making a fool of yourself and wasting your time and money and leave me the hell alone!"

He looked stricken. "But—but my Queenie. They are only little gifts of friendship. Nothing to be so upset—"

"I'm not your Queenie, and I don't give a rat's turd what you think. I want it to stop!"

I could hear voices gasp, but didn't care to look to see who was listening and how much they had heard. Raymo didn't move one inch, and I could see the horror in his eyes—horror mixed with tears. In all my twenty-eight years, I'd never seen a grown man about to cry before, but I didn't give a shit! He needed to cry! Maybe it took tears from his eyes for him to see how tired I was of his harassment. And I wasn't through. Another mean volcano bubbled up inside me. "You'd better let this be the last time you come anywhere near me, Raymo, because you can't do a damn thing for me except spit-shine my shoes!" I don't know what made me keep on, like a motor that couldn't be shut off; I was driven as I opened his bag of tamales and reached in and pulled them out one by one, all six.

"So the next time you think about going in my office and leaving flowers, or candy or any kind of fattening gifts, you'd better think long and hard about it, 'cause if you really knew the first thing about me, you little, built-too-low-to-the-ground, fool—" I hauled back and threw a still-warm tamale at him, but he ducked in time. "—you'd know that I am trying not to eat this kind of food anymore!"

I threw two more tamales at him, hitting him in the chest and on his arm. "You might be one sick and twisted chubby-chaser, but you chasing the wrong damn woman! You see this?" I pulled up the chain with Zeke's ring from my neck. "This is from my man! It's a ring, you fool! A ring! I will never be your woman, Ray! Never! So instead of trying to push up on another man's woman, try finding one of your own. One that wants a loser like you, Raymo! Stay away from me! You hear me! Stay the hell away from me!"

That was when he hung his head and walked away, headed for his own office. *Good!* I thought. And just to make sure I got my point across, I threw a tamale at his back, called him a few more names that made the crowd laugh. I didn't feel like I was through yet. I could hear my racing pulse in my ears. My chest felt like it was about to burst, and my head was a hot, throbbing room of hostility—a room of spitting anger. I was sick of him! And then, just like that, while I wasn't watching—wasn't paying attention—somebody turned the light out in my head.

Twenty-eight

Sunlight on my face pry my eyelids open. It takes a while for my eyes to focus clearly, but when they do, I see a vision of my mother. I'd know her soft, rotund shape anywhere. Her short, plump frame wore sixty-five years gracefully, the way it should be, proud and well preserved. Salt-and-pepper hair precisioned cut and tapered in the back. She has on one of her expensive silk jogging suits, the emerald green one that she sometimes wears when she goes to bingo night with her friends. Her big and faithful black leather bag is slung over her shoulders. Her back is turned to me, and it's obvious that she is struggling to open the thick curtains wider at the tall sweep of window. Somebody's bed. I'm lying in somebody's bed.

"Mama?"

When she turns around, silver hooped earrings dangle at each side of her head, and I can't miss the smile that spreads on her face—comforting, reassuring.

"You're awake." She comes closer to where I am, takes the chair next to the bed where I lay. "It's about time you woke up, sleepyhead. You've been out for hours. Had me worried half to death."

"Mama? What are you doing—?" I want to rise and lay my heavy head along her chest to feel her warmth and caring seep from her chest into me. Dry mouth. I feel as if I have slept for days, but my bed does not feel the same. And why would my mother be in my house so early in the morning? It was a question in my head, answered and quickly forgotten with the *beep, beep, beep* that was filling my ear. To the side of me, pushed back closer to the wall, I see the putty-hued monitor, the dark screen with bright green numbers, and that antsy, thin line peaking up and down. "My house? I mean . . . How'd you get in?"

"Sweetie." Mama smiled, the kind that only a mother can make look genuine at the right time. "We're not at your house, Queenie. We're at Kaiser Hospital."

"Kaiser Hospital?"

"Yes, sweetie, Kaiser." She patted my hand gently.

"But—but why? What happened?" I pull myself up some, noticing all the room's equipment. An empty bed was to my left, but I didn't care about that for noticing hanging bags of fluid and wires connected to me. Even one of my fingers was connected to a wire. And that *beep beeping* was enough to make me want to jump up and run out the building, screaming, but I should be happy to hear it, seeing how it was the sound of my own heart. *A hospital? Why? . . . I mean, how?* I had missed something in the passage of time, like what had happened.

"But. . . . how'd I get here?" Even before she could answer it, it was all slipping back to me, slipping like the slow coming of cold honey from its bottom. "Oh, yeah . . . I was at work, and I was mad. I was upset with a coworker . . . this jerk that won't leave me alone."

Mama touched my arm again, patted it. "Yesterday at work you passed out. They called the paramedics, and they brought you here. Good thing my number was on your emergency card. One of your coworkers called me."

"Dang. Am I in bad shape?" A brow raised, I was hoping to hear something about bad air seeping in through the air-conditioning ducts at work, or somebody had released some kind of potent nerve gas that makes humans dizzy and pass out, something like that. Anything. But it wasn't going to be that easy. "Am I okay?"

"For now you are."

Mama took a deep breath and let it out slowly like she was feeling the weight of the world on her shoulders. Wasn't it enough that she had a daughter living so far away from home to worry about, but now this.

"I talked a long time with your doctor, Miss Queenisha Renae."

Serious eyes locked into mine. Bad sign. Calling me by my full name was always a bad sign, and something done whenever she wasn't pleased with her girls—when her girls were falling below her motherly expectations. Like me. Laying up in some hospital bed when I had a feeling that it was all my fault to begin with—something that could have been avoided.

She sighed again. "At first they weren't sure what was wrong with you until they ran a few test and found ephedra in your system. Perhaps you were taking some kind of pills . . . diet pills containing the herb ephedra, which some people have a sensitivity to. Ephedra, so I've been told, has been known to speed up the heart and cause problems with potassium and other vital nutrients in the body. Doctor says you must not have been drinking much water to maintain a balance, because you were dangerously dehydrated."

I couldn't say one word.

"Anyway, not enough rest, not enough food, not enough water, it can put a big strain on the heart. You know heart problems run in our family."

I looked at her like she was finally telling me that I was adopted. "What? Mama, you never told me this before."

She shrugged her shoulders. "Never saw a reason to. News like that only plant seeds of worry in a person. I should know, 'cause after my mother passed from heart failure, I worried if I would be next. Worried about you, worried about your sister, and then I realized that it was God's will either way it went. So I just stopped worrying about it. When you asked about Granny, I just told you that she passed from natural causes because I didn't want you to worry like I did."

"What about you, Mama?" I was almost afraid to ask, but I had to. I had to know. "You saying you have problems with your heart?"

Mama looked hopeful. "Let's just say that if I do, I'm not claiming it. Praise the Lord. The only condition I'm claiming right now is loneliness, and that's nowhere near fatal and most often curable. In fact, I'm working on it as we speak. But let's not change the subject, Queenisha. This isn't about me; it's about you."

I couldn't look in her face, not into those deep brown eyes so much like mine. Those same eyes that always seem to know what I was thinking—reading me like fine print.

"This must be about a man. Am I right?"

I say nothing.

"It must be, because I have known you for twenty-eight years, and I have never known you to be concerned about your weight before. You were always that pleasingly plump little girl coming up and claiming that you were going to be a big and beautiful model one day. The word *diet* never skipped across your lips. So, it must be about a man."

Suddenly, I feel like I'm about ten years old again. Ten and living at home with my mother, and she has found out that I have skipped school to be with my friends. Disbelief, disappointment, maternal concern. It was all there in the creases of her warm brown face. Numb fingers play with the top cover of my bed. "Not just any old man, Mama. A special man."

"Special? Child, please." Surprise jumped in her face. "Special enough to almost die for?"

"I passed out from dehydration, Mama, not from a suicide attempt."

"Queenisha! Make jokes if you like, but you not only passed out, according to your coworker that called me, you stopped breathing for a few minutes. Yeah, that's right, we talking heartstopping here. Lord have mercy, if it hadn't been for someone at your job being brave enough to breathe in your mouth and pump on your chest until the paramedics could get there, you wouldn't even be here now, and I'd be making funeral arrangements."

"Really?"

"Yes, really!"

Someone had saved me. Now that was something to think about. I tried to conjure up in my mind who at my job would think enough to save me. Jay, my boss? As our fearless leader, Jay had an image to keep up and a certain call of duties. Saving one of his employees had to fall up under that "call of duty" and image somewhere. If not Jay, maybe Madeline in section five. Madeline ain't no fool. She knows that every Christmas I always remember to give her a nice gift—a very expensive gift, I might add. I could see her saving my behind just for that special gift at Christmastime.

"Sorry." Mama patted the top of my hand again. "Sweetie, I didn't mean to yell like that. It's just that I'm a little disappointed in you right now. And I've been so worried about you."

Calmness came back to her voice, and I could see it in her eyes, as well. "If a man loves you, Queenie, he loves you unconditional. That means your inside, your outside, big or small, imperfections and all. It has to be unconditional love because these bodies don't last forever. Youth packs up and leaves with time. Eventually, outside beauty slips away."

"Mama, don't you think I know all of this?"

"Do you, Queenie?"

I didn't answer. Couldn't.

"Remember my old friend Benita?" She chuckled lightly, looking like she was about to divulge a delicious secret.

"Yeah. Whatever happened to her?" Benita and my mother had been friends for as long as I could remember. Every Saturday they would get together with a few other female friends and play bid whist out on the patio. Drinking cold beers or ice-cold Kool-Aid, laughing and talking mess and fellowshipping like women do sometimes. This must have went on for years, with each year Benita getting wider and wider in her hips. Once, I heard one of my mama's friends joking around and talking about Benita and saying stuff like, "Girl, yo' behind big enough to sit two lamps and a small clock on." Benita had hooped, hollered, and laughed right along with the rest of the clan. Laughing on the outside, but I could see her face from my stand at the patio door, watching. Being the butt of fat jokes had hurt. There had been a look in her eyes I would never forget. Nothing was funny about that look, but time went on. Benita kept coming by our house to get together with the girls. Finally the woman was just too big to even fit through our front door and had to stop coming around entirely. "What about ol' Benita, Mama?"

"You know ol' Benita is the sweetest person you ever wanna meet. Kind and giving, too. Met this man that blew her mind. Had Benita's nose so wide open that she went on this diet to lose weight so she could be the prize. Women love to be the prize, you know. The one that's special in the relationship. Of course, nowadays things have sure changed. More men loving themselves more than they love a woman. Men love to be the prize, too. Anyway," she sighed, and paused a beat before going on. "Benita lost fifty pounds, and that man was still acting funny. Slip by her house at night, but couldn't be seen with her in the daylight. Benita didn't give up, though. Lost thirty more pounds, and that man started coming around a little more in the daytime, but he still wasn't warming up to hot for her. That crazy woman, Benita, went and had her stomach ringed or stapled or whatever the heck they do, and she is now so thin you can hardly see her standing straight behind a tree sapling."

"Benita?" *Dang. That's pretty thin.*

"Yep. Benita. Wouldn't know her if you saw her."

"Did she get the man?" My rapt attention, I felt like a six-year-old sitting around with a bunch of six-year-olds listening to the teacher at story time.

"Shoot. What she got is sick. The woman can barely hold any food in her reduced stomach now, and have to drink liquid nutrients because her body is too messed up to absorb nutrients from the little food that she can eat. And that man she did all this for—well, hmph— he still didn't want her skinny behind either. Last Benita heard, he'd run off with some young thang and made a baby. And the odd thing is, the young girl he ran off with was larger than Benita."

"Dang, mama. That is crazy." *But that was Benita*, I'm thinking. "It's not even that serious for me. I only wanted to lose a few pounds to fit into some new clothes."

"The point is, Queenie, the man never wanted Benita to begin with. If it hadn't been an issue about weight, it would have been something else: the way she dressed, or the way she chewed her steak, or the way her kneecaps looked in the winter. When a man's not attracted to you, it's never really 'bout what he says it's 'bout. Her weight was a scapegoat."

"I know, Mama, but you just don't understand." I wanted to tell her that it wasn't that way with Zeke and me. Zeke was different. He was a man who knew what he wanted in life, and knew how to go about getting it. I wanted to tell her that I wasn't trying to change who I was as a person just for him, but because for too long I hadn't faced who I was myself—a beautiful black queen trying to shed her cocoon and metamorph into the slender and beautiful butterfly that I am. I was slimming, but I was doing it for me. I wanted to tell her this, but I couldn't. How could I when I couldn't believe it myself?

"All kinds of men in the world, Queenie. Pick one that loves you for who you are, and learn to love him back. You can't go wrong that way."

"All kinds, but they aren't Zeke." I laid back into my pillow and turned my head. I just wanted to be alone with my thoughts—wanted her to leave but couldn't bring myself to say it.

"Zeke? That's his name? Umph. He must be working some strong mojo magic on you between the sheets for you to be dieting."

"Must be," I lied. Heck. I had gotten more love attention from Sweet Willie than from Zeke, but Mama didn't need to know that.

"Here," she said, handing me a beautiful silvery gift bag from her tote. "I bought you a little something."

My eyes lit up. "Mama, you didn't have to do that." I took the bag and reached down into the delicate, white tissue paper and pulled out a book. Not just any book, but the good book. Mama had bought me a new Bible. "Wow. Another Bible. Thanks, Mama." Every Christmas the same thing. Every birthday, the same thing. Another Bible. Maybe my mama was going senile and didn't know that she had given me over fifteen new Bibles. The Lord would be impressed.

"Now listen to me, Queenie. I know you hate when I sound like I'm preaching, but the truth just have to come out sometimes."

I braced for a sermon. Seemed to me like since my mother had rededicated her life to Christ and her church, she was always on my case about my lack of spiritual guidance in my life.

"I'll make it simple. Stop trying to find Mr. Right yourself, and let the Lord send him to you. You'd be surprised who he might send. Might not be the most handsome man, might not be the tallest man, might not even be the richest man. Shoots. That man might not even be perfect, but he'll be perfect for you. Prayer and belief—that's all it takes."

"I will, Mama." Anything to get her to shut up. I placed the new Bible back in its bag and placed it on the table next to my bed. Even though I believed in prayer, I couldn't remember the last time I had prayed seriously and asked God for anything. Why would God have time for me when I didn't have time for him? "I'ma start reading my new book as soon as I get home."

"Promise.

"Mama, I promise."

"Good." She smiled. "Anyway, your friends will be back up in a little while. She still looks the same, and that sister of hers is a mess, though."

"Friends? What friends?"

"Poetta," she said, eyes widening. "Who else?"

"Poe is here?" This was news.

"Don't be silly. Of course! Here," she said, rising from her bedside chair, "let me peek out in the hallway and see if they came back up. I think they went to get something to eat."

I couldn't believe Poe was back so soon. When I had left her in Arizona, the way she was acting, like I wasn't good enough to be her friend anymore, I had the feeling that she would be sending for her things so she could move in with that Brooda Mae chick and set up housekeeping. Wow, Poe was back.

"Here they come now," Mama announced, then smiled just as Poetta, and heaven forbid, her sister, Marva, came into the room.

"Queenie," Poetta said, looking concerned. "Girl, you okay?"

I smiled wanly, but I was feeling pretty good. "Yeah, right. Like you care so much." She may have been in a forgiving mood, but I wasn't ready to forgive her for her behavior in Arizona.

"Anyway," she said, with a wave of her hand. "You look good. Look like you could go home later today."

"I feel like getting up and going home right now. I can't stand all this laying around. You know me, I have to stay busy doing something."

"Yeah. I know."

Just then, a tall and devilishly handsome sienna-brown brother strolled into the room and handed Poe a pen and pad. Poe jotted down some digits—no doubt hers—and handed the pad and pen back. "Anytime after seven is fine."

"It's all good, then. I'll buzz you around seven-thirty." Smiling, he raked his eyes over Poe and strolled out the room.

"Check my baby sis out." Marva beamed like a proud hen. "Trying to push up on her an intern. A doctor in the making. And a good looking one, too."

Poe gave a sly grin. "Hey, what can I say?"

"Girl, you are something else," I say, surprise by her bold, freelance flirting. "Thought you were so broken up about Jimboy?"

"Jim who? Queenie, that was the old me; this is the new me. Had a lot of time to do some thinking while I waited at the airport. Time for a change, and that sweet, meat brother that just left is just the right thing I need to help me with that change."

"I heard that," I say, looking from one to the other. Poetta and Marva both had some kind of fancy do-rags on their heads that allowed their thin braids to hang down. In Poetta's hands were yellow roses wrapped in clear paper, half a dozen beautiful long stems. "These are for you." She placed them on the table next to my fancy hospital bed. For once she wasn't wearing a dashiki, but had on a denim outfit and white leather sneakers. Finally a different look.

"Well," Mama said, relief in her voice. "I have been here for hours and hours waiting for you to wake up. Now I see that you're okay, I feel like I can leave now. I'll call back later to check on you." She leaned over and kiss my cheek. "Get some rest, sweetie, and I'll talk to you later."

"Bye, Mama."

Poetta hugged Mama. "Nice seeing you again, Mrs. Sutton."

"Same here, sweetie, and you come to church with Queenisha sometimes."

"Yes, ma'am."

Once Mama was out the room, I looked at the two of them. Poetta and Marva. I noticed that Marva was holding a gift bag in her hand.

"You tramp, you. Yo' big behind just had to go and do something to make yo'self sick, didn't you?" She was smiling broadly, like she was glad to see that I was okay.

"I love you, too, Marva." Nothing she could say could ruffle my feathers because I knew her number. She was showing me some love in her own way.

"Well, Miss Heifer, got a little somethin'-somethin' for you." Marva stepped closer to the bed and handed me the colorful bag. "A little hope-you-feel-better present."

"For me? Ahhh, Marva, you shouldn't have." I reached inside between the thin, pink crepe paper and pulled out a sparkling do-rag for my own hair. It was made from some kind of denim material with a nice-size crystal in the middle. Smaller crystals, dazzling in the room's sunlight, dotted around it like bright stars in a galaxy. "Oh, my goodness," I said, holding it up. "I heard about these. It's a China Moon Rag. It's beautiful. This is so nice. Been seeing a lot of celebrities on television wearing 'em, and wanted one, but didn't know where to find it."

"You should have asked me. You know I be knowing where to go, girl. All you had to do was try the web site: chinamoonrag-dot-com. Check this out, the owner, Miss Tichina Arnold, we happen to be good friends, and she hooks me up with bargains on her rags."

"You good friends with the actress Tichina Arnold?" I raised a skeptic brow. "Girl, stop lying."

"Did I stutter?" Marva gave me one of her snotty looks. "Heifer, you need to recognize. Hmph."

"Yeah, right." I turned my attention to Poetta. With her white China Moon Rag on her head, she looks good, like somebody's ghetto princess. "And when did you get back, and how? And I shouldn't even be talking to you after the way you acted in Arizona."

"Queenie," she said, perking up. "I know, but I feel really bad about it. Honest. I don't know what I was thinking, but you were right about that nut, Brooda Mae. That woman was whacked in the head. Girl, after I sat her butt back in her chair and removed all that duct tape you put on her, she tried to attack me with some scissors."

"Girl, no, she didn't!"

"Yes, she did! Hell, I had to punch her lights out myself. I left after that, walked down to the corner store and called a cab to take me to the Tucson airport. Wasn't cheap, either. Missed my flight and got a cheap room for the night. Hopped a cheap shuttle flight back to Los Angeles to find you gone. Your mom called the house this morning and told me you were here."

"But how did you get in?"

"Remember the key you gave me?" She grinned wide. "Guess you forgot to take it back when you left me stranded in Arizona."

"Wouldn't have left your behind in Arizona if you hadn't been tripping behind that dizzy Brooda." I wasn't ready to forgive and forget.

"I'm sorry, okay? I'm sorry. I was wrong. I've been worried about you since your moms called me. I just want things to get back to normal."

"Did Zeke call to see what happened to me?"

Poetta sniffed, looked disappointed. "No, but I called him. Found his number on our caller ID. I called 'im twice."

"You told him I was in the hospital, right?" I search her eyes.

"I spoke to him twice. I told him twice. He said he would come see you . . . if he got a chance."

"Oh. A chance. If he got a chance, huh?"

"Said he had to take care of some important business first."

"Poe, you did tell him what hospital I was in, right?"

"Queenie, yes. Told 'im everything: the floor, the room, the bed number, the day nurse's name, and the name of the night nurse, and what their favorite colors were."

"Oh, that's funny, Poe."

"Queenie, look, I'm not trying to upset you, but I did tell him. Maybe he has other things more pressing right now. I'm sure he'll get by to see you soon."

"Girl," said Marva, trying to be cute. "You really hard up for that man, huh?"

"Forget you, Marva!"

Poetta shook her head. "Queenie, he'll come see about you. Don't be so impatient."

"Yeah, maybe so." I sighed. I watched her pull a small silver-and-black boom box from her tote bag and place it on my bedside table.

"But the heck with Zeke for now. I brought you my little boom box so you can listen to The Beat."

"Poe, you know me like a book. Steve Harvey is the beat that moves my day. Not a day goes by I don't check out my man Steve on one hundred point three, The Beat. He is too funny dealing with his Strawberry Letters and the Angels. Good looking out."

"Hey, I got your back. Just don't let none of these nightingales walk off with my box."

"For real. Don't worry."

The room was quiet for a spell, and then Marva broke the spell by saying, "Look, I'ma let you heifers talk for a while. I do believe I spotted a handsome doctor with my name written across his forehead. More beef tips for me. Be back later."

"Thank God for a minute to myself," Poetta said the minute her sister was out the room. She took a seat in the chair where mama had sat. "I love that sistah of mine, but honest-to-god that girl can work my last nerves. She wanted me to move in with her until my house is finished, but I told her no way, unless of course, you ready for me to move out yo' condo."

I shook my head. "Nah. Then I'd have to come visit you at Marva's house. I don't think I could take her cussing and calling me out my name on a regular basis. You'll do just fine where you are until yo' house is ready."

"Queenie, I am so sorry." Her eyes misted, tears lined up at the rims. "I don't know what was wrong with me taking Brooda's side over you. Can you ever forgive me for how I acted in Arizona?"

She made a funny face, but in her eyes I could see sincerity. *Dang.* She would have to pull some waterworks on me in my time of being vulnerable. Tears found their way to my eyes, as well.

"Well—I don't know, Poe," I sniffed. "I have to think about it. That was some coldhearted mess you pulled in Arizona." I reached for the small box of tissues on the table, took one, and handed it to her, then took one for myself.

"I know, and I don't blame you for hating me now. I was outta my head or something. You do forgive me?" Sniffling, she wiped at her tears.

"Only if you can forgive me for the big fool I've been. Trying to chase behind some man that I have to change who I am to be with."

Poetta nodded. "Guess we both been ice-skating on crazy."

"At least you wasn't as bad as me. I can't believe how stupid I've been, Poe."

"You're not stupid, Queenie. I've never thought you were stupid. You're just like a lot of women. You got caught up in the hype of love. We're all sensitive creatures who want to be loved, wanted, and needed, that's all. Look at me and Jimboy. I did the same thing. I think in the back of my mind I knew that he had somebody somewhere—a wife, a girlfriend, somebody. I even saw her face in my mind a few times, but I didn't want to face it. I chose not to believe it. I just channeled my mind in the direction I wanted. Thought that if I burned a few candles and chanted a few lines in a dark room at midnight, I could make him all mine forever."

I dabbed my own tears. "See this? Zeke gave me his ring to wear around my neck. He gave me my own key to his house. I think he wanted me to sleep with his roommate."

Shock flashed in her eyes. "His what? His roommate? You mean Sweet Willie?"

"Yep. That's the one. He never actually said the words, but some times you have to read between the lines. I saw where it was leading, but I was still living in expectation." I didn't mention that Sweet Willie was an almost three-hundred-pound, reddish-orange monkey. No. Not a monkey—an orangutan. I didn't dare mention that Sweet Willie hadn't been human, but had shown me more human compassion and more gentleness than Zeke had. Zeke had never lulled me into sleep with the rubbing of my feet. Zeke had never told me that I was pretty, or massaged my exposed thighs as I laid in anticipation on his big round, satin-covered bed. I couldn't tell Poe these things because they were still too painful to think about.

Poetta looked like she was waiting for me to elaborate—tell her more details about Zeke's roommate. A spicy love triangle, like some movie where I'm the minor character, when I should have been the star.

"Did Zeke try to force you to do something against yo' will? Tell me the truth, Queenie. Did he?"

"I wish. I mean, no." My eyes are misting up more, and I can't help it. "But I don't want to talk about him right now."

"I understand, Queenie."

I went quiet and Poetta did, too.

"So," she said finally, "what are you going to tell Ray?"

"Who?"

"Ray? You know, the guy from work that's crazy about you."

The *beep beep* on my machine speeded up. "Why should I tell him anything? This is partly his fault. If he hadn't gotten me all worked up with his foolishness at work, I wouldn't have blinked out."

"You make it sound like it was all Ray's fault that Zeke gave you diet pills and you took them."

"Well, no, but I don't think I have to worry about Ray anymore. Not after the way I carried on at work before I passed out. I just couldn't take it anymore. I think he'll be staying outta my face from now on. I had to do what I had to do."

She stood up and sighed. "That's too bad. Maybe you should tell him that so he can go on home, then."

"Go home? Poe, stop talking in riddles. So who can go home? Why you bringing up Ray when I'm trying to get better so I can go home myself?"

"Queenie, calm down." Poe said, back to her old self of handling my business. "Obviously your mother didn't tell you the whole story. Dr. Motley, your doctor, he's pretty cool. I talked to him myself. You passed out at work because your heart was beating too fast from diet pills. It defibbed . . . it stopped. You were clinically . . . well, dead."

"Stopped? You mean like in stop beating? I was dead?" I was frowning something awful, and I could feel it. My face had to be a twisted mask of disbelief. She was talking defib, and I was thinking she had to be telling a fib. I had heard part of the story from my mama, but it had sounded mild and harmless, like some fluke that happens with a person's health from time to time. But now, hearing it from Poetta made it ring clearer. It sounded more serious. It sounded like some life-or-death situation. Why was she doing this to me?

"Nobody at your job, and let me stress this again, *not one person at your job* rushed to try to revive you except that little guy you can't stand. Know who I'm talking 'bout, right? The one called Raymo. He was the one that restarted your breathing. He did it, Queenie. He put his lips to your mouth and blew air into your lungs. He was the one that kept pushing on your chest to keep your breathing going until the paramedics came and took you away. He rode in the ambulance with you, and he's been here at the hospital ever since. Waiting to know that you're okay."

"Poe, stop lying! Stop it!"

"It's all true, Queenie."

"No. He didn't!" I couldn't stop the tears. Water streamed down my face like separate runaway rivers. "That little—little fool of a man." I felt bad. Not only did I feel bad, I felt so ashamed. After all I had said to that man, after all I had done to that man, he had breathed air back into my lungs. He had wanted me to live even when I hadn't deserved to. What kind of sick person would do that?

"So," Poetta said, like she was some authority on the matter. "If you still think he's not tall enough, he don't have enough hair on his head, or just not man enough for you to talk to, you should at least tell 'im to his face so he can go on home and get some rest. The man looks tired, like he's just been through thirty hours of hard labor, and the baby still haven't arrived. All I'm saying is you need to talk to 'im."

I sniffed, wiped tears with the back of my hand. "I can't, Poe. I mean, how can I face him after all that's happened? I mean, I talked about him like he was some lost dog on the streets, talked about up under his clothes . . . Threw stuff at him. How can I face him?"

"You'll figure it out when he gets here, Queenie. He's anxious to see you. I knew who he was the second I laid eyes on him in the waiting room. He looks just like you described 'im. A little shorter than you, a little bald at the top, but a nice smile. Warm and caring eyes. Tall in caliber. I can tell that 'bout 'im and I just met 'im for the first time. Maybe you should try opening your eyes."

"I can't see him, Poe. I wouldn't know what to say." I sniffed, wiped more mucus with the back of my hand. "I just can't."

"Well, you'll have to tell the man yourself, because it don't look like he's gonna go home until he sees you. I'll go get 'im now, and you can tell him how you feel."

"Poe! No! Don't you dare! Poe!" But she gone.

Dang it! Now what? I kicked my feet under the sheets, pounded my fist, but little good it did.

Twenty-nine

I wished I could blink my eyes or twitch my nose and disappear. Or maybe if I could just twitch my nose the way Samantha used to do on that show called *Bewitched*, I could make it all go away. Make it all a bad dream. That way, I could be back at my house instead of in this hospital room, laying in this bed, waiting for the man I have loved to despise to come through the door and tell me how he saved my life. My life!

No. It's deeper than that. This feeling coming over me. I wish I had died. Raymo should have let me die on that office floor. That way, I wouldn't have to face him—this crazy little man that I have talked so wrong to for so long. The same one I have humiliated in front of his coworkers, embarrassed in front of mine, spit his caring back into his face like venom from some ugly serpent inside me. Even with all this, he had been the one—the only one who had thought enough of my misguided life to save it. Me, Queenie. He had done more than he realized. He had saved me from myself.

I never felt so wrong in my life. Like I'd done something so bad to another human being and there was no road to take to forgiveness. Like if Raymo was on his way into my hospital room to curse me out or spit in my face to return the humiliation I'd caused him, I deserved it. *If only I could make myself disappear before he gets here. Maybe if I just squeeze my eyes tight as possible, when I open them again I'll be at home in my own bed, happy again in the thought that it really had been a long dream—a bad dream that I had finally escaped from.*

"Please, Lord, please. Please make it all go away." I put my hands to my ears, but couldn't shut out the sound of his voice.

"I hope you are feeling better."

I shut my eyes as tight as I can and squeeze and squeeze them, but when I open them again, I'm still here in this bed, in this room with all its hospital smells, its too-shiny beige-and-white floors, and then there's him—Ray, standing at the foot of my bed, looking worried, looking concerned, looking like a man caring about a woman like me who don't deserve to be cared about. He is dressed in the same clothes I last saw him in, what was once a beautiful suit, rumpled now. He was too quiet for a few seconds, perhaps expecting me to shout some ugly obscenity or throw something at him from the table at my bedside. He is smiling, and for the first time I notice—I mean, really notice him. Poe was right. He does have the nicest smile. Just like Poe said—warm, and inviting, sincere. Not just his lips, but his eyes, as well. I see sweet hope dancing in those eyes, and I want to look away, but I can't.

"I, ah . . . I picked up some flowers from the gift shop downstairs. Yellow roses. I hope you don't mind." He laid his offering along the table.

"Thanks," I mumble, looking away to play with my hands. My eyes are restless, forcing me to look back up at him.

Ray looks like he wants to say something else, but can't. I feel like I need to say something, but what? What do you say to another human being you've been so awful to and they save your life because they were the only one of your coworkers who thought enough of you to put their mouth to your mouth and share the air from their lungs to yours? What the hell do you say? . . . Something like, "By the way, Ray, thanks for the life saving. That's some good looking out"?

Or do you do what I do and allow my eyes to mist up, feel the burn in my chest, and start crying all over again? Crying, because that's all I can do for now. And then he rushes over next to my side, finds a tissue box, takes out a couple, and hands them to me.

"Queenie, don't. Whatever it is, it will be okay. Please don't cry."

So caring, so attentive, but this don't stop my tears. I am a volcano of emotions that have brewed and simmered, peaked, and finally erupted. It all must come out: the anger, the shame, the bitterness, the shame, the I'm so much better than you, the shame, the disgust, the shame.

"No, no," he says, in a soothing voice. "Don't cry. There's nothing to cry about."

I turn my face away from his. "Ray, yes, there is."

"No, there is not. You have been so blessed. Don't you see?"

"I don't feel blessed." I sniffle, dabbing at my eyes that feel suddenly red and swollen. The *bleep-bleep*ing of the monitor kicks up a pace, summons a nurse to come in to check on me. She bustles around a minute or two before leaving back out the room.

"But you have been. Another chance for life. Not many are blessed with this." He pats my arm, gentle. There was once a time when his mere touch along my skin would have sent ripples of disgust to me, but now, there is something else. Replacement. His touch is the place of comfort along my skin, warm and reassuring.

"Ray." Turning around to face him, I watch his eyes and try to read something from them; I shake my head, trying to understand. What would make a man want to do so much for a woman that he really don't know? What would make a man take so much abuse from a woman that have shown him nothing but rejection? If somebody could just tell me that much. "Why did you save me, Ray? Why didn't you just let me lay there and die?"

He looked down at the floor, and then up at me. "It is simple, Queenie. Because I couldn't. Everyone else at that job were in shock. They all stood around, staring down at you like it was just too bad that something was wrong. Somebody kept shouting for Jay to come, but he don't come. He was somewhere else in the building, but nowhere to be found. No one seem to understand that you needed an ambulance to be called. You needed help. They all stood around, but I couldn't do it. I had to do something."

"But . . . the way I've treated you. Ray, I've treated you like shoe crud. Don't that mean anything to you?" My face is twisted as water streams freely from my eyes. "You can't go around showing concern and saving folks who treat you bad. It's not right."

"Yes, but I never took you serious. I just thought that—that when you finally opened your eyes and saw the truth, that I really care, you would be different. And I prayed."

"You prayed I'd be different? Different how, Ray?"

"I don't know, maybe nicer, maybe kinder, maybe a real friend. I prayed hard that one day we could be like friends. And if anything else should happen along . . . well, so be it."

I grinned and shook my head. "You are too much, you know that?" Surprised at my own feelings, I was feeling better. "You think you want someone like me for your friend, but you don't really know me. You saved the life of a complete stranger."

"I don't think so, Queenie. Besides," he threw in, angling his head sideways, looking cocky with a sparkle in his eyes. "If I did not save you, I would not be able to see your smile anymore at work, or the way you walk so proud through the office like you own the place, or the way you laugh and toss your head back. The light catches your eyes and looks like small stars in your face. I know your favorite color is baby blue, and it looks so nice on you when you wear it. Especially when you wear your blue Evan Picone pumps. I know you love red roses on your birthday and sometimes—our little secret, of course— you send them to yourself every February tenth."

If mild shock was registering on my face, it had a right to be there. "How could you know this?"

"And you are a romantic person at heart, but find it difficult to find a man that knows how to romance you. Not just date you, but truly romance you. You believe in God, but you are not much of a church-goer. You have plenty of friends, but only one you consider a close one, Miss Poe. We met in the hospital's waiting room, and she is nice, too. A kind person. You absolutely enjoy eating rich and fattening foods, and never thought of your size as a handicap, because you are too proud. Now, have I left anything out?"

"Dang, Ray. You been doing yo' homework." Oddly, I was impressed, a little concerned if I looked at it from a stalker's point of view, but definitely impressed.

"Queenie, I can't imagine what kind of man you would harm your health to try to lose weight for. He must be a fool to not love and appreciate you for who you are. But I am going to take a chance and say this. This may make you upset and mad at me all over and again, like always. You may want me to leave after I say this, but I have to speak my piece; so here goes: If I had a woman like you, I would not change one single thing about you. To me, you are perfect."

Well. I swallowed hard. What could I say to that? "Oh, Ray . . . What a nice thing to say to a friend."

"If I have offended you, I will leave now."

He turned to go, but this time, not hanging his head. I was glad for that. A woman wants a man—I mean, a woman wants a friend that holds his head up with pride regardless, even if that man is just a friend. A new friend.

"Don't leave." *Dang. Did I just say that? Hell yeah, I said it.* I said it again. "Ray, please, don't leave. I want you to stay a little longer, I mean . . . if you want to." Ray looked as surprised by my request as I was feeling.

"Are you sure? I don't want that special boyfriend of yours to come to this room and shoot me."

"I wouldn't worry about it." I needed to know who the real Ray is.

"Are you sure and positive?"

"Ray, yes, I'm sure. Have a seat. Stay and talk to me. I need some company."

We talked for hours, mostly stuff about growing up in Los Angeles County, and it's funny, now that I think about it. Sometimes we think we know the people that come into our lives, just by looking at them, and by hearing bits and pieces of their world snagged on our consciousness at the workplace. But truly, we really don't know them. We know only the fleshy shell that covers their existence, hides their soul. We form our opinions from what they allow us to see. Just listening to Ray talk, I learned some things about him that never would have

crossed my mind before. For instance, he wasn't typical Latino raised
by his own. He had been raised in foster care until the age of nine,
where he was adopted by a black couple with two other children. For
a long time, he explained, he had tried to hold on to his accent, thinking that it was a way of hanging on to his heritage.

"I never knew my real parents, so I used to wonder how a mother
could leave a young baby at the hospital and go on with her life, but
I learned to adjust. I just knew I was Latino, and that's all I really had.
It took a while for me to understand that the way a person talks,
regardless of what kind of accent they have, it does not make them
who they are as a person."

"Of course not," I agreed with him. Was that why his diction
seemed so different? I mused. The man was talking perfect English
like me. Such an odd man. What a trip he was, but in a nice kind of
way.

Raised in foster care. I never would have thought it about him. If
it hadn't been for the love and warmth of that family, he told me, he
would not be the man he was today. And there was more. He had
been married before—married to a black woman five years his senior,
but the marriage hadn't lasted long when she refused to have children
for him. He once wanted to be a master chef, which would explain
why he was always cooking me something. Cooking, according to Ray,
was his third passion. I dared not ask what the first two passions were.
And I had thought that working at Macy's was his only job, but no.
Ray, just like myself, had big-time ambitions, but he was way ahead
of me, with the owning of two small men's clothing stores down on
Los Angeles street downtown in the Los Angeles garment district.

"But why would you be wasting your time at Macy's?" I asked,
wanting to know the logic in it.

"For extra mad money to help open another store one day. I would
say that in the next five years, I plan to own a chain of stores specializing in men's clothing."

"Wow," my lips said. *What a coincidence*, my mind said.

Just taking a few hours out of my time was all it took. Time and
listening. Talking to Ray was more interesting than I had imagined.
The man was full of surprises. After hours of it, he told me that he

had to go home and shower and rest, but asked if it would be okay for him to come back later before visiting hours were over with.

"Sure. I would like that." Wasn't like I had someplace else to be.

"Are you sure? I don't want the lady to be mad with me."

"Ray, I'm sure." I smiled, feeling that my doing so, for once, was genuine.

Didn't have to tell him twice either. By seven-thirty that evening, dressed more casual in navy blue sweats and leather slippers, he was back with a checker board game and had snuck me in a sandwich of smoked turkey with plenty of lettuce, tomatoes, and cheese.

"You really know how to make a lady feel better," I said as I unwrapped his delightful offering. That hospital food that had been served earlier had been the pits. While I ate, we played a game of checkers by lowering my bed and using it as part of a table with me on it. I beat Ray two games, but let him win the last one.

"Only because you have been cheating, Queenie," he accused, grinning the whole time. "I should have known."

"I never cheat."

We talked, we laughed, we became what we could have been all along, no strings attached, nothing expected, nothing gained, nothing lost—just two friends sharing sweet moments of content. He asked for nothing more; I offered nothing more. Why had it been so hard for me to do this in the beginning? I wondered. A friend to talk to and listen was all he had quested.

Raymo stayed way beyond visiting hours, and before he left, he stood by my bed and looked at me with the oddest look on his face. "I have a confession to make."

I took up my water cup and sipped the coolness through the straw, my throat still a little dry feeling. "What's that, Ray?"

"I want to correct you, yes, on an erroneous remark that you made the other day before you passed out."

"Erroneous? Ray . . . I know I was out of line. . . . I was crazy that day. . . . I—"

"No, now, you must hear me out. You were presumptuous enough to make a statement about my—" He paused and cleared his throat. "—my male anatomy."

"Oh, that. Well, I didn't mean nothing by it—"

"You must hear me now. I want to say that you are greatly mistaken."

"Ray, it doesn't matter, really—"

"No, I beg to differ. At ten inches, I would have to say that it does."

I looked at him like he'd changed colors. "Ten?"

"Queenie, I did not stutter. Yes, ten."

"Would that be at its peak?" He probably couldn't see it, but a blush rushed to my face. I couldn't believe I had asked such a thing.

He smiled a wicked little smile, winked his eye, and headed for the door, then stopped and looked back at me. "Only time will tell."

That said, the seed planted, he walked out.

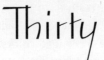

Thirty

Things have a way of working out. I could probably end it like that, but then the juicy parts wouldn't get told, and seeing how I'm telling it, I may as well tell it all.

The day I got out of the hospital, Tuesday evening, Poetta made some lame excuse that she needed my car to run errands—important errands, so she claimed. What kind of mess was that? "Whatever you have to do, Poe, it must be pretty important if you can't come to the hospital first and pick me up."

"It is," Poe said. "And I can't talk about it right now."

"Then just do it. Do what you have to do. I'll call Mama up."

"Queenie, you sure?" she asked, making sly, snickering sounds over the line.

Good grief. That girl can be so childish at times. But I knew the deal. Mr. Tony Benwell, the doctor, the new man she'd met during my three-day hospital stay, was keeping her mind pretty occupied. She had business, all right. Already the two were burning late hours on the phone and on their second date. Progress was moving along. Lord, I hope she wasn't back to her old tricks of burning candles to get some man. Anyway, she was happy, and I was happy for her. Anything to help her over that god-awful Jimboy situation.

"Yeah, you go ahead. I'll see if Mama can come. Just don't keep my ride too late." I hung up and tried my mama's line, but she couldn't be reached. Now that was odd. I could have sworn that I had mentioned to Mama the day before of my pending release. If my memory served me well, and it did, Mama was the one that told me to give her call and she would come get me. Where the heck could she be?

I was showered and baby-powdered up and lotioned down and dressed in my light gray noodle-strapped dress that Poe had brought to the hospital the day before, dressed and sitting on my hospital bed and ready to go. After being poked, prodded, injected, infused, and amused, I was told to eat sensible, induce mild exercising into my life, drink more fluids, and stay away from any kind of pills that's not prescribed for me. After three days in that place Dr. Motley, blue-eyed, gray, and balding, assured me that I would be fine after my "cardiac episode." He had no qualms about throwing in, "And one way to keep a healthy heart is to keep your weight sensible. By losing at least twenty to thirty pounds, it could make a big difference with your health and how hard your heart has to work."

"I'll keep that in mind, Doc." I thank him for his advice and medical concern. All dressed and ready to leave—but no ride. I was more than anxious to leave that place. I kept trying Mama's number every ten minutes, but there was no answer.

And if I didn't know any better, I'd swear the whole thing was planned: Poe needing my car on the very day I needed a ride home from the hospital, Mama not at her house waiting on me to call to say what time she could come and get me. Even Poetta's sistah, Marva, had something to do and couldn't come. Feeling desperate, I had called Marva, and she was talking 'bout having to take her ancient husband to the doctor to renew his Viagra prescription. The man had to be close to ninety-five, or something like that. "Yeah, right, Marva. I understand." I hung up, feeling neglected.

The person that showed up at the hospital, looking refreshed and handsome, dressed in new and perfectly creased dark blue Dockers and a dark blue polo shirt, smiling and smelling good, like always—yours truly, Ray.

"Ready to go?" he asked, standing behind that wheelchair like he was waiting on a helpless invalid to get up and plop down in it.

"Are you kidding? One more minute in this place, and I'll explode." I couldn't recall the last time somebody's eyes were so lit up with the excitement of seeing me. I hesitated for a second or two, but I got up from that bed, grabbed up Poetta's borrowed radio and my few bagged-up items, and got right in that chair, smiling back up at him. Acting like I knew how to be appreciative for a change, I chirped, "I'm ready. Let's go, then."

Worked all those years with that man, and I swear, I never thought about what kind of vehicle he would be driving. Never cared to know. I knew he always dressed impeccable—knew he always smelled wonderful, but never gave his means of transportation a second thought. If I had to think about it, I would have put him in something like a Volkswagen bug or a motorized moped. Something simple. Never occurred to me that Ray might be pushing something expensive, elegant, or sporty looking, but he was. I can't lie. My mouth sagged open when he wheeled me out to his midnight blue Cadillac Escalade, opened the door like a perfect gentleman, and there I was, sitting pretty.

"This is nice, Ray. Is this you for real?"

"Wouldn't have it no other way." He got me situated, went around, and climbed in the driver's seat.

"Notes on this must be high."

"Not if you pay cash," he replied.

"Excuse me," I mumbled. "Looks like you got it going on." The window down, a summer breeze, still warm, blew whiffs of summer into my face, whispered through my hair. Thought about getting out my China Moon Rag that Marva had given me, but that would mean fetching it from Ray's backseat. *What the heck. A little breeze never hurt nobody.* It felt good to be away from that place and on my way to my own turf.

"You hungry?" Ray looked over at me, looking content.

"A little bit. Can't wait to get back home and eat some real food for a change." I took in a deep breath and exhaled slowly. "Nothing like some home cooking."

"That's true." Ray sniffed, then added, "But rest is what you need first. The doctor said so. You are not ready to be up and about cooking. This I am sure of, so this is why I have cooked for you."

"No. That's okay, Ray. Believe me, you have done enough for me."
All I wanted was my place, my kitchén, my own bed. "I couldn't ask
you to do another thing. Wouldn't be right."

But Ray, the ever-so-persistent one who rarely takes no for an answer countered with, "Too late. It's already done. A home-cooked
meal. Dinner. Wine. The works."

"Ray, noooo," I whined. "You shouldn't have. You've done way too
much already." I don't want to go to his house, or sit at his table or
eat his food, but at the same time I know I should be grateful. After
all, isn't that what friends do when one friend does something nice,
something so unpredicted or unwarranted? And I was hungry. No way
to deny it.

Determined to do this last thing, a man on a mission, he must feed
me. "You will feel much better after you have eaten something. You
will see."

Oh, what the heck, I mused. *Humor the man.* I relax my head against
the dark gray leather headrest and flow with destiny.

His house. Ohmygawd. His house, big and magnificent, sits high
along the hilltop of Anaheim Hills. It is an older house, but well kept
and well preserved. Dark buds and pink-blossomed cherry trees stand
at each side of his lawn. Ray helped me from his vehicle and up to
his front door and opened it, where he looked—but only for a second
or two—like he wanted to lift me up and carry me over the threshold.
But he wasn't that crazy. Even persistent men like himself needed a
good back.

Inside, looking around, I didn't want to be impressed, but I couldn't
help it. Dang. Marble floors, cathedral ceiling, contemporary Italian
furniture, expensive oriental rugs. Nothing like what I had imagined.
"Wow, Ray, your place is beautiful."

"Please make yourself at home."

"Sure, if you say so."

He fed me good. Beef enchiladas, refried beans with melted,
rounded balls of polenta, and salad. Dang, that man can cook. I'm
liking that part, straight up.

"Hope this food does not spoil your diet for good," he joked, pouring more wine into my glass.

"What diet?" And being silly, we laughed like it was too funny.

We ate, we talked, we drank red wine like good friends sharing old times. And this man that I had been cocky enough to think he wasn't my type, had found a way to charm me. It was in his eyes—sincereness. It was in his smile—warm to hot, starting sparks somewhere deep inside me. It was in his gentleness—so natural and true to himself. Nothing fake about him. There was no putting on airs to show me a side of him that did not exist. And when conversation and laughter ran low, he serenaded me with, of all things, a guitar. Some old-looking thing that I could tell he was more than familiar with, him strumming the strings and singing his heart out, his own version of "Sunshine on My Shoulders" by John Denver.

I laughed until my eyes had tears, but he was so serious. "Ray, you are too much." The expression on his face, him looking so serious and singing that corny song, the sound of his voice, and maybe the wine, too, pulled something up from inside me, a deep laughter and good feeling that I hadn't known since the beginning of never. He sang another song, and I laughed until my eyes watered more, and my sides hurt, and it was okay to do so.

He would have been the perfect gentleman if I hadn't gone and spoiled it. After his singing was over, he joined me along the dark tan leather sofa. We were sitting pretty close and trying not to look at one another. But each time I looked over at him, he was looking over at me, smiling. I was smiling, too. And what he had said that day he left my hospital room about his anatomy and something about those ten inches of manhood had sprouted in my head like a tree of life that couldn't be ignored.

Ten inches. Was he for real or what? Next thing I knew, surprising my own self, I leaned over and kissed him. That's right. Just pulled his face to mine, lined our lips up, and locked them. I was caught up in some crazy spell of lust that could have been the wine, or maybe Poetta was somewhere burning candles or working some kind of wicked lust spell on us, because all I know is that I wanted him right then and there more than I had wanted anyone. I wanted to feel his warm lips along my body—and I did. We were out of our clothes in no time, our warm, sticky bodies entwined along the sofa. His head between my large breasts bobbed up and down for air before going back for more. A nipple in his mouth, his hot, wet tongue hungry on it. He kissed places long neglected and licked others that throbbed and beckoned. True, he was slightly smaller than me, but he made up for it in experience. Sitting back on his knees he rose above me and what I saw made my eyes widen and started a tiny river between my thighs. The man hadn't lied. He was short, true enough, but delightfully long, thick, and well rounded where it counted. His chest was full of dark hair, and he held himself in his hand like it was a majestic sword, a symbol of honor.

"Dang, Ray, you hung like a horse."

"Yes, but only for you, my love. You like?"

"Yeah, I'm liking."

"And you will not be disappointed."

"Sounds good to me."

We kissed some more. Slow and deliberate. Soulful kissing, you could call it. And when we could hold out no longer, we got down to the nitty-gritty of it, and dang if that man didn't make the sun inside me rise. I didn't mean to moan so loud. Couldn't help it. Didn't mean to scream his name. Couldn't help it. Something was bursting on the inside of me, over and over again, making me feel like I was losing my mind, but in a good way. I wanted to scream for mercy, but didn't.

And when it was over, we kissed and grinned. We sighed and heaved and laid there, spent, sweat glistening off our tired bodies. We both closed our eyes to sleep, but before I did, my mind had to do one last thing, my mental stats on Ray, I always have to do my mental stats on a possible keeper.

NAME: Raymundo Carlos Morales Castillo; for short, Ray.

LIPS: Perfect. Kissable sweet, too.

MARITAL STATUS: Divorced, no children, but seeking a wife.

JOB: Buyer and owner of two clothing shops.

Car: Cadillac Escalade. Nice. Very nice.

Living arrangements: Living alone, but probably not for long.

Goals: To own his own chain of stores, just like me.

We adjourned to his bedroom, where I fell asleep beside him and dreamed that I was a sleeping princess who had been awakened by the kiss of a special prince that had finally found me. I slept like a baby that night at his place, and the next, and the next before going back to my own place.

Two days later, out for a drive, I asked Ray to drive by Zeke's place. You would have thought that Zeke would have at least called to see if I ever made it out alive from the hospital, but it was days passed, and I still hadn't heard a peep from him. Not a ring on the phone, not a card. Nothing.

"Zeke? Is that the man you were dating?" Ray asked. He didn't seem too concerned about being asked to drive by Zeke's.

"Yeah. That's the one."

"And you want to go by his house?"

"Won't take but a couple of minutes. I just need to return some stuff of his." Heck, I was half expecting Ray to act jealous, but he is such a man of poised pride. *That's a good thing*, I remind myself.

"No problem," is all he said, calm and in control.

He pulled his Escalade into the driveway of Zeke's place, and I got out and straightened my lime-green sundress. I had a small box in one hand and Zeke's door key in my other. The key Zeke had given me. I thought about using it—after all, isn't that why a person gives you a key, to be used? But no. Instead, I rang the doorbell, then banged on the door until Zeke swung it open and stood there like he was face-to-face with a ghost. He had on jeans and a white T-shirt. It wasn't a look of happy to see me, nor was it a look of hating to see me. Surprise, shock, disbelief that I was still living or something.

"Queenie?"

He tried to look happy to see me, but I had sense enough to know that it was all part of good acting.

"Zeke."

"C'mon in. I was just thinking about you. How come you didn't use your key?"

"No. This isn't a social visit, Zeke. Just a couple of things I'm returning. That's all. Dropping off some stuff and picking up something at the same time."

"Things? Things like what?"

Zeke didn't get it right away, but I didn't give a hoot before I shoved the shoe box containing his ring on his gold chain, his door key, and the half-empty bottle of diet pills that almost killed me. "Here," I said, looking as serious as cancer. "I won't be needing this stuff anymore. Working on a new deal now."

"Queenie, what on earth are you talking about?"

"Working on a new me, Zeke. That's why I'm bringing back yo' stuff and picking up some of my self-esteem. I believe I left it here with you for a minute."

"Is that right?" Zeke replied, not too happy looking.

"Yeah, Zeke. That's right. Hope you and Sweet Willie have a happy life together, a merry Christmas and a happy new year. See ya." I turned and walked away.

"Hey, Queenie, wait a minute! What's this about?"

I kept walking like my ears don't work.

"Queenie, don't walk away when I'm talking to you! Is this about me not getting to the hospital to see you?"

I don't answer Zeke, because I refuse to hear him.

"I said don't be walking away from me when I'm talking to you, woman! You not all that to be acting that way. Queenie!"

It gets even crazier when Zeke leaves his doorway and marches like a soldier out behind me. I got the feeling right away that he wasn't a man that was used to women rejecting him, or igging him. He grabs my shoulder and spins me around.

"Woman, don't you hear me talking to you? What is yo' problem?! You don't come here and dump me. I'm the one that does the dumping!"

Dang. What a nasty attitude. Is this the same man I had thought was so perfect? He grabs my hand and won't let go. "Well, things change in the world, Zeke. Now I'm the dumper, and you're the dumpee. Get used to it."

"Like hell I will! Not that we had no hot relationship going on to begin with, but you don't come over and dump me. That's my job. You understand? Mine!"

"Zeke, whatever, just turn me loose, please." *What a jerk*, I'm thinking.

"Queenie, not until you tell me what's wrong now. You wanted to come to my house when you wanted, so I gave you a key. You wanted to be my special friend, and we were getting to that next, and now you coming here—unannounced I might add—and dump my stuff back in my face. What's this about?"

"Zeke, we have nothing to talk 'bout, so please let go of my hand."

"Not until you tell me what's wrong. Is it because I didn't make it to the hospital to see you? I had a gig to do and couldn't come see you. I do have to earn a living, remember?"

"Turn my hand loose!"

In no time, Ray is out of his vehicle. He is quiet as grass growing as he makes his way over to us. No loud pre-threats coming. "Queenie, is this man bothering you?"

I don't want no trouble. Really I don't. I have to put a stop to the situation before it gets out of hand. I only want to get back to the vehicle and finish our drive. "Not really, Ray," I say. "I was just dropping off Zeke's things. We can go now." Right, we can go now. I was just about to say it again.

Then Ray says, "Man, you need to get your hands off my lady!"

Zeke shot him a hostile look. "And you need to mind yo' own damn business."

Ray shot him a look that could kill. "If I drove the lady here, I guess that makes her my own damn business."

Lord help us. "It's okay, you two. Ray, we can go now." Zeke is taller and has more muscle, and I don't want to see Ray get a beat down over me. It wouldn't be right. "Let's just go now."

"And what if I don't?" Zeke don't back down as he releases my hand. "Who's going to make me?"

Next thing I know, Raymo rushes up and grabs Zeke's arm, zips, dips, and flips him to the ground. *Ouch*, my mind screams. It had to hurt because I heard the crunch of flesh and bones connecting to concrete myself when Zeke hit the walkway pavement. "Dang, Ray. You full of surprises, aren't you?"

Right then and there, I saw something in Ray I'd never seen before. He was more man than Zeke could ever be. If he was a man that would fight for me, he was man that would protect me, make me feel safe. I would have helped Zeke up, but that wouldn't be right either, so I smiled down at him and winked. "Try to have a nice day, now. You hear?"

"C'mon, Queenie," Ray held out his hand. "Let's go enjoy the day."

"Sounds good to me." I took his hand. "After all, what's the point in taking a few days off from work if you can't enjoy it?"

"Exactly. You want ice cream?" he ask as we stroll back to the Escalade, hand in hand.

"Yeah, I could stand some."

"Chocolate or strawberry?"

"If you know me, Ray, you should already know the flavor."

"Strawberry it is, then."

"Ooh, Ray, you scaring me with all this knowing so much about me. Strawberry ice cream is my favorite."

"Might put more padding on your lovely hips. You have such nice hips, you know. Good baby-making hips."

"Ray, you devil you." I giggle, feeling silly.

He is too funny. I think about his words for a spell. A mixed baby would be so beautiful. A little curly-haired girl. I could see it happening. Heck yeah. I could see it just fine. Happy in our thoughts, we drive off into the afternoon sunset.

Thirty-one

It's been months and months now, and close to a year. Time is unforgiving as it never stops to wait for no one. Poe's house is back in
order and finally, she moved back home, but didn't take long for her
doctor friend, Dr. Tony Benwell, to start taking up most of her time.
She even talking about being somebody's wife and having some babies
and all that good stuff. She is mad happy, and I'm happy for her. Looks
like love found her, too.

Sistah Marva got religion after she almost killed her fool self in a
car accident. Too much drinking and driving sent her into head-on
traffic. Dang, she was lucky. Sometimes it takes a near-death experience to bring folks back down to earth and back to truly living. She
don't curse or swear anymore. She don't date other men behind her
husband's back, and with all the cake-and-pie-baking she been doing,
the church functions and singing in the choir at Mount Zion Baptist
Church up on Crenshaw, she's not the same Marva I was used to.
Amazing.

Time is a healer and a teacher, as well. I learned a few things. I
learned that true love has nothing to do with the color of skin, the
length of the hair, the shape of the eyes. It has nothing to do with
being too big or too small. Money is okay, and having a lot of it can

be a good thing, too, but it can't buy it. Not true love. I learned that trying to change myself for a man will never help me to be who I was meant to be. And this, too, that word *never*. It's such a tricky word. I learned that you should never say never. To do so is like predicting the future—playing God with your own destiny. Who are we to say who's good enough for us to love and who's not? How can we say it without first having concrete evidence? Sex may find us in familiar places, but the true love we seek rarely seeks us. Ultimately, we may find love, true love, in the strangest places. Love is strange. That's all I'm saying. That's what I've learned.

I'm nervous. But who wouldn't be, standing here in front of the minister at Mount Zion Baptist Church. All eyes are on us. Ray and me. I'm wearing white, and I don't care who don't like it. It's a free world. My makeup is perfect. My dress is perfect. My hair is perfectly done in cascading ringlets, thanks to Poetta. One thing for sure, that girl can sure hook up some hair. She got major talent that way.

Aunts, uncles, and cousins. Folks I haven't seen in months, maybe even years. All of my friends and family and some of Ray's family, as well, are here, dressed in their Sunday best and smiling, all to witness our union. A union that almost didn't come to be. Even my sister, Kellie, flew out from Detroit for the occasion. Ray looks so handsome in his black tux. And by the time I'm saying "I do," I'm crying—crying because I'm so happy, and crying because I feel so blessed.

"I do," I say after the minister's prompt. Those two words are whisper soft across my lips, but I can feel it in my heart. I really do.

It's funny what life gives us sometimes. Certainly not always what we think we want. What I thought I wanted in the beginning was a man that would never know or care to know the real me. All Zeke saw was the shell of who I was—my not-so-perfect outside appearance. Even without his love and acceptance, I was willing. It was a price too high.

And now there's Ray. What I got was a man who cares about me, understands my soul's longings, listens to the stirrings of my heart, embraces my sorrows as if they were his. This alone can make a woman feel like she is the most special person in the whole world.

"Thank you, Lord Jesus," I mumble under my breath. "Thank you for sending me a man that gives a hundred and twenty percent." Not a perfect man, mind you, because there is no such thing as a perfect man or a perfect woman. Not really. Look at us. Ray is not perfect, but perfect for me. And when you really stop and think 'bout it, isn't that what we've been needing all along?

The High Price of a Good Man Calculator

Finding true love is great, but sometimes you have to kiss a few frogs and trudge down the wrong path to find your dream man. What would *you* do for your dream man?

1. **If your dream man was ten years younger than you, would you still introduce him to your friends and family?**
   a. Most definitely! He's my man and they'll just have to accept him.
   b. Yes, but I would make sure that no one ever finds out how old he is.
   c. No way! I'd never hear the end of it.

2. **If your mother was dating a younger man that you felt was your dream man, would you sneak behind her back to see him?**
   a. Heck, yeah! He's my dream man.
   b. Yes, but I'd make sure that I hooked my mother up with someone just perfect for her.
   c. No way. I would never do that to my momma.

3. **The man of your dreams is married with children. Would you conspire to break up his marriage?**
   a. Yes! Nothing stands between me and my man.
   b. Yes, but I'd let the kids come and live with us. I don't want to deprive the kids of their daddy.
   c. No! I don't go for married men.

4. **If your dream man had an exotic pet and you were allergic to it, would you still pursue the relationship with swollen eyes and a stuffy nose?**
   a. Yes, because once I'm in, that furry friend is out.
   b. Yes, but I'd take some kind of allergy medicine whenever I was going to be around his pet.
   c. No. I'm not messing myself up for any man.

5. **The man of your dreams has rear-ended your new car, but to date him you have to forgive and forget. Would you?**
   a. Yes, because once I'm in his bed, his car is my car.
   b. I'd forgive him completely. What's a little fender bender compared to meeting the man of your dreams?
   c. Hell no! I don't want no man who can't see where he's going.

6. **If there was a store selling dream men, and the only money you had was your rent money, would you risk being homeless for a chance at love?**
   a. Once I'm in his bed, I won't have to worry about the rent.
   b. Yes. Since we're in love we'd live together.
   c. No. I'm not giving up the last of my cash for no man. Besides he'll still be there by the time I get my next paycheck.

7. You drive your best friend to the mall, and she heads off to the restroom. Your dream man walks up and asks you to join him for lunch. Would you leave your best friend stranded?

   a. Hell yes. She's got enough money to catch the bus.

   b. Yes, but I'd give her the keys to my car and ask her to pick me up later.

   c. No, I would never do a friend like that.

8. You and your best friend are at a club when you both spot the man of your dreams. Would you move aside and give her a shot just to keep your friendship intact?

   a. Look, I can always get a new friend.

   b. I'd go for him, but I'd ask if he had a friend for her.

   c. No, no man is worth breaking up a friendship.

9. Your parents have met your dream man and made it more than clear that they can't stand him, and if you continue to date him, they will disinherit you. Would you give up your parents for your dream man?

   a. Look, there are certain things that my parents can't do for me that my man definitely can. Besides, if he's my man he's got money and I don't have anything to worry about.

   b. I'd tell my parents that I stopped dating him, but I'd still see him on the sly.

   c. My parents are important to me. I'd talk to my parents and see if there was some way to better their relationship with my man.

10. Your dream man is rich, handsome, and caring. However, he's also a ladies man with a stream of women to give you major competition. Would you be up for the challenge?

   a. Yeah, I'm up to the challenge. Once I'm in, the rest of those chicken heads will be out.

   b. Sure. Eventually, he'd learn to love just me.

   c. I don't care how handsome and caring he is, I want a one-woman man.

TIME TO ADD UP YOUR POINTS!
"A" = 15 points; "B" = 10 points; "C" = 5 points

Score	Assessment
95-150	Get yourself to a clinic—quick! The price you're willing to pay is too high. If you're not careful, you might find yourself broke and alone without your dream man or your momma.
75-90	You're a definite borderline spender. You may be prone to rationalizing your less than admirable decisions.
50-70	Sister, you've got your head on straight. No man is going to make you slap your momma!

St. Martin's Griffin